Waltz of the Heart

Stephanie Milam

Copyright © 2025 by Stephanie Milam

All rights reserved.

No portion of this book may be reproduced in any form without written permission from the publisher or author, except as permitted by U.S. copyright law.

contents

Prologue

November 1811

Cressida Martin couldn't remember much of what life was like before her father had left for France.

She sometimes liked to imagine that he had left their family home for a noble cause like other men did; to fight for King and Country. She liked to think of herself and her mother maintaining their home faithfully while they awaited his triumphant return.

But he never came back. Nor would he ever.

Cressie's mother, Mrs Anne Martin, knew it also.

Mrs Martin held herself remarkably well when in public. She had detested the narrative of the abandoned wife and preferred to think of herself as a widow. People always knew that she wasn't, but they were far too polite to mention the philandering Mr Martin to her face.

Cressie watched from her bed as her mother powdered her face with a concoction that she had made herself. Her collection of cosmetics and perfumes had long since run out, and she resorted to more economical ways of enhancing her natural beauty.

Mrs Martin had indeed been a stunning debutante, and still retained much of the beauty that had attracted the suitors to her doorstep many years earlier.

"The vicar has assured me that we will be introduced to the duke and duchess tonight, Cressie," Mrs Martin said in anxious anticipation. She pinched her own cheeks before she stood up from the small dressing table. She made her way over to the bed to stand before Cressie, appraising her with a critical brow and her narrowed grey green eyes.

"Don't you mean the vicar will be shopping me to the duke and duchess tonight?" Cressie replied, before she bit down on her tongue.

Mrs Martin arched one of her eyebrows. "Get out every one of the comments now," she instructed firmly, "for I do not want to hear a single word from you this evening that is not delicate, charming or lovely."

Cressie groaned before she threw her head back onto the bed, at which her mother scolded her for trying to ruin the hairstyle that she had just spent the last hour pinning.

Mrs Martin laughed facetiously. "It is almost as though she imagines we have fortune to spare so that she can run about like a child a little longer." Mrs Martin spoke to no one, and yet Cressie knew her mother's words were meant to plant guilt in her stomach.

Cressie was well aware of their dire financial situation. She had been since she was a child. Though, in truth, she still feltlike a child. She would not be seventeen until next April.

Cressie had not known a feeling of permanence in a very long time. She couldn't really remember it, similar to how she couldn't remember much of the time when her parents had lived together as a married couple.

She was used to uprooting herself and travelling with only a suitcase carrying every single one of her possessions. Cressie and her mother depended on the grace and generosity of friends, neighbours, and the few relatives who were still living. During the winter months they stayed in London in a flat belonging to a cousin of Mrs Martin. Cressie hated London in the winter. But she never complained.

The summer months were spent between the parishes of Brimley and Seabridge. Brimley was a small parish in Derbyshire, and it was near the estate where Cressie had been born and had spent most of her infancy and toddler years. The vicar was still good to Mrs Martin and helped her to rent a cottage that was vacated by its owners in favour of Scotland. Mrs Martin had similar arrangements in Seabridge.

Or at least, she had in the past. This past year had been their most challenging entirely. At least since the year that Mr Martin had left for France in an entirely unnoble fashion. The vicar had died, and both Mrs Martin and Cressie had felt his loss keenly. But they had also experienced the uncertainty of what they were to do until they could leave for London come the winter.

Ashwood had come about by chance. Mrs Martin had seen an advertisement for a cottage in the parish at an affordable price. The lease was only for a short time, and the price seemed accurate when they discovered the size and state of the place.

"Cressie." Mrs Martin spoke Cressie's name with a sympathetic sigh. She sat down on the bed beside her and pulled her up softly.

Cressie obliged her mother and rested her head against Mrs Martin's shoulder. Mrs Martin wrapped her arm around Cressie comfortingly.

"Nobody is shopping anyone," Mrs Martin said quietly. "We have but tonight to make the duke and duchess' acquaintance, and to grant their good favour, so that we might use this connection come the Season next year. Think of the people, the gentleman, they would know. All we need is a friend to assist you upon your debut and our problems are solved."

Cressie had heard this a thousand times before. She knew what she was supposed to do. She was well aware of her duties and obligations. Her mother had a gift for fostering guilt and getting her way. Cressie would do whatever her mother asked. But she did not have to like it.

Cressie shrugged off her mother's arm and stood up, crossing the small bedroom and walking over to the little window that was open to the chilly night air. The attic bedroom could be very stuffy, so it was necessary to air it out frequently.

"It still feels like shopping to me, Mama," Cressie said tersely. "I don't even feel remotely ready to have a husband." Cressie would never dare say it, but she felt like her mother was setting up Cressie's life to be exactly like her own. Mrs Martin was married during the London Season eighteen years earlier. She was a debutante, and Mr Martin had been a gentleman suitor.

Now Mrs Martin was a poor woman pretending to be a widow and Mr Martin was living in the south of France with a woman two years older than Cressie and their infant son. Currently, that was. Mrs Martin had her ways to seek information on him, and she didn't think Cressie knew about it. Mr Martin liked his women young, and he had at least six illegitimate children and abandoned mistresses dotted across France.

Such behaviour did not exactly encourage Cressie towards any so-called 'gentlemen'.

"My dear Cressie, we will find you someone charming and you will be happy," Mrs Martin said encouragingly. "I am certain of it. And I am confident that this acquaintance with the Duke and

Duchess of Ashwood, as well as the Dowager Duchess, will be beneficial to us. I have watched them in church. They seem like a very devoted pair."

Cressie knew that her mother meant well, but she knew in her heart of hearts that it really would not matter if she was happy in the end. Her mother would be working harder than anyone come the Season, and Cressie would be married off to the richest man they could find, one who did not care if she possessed no dowry.

They very thought sickened her, and she knew that she would struggle to remove the thought from the forefront of her mind for the remainder of the evening.

The Winter Assembly seemed like quite the highlight of the Ashwood social calendar, and nearly every resident that Cressie had ever seen since arriving was there, dancing, laughing, and frolicking away.

Mrs Martin, however, was not there for laughs. For as soon as the Beresfords were announced into the ballroom, she had Cressie by the arm and was leading her towards them with purpose.

Cressie resisted dragging her heels as her mother pulled her towards the line of people who had already assembled to make the acquaintance of the recently arrived Beresford family. She felt bashful and frustrated, among other things, and she certainly still felt like she was being shopped.

Cressie could scarcely see another girl her age in the room. She wagered they were still at home with their hems above their ankles, and not dressed as a woman as she was. Cressie wondered if their financial circumstances were not so dire, whether her mother would have insisted she come out so young? She would have liked to have thought that the answer would have been 'no'.

When Mrs Martin and Cressie came to the front of the line, she hissed in Cressie's ear, "For God's sake smile."

"Your Graces, may I introduce Mrs Martin, and her daughter, Miss Cressida Martin. Mrs Martin, Miss Martin, may I present their Graces, the Duke and Duchess of Ashwood, and the Dowager Duchess of Ashwood."

The vicar spoke formally, and both Cressie and her mother curtseyed respectfully. Cressie managed to obey her mother, and she found a smile, though she was uncertain of how nervous it appeared. Despite her aversion to being shopped, standing before two duchesses and a duke was quite intimidating.

The elder duchess was a remarkably proud looking woman, and Cressie did not feel as though she could meet her eyes. The duke appeared warmer, but the duchess possessed a lovely air about her countenance. There was great kindness in her blue eyes.

"It is a true honour to make your acquaintances, Your Graces," declared Mrs Martin, and Cressie heard the truth in every one of her mother's words. She then nudged Cressie forward, placing her directly in front of the three aristocrats.

Cressie felt her cheeks flush with embarrassment as she somehow managed to stammer, "Yes, I agree with my mother. I am d-delighted."

Mrs Martin never forgot how to behave in a ballroom. From the way she confidently spoke to the Beresfords, one would have thought that she belonged. As she complimented them, and remarked on the festivities, the duchess stepped forward to delicately take Cressie's arm.

Cressie was too surprised to know what to say.

"You look very lovely this evening, Miss Martin," she said softly as she began to walk with Cressie. The duchess led Cressie towards two gentlemen and a lady.

Cressie had seen the gentlemen before, but she had not known them. The same for the lady.

The elder of the two men was tall and handsome, his frame lean and well proportioned. His blue eyes offset his dark hair, and his skin was smooth and fair. He was standing very proudly with the lady, his lady, it could only be assumed.

Cressie had been well aware of presence of a young black woman in the village of Ashwood, just as she had been aware of the man who had become the Lady Susanna Beresford's husband. It was gossip, and Cressie couldn't avoid it sometimes. Cressie never minded gossip as it often sought out to wound the innocent. She and her mother had been the centre of a rumour or twelve whenever they were in Brimley.

Disregarding whatever the narrow-minded gossips thought of her skin, Cressie thought she was beautiful. She had scarce seen a lovelier woman in her life and could fully understand why the elder gentleman stood so proudly beside her. She was striking and poised, her skin flawlessly smooth, but one could not ignore her golden eyes as her most incredible feature. Cressie had never seen such a colour before.

While the man and the lady stood in friendly anticipation of an instruction, the younger companion appeared quite unsettled.

The younger of the gentlemen possessed a youthful yet charming face. Cressie had seen him in the village before and he never seemed to be without a cheeky smile that indicated his age and sense of humour. But he lacked it completely in this moment. Instead, he appeared quite uncomfortable, as though someone had just told him there was a hole in the back of his breeches or something. He was tall like his brother. The resemblance between the two could only mean they were brothers. Only he had not yet grown into his height as his brother had. He was skinny while his brother was lean, and he stood as though he did not know what to do with his arms and legs.

"Miss Martin, I would like you to meet my brother, Mr Denham." The duchess gestured to the elder gentleman. "And this is Miss Belle Desjardins. She is a dear friend of my family, and rather a talented modiste as you may have read in the papers, in and amongst the other drivel. Peter, Belle, meet Miss Cressida Martin."

Cressie could hear in the duchess' introduction a defensiveness to her tone as she introduced Miss Belle Desjardins. She wished that she could assure her that it wasn't necessary.

"Delighted to meet you, Miss Martin," said Mr Denham, and he seemed very sincere.

"And you, Mr Denham, Miss Desjardins," Cressie replied.

"I would also like you to meet my youngest brother," continued the duchess. "Miss Martin, meet Mr Jem Denham. Jem, meet Miss Cressida Martin."

Mr Jem looked upon Cressie then, his blue eyes strained, and his jaw tensed, as though he was clenching his teeth. Cressie couldn't help but frown as she looked upon the strange display with curiosity. What on earth was wrong with him?

Cressie had quite forgotten that her mother was behind her, and she nearly jumped when she heard Mrs Martin call, "I am sure Miss Martin is truly pleased to make the acquaintances of the brothers of the duchess!"

Cressie nearly winced at the lack of her mother's tact in that moment. She was very nearly being too obvious. The duchess was kind enough to introduce Mrs Martin to her brothers, and to Miss Desjardins, before Mr Jem made a startling announcement.

"I want a sandwich!"

All immediate eyes in the vicinity turned towards him as he promptly turned away from the party and walked off to the re-freshment room with purpose.

When the introductions were over, Cressie was led away from the Beresfords towards the edge of the dancefloor. Their position provided Mrs Martin with a good view of the room as she surveyed the couples and kept an eye on the Beresfords.

It was here that Cressie was asked for her first dance. She knew the man to be Mr Andrews, the grocer. She knew not the man's age, but he was certainly more than a decade older than her sixteen years, and the way he appraised her made her entirely uncomfortable.

How she longed for her ankle length petticoats in that moment.

Mrs Martin happily gave Mr Andrews permission to dance with Cressie, and she did so while making only polite conversation. When the dance concluded and Mr Andrews asked for the next, Cressie politely feigned fatigue, which prompted him to offer to fetch a refreshing drink for her.

Cressie used this moment to escape, from both her mama and Mr Andrews.

Of course, she did not leave the ballroom. She merely hid on the other side of the dancefloor behind the sea of attendees who were viewing the dancers.

"Pardon me, Miss Martin."

For a moment, Cressie froze, fearing that Mr Andrews had found her. But she soon realised that the voice was not the same. The voice of the man who had just spoken to her was much younger. Cressie turned around to see that it was Mr Jem who had approached her.

He was standing before her proudly, then, with his hands behind his back. Gone was the odd look on Mr Jem's face, but he still did not appear entirely comfortable. He looked nervous.

Perhaps he was as nervous as she had been when approaching the Beresfords. His youth betrayed it all the more. And quite frankly, it was something that she found very agreeable. She had felt like the youngest person in the ballroom, but Mr Jem was perhaps a similar age to her.

But while her nerves were understandable to anyone in the ballroom, she was entirely unsure of what Mr Jem had to be nervous about. He was a relation of the Beresfords. It was not as though he was being shopped around.

Cressie half expected a gentleman to want to check her teeth or measure her height in hands as though she was a horse at auction come the London Season.

"Good evening, Mr Denham," Cressie said, offering him a small smile and a curtsey.

"Oh, yes, good morning," he fumbled in returning her greeting, before he bowed his head. His eyes suddenly widened as he stammered a correction. "Good evening, that is. It's not morning. Well, it will be in a few hours, I suppose. But do you consider the hours after midnight to be the morning? I think I still consider them to be the evening. I do not wish anyone a good morning if I retire after midnight."

Cressie frowned, very unsure of what to make of Mr Jem's statement. He began to appear uncomfortable, just as he had been when they had first been introduced, and Cressie was beginning to worry that it was her fault. What had she ever done to him? They had never been introduced before this night.

"I ... suppose I consider it the morning in reality," Cressie said slowly, "though I would bid someone 'good night' when retiring after midnight as well."

Mr Jem laughed awkwardly, reaching his hand up to tug at a few of the dark curls on his head before consciously lowering his arm. "Oh, God, what is wrong with me?"

Cressie's frown deepened. Did he want her to answer that question? To look at him, there did not appear to be anything wrong with him. He was perhaps a little strange, but one could be forgiven for nerves. She recalled the cheeky smile she had seen him with in the village. He was not always this way.

"You wouldn't want to dance the next with me, would you?"

The question seemed to spill out of Mr Jem's lips in a round-about way that Cressie found difficult to discern. It was a rather backwards way of asking her to dance, or at least that was what she thought he was doing.

"I ... I wouldn't not want to ..."

It was Mr Jem's turn to frown then, before he furrowed his brow in a frustrated fashion and took a breath. "I apologise, Miss Martin. I am saying everything wrong. Would you like to dance the next with me?"

Cressie couldn't help but find herself smiling as she accepted, placing her gloved hand in his. The moment she did, she saw a genuine smile spread across Mr Jem's face. What a lovely smile it was, and it only brightened his already light blue eyes, and exemplified his young age. She did not at all feel uncomfortable at being escorted onto the dancefloor by Jem Denham, as she had been by Mr Andrews.

Mr Jem was a clumsy dancer; his long arms and legs not at all assisting him in the grace necessary to be one with poise. But

Cressie found his lack of grace to be something else endearing about him. He was trying hard, nonetheless.

The quadrille was an up-tempo dance that did not provide much opportunity for conversation between couples. Cressie was quite out of breath by the end of it and could have really used that refreshment that Mr Andrews had gone to fetch. Thankfully, though, he was nowhere to be seen.

Mr Jem's cheeks were flushed, and Cressie was certain that her own were rosy pink as well. They smiled at one another in amusement, and some of the nerves that appeared to have plagued Mr Jem seemed to vanish. He stood with more confidence, his wonderful smile warm and comforting.

"What is something that makes you feel happy, Miss Martin?" Mr Jem asked her boldly.

Cressie was quite taken aback by the question. Though her experience in ballrooms was limited, and her experience with talking to men even less, she had never been asked such a question before. Flattery, she thought, was usually the order of the day.

If her mother were beside her, she would have insisted she say something agreeable, like charity calls or children, something to make her appear amenable and marriageable.

But if Cressie was being honest ... "Swimming," she replied thoughtfully. It was not at all the only thing that could bring her happiness, but when she thought about moments in her life that had been utterly joyous, swimming in ponds had been purely delightful.

Mr Jem's eyebrows rose, before he grinned. This was a smile she recognised from the brief time she had seen him in the village. The cheeky smile. If anything, it made him appear even younger, like an ally. "I was not expecting you to say that, but now I cannot imagine anything else that I would have preferred. I love to swim as well."

"Have you ever swum in the ocean?" Cressie asked. "I long to do that."

Mr Jem shook his head. "I have never been to the seaside, but I do want to go. It seems we share an ambition."

An ally indeed. Cressie found this incredibly settling. She didn't know why sharing an affinity for something like swimming made her feel as though Mr Jem was an ally, but it did. Perhaps he could even be her friend. She had never had one of those before. She knew it was not customary for girls and boys to be friends, but neither was it usual for swimming to be the preferred hobby of a gentleman. "If you could be anywhere else in this moment, where would you be?" she asked curiously.

What would she predict? Perhaps Mr Jem had a traveller's heart. Maybe he would want to see the Continent, or perhaps the Americas or the East Indies and taste their spices. Or perhaps he was a sportsman who could teach Cressie how to ride astride. She had never learned side saddle, nor did she wish to. Though she hoped he was not a hunter. Birds were free and she hated to see them shot down.

Were she to answer her own question, Cressie would have said the seaside in high summer. And she would have no obligations to anyone. She wouldn't have a mama who demanded she marry. She wouldn't need to marry. She wouldn't have a care in the world save for running into the waves.

"I would be right here," Mr Jem replied softly.

What on earth? Why? she wondered. But her question was answered when Mr Jem's eyes met hers. Cressie knew very little of men, but Mr Jem was looking at her in such a way that it made her tongue swell in her mouth. Why was he looking at her like that? Had he always been looking at her like that and she'd only just noticed?

Mr Jem was looking at her like he admired her. Perhaps it was a little more than that. There appeared to be affection in his eyes. Was that what it was? Whatever it was, it made her stomach twist as all thoughts of her ally and friend Jem had disappeared as quickly as that had appeared. What was he doing? She didn't understand it at all.

"I must go," Cressie managed to say over her swollen tongue. "I must find my mother."

"Wait!" Mr Jem cried, holding onto Cressie's hand.

Cressie was stopped in her tracks as Jem held onto her. The expression on Mr Jem's face was as twisted as her stomach felt, as he struggled through whatever was on his mind.

"I ... I ..." he stammered, nerves and panic in his eyes. "I ... will ... will you marry me?"

Cressie gasped, so loudly it was a wonder that nobody in the vicinity turned towards them. What on earth? "How old are you?" Cressie found herself asking in an almost accusatory tone.

"I ... I'm seventeen," Mr Jem replied, looking just as shocked as Cressie was that he had asked the question.

Cressie had been right. He was perhaps only half a year older than her. Why in the world would he want to be married at their age? And furthermore, why would he want to be married to her? Mr Jem didn't know her. And she did not know him.

"No," Cressie said vehemently, shaking her head. Without saying another word, she pulled her hand from Mr Jem's and disappeared into the crowd, attempting to locate her mother once again. As she did so, she felt sick. She felt her stomach churning and tears threatening. What on earth was this feeling?

CHAPTER 1

M arch 1812

Ashwood, Hertfordshire

"Have you seen this?" Jem asked Adam, his eyes widening as he looked upon the ledger of household expenses. "Have you seen how much sugar and treacle the kitchen ordered in the last quarter?"

Adam lowered his pen and rose from his chair, peering over to Jem's side of the desk. He found the additions that Jem was referring to and he smirked. "Up is it? I would blame Grace for that. She's been practically inhaling sweets throughout this third pregnancy." Adam appeared quite amused.

While Jem had very little experience in his eighteen years in knowing the goings on in the kitchen, he could certainly see that Ashwood had ordered enough ingredients to satisfy the village for the year in only three months. Is that what pregnancy did to women? Did it make them as uncontrollable as a three-year-old staring at a dish of iced biscuits?

Of course, Jem was clever enough to keep that thought to himself. As good as his eldest sister was to him, Jem knew that he would never be too old for a scolding.

"I wouldn't worry yourself over the food spending, Jem," Adam said as he sat back down. "I don't begrudge anyone food, and what we have in excess is directly given to those in our parish in need. You have done a terrific job these last months in helping Ashwood to run more economically. Won't you come here, and I'll explain the rents to you."

Jem was the one to stand now, and he straightened his jacket and pulled at the sleeves. It was the first fine coat he had ever owned that had not been Peter's first or had been specifically for church. When his mother had first seen him dressed as he was, she had cried.

Jem Denham had certainly put in effort to growing up. He would be eternally grateful for the childhood he'd had upon reflection. There was never any expectation upon him. Not in the way that it had been on Grace to provide for them, or Peter to undertake an apprenticeship. As the youngest of the Denham siblings, Jem had been allowed to run about to his heart's content. Even as a teenager, he had rarely been without grass stains upon his knees.

While he knew that he would never lose his childhood spirit, Jem knew that if he ever wanted to be more than the youngest Denham, he needed to make something of himself.

While his family and his in-laws saw Jem's sudden ambition as a sign of his maturity, and indeed it was, there was another reason that no one knew about. No one would ever know about it.

Jem was still haunted by the way he had embarrassed himself in front of Cressie Martin at the Winter Assembly. He had nightmares about it all the time. In his dreams, he saw her laughing at him. He saw it so often that it had tainted the reality. Had she laughed at him? Had she thought him a fool? Had she thought him ridiculous?

Why ever would someone as lovely as her take a boy like Jem Denham? The fifth child of a poor family with a church education and dirt underneath his fingernails.

Jem could not even fathom what had happened in that moment. He could not believe that he had proposed. Was panic proposing something that people could do? Or could it only happen to him? All he had seen was Cressie walking away, and he had been desperate to keep her with him for only a moment longer.

And instead of saying, 'Will dance the next with me?', he'd asked her to do a little more than that.

Jem knew it was all his own fault. He couldn't blame Cressie for being just as sweet and as charming as he had imagined her to be. And when she'd told him about her love for swimming, he had seen her keen spirit for adventure in the depths of her warm brown eyes. Immediately he had sensed a kindred spirit, and it had stirred something inside of him that had excited him beyond measure.

And her beauty. Oh, Jem had lost many night's sleep over how he had ruined his chances with someone so beautiful. It was as though she did not have to try, she was so pretty. When she smiled, the act itself enough to stop the earth in its rotation, she had the most gorgeous dimples. Only hers were not in her cheeks as most dimples were. Cressie's dimples formed little craters underneath her eyes which were perhaps the most adorable thing he'd ever seen.

Jem had been determined to avoid Cressie for the next several weeks in an effort to hope and pray that she forgot about his panic proposal. Obviously, Jem knew it would not be the case, but he needed that time to settle his own pride and embarrassment.

And by the time he had been able to swallow that pride to finally apologise to her, and to find some way to address her properly with his intentions so as not to overwhelm her, she was gone.

Cressie Martin was gone.

And where? Nobody knew. She and her mother had simply packed up and disappeared, leaving no forwarding address.

Cressie had slipped right through his fingers.

Jem had been very conflicted in how he had managed his feelings after learning this. He had attempted to hide his disappointment, his heartbreak, at losing Cressie, especially after what his brother had just been through with the woman he loved. How could he equate losing Cressie to what Belle had endured? He simply could not.

Though as much as Jem endeavoured to conceal it, he knew that his powers of hiding his feelings were not very great indeed.

In the time since Cressie and her mother had left Ashwood, Jem had done the only thing he could, and that was to train under his brother-in-law, Adam, to become the Duke of Ashwood's steward. As a second son, it was a very respectable vocation for him, and it provided an excellent distraction.

It was also terrific motivation to stop him from beating his head against the wall whenever the feeling of embarrassment returned.

The truth was that Jem really did not know if he would ever meet Cressie Martin again. The odds were certainly not in his favour. Regardless of the ache that the reality gave him, he still wanted to be accomplished in some way. He wanted to be able to put his name to something.

Adam spent the remainder of the day poring over the greater Ashwood Estate with Jem, explaining the rental incomes and the lease agreements that he had with the tenants. It would be Jem's role eventually as Adam's steward to understand this information, to know it backwards and forwards, and to ensure that it was as profitable as possible. Jem had always been better at arithmetic in school, just as Peter had been, but after three hours staring at the ledger, he knew that he would need to study it again and again.

As the sun set, and Adam's study began to darken, there was a knock on the door as Grace entered with a housemaid who proceeded to light the lamps. Attached to Grace's hem was Jem's four-and-a-half-year-old niece, Perrie, who, as soon as she saw her father, clumsily sprinted towards him. Perrie darted around the desk and climbed up Adam's legs so that she could be seated upon his lap.

Adam merely chuckled as he leant down to kiss Perrie on top of her brown mop of curls. "I hope you haven't missed me too dreadfully today, Perrie."

"Oh, no," replied Grace facetiously. She folded her arms across her chest and rested them upon her swollen belly. "She has only been asking for you every fifteen minutes since breakfast. She would not even sleep today. Unlike Lily who does as she is told."

Jem smirked. As Perrie had grown older, and her personality had become more apparent, he liked to think that his niece had inherited a little something from her Uncle Jem. He had been a little bit of a hellion as a child ...

... and as a young adult.

Perrie Beresford had a mind of her own and a will to match.

One would never guess by looking upon her angelic face.

"I will always consent to my Perrie visiting me," Adam teased, squeezing his daughter tightly. "And you, of course, Grace."

Grace laughed sarcastically, though she did wear an amused smile.

Jem's eyes flicked between the two, and he hated that he felt a pang of envy. It was such an ugly emotion, and he understood why it was a sin. He would never begrudge his sister her happiness. Grace had always looked after Jem and their other siblings, and she deserved everything that she had.

And what she had was so beautiful. She had a decent husband, a true gentleman, one whom Jem was proud to call brother. They shared such ease in communication where they could be teasing and silly, and yet serious and loving. And they worked together to raise their children the best that they could.

And nobody had panic proposed.

Jem wondered what Grace would have done had Adam panic proposed to her. In knowing his sister, she would have accepted. She had always loved Adam.

And that realisation hurt Jem unnecessarily as he knew that Cressie did not love him. Of course, she did not. She had only met him twenty minutes before the panic proposal.

"Are you alright, Jemmy?" Grace asked. "You seem quite lost in thought." She came to sit on the arm of Jem's chair. Jem immediately jumped up, having not even realised that he had remained seated when his sister had entered the room. The sudden disruption to the weight caused the chair to topple, and Grace suddenly fell to the floor.

It happened too quickly for anyone to do anything. Jem could only watch as Grace threw her arm out to break her fall. She landed awkwardly on her knee, before stopped herself with her hands, doing anything she could to protect her belly.

"GRACE!" Adam cried as he threw back his chair and whipped Perrie out of the way, setting her on the floor before he tore around his desk.

Jem stood motionless in shock.

"I'm fine!" Grace called from the floor. Once she had stopped herself from falling, she shifted onto her rear and brushed her hands together. "I'm honestly alright!" she said again as Adam fell to his knees, his hands fluttering over her with no obvious idea of what to do. But then they stopped, hovering a mere inch from her stomach.

Even with his back to him, Jem could see that Adam was frozen in fear. Jem was going to be sick. This could not be possible. What had he done?

But Grace settled everything. There was a smile on her face as she cupped Adam's in her hands. "Hush," she cooed. "I'm fine. I fell not even a foot. He's fine. I feel him. Here." Grace reached for Adam's frozen hand and placed it against her stomach. They were both silent for a moment, Adam's shoulders rigid, before they both exhaled a breath of relief.

"Oh, thank God," Adam whispered, before he leaned forward and placed a hard, relieved kiss against Grace's lips.

Perrie promptly burst into tears. Jem could have done the same.

"Oh, Perrie dear," Grace murmured sympathetically as she extended one of her arms, beckoning her daughter closer. "Come here. Come to Mama."

Perrie stumbled over to her parents and settled herself between them and she was quickly cocooned within their arms.

"Grace," croaked Jem, his voice nearly unrecognisable it was so thick with emotion. Could he really have been so swept up in his own envy and embarrassment that he neglected his pregnant sister's welfare?

The moment Grace heard her name spoken in such a way, her head snapped around. Her face fell and her brows furrowed with maternal-like sympathy.

"Jemmy!" Grace said firmly. Her tone was nearly chastising in a way. "It was an accident. Do not you blame yourself for anything. I could have quite easily sat down in the vacant chair." She nodded towards the empty chair that was beside the one Jem had been sitting in.

What if the baby had died? That happened, didn't it? Babies could die because of falls like that. What if he'd caused that because he'd been so careless? This was Jem's problem. He'd never had to worry about anything and –

"Jem!" Grace cried insistently, interrupting Jem's panicking.

Jem met his sister's blue eyes. "Grace, I am so sorry."

"I'm alright!" she assured him. "Perfectly fine. A little stumble is all. Adam, will you help me to my feet, please?"

Adam shifted off of the ground, delicately manoeuvring Perrie, before he gently pulled Grace to her feet. Adam swung Perrie up into his arms then as Grace came to stand before Jem.

Jem towered over his sister, but she still looked upon him as though she was taller. There was eleven years between them. The years carried more weight than the thirteen inches in height.

Grace stared at Jem, the furrow of her brow deepening as she appraised him, as she looked into him. Pursing her lips, she threaded her arm through Jem's and pulled him towards the door. Over her shoulder, she said, "Will you take Perrie to the nursery and wake Lily for me?"

"Anything," breathed Adam, his voice still shaken.

Grace smiled as her focus turned back forwards. Adam brushed past Grace with affection as he and Perrie left the study in the direction of the nursery, while Grace and Jem walked towards the first-floor landing. They were alone in the large gallery hall, save for the wandering eyes of the portraits that hung on the walls.

"Jemmy, what's wrong?" Grace asked gently. "Won't you tell me?"

"I nearly hurt you, Grace. That is what's wrong."

Grace tsked. "I am fine!" she promised, before she stopped in her tracks and seized Jem's hand. She thought for a moment before she found the right position, and pressed Jem's palm against her swollen stomach.

Jem felt nothing for a long moment, and his stomach nearly came up through his throat. But after the longest minute of his life, he felt something brush past his hand, before he felt a direct pulse, a kick.

"Your nephew is just fine, as is his mama."

Jem did feel genuine relief in feeling the baby's movement. He'd never felt anything like that before, and a smile tugged at his cheeks because of that miracle. "A boy, is he?" he whispered.

"I do not know for certain," replied Grace. "But it certainly pleases my mother-in-law to hear me refer to him as such. It feels different. It feels like a boy. But I know that if I have another girl, then she will be just as adored as my first two." Grace sighed. "But I know it is not just our welfare that wholly occupies your mind. I know something is wrong, Jem, and it hurts me to see you not acting like yourself."

Jem resisted hissing. Grace deserved no such reaction. How did he act before? Like a child? A child who did not know how to behave around beautiful young ladies. A child who panic proposes ... an act which probably drove Cressie from Ashwood.

"Do you know who you remind me of?"

Jem met his sister's knowing gaze. "Who?"

"Me," replied Grace. "Me when Adam left for school all those years ago. Broken-hearted and missing my favourite person."

Jem didn't say anything. But his face probably spoke for him.

"Peter told me, in so many words, that you rather favoured Miss Martin," Grace continued softly.

Traitor.

"Is that what is troubling you, Jemmy? Is it Miss Martin's absence?"

Jem managed a stiff nod. That was indeed troubling him. That and the fact that he had humiliated himself by ... panic proposing.

Grace pulled him into a tight hug. "I wish you would have said. I would have helped you in any way that I could have. Even if it is to just be an ear to listen."

Jem really did not know what could directly help him save for deeply apologising to Cressie for his foolishness and praying that she did not laugh at him like she did in his nightmares.

"Pardon me, Your Grace."

Jem and Grace were interrupted by Mr Cole, the butler, who stood several feet from them having come from the direction of the landing. In his hand was a silver tray with a letter upon it.

"Not at all, Mr Cole," said Grace, never losing the respectful way she had addressed the butler when she had been a housemaid at Ashwood. "What is it?"

"And express has just arrived from London for Mr Denham."

A letter for him? Jem frowned as he stepped forward to claim the letter, thanking the butler as he did so. Mr Cole bowed his head before departing. Jem recognised the handwriting immediately but turned it over to be certain.

"It's from the traitor," Jem muttered.

"The what?"

"Peter," Jem quickly corrected himself. "I wonder what is so important that he felt the need to send an express."

CHAPTER 2

March 18, 1812

Dear Jem,

I hope this letter finds you, Mother, and our family well, as always.

Belle and I are settling into our new home and are enjoying filling it with things that belong to us. I am especially enjoying seeing Belle take command of her own space and asserting her opinions and her authority over what is hers. It truly delights me.

But I must confess, writing to inform you of the progress of Belle's dress shop or our flat was not the purpose of this letter. I returned home this evening to some rather interesting news that I thought you would most definitely care to hear.

Belle was visited by two customers only this afternoon with whom we all share an acquaintance. Mrs Martin and her daughter, your Miss Cressie, came to order a ballgown for the latter's debut for this upcoming Season. It seems she did not fall off the face of the Earth after all! She is in London and preparing to enter into the marriage mart that is London in the summer.

What you do with this information is entirely up to you, brother, but I thought you would want to know. While I do not know the particulars of your acquaintance with Miss Martin, or how you parted, I do know that you were terribly fond of her, and that her absence has caused you pain.

No matter how we both enjoy vexing each other (you more than me!), I do sincerely wish for your happiness and felicity in your future union. Be the lucky woman Miss Martin, or another.

Should you decide to descend upon London in the near future, know that your brother and sister-in-law would be happy to host you. However, if you would prefer not to encroach upon the hospitality of two newlyweds who are so enjoying their privacy, I would tell you that my bedroom in the home of Jack and Claire is currently vacant.

I look forward to your reply.

Your brother,

Peter

Jem had read his brother's letter at least five times before he had left for home, and another time through before he had walked through the door of the Denham family home in the Ashwood village.

Jem had begun the letter dryly, truly wondering why his brother had sent an express to inform him of the progress of the dress shop. While he was certainly pleased for his brother and new sister-in-law, Jem had very little interest in silks and satins. But Peter had predicted this, and the true purpose of his letter had floored Jem.

The very idea that he knew exactly where Cressie was felt ... troubling. He felt extremely unsettled in his stomach, which was not the way he imagined he would feel if he had ever had the chance to see her again. But Jem presumed that he felt this way because of his terrible conduct at the Winter Assembly, and he knew that the feeling would never allay unless he apologised and corrected his behaviour.

On his walk back to his house, Jem's thoughts had momentarily strayed away from his own desire to correct the faux pas that was his panic proposal and had settled on the purpose of Cressie's being in London.

Cressie was in London to find a husband.

Cressie was in London to find a husband.

If he had not already felt ill, Jem's stomach churned.

The beautiful young woman, the girl with the curly, golden mane, and the warm brown, dimpled eyes who yearned to swim in the ocean, was going to be married off to someone ... someone who didn't understand her ... or someone who had no desire to.

Jem certainly didn't know Cressie as well as he would have liked to, but he certainly had the desire to. In their brief meeting, he had seen her spirit in her smile and the way her eyes flared when she spoke of something she longed to do. Cressie's spirit flowed within her veins and Jem's own yearning to know her had certainly never dissipated.

What made him sick was the vision of an old, portly gentleman seeing the beauty that was Cressie and marrying her to stow her on a mantle with his other trophies that gathered dust.

Jem was certainly no gentleman, but ...

"Jeremy Denham!" The door to his house swung open, and his mother stood in the entryway admonishing him. "What are you doing lurking about thus? I saw a great tree of a man skulking about from the window and I thought a marauder had come upon us all! Walk in the door properly, would you?"

Jem had quite possibly heard his mother use his given name five or six times in his life. It almost sounded foreign to him; Jem was so unused to hearing it. He had once posed the idea to his family that he would start going by his full name in an attempt to sound more refined and ... gentlemanly. But his family had quickly squashed that idea. They could never see him as a Jeremy. He would always be Jem. Or Jemmy, when they felt particularly inclined to baby him.

Jem obliged his mother and entered into the house, bending down to kiss her cheek. Mrs Denham was not satisfied with that as she quickly secured her youngest born child into a tight hug, before she kissed him several times on his forehead.

Jem was the farthest thing possible from a gentleman.

"Mother," he grumbled. "I am not an infant."

Mrs Denham laughed. "Says who? You are my baby whether you like it or not." But she did released Jem, who promptly righted his posture and straightened his coat. Mrs Denham pursed her lips as she appraised Jem. She left her cane leaning against the door as it closed and reached up to brush off his shoulders. "So handsome," she mused. "When did you get so handsome?" She smiled. "Come now. Supper is almost ready Amélie has been working her usual wonders in the kitchen. Alex had brought over a new ingredient that he has been cultivating. She had prepared something called an avocado pear. Have you ever heard of it?"

Jem adored his mother. He would always greatly respect her for the childhood that she had made certain he would enjoy. Jem never knew the troubles that some of his other siblings had faced, and he knew that he had been greatly protected by them all because of the age he had been when his father had died.

What frustrated Jem now in living at home with his mother was that he felt like a child, and not like the young man he longed to be. While he would never be a gentleman, he certainly had the ambition and motivation to make his way in the world.

He had felt more frustrated than ever seated at the table with Mrs Denham and Amélie with the knowledge that Cressie was in London husband hunting. And that was nobody's fault except for his own. Had he not panic proposed, he might have artfully formed an attachment to Cressie, and she in return. Instead, he had frightened her off.

Perhaps he had decided the minute he had read Peter's letter that he would be travelling to London, because his plan was firm in his head by the time that he had consumed his supper of avocado pears and plantains.

Jem was early to Ashwood House the next morning in a deliberate plan to catch both Grace and Adam together. They could always be found in the nursery in the early morning spending time together as a family before Adam went to his study to work.

Jem knocked on the door and opened it when he heard his sister's soft call to enter. Inside the nursery he found quite the scene of a father who doted upon his daughters. Adam sat before a great doll's house that had been gifted to Perrie by Cecily last Christmas. Jem's niece, Jackie, had been given an identical one that she would share with Maria when she was old enough. Lily was seated upon Adam's lap as both girls smothered their father with commands about which dolls could go where, and what furniture belonged in what room.

The dark haired two and four-and-one-half year olds had quite the control over their father, and Perrie, who would be five in September, seemed to know how to get her way already.

Grace smiled at Jem in greeting. She was seated in a rocking chair in the corner, her hands resting on her belly. Seeing her sitting there happily filled Jem with relief that no serious injury had been caused by the accident the day before. "Good morning,

Jem. You are here early," she remarked. "Did you have a sudden desire to play dolls?"

Adam turned his head and smirked. "Do join us," he encouraged. "Miss Pimsy is about to marry Mr Porky."

"Papa!" exclaimed Perrie, shock covering her sweet face. "Mr Porky isn't marrying Miss Pimsy! Miss Pimsy is the bridesmaid! He's marrying Miss Belle because she has the prettiest dress." Perrie shook her head at her father, as though he had missed the terribly obvious. "Here, Lily," Perrie held out one of the dolls to her sister, "you be Mr Porky because Papa keeps getting it wrong."

"Perrie, do not tell your sister or your father what to do," scolded Grace.

"But Mama!" cried Perrie, her blue eyes widening at her mother's sudden admonishment.

"But Mama nothing. Stop being a dictator, or we shall have to rename some of your dolls. Caesar and Brutus come to mind."

Adam sniggered at Grace's joke and Perrie was indeed most put out. She sighed dramatically as she reluctantly allowed Adam to re-join her game before graciously allowing Lily to be the Belle doll.

"You sound more like Mother every day," Jem observed as he sat down on Perrie's bed, the one nearest Grace's rocking chair.

Grace laughed softly. "Good. We five turned out well enough, did we not?"

Jem certainly thought his four elder siblings had become well-rounded and established adults. He was yet to join them. But he desperately wanted to. He wanted to be a man worthy of someone like Cressie.

Jem had considered lying to his family about his desire to go to London, but as soon as the thought had entered his mind, he had known it was the immature thing to do. After all Grace and Adam had done for him, he owed them the truth. And perhaps if they knew, they might be able to help him.

"I came here earlier this morning to share with you what Peter had written to me about in his express yesterday."

"Oh?" Grace inquired curiously.

"What express?" asked Adam from the doll's wedding.

"No, Papa, you must say 'man and wife'!" corrected Perrie.

"He wrote to tell me that Belle will be making the debutante gown for Miss Cressie Martin for the upcoming Season," Jem continued, his tongue nearly tripping over her name. "She and her mother are in London ... husband hunting."

Grace's lips parted in shock, and Adam's head turned towards them with his brows furrowed.

"And how do you feel about this news, Jemmy?" Grace asked after a moment.

"Sick." Jem couldn't hide the truth. It was most certainly etched all over his face.

Grace recoiled at his blunt answer, but she still appeared terribly sympathetic. By the way Adam did not appear shocked at this revelation made Jem realise that his entire extended family had most definitely been gossiping and fretting about this behind his back.

"Oh, Jem," murmured Grace.

"I came to ask if you knew ... if either of you knew if someone like me could go to London. Can men who are not gentlemen participate? Is it possible to meet with debutantes if you are not a rich lord with ten houses and three hundred servants?"

Adam's face softened and he offered Jem an encouraging smile. "Of course, it is. Half of the aristocracy haven't two shillings to rub together as they manage their fortunes so poorly. The Season is all about connections. Who knows whom? And luckily for you, dear brother-in-law, you happen to have a wonderful connection or two."

"I have only been to London the one time, but when I was there, I can heartily agree. Everybody was concerned about who had the best connections and who could secure them introductions," added Grace. "Quite frankly, I found the whole experience to be very superficial."

"But you would come?" Jem deduced from their explanations. The right connections would see him meet Cressie Martin again. "You would come to London with me?"

An expression of something crossed Grace's face that told Jem she was unsure of the idea. He final statement about London did give off the air that she had not necessarily enjoyed her time there. Perhaps that was the reason she had never ventured into Town since.

But Grace's sympathy returned as she looked to Adam. "What do you think?" she asked him.

"I won't have you do anything you do not wish to," Adam replied. "You will only be two months from delivering our child, as well."

Jem chastised himself for making such a selfish request, having momentarily forgot that his sister was expecting. "Grace, forget I asked," he said dismissively. "Never you mind it."

"No," Grace said forcefully. "No, I think it will be alright. I want to go. I have nothing to be afraid of or ashamed of. Besides, I imagine your mother would enjoy a trip to London for the Season, and I know Cecily will do everything in her power to look after me." Grace's eyes returned to Jem. "And I will do everything in my power to help you and Miss Martin find your way to one another."

Chapter 3

"**I** think a little tighter, perhaps a half inch there ... at the bust," Mrs Martin mused as she inspected Cressie's gown, or what would be her gown when Belle Desjardins was finished with it.

Cressie could not believe how quickly Miss Desjardins, or Mrs Denham, she supposed, had worked, to create the bones of her debutante gown. The Season's opening was imminent, and Mrs Martin had visited nearly every modiste in Town to procure a gown, but she was unable to get any credit. The news that Belle Desjardins was opening a shop for couture gowns was fortuitous, and the kind-hearted lady had done them all a great service. Mrs Martin was certainly paying for her services, but Belle Desjardins had not charged them anywhere near what a gown such as this would usually fetch.

"Are you certain, Madame?" Miss Desjardins asked with an uncertain brow. "Her measurements are correct. I would worry that tightening the bust would make the gown ... indecent."

Cressie felt her cheeks flush a crimson red. What was her mother thinking of? Such a request stank of desperation. Cressie understood her mother's desperation, certainly, but she did not want to walk into the Season dressed like it! Having to debut and marry in itself was horrid enough.

Miss Desjardins worked diligently during the fitting, managing Mrs Martin's requests with gentle professionalism as she refused them. Cressie couldn't help but admire her tact. It was obvious to anyone that Miss Desjardins knew what she was doing. She was certainly an incredibly talented dressmaker whose eye was second to none. She did not need external opinions, especially from anxious mothers.

Cressie, however, still felt the sense of shock in her stomach as she saw the thin gold band on Miss Desjardins' ring finger. Cressie remembered her standing beside the elder Mr Denham at the Winter Assembly last November. She then, of course, saw the newspapers that spread her awful experience about the country for the next month. If she suffered, or if she was still suffering from the pain of it all, it did not show on the flawless face of Belle Desjardins. Hearing Miss Desjardins reveal her marriage had startled Cressie.

But thoughts of the Winter Assembly, and thoughts of the name 'Denham', sparked another memory in Cressie. She thought of the boy who danced like a newborn fawn, but whose eyes and smile were filled with youthful vibrance. Cressie's thoughts often drifted to Mr Jem when she was sitting idly. How could they not? It was not very often one received a proposal, especially in the way that Cressie had received it from Jem Denham.

The whole ordeal still confounded her, and to this day she certainly had no idea what Mr Jem had been thinking of proposing to her after such a short acquaintance.

Cressie's initial shock regarding Mr Jem's proposal had faded. She still vehemently maintained her position that someone his age ought not to be marrying if he did not need to, just as Cressie had no desire to. Cressie was not at all certain that love would even persuade her to marry, not that she had much say in the matter. What she felt mostly now when she thought of Mr Jem was sadness and regret at how she had rejected him. Cressie had never been proposed to before. She had never been the subject of romantic interest before. She could blame her youth and inexperience, but she still knew how to behave, and turning her back on a young man who had done nothing remotely cruel to her was wrong.

Cressie wondered if she might ever see Mr Jem again. In meeting with Belle Denham, here and now, the idea was at the forefront of her mind. Should she ever meet with him again, Cressie would apologise and be done with it.

Cressie was quite certain that after quashing her guilt, her mind would never trouble her with thoughts of Jem Denham again.

"Oh, Cressie, my dear, you are going to be the most beautiful debutante this Season. I just know it." Mrs Martin clapped her hands together with pride as she took a step back to take in Cressie's appearance.

It hurt Cressie to see her mother so excited for her, because it meant that her determination and resolve to fight Mrs Martin fizzled. When she saw such hope in her mother's grey-green eyes, Cressie saw her own fate. No matter what, she would be wed before the Season was over. To whom, she had no idea.

Cressie prayed the man would not be an ogre.

Her head turned towards the sound of laughter. It sounded faintly outside, and peering through the front of the shop, Cressie saw a handful of children running past the window. What were they playing? What were they laughing about? Whatever it was, they sounded jovial and free from care or worry, or burdens to marry.

Cressie longed to join them. She longed to run. She didn't remember the last time she had moved faster than a lady-like promenade.

"Don't you agree?" Mrs Martin asked Miss Desjardins. "Is not my daughter a true beauty?" Mrs Martin had mentioned several dozen times how Cressie's beauty was as good as a dowry for some gentlemen, and that they would be relying upon her fair face and handsome features to bewitch her suitors into not caring for a dowry.

Miss Desjardins smiled politely. "Miss Martin is très beau," she agreed. "Would you care to wait out in the shop, Madame?" Miss Desjardins suggested to Mrs Martin. "I will assist Miss Martin in changing."

Mrs Martin nodded gleefully as she flitted back out into the shop. Cressie could see from where she was standing that her mother had immediately found a bin of fabric bolts and was inspecting the patterns with keen interest.

Miss Desjardins helped Cressie to step out of the gown in silence, before she spoke under her breath.

"Are you excited for the Season, Miss Martin?"

From the tone and volume of her voice, Cressie could tell that Miss Desjardins did not want Mrs Martin to overhear the conversation. What did she expect Cressie to say? Was Cressie really so transparent?

Her eyes found her mother once more and Cressie bit down on her bottom lip. Cressie's heart told her to fight, but her head told her to grow up. When she thought of what her mother had been through, and what she had done to essentially survive throughout her entire childhood, Cressie felt immense guilt for stomping her feet like a child when Mrs Martin spoke of her marriage.

Cressie understood she would need to marry eventually. All women did. For what were they without a husband? She would be seventeen soon. She was certainly not the youngest bride there ever was, nor ever would be.

Mrs Martin had sold every possession they had of value, giving them enough to participate in one Season, and one Season only. They bore a respectable name, even if the man who had given it to Mrs Martin was not at all gentlemanlike. They had taken a small but comfortable house for the summer off the main street of Grosvenor Square, and would be in a fit situation to receive callers.

It was certainly a charade, and one that would leave them destitute at Season's end if Cressie did not marry.

It was a heavy and heartbreaking burden weighing upon her young shoulders.

Cressie didn't want to marry. She wanted to run and swim and play and laugh and live.

But Cressie needed to marry, and she hated every bit of that knowledge.

Taking a breath, Cressie put on a smile, and replied, "Terribly. I cannot wait."

A fortnight later, Cressie sat at her dressing table, staring at her reflection, hardly recognising herself. She suddenly didn't look like a girl. Cressie certainly still felt every bit a mere girl, but she didn't look it. She looked like a lady ... and one who would not dive into a pond and splash about at her first opportunity.

Cressie's pale blonde hair was fastened in a style so intricate, it had taken the maid an hour and a quarter to complete it. Soft curls framed her cheeks which were flushed with rouge. The same rouge had been applied to her lips, which were the colour of pink roses.

She sat in what was perhaps the most exquisite dress she had ever seen, and certainly had ever worn. The white masterpiece featured a beaded bodice that fit her perfectly. The tulip sleeves were soft and weightless, and the skirt was made up of a half dozen layers of floating silk that had such elegant movement when she walked, Cressie would not have minded promenading.

The only part of herself that Cressie recognised were her dark brown eyes, which stared back at her showing her fear at what was to happen this evening.

Cressie was to debut. She was to be escorted into a grand hall before the queen and presented to all as a marriageable prospect. They were then to attend a ball. Their first invitation of the Season had arrived a week ago, and Mrs Martin had paraded it in front of Cressie's face as proof that making the acquaintance of the Duke and Duchess of Ashwood had been as important as she had originally said.

The duke and duchess were giving the opening ball of the Season. Cressie was already anxious to be attending a ball at all, but in knowing that she might once again meet with Mr Jem only increased her apprehension. She did not at all understand why, when she had so previously convinced herself that apologising to Mr Jem would allay all feelings of guilt.

"You are an angel, an angel," gushed Mrs Martin as she looked upon Cressie with tears in her eyes. "I cannot tell you how proud I am of you, my beautiful Cressida."

Cressie really had no idea what to say to her mother. She supposed she was glad that her apparent beauty pleased Mrs Martin, but she could not bring herself to say, 'you're welcome' for agreeing to debut when all she wanted to do was run away. She wondered if it would always be such a battle between her head and her heart.

Mrs Martin produced a necklace as she came up behind Cressie. She laid it delicately around her neck and fastened it at the back. "This was the necklace your father gave to me when we became engaged during my Season," Mrs Martin explained. "I had the diamonds replaced with glass long ago, but the setting remains beautiful, just like you. I hope it brings you infinite luck, as it did me. After all, it led me to you."

Tears sprung to Cressie's eyes as the familiar guilt weighed in her chest.

Mrs Martin kissed Cressie's cheek as she rested her hands on her shoulders. "I am certain you will fall passionately in love this season, my dear. I am certain that when it happens, marriage will not seem like such a foreign frightening thing to you as it does now."

"I don't know if I agree with you, Mama," Cressie whispered.

"Just look at you," replied Mrs Martin. "Any man would make a fool of himself to have your heart. And the gentleman who does secure it will be a fortunate man indeed."

Jem had never been in such a room in his life. Not even the grand halls of Ashwood House could compare to the Royal Court. And here he, the fifth child of a tailor and his wife, stood in a sea of England's elite and genteel, not fifteen feet from the queen herself. Jem could hardly breathe, let alone form coherent thoughts.

Adam, and now Grace, belonged to this world. They, alongside Cecily, were received by the people in this room as one of their own. Jem felt like quite an imposter dressed in an old suit of Adam's that his mother had altered for him.

And as the debutantes began arriving on the arms of their escorts, Jem wondered if his facial expression mirrored theirs.

They, too, looked like they might be sick on the hems of their terribly elaborate gowns.

"You stand up tall now, Jem," Grace whispered, only for him. "Cecily gave me some very valuable advice during my time in London several years ago. People will say what they will, and it is those who talk who envy us most. Waste not your time dwelling on the follies of others, but on your own endeavours."

A small smile twitched at the corner of Jem's lips.

"Do not forget the second part of the advice that I gave you, Grace," murmured Cecily, having overheard Grace's words.

Both Grace and Jem's heads turned towards Cecily.

"Waste not your time dwelling on others, of course, but should anyone require a dressing down, I am perfectly contented to spend my time doing the Lord's work." Cecily smiled smugly. "It's been quite a while since my tongue has delivered a lashing."

"Cecily!" admonished Grace, but Jem could hear the amusement in his sister's voice.

What an ally his sister had in the dowager duchess. Jem certainly would never wish to go against a woman like her.

"The Honourable Miss Jane Hartfield, escorted by her mother, the Lady Hartfield."

"Miss Catherine Allerton, escorted by her mother, Mrs Allerton."

"Lady Mary Liston, escorted by her mother, the Duchess of Kenwood."

The debutantes were announced one after the other, and all floated down the aisle as pictures of nervous beauty before they came before the queen to curtsey and receive her nod of approval.

"It seems only yesterday I walked into this room with Susanna for her first Season," mused Cecily. "You will blink, Grace, and suddenly it will be you and Perrie walking into this room upon her debut."

"Not bloody likely," muttered Adam. "I will glue my eyelids open if it only takes blinking for that to happen. Perrie is four."

"Going on fifteen," retorted Cecily with a sly smile. "Every day I grow curiouser and curiouser about the sort of match my eldest granddaughter will make. And then, of course, there is Lily who —"

"Who is only just two!" hissed Adam as he interrupted his mother. "Stop frightening me with images of my daughters leaving my house."

Grace held onto Adam's arm comfortingly as she leaned into his side. Adam seemed to visibly relax as she did this. Meanwhile, Cecily seemed very pleased with herself. Jem had no doubt Cecily could handle any one of these aristocrats with her eyes closed.

Jem had been so distracted by the quiet argument between Adam and Cecily that he was quite startled when the next debutante was announced.

"Miss Cressida Martin, escorted by her mother, Mrs Martin."

And there she was.

They were once again in the same room, and Jem stared at her openly. How could he not?

Cressie appeared like an angel in white, draped in a gown so soft and stunning it only accentuated her natural beauty. She walked on her mother's arm, her doe brown eyes focussed forward as she moved towards the queen.

She did not see him, of course, but as she neared him, and Jem could better study her face, his initial trance lessened. At a glance, anyone would see what a beautiful creature was Miss Cressie Martin, but upon closer inspection, Jem could see a tightness in her eyes and a stiffness in her jaw. Her posture was rigid, and her mother's grip was tight, as though Mrs Martin was preventing Cressie from turning around and running in the other direction.

But she walked past him gracefully, making it down the aisle of aristocrats to curtsey deeply before the queen, who in turn, have her a nod of approval, as she had done for the other debutantes.

"Belle has outdone herself," marvelled Cecily quietly. "That gown is divine."

While Jem would never disparage his sister-in-law's talents, he was quite of the opinion that in this case, it was the lady who maketh the gown.

"A fine choice indeed, Jem," whispered Grace. "I hope she is deserving of you."

CHAPTER 4

It had been five long years since the Duke and Duchess of Ashwood had made an appearance in London for the Season. Their invitation to the opening ball of the summer had become one of the most coveted in a long time, and each invite had been responded to rapidly with eager acceptances. Jem had kept a sharp eye out for the acceptance of Mrs Martin and her daughter, and it had promptly arrived.

Though the wiser of the ton knew many would be making an appearance to gawk at the duchess, as Grace had been the 1807 Season's favourite topic of gossip. The union between the duke and the housemaid had been touted by many to fail. How long would it be before the duke spurned his 'flavour of the month'? Such were the questions asked by those of whom who were not intimately acquainted with Adam and Grace. They had certainly proved the aristocracy wrong, having been happily married for five years and a half, with their third child expected in the next few months.

Jem clearly had been living in naïve fairyland in Ashwood, as he really had had no idea of the level of trouble and gossip the rich folk had caused Grace five years earlier. Cecily had spent a great deal of the afternoon raving about it, targeting her bitterness at the situation at Jem as he was the only one in the vicinity to hear her.

Cecily claimed that she was sharpening her knives, and her tongue, in preparation for that evening's festivities.

Jem had previously thought that he was the one with the most nerves surrounding the upcoming ball, but in seeing his elder sister, Jem felt immensely guilty. After all, it was he who had bade her come to London in the first place. Grace was doing all of this for him so that he might have a chance to reacquaint himself with Cressie. In her condition, Jem wanted to tell Grace to go home. He also wanted to fall at her feet in gratitude. He would in fact.

Grace resurfaced a little while later, dressed immaculately in a gown that both flattered and modestly concealed her growing figure. Her brow was stern as she spoke to both Mr Cole and Mrs Hayes, ensuring that the preparations were in order. Servants scurried about moving furniture and fixing candles while the foot-men assisted the musicians with their instruments.

"Grace, would you like to sit down?" Jem asked his sister carefully.

Grace frowned at him, before she exhaled and smiled knowingly. "I am alright," she promised. "People will say what they wish to. It will not change anything. Though, it will always bring me comfort to know that I have Cecily Beresford behind me. Nobody knows better how to dress down a matron of society than her."

"I take that as the highest possible compliment, dear Grace," Cecily announced, having heard her comment from across the ballroom.

"And I meant it as such!" called Grace.

An hour before the guests were due to arrive, Jack and Claire arrived, shortly thereafter followed by Peter and Belle. Both ladies were dressed in impeccable ballgowns, which could only be of Belle's creation. Belle really was a walking advertisement for her business.

Jem greeted his family members with welcome relief, feeling grateful to have familiar faces in the vicinity as he took his first fawn-like step into the deep waters of London society.

"You must quite be the favourite of Grace's to bring her back to London," mused Jack. "Or perhaps my dear sister-in-law is merely the romantic and she is desperate to see her brother swept up in a felicitous courtship."

"Of course, he is. Jemmy is the baby of the family," chuckled Claire as she clutched onto the arm of her husband. "Though I know we are all itching to meet with your Cressie Martin. I am anxious to see her. Peter told me that he and Belle met her at the assembly last November."

Of course, Peter did. He was a traitor. "She is not my anything," Jem snapped at Claire. "And you would do well not to call me 'Jemmy' in front of her, or baby me, or anything else!" Nobody knew what a fool he had made of himself at the assembly, and he would be truly grieved if his family made him appear to be an even greater fool.

Jem felt the need to take back his relief at seeing the familiar faces of his family.

Peter seemed to sense Jem's embarrassment. "Relax, Jem," he urged. "Your family will all be on their best behaviour. Though I would like to have it pointed out that upon my first encounter with Belle at Ashwood, you sat there laughing at my every folly from across the table."

"That was different!" Jem said exasperatedly.

"How so?"

"That was you and this is me!" he retorted.

Jack burst out laughing and Peter grinned.

Belle rubbed Peter's arm as she said, "I have seen Miss Martin a few times since she has arrived in London. I sense she is not happy to be here. I believe her to be sad even. Her mama seems to be the one who is most excited for her debut. I am certain that if you are sensitive to Miss Martin's feelings this evening that you will renew your acquaintance most successfully."

From what Jem had heard from Cecily, Cressie's dynamic between herself and her mother was not at all foreign in London. But thinking back to their conversation, he wondered if she would rather be swimming than dancing. He would certainly endeavour to be sensitive. "You are my favourite sister," Jem told Belle sincerely, "after Grace, of course."

Belle giggled as Peter slapped Jem on the arm. "You know you have us all as allies this evening, Jem."

"We cannot help but tease our youngest brother," added Claire, "but you know I wish you everything that we have managed to find."

"I might blush," Jack teased his wife, leaning in to kiss her temple.

"Jack! Claire!" Cecily voice called from the door of the ballroom as she walked in with the confidence and purpose of a queen. "And you have brought Peter and dear Belle with you also. Welcome!"

Jack separated from Claire briefly to receive his mother. Cecily received his kiss on the cheek warmly, as she looked around them expectantly.

"Where are my granddaughters?" she demanded to know with a frown on her face.

"Oh, well you know our two," Jack sighed, shaking his head with disappointment. "Jackie's drunk and passed out in her bedroom and Maria is at White's playing cards. She may be only nearing one, but her talent at the tables is to be revered. I am as disappointed as you are, Mother, but what are we to do?"

Cecily pressed her lips together firmly as Peter did his best to stifle a laugh. Claire rolled her eyes, but there was a hint of a smile in her eyes.

"They are at home in bed, Your Grace," Claire interjected, "but you are most welcome to join us tomorrow for luncheon. They will be most excited to see their grandmamma, Jackie especially."

"Claire's in denial, Mother," complained Jack. "She can't control the drunkard or the gambler any more than I can."

"Sarcasm rarely passes as wit, Jack Beresford," Cecily quipped.

"Oh, Mother, I heartily disagree." Jack grinned wickedly.

Cecily shook her head. "Thank you, Claire. I should very much like to join you. I hate to think how my girls have changed since I saw them last. Have I told you what I have decided on as a birthday gift to myself for this year?" she asked Claire as she stepped forward to claim her arm.

Claire looked quite suddenly shocked at Cecily's attention, but the dowager duchess did not seem to notice. Cecily pulled Claire away from Jack and took her on a turn about the room.

"I shall be commissioning a portrait of my grandchildren to be painted at Christmastime. Both Grace's and Susanna's little ones will be here by then and I shall have all six together," Cecily planned gleefully.

Jack smirked, before shaking his head. Jem was glad for the distraction, even if his nerves were still up in his throat.

An hour later the halls of Ashwood Place were filled with London's elite. It seemed every thirty seconds another lord, lady, countess, marquess or baron was being introduced into the ball.

Jem had never felt so extraordinarily plain before, and he did not think that it had ever occurred to him just what a duke or a duchess was. Grace had always been his elder sister, even when she had married Adam, but seeing the people among whom she outranked, or ranked equally, was bewildering.

Jem was wearing his very best of suits, and he knew that aesthetically, he did blend in well with the gentlemen, even though he was not one. The ladies were all draped in luxurious cloths and jewels and effortlessly glittered in the bright candlelight of the Ashwood ballroom.

The musicians played their strings beautifully, and the dancers had already taken their places for the first of the evening. In standing at the edge of the ballroom, Jem was in prime position to view the entrance, but he was also privy to the snide conversations shared between the guests who were not dancing.

"I see Lord Harding has already secured Miss Denny's hand for the first dance," sneered one. "Does he not know that she is only to share in five thousand pounds when her father dies? She had six siblings and her father appears to be in excellent health. I wonder why Lord Harding wastes his time."

"Oh, I quite agree, Agatha," chimed in the first's conversation partner. "And Miss Denny is hardly anything to look at. What unremarkable features, indeed."

Jem followed the two ladies' line of sight to lay eyes upon a couple who could only be the Lord Harding and Miss Denny in question. Indeed, they looked like a young couple rather enjoying the other's company. Lord Harding was smiling, and Miss Denny was blushing as she danced.

Jem was about to dismiss the two women as ridiculous and jealous before walking away when his ears suddenly pricked up at hearing the mention of Grace.

"How altered the Duchess of Ashwood appears this evening," commented the first, Agatha. "So pale and unsightly. She is not fit to be seen. I suppose that is what five years in the country will do to a maid. I do pity the poor duke having to hide the shame of her away. What an embarrassment."

Jem looked upon the woman with astonishment, as they could certainly not be referring to his sister! No matter how nervous she was about this evening, Grace stood at the entrance of the ballroom on Adam's arm, greeting her guests with a beautiful glow that could only be attained through impending motherhood.

Not fit to be seen. An embarrassment. What utter stupidity.

"She has kept the duke away from London all these years as well," continued her friend. "I hear he remains quite faithful to her. Very peculiar, indeed. I wonder what beguiles him so," she mused with a distasteful tone. "But then, did we all not wonder this five years ago? It seems housemaids nowadays do so much more that lay fires and change linens."

Jem's tongue seemed to swell in anger as he couldn't find the words to admonish the two women for insulted the duchess, his sister, in her own house. Jem was fortunate, though, that the dowager duchess had also been nearby. Cecily appeared beside the two women with a saccharine sweet smile and a deadly stare.

"Good evening, Lady Thornbridge, Mrs Clymoth," Cecily greeted.

Jem could see the blood draining from the faces of the two women.

"Your ... Grace," they both stammered.

"I could not help but overhear that you had some concerns surrounding my son, the duke, and my daughter-in-law, the duchess," Cecily said sympathetically. "While I thank you for your anxious interest in the duke's fidelity, I can happily assure you that he remains very devoted to his beautiful wife and their children." Cecily placed a condescending hand on the arm of the first woman, Agatha. "Though, I cannot say the same for your husband, Lady Thornbridge. I heard your recently dismissed scullery maid was lately delivered of a child that bore the striking image of Lord Thornbridge. The poor child, indeed. No innocent creature should have to suffer that nose." Cecily smiled. "Good evening to you both."

Jem stared openly at the exchange. He had heard time and time again that Cecily Beresford knew how to operate within ballrooms such as these, but to witness it firsthand was something else entirely.

Cecily subsequently noticed Jem's presence, and she offered him a cunning smile. "And that is how it is done, young Jem," she said coolly, before moving past him to greet an old acquaintance.

Moments later, the next guests were announced into the ballroom.

"Mrs Martin and her daughter, Miss Cressida Martin!"

The volume of heads turning did not increase as it did when an eligible peer was announced into the room, but Jem's head certainly did. There she was. Cressie walked into the ballroom on the arm of her mother, dressed in a gown of rose pink, her blonde hair affixed with flowers of the same colour. Cressie and Mrs Martin were immediately received warmly by Adam and Grace, and Mrs Martin looked incredibly grateful for the renewed acquaintance.

An attendant assisted Cressie in fastening her dance card to her wrist before they were moved along as the next guests were waiting to be greeted by the duke and duchess.

Lord, she looked beautiful tonight. She looked beautiful always, but tonight she was especially lovely. From where Jem was standing, her skin looked like flawless porcelain, save for the healthy flush in the apples of her cheeks. Her hair shone under the candlelight as she looked up to marvel at the chandelier above them.

Though the announcement of Cressie's name had not sparked the attention of many, Cressie's appearance had begun to turn heads. Like they whispered about Grace, they begun to whisper about Cressie.

"So lovely. So young. A pity about her lack of fortune."

"Good family on her mother's side. Her face should certainly find her a suitor or two who would not want for a sum."

"Really, fancy her mother launching her when she is only what? Seventeen? And with no dowry, the poor child does not stand a chance."

"What a beauty. She will certainly be a prize, to be sure. I wonder what would make a girl like her blush. Who do I have to shag to arrange an introduction?"

The last comment was not spoken by one of the gossips, but by one of the gentlemen, though by the tone of his voice and the wickedness of his brow, the man barely warranted the name.

Jem managed to swallow his nerves and find his feet as he moved away from the edge of the ballroom and started towards where Cressie and her mother were taking in the splendour of the occasion. Jem was not the only man making his way towards Cressie, and this knowledge made his legs move faster. Owing to the fact that he possessed disproportionately long limbs, he reached the Martins first, almost accosting them in his ambition to beat his fellow suitors.

And suddenly, Jem came face to face with Cressie after several long months of wondering exactly what had happened to her. And his tongue swelled once more.

Cressie's deep brown eyes widened in recognition, her brows rising as her lips parted in surprise. "Mr Jem!" she gasped.

"Mr Denham," greeted Mrs Martin with a little more composure than her daughter, though she, too, appeared a little affronted at Jem's sudden appearance before them. "How nice to see the brother of the duchess again."

"Ladies," Jem managed to finally say, bowing his head, taking a moment to look down at his feet while taking a breath, before standing back up straight and ordering himself to behave normally. "I am pleased to see you both again, as well." His eyes flicked to Cressie's, and she was looking upon him intently with an undiscernible expression.

Was it pity? Was it compassion? He was loathed to think it was pity. Jem was not at all certain his pride would survive it. But Jem dismissed this. His pride would survive it. It had to. Jem was determined to make amends for his ridiculous faux pas and present himself to Cressie in a better light.

"Miss Martin, would you do me the honour of dancing the next with me?"

"Oh," breathed Cressie, before she looked to her mother.

Mrs Martin gave her permission with a nod as Cressie extended her gloved wrist to him, from which her dance card dangled. Jem signed his name to the Cotilion.

The musicians played the final notes of the first dance as Jem finished his signature. When he was upright again, he extended his arm to Cressie, and was thankful when she placed her hand on his forearm. Out of the corner of his eye, Jem spied Grace watching him with a proud smile at the entrance. Jem was certain that his siblings and their spouses were likewise watching from wherever they were in the ballroom.

While Jem thought that he would be the first one to speak, as soon as they were out of reach for the ears of Mrs Martin did Cressie speak to Jem with fervent concern. "Oh, Mr Jem, I am so pleased to meet with you again. I have been in dreadful disarray every time I have thought of you since last we met at the Winter Assembly."

Jem's pride foolishly swelled at the thought that Cressie had thought of him during their time apart. Reality quickly settled him as he sensed the sympathy and regret in her voice.

"What on earth do you have to be in disarray about, Miss Martin?" Jem asked with genuine confusion, his thoughts leaving his mouth without volition. "It was I who assaulted you with my own foolishness." Jem immediately regretted his words. Why was he trying to convince her of his own folly?

Cressie frowned momentarily before she shook her head. "No, no. You must understand that nobody has ever spoken to me in that way before. I didn't know what to do or how to behave, and I know that is not excuse for my behaviour, but I do sincerely apologise for turning away from you as I did. I hope you can find it in your heart to forgive me. In seeking me out thus I do hope that means that you possess a forgiving heart."

Jem could not quite believe what he was hearing. Cressie was anxiously apologising to him. He could see the anguish in her eyes as she spoke. There was indeed guilt in their doe brown depths.

Much of Jem's own apprehension seemed to melt away as he became determined to settle her, and to take away any unnecessary and ridiculous guilt that she was feeling.

"Miss Martin, please," he murmured softly. "You have nothing to apologise for. I wanted to apologise to you for my own abruptness. I did not mean to alarm you, and I can assure you that I was most embarrassed by my own actions. I ... I realise what an extraordinarily odd thing it was to do to ..."

"Propose to me?" Cressie interjected, finishing Jem's sentence as his own words failed him.

"Yes," Jem nodded, replying awkwardly.

Cressie bit down on her bottom lip as she looked up at him in study. "I think we are both too young to be in this world of balls and suitors and marriage," she mused.

"I don't know," returned Jem. "I have seen enough happiness in marriage to know that if one has the opportunity, one should not waste any time in being with the one they love."

Jem was suddenly impressed with himself. That was said in a remarkably smooth manner. And he had not even had a drop of champagne. Whatever it was that was flowing through his veins, he prayed it continued.

Cressie frowned as the musicians began to play the opening bars of the Cotilion. Both she and Jem took their places in the sequence. "You are not suggesting that you have already been married at your age, are you, Mr Jem?"

Jem openly chuckled as they stepped forwards towards each other, spinning around each other, his breath momentarily catching as he held Cressie's small hands in his. "No, certainly not. I refer to my sister, Grace. She —" It suddenly occurred to Jem that he ought not to be discussing his sister's affairs in the middle of a dance sequence among those who probably would enjoy spreading gossip about the duchess.

"The duchess seems very devoted to the duke, and he to her," Cressie observed with a smile, the dimples under her eyes deepening.

Jem managed to fumble his way through the remainder of the dance, and he was once again regretful that he was not at all a graceful dancer. He could feel that his cheeks were hot with embarrassment as the music ended and he bowed to Cressie. Cressie, in turn, curtseyed.

"Truthfully, Mr Jem, you dance like a fawn and I find it to be a very redeeming feature in you." Cressie stood a few feet from him with her arms at her sides, seemingly possessing no qualms at offering a man a compliment.

Jem did not know whether it was boldness, naivety, or a combination of the two that allowed Cressie to speak so openly. Whatever it was, he admired it.

"Truthfully, Miss Martin, I feel very out of place here," he confessed.

Cressie's eyes softened. "Truthfully, Mr Jem, so do I. I feel as though it is in my nature to be unladylike no matter how my mother tries, and I worry that there is a rather large part of my will that wants to deliberately do something childish just so that I might feel a little bit more like myself in this dress."

Jem found it extraordinary that this young woman could make his stomach sick with nerves, and yet he could talk to her, say things to her as though they were old friends, and not relatively new acquaintances. He believed that Cressie felt this way, too, or else she would not speak with him so openly without fear of a consequence. Not only was she outwardly beautiful, there was something overwhelming enticing about her spirit. He was quickly believing her to be a kindred spirit.

CHAPTER 5

Cressie's anxieties surrounding her conduct towards Jem Denham were settled in how he had received her apology, and in how he had apologised for his own actions as well.

Because of this, she was unsure of why her stomach still felt as though it were tied in knots in his presence. If he was not angry with her, or ashamed of her behaviour, then why did she still feel so odd?

"Would it ... would it be too presumptuous of me to ask for a second dance, Miss Martin?"

Cressie's knotted stomach flipped over as she nodded, and she gladly took Jem's arm as he led her back into the sequence of dancers. As she stood across from him, Mr Jem smiled at her. It was a smile of youthful vibrance and spirit, and Cressie found herself quite breathless in receipt of it.

Cressie did not look away from Jem Denham's ocean blue eyes throughout the entire dance. Of course, Cressie had never seen the ocean, but the hue of his eyes was what she imagined it to look like. Mr Jem did not look away from her eyes either, no matter how he stumbled through the steps.

Her own amused smile teased at her lips as she once again thought of a fawn dancing. Mr Jem was so tall, with such long arms and legs, that the image could not quite escape her mind when she danced with him. She had told him as such, and she quite meant it. Cressie found it to be an extremely favourably quality. Somehow, Mr Jem's lack of grace on the dancefloor made Cressie feel oddly safe in his presence.

Though, this notion of safety did nothing to quell her tight, uneasy stomach.

"I believe I should be offended at your laughing at me, Miss Martin," Jem murmured to her when the dance finished as they all applauded the musicians.

Cressie's eyes widened. "Oh, no. I would never," she promised him.

"Do not worry. I am glad to be able to make you laugh, even if it is at me." Mr Jem smirked as he bowed his head to her.

They looked at one another then, unsure of what to do next. Cressie imagined that, like her, this was the first proper ball that Mr Jem had attended. Despite being the brother of the duchess, his young age had to have meant that he was excluded from occasions like this until now. What would he had gotten up to while the aristocrats in his family danced and dined? Cressie could sense Mr Jem's spirit, and she wondered, or rather hoped, that it was as childlike at hers.

Cressie's own unladylike spirit wanted to run away from this ballroom. Not out onto the street, but to run upstairs, to explore and poke around nosily in rooms that were shut away. Such silly, clandestine behaviour excited her, and she got the sense from Mr Jem that he would be very agreeable to such a suggestion.

It took her mother appearing beside her to remind Cressie that she was, in fact, a lady, and to be alone with a man was entirely unacceptable. Her heart sank, and it joined in on the congealed, tangled mess that was her stomach.

Mr Jem's back straightened in the presence of Mrs Martin, and he bowed once again to her. "Your daughter is a lovely dancer, Mrs Martin," he complimented nervously.

Mrs Martin offered a polite smile. "Yes, she is indeed," she agreed. "Good evening to you, Mr Denham." She smoothly threaded her arm through Cressie's and began to lead her away.

Cressie anxiously looked over her shoulder at Mr Jem, where he offered her a warm, understanding smile. He nodded his head, before he turned in the direction of his sister.

"You cannot allow one man to singularly command your attention, Cressie," her mother murmured to her. "We do not want the gentlemen here thinking that your affections have been captured already."

Cressie recoiled at the notion, almost affronted at her mother's insinuation. She was being ridiculous. That was not at all what she was doing. Cressie merely enjoyed Mr Jem's presence and smile and spirit and demeanour. There was certainly no affection, and she was confident in this assessment owing to the fact that her stomach seemed to be seized quite painfully as she thought of Mr Jem and the idea of affection together.

"I have someone that I would like to introduce you to. I secured my own introduction from the duchess while you were dancing. He is a Mr Everett Delaney." Mrs Martin's tone was hushed but excitable. "He is a landed gentleman originally from Suffolk, I am told, but he has made his fortune in Yorkshire with several cotton mills. He is in search of a wife this Season."

An overwhelming feeling of dread quickly filled Cressie as she sensed her mother's scheming, good intentioned as she was. It was only the first ball of the Season. How many more Everett

Delaney's would she be forced to meet? And which one of them would she be encouraged to wed? She only prayed Mr Delaney was not an ogre.

Mrs Martin nonchalantly led Cressie over to a well-dressed gentleman standing with an older couple. He looked rich and distinguished to be sure, but he also appeared old. Cressie was certain that her mother would chastise her for thinking a man who would have to have been in his mid-thirties old, but as she was not yet seventeen herself, this gentleman was old.

Mr Delaney noticed Mrs Martin's presence immediately, and he smiled a charming smile. He had an elegant face with handsome features, and he carried himself with an air of superiority and grace. His hair was thick, and dark blond in colour, while his eyes were a cool grey. They found Cressie immediately, and his smile widened.

Cressie's mind unwittingly compared it to the smile she had received only moments ago from Mr Jem. She felt nothing of Mr Delaney's spirit in his smile. She had no desire to run amok with him, though she was certain that a man who held himself with such poise had far better things to do than find mischief. But it was unsettling not to sense this man's spirit. Did he have any?

"Mrs Martin, how lovely to see you again so soon. And I see you have brought me a lovely flower," crooned Mr Delaney smoothly.

Mrs Martin laughed musically, seemingly charmed by Mr Delaney's compliments. "My Cressida is very lovely, is she not? You are quite perceptive, and very kind, Mr Delaney," she responded. "But allow me to introduce my daughter to you properly. Mr Delaney, this is Miss Cressida Martin. Cressida, may I introduce Mr Delaney."

"I am delighted to make your acquaintance, Miss Martin," Mr Delaney bowed to her, and Cressie suddenly remembered to curtsey.

"And I yours, Mr Delaney," Cressie replied automatically, and rather unenthusiastically. A side glance from her mother prompted Cressie to put on a charmed face. She was not in this ballroom to suit herself.

"I would be truly honoured if you would grant me the next dance, Miss Martin, if you are not engaged already."

"Cressida would be delighted, Mr Delaney!" exclaimed Mrs Martin. "And she is certainly not engaged."

Mr Delaney stepped forward, his movements graceful and poised, and offered his arm to Cressie. With a nudge from her mother, Cressie placed a hand on his arm and allowed herself to be led towards the dance floor by Mr Delaney.

"Are you enjoying the evening, Miss Martin? I am finding the festivities animated indeed."

"I ... yes," Cressie managed to say, stumbling over her words. "It is a lovely party." She stole a glance up at Mr Delaney, and she found that he was looking upon her with his focussed, confident eyes. Cressie could not quite determine what he was thinking. To be polite, she asked, "Are you enjoying the evening?"

"Oh, most definitely," he replied.

Mr Delaney was a fine dancer who never put a toe out of sequence. He was light on his feet and led Cressie with expertise and experience. Cressie knew that she ought to have been impressed, but she couldn't help but wonder why she wasn't.

"I am certain your drawing room will be filled with gentleman callers tomorrow," Mr Delaney commented.

"Oh, I hope not," Cressie responded without thinking. The moment the words had escaped her lips, she blushed. She had not even begun to think of the prospect of having gentleman calling on her. What on earth did one speak about? Marriage, probably. Cressie managed to stop herself from shuddering and composed herself well enough to correct her slip of the tongue. "Our drawing room could not possibly fit more than one or two callers."

Mr Delaney chuckled. "Well, that is pleasing news," he replied. "I am in London this Season to select a ... a flower for my garden," he put delicately. "I should be incredibly honoured if you would allow me to call upon you in the morning so that we might speak again in a room a little quieter than this one."

Cressie managed to hold her tongue this time, and she did not allow herself to say what had first popped into her mind. This was what was meant to happen. This was why she and her mother were in London. Perhaps she had no sense of Mr Delaney's spirit yet. Maybe it would come if they spoke again. And just maybe at the next ball she would meet someone who would not be quite so old, or quite so preoccupied with flowers. Cressie imagined herself more like a bird that could fly. Or a bird that wanted to fly but whose wings were clipped.

"I ... I would welcome your visit, Mr Delaney," Cressie said, stammering through her acceptance.

Mr Delaney offered her an amused smile. "Excellent."

Mr Delaney arrived at the Martin residence promptly the next morning at ten o'clock. Mrs Martin had already had Cressie up and dressed, and she was as proper as she ever had been at that time of day.

Mr Delaney was led to the small drawing room by their servant, Nelly, whom they had employed for the summer out of necessity for appearances. He arrived with two beautiful bouquets, a large one for Mrs Martin, and a smaller, tasteful arrangement of tulips for Cressie.

"I did not ask for your favourite blooms, Miss Martin. I thought I would bring you my favourites." Mr Delaney sounded very satisfied with himself. "I can see that they are your favourites, too."

Cressie did think that the pink flowers were very pretty, but if she thought of her favourite flowers, she thought of the wild ones growing in fields that brushed against her petticoats as she ran.

"You are very kind, Mr Delaney," Cressie said gratefully as she brushed her fingertips over the silky petals.

Mrs Martin sat in a chair by the window, her embroidery in her hands, though Cressie knew that while Mr Delaney was present, not a stitch would be made. She and Mr Delaney both sat down on the settee, a few feet between them as they turned in towards one another.

"I find that I have thought of little else but our dance together last night," he began, exhaling through a surprised smile. "You are quite an enchanting young lady."

Was Cressie supposed to return the compliment? She wasn't sure. What was polite? It would be an out and out lie if she told him that she had thought of little else but him? Why, she had dreamed of fawns the night before! And as soon as the thought popped into her head, it had fallen out of her mouth. "I have been thinking about deer!"

Mr Delaney frowned, perplexed. "Deer?" he repeated. "Are you fond of venison?"

And at the mention of venison, Cressie was shocked into realising that she would never touch such meat again. "Fawns," she persisted, with no sense of control over her own tongue.

"Cressida is quite the naturalist, Mr Delaney!" Mrs Martin called anxiously. "Always reading and caring about God's creatures! She possesses such a compassionate heart."

Mr Delaney appeared pleased. "I should like to shoot such a creature for you one day, Miss Martin. It would be my honour."

Cressie was utterly horrified at the notion, and Mrs Martin noticed this immediately. She abandoned her embroidery and rushed to the back of the settee, placing her hands on Cressie's shoulders. "Oh, Mr Delaney. You have shocked Cressie most considerably with your thoughtfulness. She would be delighted to receive whatever you send when next you hunt."

No. No, she would not. What if he sent her a fawn? Cressie jumped when she felt a pinch on the back of her neck, and she dismissed her panicked thoughts. She was supposed to be being polite.

"Perhaps you could just look at it," Cressie suggested feebly. "You need not shoot anything."

Her comment seemed to amuse Mr Delaney considerably, and he laughed heartily. Mrs Martin joined in.

"Oh, Miss Martin, what a delicate heart you have indeed." He certainly seemed gratified with Cressie's comments, even though she, herself, felt as though she was stumbling rather terribly through the conversation.

Their conversation did, thankfully, move away from hunting and fawns, and Mr Delaney spent the next half hour telling Cressie about his success in the north with his cotton mills, and the rather palatial Yorkshire estate that he had recently purchased. Cressie responded with appropriate enthusiasm when he gave her the opportunity to respond.

In speaking with Mr Delaney, Cressie was able to decide that he was a very self-assured gentleman who was rather concerned with himself. Though, she supposed that was confidence, and she could not dismiss a man for having confidence.

She thought him pleasant and charming enough, but she felt nothing when she thought of romance. All she could think of was the fact that he was some two decades older than her. Would not he be more satisfied with a lady with more experience?

Cressie was quite certain that he would find someone better suited to him during the Season.

When Mr Delaney took his leave of them, he surprised Cressie by taking her hand and kissing it. Cressie's arm fell practically dead in shock at his actions. He was kissing a dead limb. But he did not seem to notice.

"I look forward to seeing you again, Miss Martin." Mr Delaney smiled once more, before offering Mrs Martin his compliments for her hospitality. And then he was gone.

"What a charming young man, Cressie," Mrs Martin declared.

"Young?" repeated Cressie. "Mama, he could well be older than you!"

Mrs Martin tsked. "Pish posh," she said dismissively. "It does not hurt for a gentleman to have some years and worldliness. They are matured and ready to support a wife and a family. I thought Mr Delaney was perfectly lovely."

Cressie physically bit down on her tongue to stop herself from suggesting to her mother that she marry him. She sat down in a huff on the settee and knitted her fingers in her lap.

Mrs Martin sighed sadly and sat down beside her. "Darling, you will know such happiness when you are married. You will know what it is to be the mistress of your own house. You will know security. You cannot know how it pains me to have failed to give you that surety. I feel like I have failed you, and I am trying to mend it now."

Guilt stirred in Cressie's stomach. "Mama," she whispered. She didn't want her mother thinking or feelings those things.

Mrs Martin put an arm around Cressie's shoulders and kissed her cheek. "Everything will be alright. Do not you worry."

Nelly knocked on the door to the drawing room and both Cressie and Mrs Martin looked up.

"Another caller for Miss Martin, ma'am. A Mr Denham is here."

Mr Jem stepped into the drawing room carrying an expensive bouquet of flowers in one hand, and a velvet drawstring bag in the other.

Both Cressie and her mother stood up immediately, and Cressie felt as though a terrible weight had been lifted off of her shoulders now that she was standing in the presence of Mr Jem again. She felt his vibrance immediately, even if there was a nervous energy about him, and it made her smile. Her friend was there. It was so lovely to feel that a friend was near.

But the moment after she smiled, Cressie felt her stomach begin to tense and gurgle. Was she hungry? Perhaps that was what was wrong with her?

"Good morning, Mr Denham," greeted Mrs Martin, quickly putting on a pleasant smile.

Mr Jem bowed to her, and then he bowed to Cressie. "Good morning to you both. I hope you are well, and I apologise for calling unannounced."

"Certainly, you are welcome," Mrs Martin beckoned him into the room, before she wandered over to her chair by the window with her abandoned embroidery.

Mr Jem looked between Mrs Martin and Cressie rather awkwardly, before he made his way over to Mrs Martin at the window. "I have brought these for you, Mrs Martin." Mr Jem held out the bouquet of flowers to her.

"Chrysanthemums," Mrs Martin murmured as she appraised the bouquet. "Did you know, Mr Denham, on the Continent, chrysanthemums are the symbol of death, and are given to mourners?"

Cressie watched as the blood drained from Mr Jem's face. She felt a great deal of sympathy as she presumed that he had selected the blooms for their beauty alone. She had never known her mother to be cruel, but she felt that Mrs Martin was deliberately trying to make Mr Jem feel uncomfortable.

"Oh ... I ... uh ... I meant no offence," stammered Mr Jem.

Mrs Martin offered him a small smile. "Of course not. Nelly, would you put these in some water by the flowers from Mr Delaney? Thank you," she said, as their servant collected the bouquet.

"Won't you sit down?" Cressie asked him, motioning to the settee. She took a seat herself and Mr Jem quickly crossed the small room to join her. Cressie felt an immediate need to bring Mr Jem's smile back.

"I hope I am not being rude. I didn't know I was supposed to ask," he told her quietly. "It seems silly now that I say it out loud, but my sister told me that I should have asked if I would be welcome to call upon you today."

"You are forgiven, Mr Denham," called Mrs Martin. "Cressie's suitor has already been this morning. You have not interrupted."

A flash of emotion crossed Mr Jem's face before he composed himself. Cressie wanted to tell him, and her mother, that she did not consider Mr Delaney a suitor, but she knew that she would be chastised for speaking inappropriately.

"My sister told me that flowers are customary gifts. I ... I thought the white ones were nice. I've never even heard of chrysanthemums."

Cressie's eyes flicked to her mother. Mrs Martin was pretending to embroider, but her eyes were down. She leant in closer. "They are nice. Mourners on the Continent have excellent taste."

Cressie felt a spark of glee when a smile teased the side of Mr Jem's lips. "I appreciate your grace, Miss Martin. It well and truly makes up for my lacking in that arena."

Cressie had but one thought, and it was again of a fawn.

"Grace told me I ought to bring two bouquets, but I thought you might like this a little more," Mr Jem continued, bringing the velvet back into his lap. Cressie's curiosity was piqued.

"How kind of you to bring a gift for Cressida," Mrs Martin called over to them. "She is a modest young lady. I hope you did not spend a fortune. Did you?"

Cressie shuddered at her mother's tactless way of inquiring after Mr Jem's finances. That was what she was doing, was it not? Was it not rude to ask after the value of a gift?

"On the contrary, Mrs Martin, this did not cost me a penny," Mr Jem replied.

"Oh, how terribly savvy of you," replied Mrs Martin. "Though, I am certain, as the brother of the duchess, you would have vendors chomping at the bit for your business." She laughed, but she was still fishing shamelessly.

Mr Jem shook his head rather uncomfortably. "My sister and brother-in-law rarely frequent London. This is my first time to Town. I do not think any vendor would have a clue who I was."

"Mama!" Cressie said firmly, giving her mother a frustrated glare. Did not Mrs Martin realise she was being rude to a guest?

Mrs Martin acquiesced, and went back to faking her embroidery.

"It really did not cost me anything ... does that matter?" Mr Jem wondered as he loosened the strings on the bag.

"No!" promised Cressie.

The small smile that had appeared on Mr Jem's lips a moment ago increased, and Cressie mirrored his happy expression.

"I turned eighteen a little while ago. My sister-in-law, Belle, gifted this to me for my birthday. I loved it, I love it, but I think you will love it more." Mr Jem put his hand into the bag and withdrew a rather remarkable object. "It is a conch shell," he informed her. "Belle collected it on a beach and brought it back from a country called Haiti in the Caribbean."

The shell itself was a glorious pale orange colour, covered in little black markings and natural bumps and spikes, twisting over itself to protect its glistening pink interior.

Cressie audibly gasped at the beautiful shell and was entirely mesmerised by the fact that this glorious object had been found on a beach and had touched the sea.

Mr Jem placed the shell into Cressie's hands. She immediately ran her fingers over the rough texture of the outside, before feeling the shiny, smooth texture on the inside.

"I remember you told me that you longed to swim in the ocean," Mr Jem continued, and in that moment, Cressie did not care that her mother had heard her fanciful dream. "Did you know that shells are magical?"

"Magical?" repeated Cressie.

"Place it to your ear," he encouraged.

Cressie immediately obeyed him and placed the cold shell to her right ear. Immediately she was overwhelmed by the whoosh-ing sounds that she could hear. It was as though there was a storm inside of the shell! She pulled it away quickly to ensure that the weather had not turned, before she placed the shell back to her ear, and sure enough, she heard it again.

"It's the ocean," Mr Jem explained. "What you hear is the sea, where this shell has come from. I thought ... I thought it might help you to imagine what it would be like to swim in the sea, to tide you over until you can do it in reality."

Cressie stared at Mr Jem, her mouth wide open in utter amazement, as tears began to roll down her cheeks.

CHaPTer 6

Jem felt such a deep sense of pride as he watched the tears fall from Cressie's expressive brown eyes. Ordinarily he would have thought it a great sin to make a lady cry, but he could see from the look on her face that what he had done had meant a great deal to her.

Cressie was seated not two feet from him, the conch shell still pressed against her ear as she listened to the sea for the first time. She smiled as she cried, with the dimples underneath her eyes forming utterly endearing craters.

Her reaction to his gift tugged at Jem's heart a great deal. He already cared for Cressie. He had done from afar ever since he had laid eyes upon her. But he hadn't known her, not really. There was still much of Cressie Martin that remained a mystery to him. But with each meeting, she showed Jem the type of person that she was.

Cressie was a beautiful soul who wore her heart on her sleeve. She was tender yet spirited, and in that moment, she was someone who believed in the magic of seashells. Jem found it truly difficult not to adore her immediately.

"I cannot believe this," whispered Cressie, her voice filled with wonder as she kept the shell to her ear. "It's the sea. It really is the sea. It is exactly how I imagined it, and nothing like it as well. You gave me the sea, Mr Jem."

Jem wanted to tell her to call him by his name, just as he wanted to ask if he could call her by her Christian name, but he knew not to push his luck with Cressie's mother sitting nearby, listening to every word they spoke.

Jem had visions of really giving Cressie the sea. He, himself, had never been either, and he could see the scene clearly in his mind of the two of them running into the blue ocean waves, laughing uncontrollably.

"I am glad you like it, Miss Martin," Jem murmured sincerely.

"I love it," Cressie said earnestly.

"It is a very kind gift, indeed, Mr Denham," called Mrs Martin. "I am certain Cressie will find a place to keep it where it shan't be broken."

Cressie seemed to ignore her mother's comment, and Jem offered her a quick nod in acknowledgement before turning his attention back to Cressie. She lowered the shell and held it in her lap.

"You have a big family, I think," Cressie stated. "What must it be like to have extended members from all over."

"I do," Jem confirmed, nodding. "I am the youngest of five children." He hated that his voice sounded as though he were admitting a vice rather than a fact. He knew that he did not look any older than his eighteen years. He did not want Cressie to see him as the baby his siblings did.

"Five," breathed Cressie, marvelled. "My, how lucky you are. I do not have any siblings ... well, I suppose I do, but —"

"Cressida!" silenced Mrs Martin firmly, and Cressie stiffened at her mother's sudden harsh tone.

Jem's brows furrowed as he sensed a rather sensitive subject within the Martin household.

"Sorry, Mama," Cressie said sheepishly. She took a breath before her brown eyes returned to Jem's. "I have grown up an only child. I cannot imagine what it must be like to have so many siblings."

Jem chuckled. "I think my instinct would be to offer you the one who is vexing me the most, but I do joke. I know I am very fortunate." Extraordinarily so. Jem would never forsake his sisters or brother, for he knew it was his elder siblings and their sacrifices that made his childhood as carefree as it was.

Cressie giggled. "It was happy then, your home?" she asked.

Jem nodded with a fond smile. "Yes," he confirmed. "It was not always easy." Despite the fact that his mother and siblings had often tried to protect him from their hardships and woes, he had known that there had been times which were very tough. "But I am very grateful for my family, and for the in-laws my siblings have brought into our family. They all chose exceptionally well."

"I remember you saying your eldest sister in particular had made a wonderful love-match," Cressie recalled.

"But, of course," exclaimed Mrs Martin. "The duke and duchess' love-match is clear for all to see. I imagine, Mr Denham, that the duke favours your family extraordinarily."

By the window, Mrs Martin's back was straightened as she leaned towards Jem and Cressie, as far as she could go without leaving her chair. Her eyebrows were raised as she awaited an answer. Jem resisted frowning uncomfortably. He rather hoped that he was being too sensitive to assume that Mrs Martin was inquiring after the level of financial support that the Denhams' received from the Ashwood estate. That was rather a personal question, was it not?

"The duke is a kind and attentive master of the Ashwood estate, ma'am," Jem replied carefully. "In fact, he has been gracious enough to take me on as his apprentice. I am training to be his steward so that I might one day manage his affairs."

Jem had been proud to share this information, proud to state how he was planning on rising up in the world. One had to be clever to be a steward, and Jem was clever. He would always enjoy making fun, but he was not a fool.

But the moment it had left his lips, he felt his stomach fall as he saw the look on Mrs Martin's face. Disappointment.

"A steward?" she repeated, her voice no louder than a whisper.

"Mr Jem." Cressie commanded his attention with a rather forceful tone. Her brow was stern as she glanced at her mother before devoting her attention to him. "I have formally met all your siblings but one, is that not correct?"

"Y-yes." Jem tore his eyes away from Mrs Martin, but a sick feeling was bubbling inside him. He was not a gentleman, he knew this, but he was trying. Jem was trying to make his way up in the world, to gain respectability and a position. He wanted to be good enough.

"Won't you tell me about her? And your mother and father?"

Jem could see Cressie's heart once more, the tender thing it was. It might as well have existed outside of her body she showed it so purely. Jem wanted to tell Cressie about his family, and he wanted to learn about hers. He wanted to know all about how she had grown up, and how it had come to be just her and her mother. He had not missed her comment about having siblings in some sort of way. But he couldn't talk to her in the way that he wanted to in this room. Jem was determined to find another opportunity.

The moment the door to the drawing room closed and Mr Jem was away, Mrs Martin flocked to Cressie's side, seizing hold of her hand in desperation.

"Oh, Cressie," she practically moaned. "A steward? Though, of course, he is but an apprentice! He is not even a steward yet!"

"Mama!" snapped Cressie as she whipped her hand out of Mrs Martin's reach. She returned to the settee where she seized the conch shell. Just holding the precious object made her feel incredibly warm.

"Oh, my darling, I will never deny that Jem Denham is charming young boy, but he is exactly that! He is a boy!"

"I know that!" Cressie exclaimed. Mr Jem was a boy, the same as she was just a girl. They were both young and she sensed they had the same spirit. She wanted Mr Jem to be her friend, even if it was rather unorthodox. She already liked him better than any other man she had had occasion to meet. "Mama, did you not realise that you were being terribly rude?" Cressie admonished.

Mrs Martin recoiled. "I would watch your tone, young lady!" she scolded. "I was doing no such thing. If you are referring to my line of questioning, I am certain you can understand why I inquired seeing as we learned Mr Denham is nothing but a future steward."

Cressie felt a spark of anger in her chest when she heard the words 'Mr Denham' and 'nothing' in the same sentence. "Mama, you are being cruel, and you are never cruel."

Mrs Martin sighed sympathetically. "I am not being cruel, Cressie," she said calmly. "I am being realistic. I truly believe that Mr Denham is a fine young man ... but for someone else. For his own prospects, he needs to secure a match with wealth, for he has none of his own. You would not be the right sort of woman for him either." She shook her head. "I believed that as the brother of the duchess he might have some land or some form of income from the estate, but this does not seem to be the case. I am sorry, dearest. I truly am. But I think we can both agree that for our needs, Mr Denham is simply not right."

Cressie felt her frustration brewing. She was not thinking of marriage! Cressie knew that she would have to marry someone like Mr Delaney at some point, but for the interim, she had found a friend whom she liked immensely. Cressie had never had a friend before. She and her mother had never lived in one place long enough for her to form such connections. But she knew that had she had a friend, and had her mother dismissed them as she was dismissing Jem Denham, then she would have acted in exactly the same way.

Mrs Martin reclaimed Cressie's hand, pulling one away from the shell as she guided them both down to the settee. With her other hand, she cupped Cressie's cheek and forced her to look into her mother's sympathetic grey-green eyes. "I wish things were different for you, Cressie," she said softly. "You cannot know how I wish this. I wish that I had been the sort of woman who could keep our family together so that you might have had the opportunities that you deserve. But I have done the best that I could. I hope you believe that. This year, this Season, is our one chance. We have not the funds to make it another year. We have not the funds to make it beyond the summer, and I know you know that. I hate that I have put this onto your shoulders, I hate that I have burdened you, but I know that you are beautiful and sweet enough to make a fine match that will give you the life that I could only dream of for you."

Mrs Martin's change in tone weakened Cressie's resolve to scold her mother for her cruelty, and she was harshly and epically reminded of their circumstances. Guilt festered within her as she remembered exactly what her mother was trying to do. Cressie gripped onto the conch shell even harder.

"Young Mr Denham is simply a boy," Mrs Martin continued quietly. "And if good intentions were enough to fill a household's coffers then he would certainly be a wealthy someone. Mr Delaney, on the other hand, is a mature and distinguished gentleman. He has money and property and is in the sort of position to support and care for you. Now, I am not saying that he shall be your match, as you may well find another gentleman you like better, but Mr Delaney is the more sensible match. You understand what I am saying, don't you?"

"I understand, Mama," Cressie murmured. But despite understanding, Cressie felt entirely unprepared to give Mr Jem up. He was her friend, and he had given her the ocean.

CHAPTER 7

"What do you think, is blue my colour?"

Jem dramatically draped a length from one of Belle's bolts of fabric against his torso and flapped around, deliberately trying to elicit a laugh from his brother and sister-in-law.

Belle giggled. Peter snickered, shaking his head, before he called Jem a, "Muttonhead."

"Blue is certainly your colour, Jem," Belle encouraged with a laugh. "I shall sketch something for you immediately. Do you prefer tulip or trumpet sleeves?"

Jem pursed his lips. He really had no idea what a tulip sleeve was, but the very word reminded him of the bouquet of tulips that had been sitting in Cressie's drawing room when he had arrived, next to which his mourning bouquet of chrysanthemums now resided.

He shook off his embarrassment over the whole affair and said, "Trumpet, I think. They sound terribly noisy and irritating. I should like to march through Peter's office wearing them constantly."

"Of course, you would." Peter rolled his eyes with an amused smile on his face. "You should sew bells onto his boots and a tambourine onto his bonnet to complete the ensemble, Belle."

"I shall certainly be the best dressed deb at the ball," Jem joked. He then rolled up Belle's fabric and stowed it away in the bin in which he had found it.

It was after eight, and Belle had long closed her shop for the evening. Considering she had not been open for long, it looked like a very established dress shop. They had done well to organise it in the time that they had. Jem's only reference for a dress shop, of course, was Belle's table in Mr Andrews' grocer shop in Ashwood where she had mended rips in hems and sewn buttons onto coats for the villagers. This was the establishment in which she belonged.

Peter had also returned from his work at Beresford Press for the day, and they had entertained Jem for supper that evening. Rather, Jem felt that he had imposed himself upon his brother and sister-in-law by annoying them until he was asked to stay.

He was staying with Grace and Adam at their home in Grosvenor Square. But he had not been home since calling upon Cressie at her home that morning. Jem knew that his sister would have been anxious for news as to how the visit had gone, and Jem was not yet ready to tell her that it had been a complete and utter disaster.

Of course, his interactions with Cressie had bene wonderful. He had loved conversing with her, even if they could not speak properly with her mother listening nearby. But in confessing his position, or lack thereof, Jem was almost certain that he had ruined his chances at ever being seen as a serious suitor of Cressie's. It was clear that she already had another suitor as well, and by the way Mrs Martin spoke, she approved of him.

Jem, Peter and Belle were gathered around Belle's large work-table. It was littered with her sketches and materials for the project she was working on. On it were collections of buttons and scraps of fabric and offcuts of cotton. It looked like organised chaos. Jem picked up a smooth, white stick and flipped it between his fingers.

"What's this for?" he wondered aloud.

"It is a whale bone," answered Belle.

Jem flinched, dropping it instantly as though it had burned him. "What on earth do you need a whale bone for?"

"They are used in ... women's stays," Belle replied delicately.

Jem felt entirely ignorant. "A woman stays where?"

Peter burst into a fit of laughter, so much so that he rested his forehead against Belle's shoulder as his wife huffed. Belle hushed him.

"They are fitted in ladies undergarments, Jem," Belle explained. "A stay is something that a woman wears underneath."

Jem felt his ears turn pink as he averted his eyes. He made a promise to himself to never question Belle over an object in her shop again. It would be safe to assume it belonged to a woman's unmentionables and it was none of his business.

Well, in truth, he had no desire to ever appear so green in front of his brother again. Jem wanted to whack the hysterical laughter right out of Peter's mouth.

Thankfully, Belle seemed to be clairvoyant and she playfully slapped Peter's chest to get him to stop, before she admonished him in French. Jem, of course, did not speak French, so he could only hope that it was a scolding.

Peter's amusement calmed, and Jem saw a flash of sympathy in his brother's eyes. Where had that come from? "Are you ever going to tell us how your call went this morning?"

Jem stiffened. "How do you know about that?"

Peter pursed his lips for a moment, before he said, "Claire called upon Grace this morning, who must have told her about it, as I heard about it when she came to the publishing house with the girls to visit at luncheon."

Peter had only just rested his forehead on Belle's worktop. Jem promptly banged his head against it and groaned. He heard Belle scurry around the bench to hold onto his arm with concern.

"Ça vas aller, Jem," she told him in worried yet assuring tone, even if Jem didn't know exactly what she was trying to say.

"Did all of you somehow miss the family meeting about discretion?" Jem moaned from the table. "Or the sermon? I am fairly certain I have sat through and endured countless lectures from the vicar about the sinful pastime of gossip." Not that the Ashwood parish was known to adhere to such rules. There, gossip was a competitive sport.

"Jemmy," Peter appealed.

"Do not condescend to me."

"Ordinarily I would poke fun at how the shoe is certainly on the other foot between us now, as it is usually you making me writhe with embarrassment, but I can assure you that is not my intention," Peter promised. "I just wanted to ask in case you wanted to talk about it."

"Condescend?" Jem heard Belle whisper in a questioning tone, as though she were looking to Peter for the definition. "Condescendant," she then answered her own question in realisation. "Oh, no, Jem!" she insisted.

Jem peeked up into the concerned golden eyes of his brother's wife. Even if he was irritated with his siblings as their gossip mongering, he didn't ever want to distress Belle. He reluctantly straightened his back and stood up to his full height, before taking a breath and uttering, "I am not enough."

"What?" both Belle and Peter exclaimed.

"You heard me," he said stiffly. "I told her mother, Mrs Martin, rather proudly, I might add, about my ambitions to rise up in this world as Adam's steward. I might as well have told her I was a gravedigger for the look of disappointment she had on her face." Jem was not a fool. He knew he was not a fool, and he knew that the brains in his head would make him an effective steward. He knew that eventually he would be indispensable to the Ashwood estate. He would rise up and be an amiable man.

Jem knew that he was not a gentleman, but he had at least hoped that he could be seen as respectable.

Peter's face fell, and Belle's look of anguish only intensified. Her brows could not furrow any further.

Peter finally found his tongue after a minute of silence. "Mrs Martin may have been disappointed, and unjustly so, but was Miss Martin?"

Jem could immediately shake his head. In fact, just thinking of Cressie and her beautiful reaction to the magic of the conch shell warmed his insides, as though he had just drunk a pitcher of hot milk. Cressie didn't seem disappointed at all. Cressie ... Jem dared to believe ... did not mind a bit.

"No," he breathed.

"Well, there you have it. That's all that matters," Peter insisted. "Jem, I can assure you that many matches have been made on much less. You have as much right to pursue Miss Martin as any other man. And I was watching the two of you last night, and I could see that she was ..." Peter wrestled with finding the right words, "... bloody delighted in your company. Mothers only want what is best for their children, and I am certain that you will be able to prove yourself to Mrs Martin. Do not give up or allow your confidence to be dashed because of this. Despite our tendency to spread familial information like wildfire, you have a family around you to help."

Jem wanted to whole-heartedly believe his brother, but he couldn't help but feel his mind resist. Not after seeing the look on Mrs Martin's face. Somehow, he could not foresee her ever thinking Jem was good enough, even if Cressie felt otherwise.

Oh, the idea of Cressie thinking of Jem for her excited him beyond anything else. Jem took a deep breath as the vision washed over him.

"I am being a pessimist," he realised.

"You certainly are," Peter agreed.

"You must have faith," encouraged Belle. "No matter the hardship, no matter the trouble, things do come right in the end, I promise you." Her tone spoke of a world of experience.

Jem hated to think of Belle's lived experiences, but there she was, there both Belle and Peter were, as living proof that even the worst of odds were worth a little belief.

Jem did not escape Grace's inquisitions when he arrived back at Ashwood Place, but he managed to present the day's events to her in a slightly more positive light then had to Peter and Belle.

In the time between balls, Jem learned that many members of the ton spent time promenading. Cecily defined it as 'walking to be seen'. Though for the next few days, Jem had not been able to go. Despite being in Town for the season, he and Adam still had work to do. Jem did not begrudge his responsibilities for a minute, even if he would have liked another opportunity to talk to Cressie. As he sat in Adam's London study, he truly felt as though he was proving himself by the minute.

He needed to have hope.

Cressie had never been so finely dressed for walks in her life then in this first week of the Season. In what would have been a country ballgown, she and her mother walked through Hyde Park along with the rest of the aristocratic ladies and gentlemen, nodding and curtseying to every lady and gentleman they passed.

Mrs Martin seemed terribly excited by every gentleman they passed who appraised Cressie with a critical, and admirable, eye.

Cressie, on the other hand, felt as though she were at a horse auction. Had she had the legs of a thoroughbred she would have made a run for it an hour ago.

She did, however, keep an eye out for Mr Jem. Cressie wanted to speak with him again, and she wasn't certain she could wait for the Fentonbury ball that would be taking place in a few days. She, of course, wanted to ensure that he was not terribly wounded by her mother's remarks of the other day, but she also wanted to continue their acquaintance.

But Cressie had not seen him. Not since he had come to call the day after the Ashwood ball. It disappointed her. Greatly. She did not at all understand this disappointment as she had never felt anything like it before.

Mrs Martin brought Cressie out of her thoughts when she shook her subtly. "Cressie, look. It is Mr Delaney coming right towards us. Smile. Smile," she insisted.

Cressie smiled. Or at least she hoped whatever expression on her face resembled a smile as it was perhaps the most dishonest smile she had ever given. Cressie was in no mood to pretend as though she enjoyed the company of Mr Delaney, even if he had done nothing to offend. He simply was not the man that Cressie wanted to converse with.

But she would try not to be rude, for her mother's sake.

Mr Delaney approached the two ladies with a cheerful smile. He walked confidently with long strides, dressed immaculately in navy and gold, before he removed his top hat from his head as he bowed to them respectfully.

"Mrs Martin, Miss Martin, how delighted I am to see you both." When he looked up, Cressie noticed how his grey eyes wandered down her frame. When they returned to her face, they almost looked ... well, she could not be certain ... but hungry. She didn't quite understand that as there was no food to be seen, but it made her uneasy.

"And how lovely it is to see you as well, Mr Delaney," Mrs Martin replied musically. "My Cressida is happy as well." Mrs Martin nudged Cressie subtly for an agreeable response.

"Oh! Oh, yes, Mr Delaney. I am terribly happy to be having my teeth checked and my height measured in hands."

Cressie's concern regarding Mr Delaney's eyes had lowered her guard over her tongue, and her thoughts surrounding the horse auction of a promenade had slipped out without her realising. She bit down immediately, so hard that she could taste blood.

Mrs Martin looked mortified, while Mr Delaney appeared quite perplexed at Cressie's response. Mrs Martin was the one to recover first. She let out a burst of laughter that was entirely false. "Oh, Cressie! What a wit you are! My daughter has such a sense of humour, Mr Delaney. Such an agreeable quality, I am certain you would agree." There was gravel in her voice, and Cressie knew that she would be in receipt of a scolding later.

Mr Delaney laughed lightly. "But of course, Mrs Martin. I am certain that Miss Martin would be happy to hear that she is lovelier than a horse this fine afternoon."

Cressie managed to reply in a manner that would much more please her mother. "I thank you, Mr Delaney," she murmured.

"Would you care to promenade with me, Miss Martin?" Mr Delaney subtly held out his arm.

Mrs Martin was the one to practically loop Cressie's arm through his. Once she was on his arm, Mr Delaney moved them off, while Mrs Martin walked several steps behind.

Cressie had never done this before. She had never walked with a man. But she decided right then and there that she did not like it. She felt out of control, led by a man whom she did not really know. And yet she felt no sense of authority to be able to say 'no'.

"Will I be seeing you at the Fentonbury ball, Miss Martin?" Mr Delaney asked.

"Y-yes," Cressie confirmed. "Mama and I have accepted our invitation."

"Excellent," replied Mr Delaney. "May I then be so bold as to ask for your first two dances?"

Women were not allowed to refuse a gentleman. Not unless they were previously engaged to another. It was the height of rudeness, or so her mama had told her. Cressie once again had no authority, no choice but to say, "Yes."

Mr Delaney seemed very pleased with her response as he brought his other hand over to pat the top of hers, in almost a petting motion.

"I so look forward to your company, Miss Martin."

CHAPTER 8

C ressie and her mother were announced into the Fentonbury ball, much like they had at the Ashwood ball. The ton
were once again dressed divinely, the musicians were playing a
welcoming aria and servants were making their way around the
room carrying trays of expensive champagne. Cressie was helped
to fasten her dance card around her wrist, and her mother was
quick to scrawl Mr Delaney's name beside the first two dances.

"I wonder where he is," Mrs Martin murmured as she dropped
the pencil. She subtly craned her neck to survey the ballroom.

"Is it a good idea to be so often seen with the same gentleman, Mama?" Cressie asked quietly. Ever since she agreed to the
dances, Cressie had felt the obligation hanging over her like an
omen. She had never looked forward to anything less than attending this ball, and in her heart Cressie knew that was ridiculous. She
had personally experienced far worse, and really, dancing with a
gentleman was not a terrible fate.

Cressie theorised that she disliked what Mr Delaney represented far more than the man himself. Really, he had done nothing
to offend save do exactly what gentlemen were supposed to be
doing during the Season. Cressie just had no interest.

She just wanted to talk to Mr Jem again.

Mrs Martin petted Cressie's arm as she took it to lead her into the ballroom. "Of course not, dearest," she agreed. "We shall not be settling on anyone so soon. But we must be clever. You and I both know that your lack of a dowry will render you an impossible match to many of the eligible gentlemen here. When wealthy men take an interest in you with no fear of your lack of fortune, we must encourage it."

Cressie interpreted her mother's answer to mean that they absolutely would be encouraging Mr Delaney's interest.

As they moved through the crowds, Mrs Martin and Cressie were dutiful in greeting and paying their respects to the many senior members of the aristocracy whom they had made the acquaintances of at the Ashwood ball or during their many promenades throughout the week.

And then they came to the Duke and Duchess of Ashwood. Cressie immediately noticed the duchess appeared a little less comfortable than she had been at her own ball. She was being supported by her husband, but then, Cressie thought, she was quite obviously with child, and she understood that this could be a very trying and tiring experience for a lady. With them was Mr Jem.

The moment she spotted him, Cressie felt a ridiculously wide smile spread across her face, and this was directly in response to the fact that he was smiling at her also. She saw it immediately. His youth, his vibrance, his spirit.

"Mrs Martin, Miss Martin, how do you do this evening?" asked the duke.

Both Cressie and her mother curtseyed. "We are both very well, I thank you, Your Grace," responded Mrs Martin dutifully. "We are pleased with the Fentonbury ambience, but I do believe that nothing could compare to your attention to detail, Your Grace," Mrs Martin complimented the duchess.

The duchess smiled, albeit bashfully, before saying, "I will pass on your compliments on to the dowager, Mrs Martin, for she saw to every detail of the Ashwood ball. I find myself quite unaccustomed to Town. I have lived in the country all my life."

Her candour surprised Cressie, but she admired it all the same. She supposed she felt quite the same. The pace of London was unlike anything she had experienced.

In an act that was quite uncommon for the aristocracy, particularly in public, the duke leaned over and kissed the duchess' temple, before cuddling her into his side. Cressie found that she quite adored the duke's display of affection for the duchess. Theirs was clearly a love match in every way.

The duchess appeared comforted by her husband's actions, and she smiled. "You, of course, remember my youngest brother, Jem Denham." She gestured to Mr Jem, who was standing to the side of the interaction.

Cressie did not need any reminding. Jem stepped forward now that he had been invited, and he bowed his head to both Mrs Martin and Cressie. Cressie couldn't help but notice his face harden ever so slightly when he looked at Mrs Martin, and she worried he had a sour taste left in his mouth after his call earlier in the week. Her mama had been rude, even if she had not meant to be.

"Yes," replied Mrs Martin with a polite smile. "How are you this evening, Mr Denham?"

"I am well, thank you, Mrs Martin," replied Mr Jem formally. "I am glad to see you both in attendance. Uh, Miss Martin," he said, clearing his throat, "would you do me the honour of dancing the first with me tonight?"

Cressie could hear the nerves in Mr Jem's voice, and she absolutely knew he was nervous to ask because of how Mrs Martin had behaved. But Cressie ... the moment he asked, she felt a resurgence of pain in her stomach. It alarmed her.

But then, she thought, if she was coming down with an illness of some sort, then perhaps she might be able to escape dancing with Mr Delaney. Cressie was not above being theatrical.

Before Cressie could answer, however, Mrs Martin was quick to explain why Mr Jem's request was impossible.

"How kind of you to ask, Mr Denham, but I am afraid Miss Martin is already engaged for the first two dances."

Mr Jem did not show disappointment, even if that was what he felt. But it was what Cressie was feeling. She felt it upon her shoulders. She would have much rather danced with Mr Jem.

"A Mr Everett Delaney is Cressida's partner," continued Mrs Martin to the duke and duchess. "Are you familiar with the gentleman?"

"No, I cannot say that we are, Mrs Martin," replied the duke. "I should look forward to making his acquaintance this evening should the occasion arise."

"Are you engaged for the third dance, Miss Martin?" Jem then asked.

Cressie's smile returned as she shook her head. "No, I am not engaged." She held out her wrist, from which her dance card dangled. Before everyone, Mr Jem stepped forward and signed his name beside the third. Cressie watched as his hand paused beside the fourth dance, but he dropped the card.

"Come, Cressie," urged Mrs Martin. "We must not monopolise the duke and duchess when I am certain they have many friends to greet. Do enjoy your evening."

As soon as they were away from the Beresfords, Mrs Martin whispered, "Cressie," in a warning tone.

"I was not engaged, Mama," Cressie retorted, "and I have no broken leg nor dippy tummy to warrant a polite refusal." Not that she would ever refuse in the first place.

"Yes, yes," sighed Mrs Martin.

Jem immediately turned to his sister the moment that Cressie and her mother were away and asked, "Who is this Mr Delaney?"

"Jem, this might as well be my first time in London, the same as you," replied Grace. "I really know nary a soul in this ballroom."

"I've heard of him," interjected Adam. "His family are an old one, but I believe he's made quite the name for himself in cotton production. I've never met the man, however."

Jem wondered if he would be the same man that Cressie had danced with at the last ball. His suspicions were confirmed a moment later when a gentleman approached Cressie and Mrs Martin. He was an older man, definitely older than Adam, though he carried himself with an air of self-importance.

He was certainly a good-looking gentleman, with distinguished and elegant features. Jem, in particular, spotted the healthy side whiskers growing on either side of his face. Jem, himself, was incapable of growing them at his age.

Cressie was incapable of shielding her thoughts. Though she smiled, Jem could see what she was thinking through her expressive brown eyes. He could see them all the way from where he stood. She didn't want to dance with this man. She did not even seem to want to speak with this man.

The selfish, and perhaps the immature, side of Jem was pleased with the knowledge. However, his greater concern was for Cressie. She was clearly in a situation she did not want to be in out of social obligation.

"Evening all," Jack said cheerfully as he joined their small party, Claire on his arm.

Claire came forward to kiss the cheeks of both Grace and Adam, before she stopped at Jem and murmured, "You look very handsome, Jemmy."

Jem grinned at his sister.

"Are Peter and Belle not here?" Claire wondered, searching the immediate area. But the moment the question was asked, Claire seemed to realise her answer. Peter and Belle had been invited to the ball the week before because it had been hosted by Adam and Grace.

"Belle is good enough to design the dresses for half of the women in this room, but she is not good enough to dance among them," Grace murmured with an edge to her voice.

"Well, who do you think is having the grander evening, then?" pondered Jack. "The men here wearing girdles, or Peter and Belle at home enjoying a night of newlywed exertion?" Jack winked.

Adam chuckled. "Put on a few stone, have you?" he asked teasingly, swatting his brother's stomach.

Jem's attention slowly left the conversation as he watched Cressie take her place among the dancers. She truly was a graceful dancer. She floated across the floor; her delicate movements only accented by the soft flowing silks of Belle's dress. Her partner danced with the same grace and experience. He guided her expertly.

But Cressie never looked at him.

And Jem took confidence from that. His confidence had been shattered and repaired many times this week, but he was determined to have faith. As Belle had told him the other night, everything would be alright in the end.

At the conclusion of the second dance, Jem walked away from his family without saying 'goodbye'. He did not even think to when he had Cressie on his mind.

"... dance so remarkably well, Miss Martin," Mr Delaney complimented as Jem approached. "With the grace and maturity of someone well beyond your so very few years."

The comment made Jem stop a few steps shy of the couple. A deep frown settled into his forehead as he mulled over a deeply disgusting thought. Was Mr Delaney acknowledging how young Cressie was? Furthermore, did he enjoy that Cressie was as young as she was? There had to be at least twenty years between them! This man would have been sowing his wild oats as Cressie was being nursed.

With the authority of someone well beyond his years and station, Jem marched the final few steps to approach Cressie and Mr Delaney.

"Excuse me, sir," Jem said formally, "but I believe I have engaged Miss Martin for the next dance."

The man's cold, grey eyes appraised Jem very quickly with a quick flick up and down his person. He arched one of his brows as a small smirk teased at his lips, as though Jem amused him.

"I don't believe we have met," Mr Delaney said coolly.

Jem had no desire to formalise the introduction, but Cressie had other ideas.

"Mr Delaney, please allow me to introduce Mr Denham. Mr Denham, this is Mr Delaney," she introduced.

"Denham, Denham," Mr Delaney pondered, furrowing his brows a little as he thought. "I don't believe I recognise your family name, Mr Denham. Do you represent a smaller estate?"

Jem was taller than this man. He was taller than most men. But the way Mr Delaney was looking at him was of a schoolmaster lecturing a naughty student. Any minute now the cane would have been brought out to punish Jem's knuckles.

"I represent the Ashwood estate, sir," he replied. "My family are connected with the Beresfords twice over. Should you desire a family tree, I encourage you to make yourself known to the Duke of Ashwood. The lady and I have a prior engagement. Good evening to you."

Heart beating erratically, Jem stepped forward and claimed Cressie's arm, before immediately leading her away from Mr Delaney and towards the dance floor. The moment they were out of earshot, Cressie gripped Jem's arm with her other hand to stop him.

Jem was in a bit of a state of shock as he looked down at Cressie. Her brown eyes were wide with delight and she giggled with such humour. Her beautiful undereye dimples were on show, and Jem was pleased that it was he who elicited a smile happy enough for them to appear.

"I do not know where that came from," he confessed. "I've never spoken to anyone like that in my life." He could still actively hear his pulse thumping in his ears.

"That was brilliant," Cressie declared gleefully.

Jem couldn't help but grin in knowing that he had impressed her, even if he had been dreadfully rude. What did it matter? The man probably deserved it. "Really?"

Cressie nodded. "Come on, the music's starting," she urged.

As the musicians began to play the first few notes of the third dance, Jem and Cressie quickly took their places in and amongst the group of dancers.

As they stepped forward to begin the sequence, Cressie confessed, "I don't like this song. I find it a little droll."

It was an awfully slow piece of music that required the dancers to move about as though they were towing an anchor behind them. It was not fitting for a clumsy dancer like Jem, even if he was doing his darndest to concentrate on moving smoothly.

Jem grinned as an idea struck him. As he and Cressie turned in the sequence, he sang under his breath to the tune of the song, "There once was a rabbit named Cressie, who was so unbelievably messy."

Cressie gasped, but she beamed, and leaned into him ever so slightly to better hear the next lines of his silly song.

"Her favourite food was some carrots, and then she befriended some parrots. But she ate so many that she turned orange, and that turned her into a ..." Jem paused as he racked his brains to find something that rhymed.

Norange? Gorange? "Door hinge?" he sang, sounding very unsure of the word.

Cressie laughed, so much so that she drew the attention of several onlookers. But she didn't seem to mind at all. Jem didn't either. Cressie laughing was beautiful, and it was the easiest he had ever seen her.

"Go on!" she urged as they spun around one another. "What did Messy Cressie do next?"

"She found a fine hare called Jem, who wanted to be her best friend. So, he asked her to dance, and he learned how to prance. And they danced ever after. The End."

Jem reeled off whatever ridiculous rhymes popped into his head, and Cressie listened to every word with eager amusement. When he had her alone, Jem wanted to talk to her. He wanted to ask her everything that he couldn't while her mother was listening. But somehow, in this moment, this was better. Jem wasn't panicking, nor proposing. His nerves were elsewhere. He was able to be his usual self, humour and all, and he could make her laugh.

Jem kept her giggling for the entire dance, whispering silly things into her ear, or making up further ludicrous adventures for Messy Cressie. But the end of the dance came too quickly. When they stood back across from one another, Jem could see that Cressie had tears in her eyes.

He wondered when the last time she had ever laughed so much that she'd cried. He felt such unbelievable pride, and such un-believable faith. As he looked upon her, he knew, he knew that everything would be alright. One did not find their kindred spirit every day.

"You gave me the ocean this week, Mr Jem, and now you invent Messy Cressie for me." Cressie grinned, shaking her head in dis-belief. "You are a very unconventional gift giver, but I find I enjoy each present more and more."

"I wish you would call me 'Jem'," he uttered.

Cressie pressed her lips together, before she nodded. "Perhaps you may also call me 'Cressie' when no one can hear. Mama ..."

"I know," Jem said, interrupting her. "I know, Cressie."

CHAPTER 9

"People were taking note of you last night, Cressida." Mrs Martin rarely used Cressie's full name when they were not in company. Her tone immediately alerted Cressie to the fact that her mother was displeased. "I did not say anything last night as we were tired when we returned to the house, but I must address it now."

Cressie looked upon her eggs sadly. "Mama," she appealed, but she had nothing to offer in her defence that would appease her mother.

"I forget sometimes that you are not yet seventeen, and that you are a very young almost seventeen-year-old. I did my best to prepare you for your first Season, but I can see that I have not done well enough. Cressie, darling, we have been overthis. You cannot be seen to be laughing and joking with a man so openly. It speaks of intimacy beyond propriety!"

Cressie felt guilty, and only because she was supposed to. But really, it was not sincere. She had had a marvellous time at the ball the previous evening, and it had solely been because of Mr Jem ... Jem, as he had bid her call him, and his wit. What true harm could there be in a young man entertaining a lady with silly words?

She had laughed openly, and probably as hard as she ever had done. Cressie could not recall ever laughing so hard that tears had fallen from her eyes. And Jem had laughed, too.

Cressie had never known a man by his Christian name before, and to think of Jem as simply Jem was quite exciting. She didn't quite understand why it excited her, but it did. It was the same feeling she experienced when Jem called her 'Cressie'. No man had ever called her just 'Cressie' before. Perhaps her father had at some point in her life, but she had not been old enough to remember it.

Cressie very much liked that Jem knew her as such, and she felt very proud of the little secret that they shared.

But in looking into her mother's distraught grey-green eyes, she knew that such pride was inappropriate in that moment, and that she ought to replace it with shame, even though she had no desire to repent.

"We were only laughing, Mama," murmured Cressie.

Mrs Martin sighed. "And did any other gentleman ask you to dance afterwards?"

Cressie had rather thought it fortuitous that she had not been sought after by another gentleman as it had given her more time with Jem. She had not thought about it from horse auction perspective.

"I want you to have options, Cressie," insisted Mrs Martin. "I want you to use your beautiful face and your effervescent, youthful charm to collect as many worthy suitors as you can so that you may have your pick of who would make you happiest. But if you behave in such a way again, many will think you spoken for, and by a man with nought but two shillings to rub together."

Cressie knew that she needed to agree with her mother, but everything in her body was willing her to bag her head down on the table in frustration. Spoken for. What sort of an idea was that? How she hated the very notion of someone speaking for her.

"I know I do not need to remind you of what is at risk for us, Cressie."

Cressie did groan then, an unintendedly so. She gasped as soon as the noise had escaped her lips.

"I know I must exhaust you with worry about our impending ruin," uttered Mrs Martin coolly, with an element of hurt in her voice.

Cressie's appetite for her breakfast disappeared. She didn't like at all that her memories created with Jem from the night before were meant to be tarnished with guilt. She refused to do it. Perhaps it was naïve of her, but if her being seen laughing with her friend alarmed a potential suitor then Cressie would have no interest in anyone so fragile.

Cressie wished she was of age. If she was, then all of this would be her choice. She would refuse it all and travel to France. She would travel to France and locate her father and demand he return her mother to the situation she was promised upon their marriage. She would demand her dowry which would give her freedom to choose her own husband. Or better yet, she would demand an inheritance and live as a spinster, perhaps marrying at eight and thirty if she so desired.

Instead, she was seated in a small house in London, a little over a week shy until her seventeenth birthday, and very far from achieving any of that. She would be long married once she reached the birthday where she would be considered of age.

A knock on the door of the small dining room captured the attentions of both Mrs Martin and Cressie, and they turned to see Nelly. "Begging your pardon, ma'am, but a Mr Delaney has called to see Miss Martin. I've told him to wait in the drawing room."

All remnants of their quarrel were forgotten when Mrs Martin stood up abruptly, nearly knocking her chair onto the ground with the force. "Oh, thank God!" she cried, cupping Cressie's cheeks suddenly. "But, you are not yet fit to be seen!"

It had been a rather slow morning and Cressie's hair was still fixed in a sleep plait, and only because it was only twenty past nine. Mr Delaney was early. And eager.

And he was also not Jem. Cressie found that she felt disappointed that Mr Delaney was not Jem.

Cressie learned that morning that it was expected for fashionable and desirable debutantes to keep their suitors waiting for at least half an hour before they made their entrance. Though Cressie felt it completely rude to keep a guest waiting, she found herself entirely satisfied if it meant she did not need to make conversation with Mr Delaney for a further thirty minutes.

Both Nelly and Mrs Martin worked on Cressie's hair at great speed, fluffing and pinning curls until they were just so. Cressie was buttoned into one of the stunning day dresses that Belle Desjardins had made for her and when it was nearing ten o'clock, she was deemed ready to receive Mr Delaney.

As Cressie descended the steps, she went over topics of conversation in her head. She wanted to be able to distract Mr Delaney so that he did not pay her uncomfortable compliments. In fact, when she spoke with Mr Delaney, she understood why it was that gentleman claimed a lady was 'spoken for'.

Mrs Martin entered the room first and greeted Mr Delaney warmly. Cressie followed to find Mr Delaney standing by the settee with a gift box in his hand. It was tied with a golden ribbon.

The moment he saw her, Mr Delaney smiled and bowed his head. "Miss Martin, how well you look this morning."

Cressie, whose cheeks still hurt from all of her mother's pinching, managed a smile and curtseyed before the gentleman. "How kind of you to call, Mr Delaney," she replied dutifully.

Mr Delaney seemed to appreciate the flattery. Mrs Martin retreated to her chair by the window as they both sat down on the settee. Cressie found herself nearly hugging the arm so as to keep as much distance between them as possible.

"I have brought you a gift," Mr Delaney continued. He held out the box to her. "Something sweet, just like you."

Cressie's tongue swelled in her mouth as she was unable to respond. She accepted the box with an awkward smile and sat it on her lap. "Th-thank you," she managed to stammer. She pulled on the silk ribbon and abandoned it, before lifting the lid off of the box. Inside was a small tin with a confectioner's stamp embossed. Cressie had never heard of them, but just by the look of the crest, the sweets seemed an expensive treat.

"How generous of you, Mr Delaney." Cressie hoped that her voice sounded gushing, otherwise her mother would scold her about it afterwards.

Mr Delaney's grey eyes flicked towards Mrs Martin momentarily, before an expression that Cressie could not quite discern spread across his face. "Allow me," he murmured, taking the box from Cressie's lap, simultaneously edging closer to her. He gently lifted the lid off of the tin to reveal an array of fine confections, chocolate and the like. He selected one at random and held it between his thumb and forefinger. "Open," he commanded so quietly that he might well have mouthed the instruction.

Cressie's eyes widened. An immediate chill travelled down her spine at the very idea of what he had asked her to do. It set her whole body on edge, and a terrible rush on unpleasant nerves filled her stomach. She didn't know what to do. Was she allowed to refuse? She dared not look to her mother. She already knew the answer. Of course, she could not refuse.

But Cressie's facial expression betrayed her, and Mr Delaney laughed quietly, before his arm dropped, and he returned the chocolate to the tin. "So young," she thought she heard him utter.

"It-it is a beautiful tin!" Cressie suddenly said, almost frantically. "I should certainly like to save it to put things in. I am certain Mama and I will enjoy them. Thank you."

"Are you a collector, Miss Martin?" Mr Delaney asked as he stowed the tin on the small table in front of them. "I am a collector myself. One might even call me a purveyor of beautiful things." He smiled as his eyes looked over her.

Mr Delaney seemed rich enough to collect jewelled trinkets and the like. She supposed her mama would be pleased that he could afford to amass such a collection. "No, I am not a collector," Cressie replied. They had never had the means to be collectors of any sort. Cressie, really, possessed very few material things beyond the necessities. "What sort of things do you collect, Mr Delaney?" she asked politely.

"Flowers in bloom," he mused quietly.

Even in greenhouses, Cressie didn't know if flowers could bloom all the time.

"I very much enjoy your company, Miss Martin," Mr Delaney then said, in a tone a little louder. "You possess an air about you that has certainly been missing from my circle of acquaintances."

Mr Delaney did not wait for Cressie to respond, and thankfully so, as she did not think that she could have convincingly returned the compliment.

Instead, he went on to describe the palatial estate he owned in Yorkshire in great detail. He told her about the drawing room and the parlours and the music room and the library and the billiards room, "not that you would ever need to go in there," he chuckled.

Mr Delaney's presumptuousness caused Cressie's breath to catch in her throat. Was this how it was done? This wasn't a proposal, was it?

The very idea shocked her beyond belief.

"Yes, yes, I can see your surprise," Mr Delaney continued, "but there are fourteen guest chambers to be certain!"

Cressie wondered what Jem's home was like. She vaguely knew of his family, though she had never been introduced to his mother, and the whereabouts of his house in the main part of the Ashwood village. She could picture the cottage in her head, right down to the newly painted blue shutters. Even the thought of it was enjoyable. She wondered what it would be like to go inside a house that was warmed not only by the hearth, but by its people.

When Mr Delaney finally took his leave, Cressie breathed a sigh of relief. She would never be rude on purpose, but she really did not care to hear any more about his collections or his billiards tables. And she certainly would never care to be fed as though she were an infant.

"Well, we can thank God that your antics with Mr Denham last night did not dissuade Mr Delaney!" Mrs Martin exclaimed cheerfully when they were once again alone in the drawing room.

Something told Cressie that God had very little to do with it. "Mama, I don't think I like him very much," she confessed.

Mrs Martin frowned. "But why?" she asked. "He is handsome and wealthy and well connected. He speaks very well from what I have heard. He has not said anything to offend you, has he?"

Cressie chewed on her bottom lip. She did not exactly understand why she could not warm to Mr Delaney save for her objections about his age. The way he made her feel was not comforting. "Well, no –"

"Exactly," interjected Mrs Martin. She stepped forth to cup Cressie's cheeks. "Give it time, dearest!" she encouraged. "You still have lots of time."

Cressie found herself waiting by the window for the remainder of the day. Waiting, she knew, for Jem to call as he had after the first ball. She wanted him to call.

But he never did.

While she had felt uncomfortable in Mr Delaney's presence, the lack of Jem's presence was discouraging to her.

When it was nearly five in the afternoon, a letter arrived that Cressie intercepted before her mother or Nelly could know of its coming. It was not delivered by a postman, but by a servant dressed in fine livery.

The letter was addressed to her. She did not recognise the seal, but the intricate 'A' stamped into the back of the letter could have only been from the Ashwood estate, could it not? Jem was staying with his sister, the duchess, after all.

Cressie clutched the letter to her chest and ran with it, finding the only quiet place she could where she would not be disturbed by her mother. She sat down on the floor of the larder beside a sack of potatoes as she broke the seal.

She unfolded the letter and looked immediately to the signature to see that it was signed 'Jem'. A happy smile spread across her face as her eyes returned to the beginning of the letter.

Dear Cressie, he wrote.

I do not feel as though a call today would have been well received by members of your household. But I could not let the extraordinary time I had in your company last night go without sending you a gift.

The gift of my immense poetic skill.

Please imagine I am clearing my throat as I recite these verses to you.

Cressie giggled as she heard it in her mind as clear as anything.

The Adventures of Messy Cressie, Vol II.

Messy Cressie was the loveliest rabbit,

And she really made quite the habit,

Of laughing at Jem's jokes,

And eating egg yolks,

And all of this on the Sabbath.

But fear not, she is not a blasphemous bunny,

This writer only needed the rhyme to be funny.

The hare, Jem, wished he could be there to see,

If his rhymes seemed just as silly to thee,

And if they made her brown eyes go runny.

I hope to meet you again soon.

Yours,

Jem

Cressie had to wipe her eyes. Jem had certainly succeeded. She clutched the letter to her chest and smiled, basking in the feeling that filled her that she could not quite name. But in that moment, she became a collector. A collector of poetry, by one particular poet.

CHAPTER 10

Jem attended two further balls following the Fentonbury soirée, and was unsuccessful in securing a dance with Cressie at either of them. He was not at all certain how Mrs Martin had managed it, but she had filled Cressie's dance cards entirely before the commencement of the actual ball.

Jem's authority on this was sound as it had been Cressie herself to tell him this in the very brief moments that he had managed to speak to her, often in passing as she was handed off to her next suitor for a quadrille.

In watching her dance with a dozen gentlemen, Mr Delaney more than most, Jem ought to have felt jealousy. Of course, he did feel envy as any other red-blooded man would, but he did not feel jealousy. This was because it was apparent that Cressie would rather have been plucking chickens then spending time with any one of the fine aristocrats who sought her attentions.

But she didn't look at him the way that she looked at them. That was what saved Jem's heart from the anguish of jealousy. Her brown eyes filled with pleasure and enchantment whenever he was near, and it was only him who could provoke a smile in her that would show her adorable dimples. At least, Jem allowed himself to think this way. To hope this way.

Despite her lack of fortune, Cressie had a natural and effortless ability to be endearing and amiable. Those who could afford to marry for beauty saw Cressie as a fine prize.

Jem did not see her as a prize. She was not a thing to be collected or kept.

On the twenty-eighth of April and nearing one month into the beginning of the Season, Adam and Jem kept busy in the study. Despite being in London for the social festivities, the estate would not run itself and Jem was still committed to his vocation. It took Cecily marching in an hour or two before luncheon to announce that they all would be going for a promenade to pull their eyes from the ledgers.

Cecily was closely followed by Grace, who appeared less than impressed with the idea.

"Mother, we have work to do," Adam replied to Cecily idea dismissively.

"I don't believe I asked for a negotiation," Cecily retorted. "I am in no mind to be cooped up indoors today. Look at your wife. Look how sallow she appears having seen no sunlight."

Grace flushed as her eyebrows furrowed. "Your kindness knows no end, Cecily," she murmured.

Adam huffed as he abandoned his quill. "Anyone who believes my wife to be sallow is an idiot."

"Good!" enthused Cecily. "Tell that to the Marchioness of High-bury when we promenade, for that is exactly what she said about Grace at the ball two nights ago."

Jem frowned deeply, feeling anger and frustration bubble inside of him at the littleness of some people. Why did his sister offend them so?

"I really did not need to hear that," muttered Grace as she made her way to an empty chair before the desk, lowering her larger frame into it gently. As soon as she spoke, Adam left his chair and made his way to her, standing behind her and placing his hands on her shoulders protectively.

"I have no doubt in my mind that you dressed down the Marchioness of Highbury as soon as that unjustified comment was made, Mother," Adam theorised.

Jem recalled the first time he had heard Cecily verbally tear some of Grace's critics apart. Cecily could be vicious, and rightfully so.

Cecily sighed. "Of course, I did," she retorted. "I asked after her grandson. The illegitimate one her son bore by a prostitute." She tsked before sighing once more. "Adam, you do not know these people as I do. The best revenge is to force feed them your happiness. My son imminently expects his third legitimate child."

"So, from what I understand, you desire to prove to the Marchioness of Highbury that you have ... won?" Adam deduced.

Cecily huffed. "You are as contrary as your father used to be," she scolded. "We are to promenade immediately. Dress!"

Cecily got her way, but she usually did. Within the hour, the family were among the many, many families who used their days to walk through Hyde Park, politely nodding and smiling at others, remarking on the weather and asking after the health of absent family members.

Adam and Grace walked in front, which left Jem to escort the dowager. He felt intimidated to be walking with a woman like Cecily Beresford on his arm. It almost felt like walking with the queen. She was distinguished, respected and superior, and people bowed and curtsied to her as they passed.

"You look so much like your father, Jem," Cecily murmured softly.

Jem was so taken aback by her remark that he was certain her had heard wrong. It was not until he looked down into Cecily's eyes that her comment was confirmed.

"I didn't know you knew my father," he managed to stammer in reply.

"Not well, but I did," Cecily returned coolly. "He mended a hem for me once when I was a little younger than you. I see him in you."

Jem wondered what it must have been like for his father to attend to a distinguished lady like Cecily when he was but a country tailor. He wondered a lot about his father, actually.

And it almost brought a tear to his eye to hear someone mention him or connect Jem to him. Most of his family seemed to forget that Jem had been so young when their father had passed away. He didn't have the ability to remember as they did.

"I want to know how you are going in your pursuit of Miss Martin," Cecily continued, not waiting for Jem to respond. "You might be surprised to learn that I am, indeed, a fan of young love."

Jem found that he had very little control over his tongue as he found himself divulging all to the unlikeliest of ears. Cecily listened intently to Jem's story of affection, and his perpetual hope. He did not, however, tell her of his poem. While he knew it was terribly silly, Cressie had loved it. She had told him so herself, and he liked that they shared a little secret that belonged to the two of them.

"If I can offer you anything, Jem, let it be this. When all is lost, the heart is constant. It remains constant, always. I know this to be true."

Jem silently thought of Cecily's lost husband. She had known true love and loss.

"Only a fool allows others to get in the way of true constancy."

In the distance, Jem spotted Cressie and her mother walking together under the shade of a parasol. Cressie was dressed in a white day dress with a blue sash being the only drop of colour on her.

"Only a fool, eh?" Jem uttered under his breath.

Cressie had fond memories of her sixteenth birthday. Of each of her birthdays, really. All of them consisting of her wearing a dress that was hemmed above her ankles as she celebrated as a child.

Today she turned seventeen, and she was spending the day promenading in a dress that showed all that she was a woman of marriageable age.

It was her worst birthday ever.

Cressie had told her mother as such, and Mrs Martin had accused her of being ridiculous.

"Think of it this way," Mrs Martin said to her as they walked, "next birthday you will celebrate in a fine house with a husband who adores you.

Cressie scowled, and Mrs Martin promptly instructed her to remove the expression.

They walked, curtseyed and conversed with the parties they passed. Cressie tired of being 'delighted' to see any of them again very quickly, and found her attention wandering as Mrs Martin laughed musically at a tasteless joke made by a gentleman whom Cressie had quite forgotten them name of.

She was so distracted that she was quite startled when a young boy bumped into her, knocking her into her mother's side.

"Oh, goodness!" cried Mrs Martin.

It took Cressie a moment to realise that the boy, who was now running away from them, had shoved a piece of folded paper into her hand.

"Urchin!" shouted the unknown gentleman, a Mr Smith. "Are you quite alright, ladies?" he asked. "The streets are filled with ragamuffins like him. I only hope he has not pinched anything valuable!"

As Mrs Martin assured him that they were unharmed, Cressie subtly turned her body to conceal that she was unfolding the note that she had been slipped.

Messy Cressie, can you find a way to escape and meet me at the park entrance?

It wasn't signed, but it did not have to be. And the very idea filled her with a sort of thrill that was becoming all too familiar. Cressie did not know at all what was happening to her, but what she could understand was that talking to Jem, however briefly, at these last balls had made her happier than dancing with any one of the gentlemen her mother had insisted upon.

"Mama, I dropped my handkerchief a way back, I must go and fetch it!" Cressie said suddenly, coming up with the first excuse that popped into her head.

"Won't you allow me, Miss Martin?" offered the nameless gentleman. "I would be honoured to be of service to you."

"You are too kind, sir," replied Cressie, "but only I know our path and I will not be long."

Mrs Martin frowned. "Why didn't we bring Nelly?" she asked under her breath. "Quickly then, Cressida," she permitted, nodding her head.

Cressie did not wait for her mother to change her mind as she turned on her heel and walked swiftly back the way they came.

Though following their path, she was heading towards the park entrance.

Her stomach fluttered and her heart thundered as Cressie tried to appear as nonchalant as possible, so as not to appear that she was running off to meet a man alone which, of course, was exactly what she was doing.

But Cressie's excitement was far too loud to hear the anger that she knew her mother would have when she found out.

When Cressie reached the entrance to Hyde Park, she looked around, searching her surroundings anxiously for a tall, dark haired man. There were plenty of people about, all occupied with their own agenda of being seen, but none were Jem.

"Psst!"

Cressie's attention was caught by a hand waving out the dropped window of a small hackney. Had that sound come from there?

The hand at the window was swiftly replaced by the head of the man she most wanted to see. He only briefly showed himself to her, before he beckoned her again with his hand.

Taking a deep breath, Cressie looked around to ensure that nobody was directly watching her. And then she darted over to the hackney, the door opening for her just in time to practically launch herself inside.

Cressie tripped on the step and fell into the hackney, quickly feeling Jem's hands on her arms and back as she all but laid across his lap. He helped her to right herself, and before she knew what was happening, she was staring in his blue eyes from only a few inches away.

What on earth was she doing?

And why on earth did she have no desire to go back?

Cressie had never been this close to Jem before. She had never been this close to any man before. Jem was so tall that it was quite impossible to look upon his face from this distance during normal functions. Lord, his eyes were exactly what she imagined the sea to be.

"You came," he breathed.

"You asked," she returned.

A smile tugged at the corner of Jem's mouth. "Only a fool," he seemed to mutter to himself.

Cressie wasn't certain who the fool was, but she knew that they both would be fools in the eyes of everyone if they did not get away quickly. And the very notion that the idea of escaping was in her head shocked her ... and excited her terribly.

Jem seemed to read her mind as he banged on the roof of the hackney with his fist. Moments later the carriage took off and Jem helped Cressie to the seat beside him. The feeling of his hands on her only increased the flutters in her stomach.

"This is madness," she whispered.

"I know," Jem assured her.

"But I don't mind. It's my birthday today."

"April twenty-eighth," he mused, as though he was committing the date to memory. "Then let my gift to you be a day of madness."

CHAPTER 11

Despite having been in London for a month, Cressie felt as though she was seeing all the streets anew as they flew past the hackney's windows. As the distance between Cressie and her mother grew, she knew that her guilt ought to have been growing. But in that moment, she couldn't feel it. All she felt was excitement. She felt it coursing through her body.

Cressie finally tore her eyes away from the window and looked at Jem. He had been watching her, a smile on his youthful, handsome face. She could see the same excitement there. They mirrored each other. It made her laugh, which drew an amused grin from him.

As they laughed and looked at one another, Cressie felt her stomach seize, as it had done so many times before, only this time she was beginning to understand the cause.

"Where are we going?" Cressie asked him, becoming aware that she really had no idea where he would be taking her.

"Hixham," replied Jem. "It's not far, or so I am told. The Ashwood butler informed me that it is there that we might find some Caribbean food."

"Caribbean food?" repeated Cressie, sounding surprised.

"It is unparalleled," he told her emphatically. "Never will you taste anything more flavourful in your life. Did you ever happen to read about when Lady Susanna married Alex Whitfield? Truthfully, I hope you did not as what the papers reported was mostly vile, but when Alex returned to England, he brought his mother along with him as she now lives in Ashwood with my mother and I. Madame Amélie ensured that I was never late home for my supper again." Jem chuckled to himself.

Cressie found herself suddenly entranced by Jem's story. It was spoken so simply, so offhand, in such a casual way that one would share titbits of information about themselves. It occurred to Cressie, then, that she really had never spoken to Jem much about his life or his family. She had never had the opportunity to, of course. But she found that she utterly adored receiving it, alarmingly so. She wanted to hear more as a multitude of questions bubbled to her lips, but she resisted shouting them all at once as these feelings overtook her.

"What is your favourite dish that Madame Amélie prepares?" Cressie asked, impressing even herself with her controlled tone of voice despite her desperation to engage. What on earth was the matter with her?

"Soup Joumou, undoubtedly," Jem replied immediately, without having to think for long. "It is a delicious soup of meat and vegetables and one could smell it wafting through the village a mile away." Jem smiled fondly, before he asked, "Pray, tell me. What is your favourite dish to eat?"

Cressie wasn't at all sure that she had something to compare to Jem's partiality for Madame Amélie's cooking. She certainly had no fond memories of family dinner tables or traditional meals. She and her mother had often benefited from the mercy of friends and their meals as she had grown. There had never been any abundance of food, nor had they ever had the means to purchase expensive cuts of meat. Cressie had never eaten a meal, let alone taken tea, in public before as they would never have been able to justify the cost. Mealtimes were never an occasion, Cressie realised. They were a source of stress for her mother. A side of mutton and potatoes, if that was all they could manage, were a means to an end.

Cressie knew that she was fortunate in that she had never gone hungry. But she was a little sad in that moment in realising she had no connections to a family supper.

"What have I said? Are you alright?"

Jem's questions were fired at her in quick succession as Cressie realised her face must have been betraying her realisation.

"Do you want me to have the carriage turned around? Do you want to go back? You need only say the word, please."

"I don't have a favourite dish," Cressie said in reply, meeting his blue eyes after having looked away. Her voice seemed to immediately settle him. "Perhaps I will after today."

The carriage brought them to a small borough of London that Cressie had never been to before, nor had she known it to exist. It was very unlike Mayfair in that it was very tired, the buildings in various states of disrepair. Cressie could see that holes had been patched with planks of wood and nails and the thatches of the rooves appeared old and weathered. The people were dressed like the working class, and the majority of them appeared to be from somewhere else, as evidenced by their deep skin tones.

Cressie didn't mean to stare, but she couldn't help it. She had never seen anything like this place before.

"You will find that many of these people have come to be here not of their own volition," murmured Jem. "Them, their parents, their grandparents. A great injustice, a great cruelty has occurred."

Cressie felt terribly guilty for staring at them as the carriage moved past them at a slow walk. They were people moving about their business on the street, just as the people did in Hyde Park, only these people appeared to have business that mattered.

"Do we ought to go somewhere else?" Cressie worried quietly. "Perhaps they will not want us here. I ... I wouldn't know what to say."

"Do you know much about the slave trade? Do you think poorly of them?"

Jem's question was not at all asked in a malicious or judgemental tone. He was merely wondering. But Cressie could not help but be affronted.

"Not at all!" she exclaimed. "No! How could I? Truthfully, I know very little about slavery." Cressie felt foolish admitting that to Jem when he was clearly learned about the subject. "But I know enough to understand the great cruelty in one man owning another."

"I do not think I know nearly enough either," replied Jem in a reassuring tone. "I only know what has been voluntarily said by Amélie, Alex, and my sister-in-law, Belle. I would never ask as it would feel insensitive. But in knowing them, and their experience with white people, blancs, as they call us, it is that respect and humanity go a long way. What is done cannot be undone, but respect and humanity are where we start."

Cressie was terribly impressed by the maturity in Jem's usual youthful demeanour. She admired it immensely. It also helped to allay some of her anxiety about stepping foot into an area like Hixham.

Jem paid the hackney driver to wait for them as they stepped out onto the street. The smells were certainly different, but Cressie could isolate some of the food aromas. Jem joined Cressie at her side, and he offered her his arm. Nobody knew them. Nobody knew that Hixham was where they had found themselves. They could walk together without consequences.

Cressie's stomach flipped as she took Jem's arm, and she could have sworn that she saw a proud flush momentarily fill his cheeks. It was quickly replaced with a wicked sort of smile.

"I don't think you have any interest in promenading, in Hyde Park or anywhere," Jem theorised. "Come on," he urged.

Before Cressie knew what was happening, Jem had begun to run. His long legs took big strides and Cressie sprinted to keep up with him, one arm through his and the other holding her skirt up out of her way. And she loved it. Running down the street alongside Jem, passing people who looked upon them like they were mad, of which they probably were, was fun. Cressie had been craving fun. She had been yearning for fun for years.

Cressie found herself laughing as she puffed. She had not run this way since she was a child. In fact, she could not ever recall running in such a way, and certainly never with a young man. Despite her heart pounding in her throat as she felt the consequences of the exercise, Cressie knew that people were meant to move this way. Promenading with one's nose in the air could never be the order of the day.

Jem abruptly stopped her, throwing his arm out across her stomach and holding her at her waist when a small child suddenly ran out in front of them. Cressie would have fallen over her own feet were it not for Jem's steady arm.

The little girl, who could not have been more than five years old, was quickly collected by her mother, who wore an expression of shame on her young face as she manoeuvred her daughter out of their way, apologising to them in a language that sounded like French.

Jem gave the woman a warm smile and used his free hand to tip his hat as a mark of respect. "Please pardon us, madam," he replied.

The young woman was visibly stunned by such behaviour, and Cressie's rapidly beating heart sank. Men tipped their hats to her all the time. It was expected. If a woman ever was to enter a room it was the custom that a man stood for her. It was basic respect and good manners. Cressie often resented her existence and yet she had never known disrespect.

And this poor woman knew none of it because ... because of people without humanity.

She did not stay. She probably thought Jem was mad. She hurriedly ushered her daughter away from Jem and Cressie and left them alone.

"It makes our problems seem fickle, does it not?" she posed to him.

"No," Jem told her emphatically. "Just because someone has experienced something terrible, it does not mean that your own woes are invalid. We have a right to feel the way we do."

"Is that Madame Amélie wisdom?" Cressie asked.

Jem shook his head. "No, it is something that I have worked out for myself."

Despite the Ashwood butler's assurance, there were no public houses in Hixham where one could purchase a meal, or at least none that they both could see. They walked back to the hackney, the both of them out of breath from their run, and Jem asked the driver to take them to another location quietly. Cressie presumed that she was not allowed to know.

"I meant to find your new favourite dish and I have dismally failed," Jem playfully chastised himself. "A very happy birthday indeed."

"Perhaps nothing could compare to Madam Amélie's cooking," Cressie replied.

"Perhaps not," Jem agreed thoughtfully.

Turning to him, Cressie said, "It really is a happy birthday, though. Now, at least. Just to have laughed and smiled and had a little fun was all I needed."

"I hope this doesn't make you bashful or feel affronted, or make me seem forward, but I want to tell you that you have a beautiful smile." Jem's voice thickened as he spoke with sincerity, and Cressie immediately saw the reservedness in his eyes.

She wondered if he was thinking back to the night of the Winter Assembly where he had proposed to her shortly after their meeting. In thinking of it herself, Cressie was very startled to feel an immediate pull towards Jem. She quickly managed to refocus herself as she managed to say, "Thank you." The moment she saw his shoulders relax, she felt her own smile grow, as though it was tied to his happiness in some sort of way.

"It is those that I like, that are my favourite," Jem mused sheepishly.

"What?"

To her surprise, he raised his hand carefully, before gently brushing the tip of his index finger over the delicate skin underneath her right eye. She knew immediately what he was talking about. Cressie had never before thought of the dimples in her cheeks with any sort of partiality. They were a feature of her face, the same as her brown eyes or her curly hair. But they were Jem's favourites, apparently, and the thrill that information gave her was almost ungodly.

"My father has them, I think."

Cressie had not known where on earth that statement had come from, but it had escaped her lips without her realising. The moment it had, her eyes widened.

"Your father?" Jem prompted gently.

Cressie couldn't help but nod. "I don't remember. I look like him in some ways. That is my theory, anyway. My eyes are brown, and Mama's are not. I have heard before that such things as dimples are hereditary and Mama does not have them, so I believe that he does."

"You speak of your father as though he is still alive," Jem murmured, the question evident.

Cressie felt a terrible numbness as she confessed, "He is alive." She looked at Jem and saw the tenderness in his eyes. "He is alive," she said again, her voice stronger. "He deserted my mother, he deserted me, when I was very young. He ... he did the same thing many times to many women over the years, but he now lives in France with a woman. There could be many more children, I don't know."

"I am sorry, Cressie," Jem said softly. "He is no father."

"But he is," Cressie retorted, and she hated that she sounded indignant. She never wanted to appear like a petulant child. "He is my father, the only one I have, and he doesn't love me." Cressie cupped her hand over her mouth as she spoke the words, completely shocked at her own confession.

She had never uttered such a thing before. How could she when she had only her mother to talk to about this? Her mother's suffering was far greater than Cressie's, and so she had never considered her own feelings on the subject.

And in this moment, they had simply fallen out of her.

Despite what her mother had endured, Cressie's feelings were not invalid. Jem had told her this only a short while ago. Despite this, she still felt selfish for thinking it. She felt selfish for feeling her own pain in her father's abandonment. She felt selfish for grieving the fact that the only father she had loved himself more than he did her.

"I wonder if he even knows that I am seventeen today," Cressie whispered. "Does he ever wonder if I am still alive? He's never written."

"Cressie," Jem said in a pained voice, "he is no father. He is a fool. And what you have lacked in paternal love is entirely undeserved and unfathomable." Jem took hold of Cressie's hands and squeezed them, capturing her attention. "Believe that you are deserving, though, for you should be treasured."

Cressie's lower lip began to tremble. Tears began to well in her eyes. She didn't know what to do or say as his words washed over her.

"No, no, tears will not do on your birthday," joshed Jem as he smiled at her with warmth and sympathy.

"Tell me of your father." Cressie had not meant for her question to sound like a demand, but she spoke a little forcefully.

Jem nodded slowly as he took a breath before beginning. "My father's name was Edward Denham. He was a tailor, and we were very poor. But I never knew that as a child. We never felt it. I think as the youngest of all my siblings, I was protected from it. But in what I remember of my father, there was always happiness. That is all I remember of him. Feelings," Jem confessed. "I remember how I felt when he was there, when he was home. I remember being happy to see him. I remember laughing when he said something funny. But I don't remember him as my brother and sisters do. I was only seven when he died. I forgot his voice, his laugh, his face long before I realised that I should have been forcing myself to commit them to memory. It's hard to believe that we are capable of forgetting such important details, but we are.

"I don't remember him, and that pains me very much sometimes, and I feel envious of my siblings when I know they have special moments that they can recall whenever they want. I used to wonder if that meant that I didn't love him as much as my siblings did."

It was Cressie's turn, then. She removed her hands from his, only so that she could place them on top of his hands in comfort. "I am so sorry for your loss, Jem," she said softly. "Of course, you loved him. Your pain and loss are real, and I should not have been callous in talking of my father –"

"Cressida Martin," Jem snapped, his tone firm, yet teasing. "Weren't you listening?" His eyebrows rose in questioning. "Someone else's pain does not negate your own.

With just a little teasing, he had quashed her anguish, and he had changed the air entirely in the carriage. They had both bared their hearts to one another and shared something that Cressie was quite confident that they had confided in anyone else. And yet Jem was still able to bring a smile to her face.

"Don't call me 'Cressida'," she instructed sheepishly, "or I shall be forced to call you ..." It suddenly occurred to Cressie that she was not at all certain of what 'Jem' was short for. "... Jemothy?"

Jem burst into a fit of laughter so violent that it shook the carriage. Cressie clamped her lips shut as she frowned.

Cressie had not been the only one to cry on this journey. Jem laughed so much that he, too, began to tear up. He quickly used the sleeve of his coat to dry his eyes.

"I am not very good at being ladylike. I will hit you in a minute," Cressie warned.

Jem wheezed as he got control of his laughter, clutching onto his stomach. "Jeremy," he managed to correct her. "My given name is Jeremy."

"Oh." Cressie flushed crimson. That had been terribly obvious now that it had been pointed out to her. Where on earth had she plucked 'Jemothy' from? That wasn't even a name.

"I won't have you embarrassed, not on your birthday," Jem urged. "Will it cheer you to call me 'Jemmy'?" he asked. "My family call me that sometimes and it irritates me to no end. I feel like an infant."

Cressie felt herself smirking as the name sat on the tip of her tongue. Jem was watching her intently. But the seconds went by, and Cressie felt her smirk fading with every moment as they simply looked at one another. They were still holding onto each other's hands, and Cressie became increasingly aware of his thumb brushing over the backs of her knuckles.

She swallowed. Loudly.

Jem did as well as Cressie's eyes briefly dropped to the lump in his throat bobbing.

The carriage suddenly slowed, and both of their attentions were diverted to the window, snapping the tension in the air.

"We're here," whispered Jem.

CHAPTER 12

J em still could not quite believe that Cressie had agreed to accompany him on this most foolish outing. No matter the fun, or the hope it gave him, she was still a lady and she was with a man unchaperoned.

That was where the hope was coming from. She had come with him. Surely Jem could not be imagining the way her brown eyes were looking at him. Did she feel what he did? Could she sense this burgeoning attachment between them? It felt like a string that was hardening with every passing moment, turning from cotton to an unbreakable steel.

The carriage had brought them to Bushy Park, near Hampton Court Palace, namely to visit the remarkable fountain that was situated in the gardens. Being new to London himself, Jem had not known about this place until he had made some subtle inquiries.

By the look on Cressie's face, it was well worth the risk.

Jem jumped down from the hackney first, before helping Cressie out into the beautiful afternoon sun. He once again paid the driver to wait for them as Cressie took his offered arm to venture further into the park.

They were some ten or so miles from the centre of London. The park was certainly populated on a beautiful day like this, but not by the folk frequenting London for the Season. They rarely ventured beyond Mayfair. There were plenty of couples walking, as well as families with their children, and Jem felt as though he and Cressie were one of them.

Nobody knew them, and so nobody looked at them.

The park was a wide expanse of lawns and mature trees, sheltering the masses in shade with their full summer canopies. The gravel path crackled underfoot as they walked.

"I much prefer this park to Hyde Park," Cressie confessed. "Hyde Park is beautiful, but the eyes ..."

"I know exactly what you mean," Jem replied. Of course, he had not been subject to the stares, but his sister had, and he had seen how uneasy it had made her. He couldn't imagine what the stares and gossip would be like for a debutante like Cressie.

The moment Jem heard a drop in Cressie's tone, he knew that he needed to do something. It had been his idea already, but now was the time. He dropped Cressie arm only for a moment before collecting her hand in his. This surprised her, and she looked up at him with confusion and anticipating in her eyes, a small smile of excitement teasing at the corner of her lips.

"We do not promenade, remember?" Jem flashed her a devilish grin before he took off in another run, pulling Cressie along behind him. Jem ran as quickly as he could, feeling his boots kicking up the gravel behind him.

Cressie sprinted alongside him, using her free hand to hold onto her bonnet and their entwined hands swung in between them. For someone so considerably shorter than he was, she was a remarkable runner, and she kept up with a gleeful smile on her face.

Jem had spied it when he heard her laugh with delight. Looking to her, he saw her brown eyes were wide with delight, her smile so big it touched her eyes, and those beautiful dimples were nestled deeply in her cheeks. She was beauty's definition.

Returning his focus forward, Jem continued to run as the Diana Fountain came into full focus. Situated in the very centre of a great expanse of lawn, the enormous fountain was a serene and hypnotising finish line. The golden nymph that stood in the centre almost beckoned them. Jem slowed down as they approached the edge of the water, and Cressie nearly stumbled herself. Jem instinctively caught her, his hands releasing hers to grab a hold of her waist before he realised that holding her hand was scandalous enough.

But Cressie didn't seem to mind, and the very fact that she did not appear affronted by the contact only encouraged Jem's hope that he was not alone in his feelings.

The sounds of the fountain were so peaceful, and Cressie looked over it with awe, her cheeks red from the run. Jem was certain his own appeared the same.

"It is not the seaside, I know."

Cressie suddenly looked up at him, her brows furrowed. "What?"

"You told me that you always longed to swim in the sea," Jem recalled. "The Diana Fountain is not the seaside, but it is better than the Thames."

Had Jem wanted to give them both cholera, then he would have taken her on a swimming trip in the Thames, but that did not seem very romantic.

Cressie still looked utterly confused, and it only increased the thrill that Jem felt travelling down his spine. He grinned. Perhaps it was mad. Perhaps she wouldn't like it. But something inside of him was telling him that this was the right thing to do. This was fun. This was silly. And Cressie was someone who longed for fun.

They would certainly be looked at now, but they were still lucky that nobody knew them.

"Won't you swim with me, Cressie?" he asked in an almost taunting tone, abandoning her side so that he could step into the fountain. The moment he did, he felt the water fill his boots and soak his socks and the bottoms of his breeches. It would have been horrid had the look on Cressie's face not been so amusing.

She was staring at him in utter shock as he waded into the fountain, more and more of his ensemble becoming saturated by the second.

"What are you doing?" Cressie hissed yet yelled. "Have you gone mad?"

Jem let out a laugh as he held his arms out to her. "We've all got to make a little time for madness."

Cressie's smile was one of disbelief and wonder. And it was beautiful. "Your spirit is something else entirely, Jem Denham," she remarked, before she shook her head and bent over to lift up her petticoats to her calves.

With first her left, and then her right foot, Cressie stepped into the fountain, her mouth forming an 'o' shape when the cold water began to soak through her stockings and shoes.

And then she laughed as she released her skirts, letting them drop down into the water with a shrug of her shoulders.

Over Cressie's shoulders, for the briefest of moments, Jem could see that passers-by had begun to stop and stare and question as to what these two fools were doing. But Jem could not convince himself to care at all. His vision quickly refocused to Cressie, and Cressie only.

Cressie's laugh was musical and joyous as she began to wade through the fountain towards him. Jem could visibly see her shoulders relax and a considerable weight lift off of them. In looking upon her now, Jem did not think that he had ever seen her without that unknown burden. She looked young and happy and free.

Just as Cressie reached him, as she took her final step before she would be before him, her foot caught in the water laden hems of her dress. Her laugh vanished momentarily as she lost her footing, and she stumbled forwards. In a panic, she reached out for whatever was nearest her, and that happened to be Jem. Jem could not do anything but be pulled down into the shallow water of the fountain with Cressie, and before either of them knew it, they were soaked up to their necks in the cold water of the fountain.

They both held onto each other, staring at one another in surprise at what had just happened, and quite in shock at the fact that they were soaking wet.

Jem felt Cressie's fingers tightening on his forearm as they both managed to stand up on their knees in the fountain, his eyes unwittingly dropping to follow a stray water droplet as it travelled across her collarbone. When he met her gaze once more, Cressie's pursed lips were smirking, and she cracked. What erupted from her was the most amusing snort of laughter, and it made him break, too.

Jem managed to climb back to his feet, and he helped Cressie to stand as well. She soon reached for the ribbon underneath her chin, and she pulled at it to remove her bonnet. The water had dampened the curls at the nape of her neck. Her dress was soaked through, but she was wearing layers enough that she did not appear indecent, only slightly ridiculous.

But no more ridiculous than he.

As her arms dropped to her sides, Cressie remarked, "This is the best birthday I have ever had. Thank you."

Jem beamed a triumphant grin as he saw the truth of Cressie's words in her eyes. And in that moment, he wanted nothing more than to take her to the seaside to experience the ocean for real. What he would give to see that look of pure and utter joy on her face once more.

This precious being in front of him deserved to feel true happiness every day.

After departing the fountain, they both found a sunny yet slightly secluded spot on the lawns in the park to sit and dry. They had a tranquil view of the gardens, a perfect spot to watch the world go by.

"This is the greatest day of my life, I think." Cressie's voice was soft and decided beside him. She then stretched out her legs in front of her and fanned her skirt as much as she could to allow the sun to dry her, as though she was suddenly trying to avoid her confession.

Jem sensed a sudden sadness in her, and it seemed peculiar owing to her positive confession. "What is it?" he prompted gently.

Cressie's hands paused on her skirt as she took a breath. "I haven't had many days like this. Any days like this," she corrected herself. "My ... my father's actions made many things impossible for my mother and me. There was never any money and we never could ... I never could ... oh, that sounds terrible." Her final comment sounded as though she were chastising herself for thinking something.

Jem leaned closer. "Cressie, tell me," he urged.

Cressie pursed her lips together guiltily as her brown eyes flicked to his. "I feel like my childhood was stolen from me."

The moment the words escaped her mouth, Jem could see how Cressie felt terrible for thinking them. But she needn't. "You seem to punish yourself for having self-regarding feelings," Jem observed sympathetically. "It is not a sin to care about yourself and the weep for the wrongs that have been done to you. Or to mourn for what you have lost."

Cressie sat with his words for several minutes. She breathed evenly as she thought, and what Jem would have done to have known those thoughts. "I do mourn," she whispered. "I mourn for the years I should still have in the shorter dresses of youth. I hate that my father's choices have taken away my own. I hate that I have to be taken away." Cressie's voice shook. "I am terrified of being taken away from my mama to a place belonging to a keeper I do not even remotely like."

There it was. There was Cressie's reason for being in London. Or rather, there was Mrs Martin's reason for being in London. Though, her reason was not so different from the dozens and dozens of other debutantes around. They had indeed fallen upon hard times through no fault of their own, and Mrs Martin needed Cressie to be married to alleviate that burden.

It was as clear as anything that Cressie felt trapped. She had no say in the matter. She was a victim of both her parents.

Her blackguard debaucher of a father had abandoned his responsibility of a wife and child, and her mother was using her to solve their problems stemming from this fiasco of a union.

Jem's mind was racing, but he forced himself to focus on one key point that Cressie had expressed. She was terrified of being taken away by a man she didn't like. If marriage were inevitable, would it be possible to quell some of her fears if she managed to find a man that she did, in fact, like?

Jem wanted to save her, to take her away from the pressure and burden of both Mr and Mrs Martin. He wanted to take her to the seaside and run through gardens and make her laugh and show her the fun that he had had in his own unburdened youth.

Jem felt the words coming up his throat before he knew what was happening. But he caught them before it escaped his mouth again this time. He would not panic propose again, not unless he was certain that she would accept.

Instead, he managed to say, "I would have you find a partner, and not a keeper."

CHAPTER 13

As Cressie looked up into the crystal blue eyes of Jem Denham, there could be no contradicting what she saw there. It was an intensity that she could scarcely describe and could certainly no longer deny.

What she saw was great feeling, and Cressie could be certain of this because she felt it, too. She felt it immensely, suddenly, all at once, and perhaps, all this time.

It was immediately overwhelming to become awash with such attachment to the young man sat in front of her. It was almost enough to distract from the fact that Cressie had not pieced together Jem's own regard for her.

The man had proposed last November, Cressie!

Cressie gasped. She could see it all in his eyes, his beautiful ocean eyes. Oh, the ocean! He had remembered and he had tried to give it to her that very day. Oh, oh!

Was it love? Cressie didn't know what love was supposed to feel like, but was it this? She ... she wanted to be closer to him, to hold his hand as he had held hers in the carriage. But there was more, she wanted more. She wanted his smiles and laughs, she wanted them all. Suddenly the thought of the Season and all the other pretty ladies spinning in their skirts became unbearable. She wanted to hear everything Jem had to say and more. Cressie wanted to ask him so many questions that she promptly forgot them all. And she wanted to tell him everything in return. She wanted Jem's questions, and she wanted to share her heart as she had been during their day.

Jem had proposed last November. The thought circled her mind uncontrollably, and it made her wonder, hope, if he loved her, too. Cressie thought it was love. She hoped it was. Because it felt wonderful and terrifying and confusing all at once.

Cressie could not imagine binding herself to a keeper. The very thought of being kept sounded abhorrent to her. And Jem had said it himself. She ought to find a partner. Was that what he would be? Did he wonder this himself?

"You look as though you have sucked on a lemon," Jem murmured, a bashful tone in his voice. "I hope I was not too presumptuous, but I fear I have been. I have taken far too many liberties today already."

Cressie seemed to stumble over her own tongue as she realised Jem thought that she was reacting poorly to his last statement. What on earth would he think if he could read her mind in this very moment? Certainly, he would think that Cressie was half mad for how fast her mind was racing.

"No!" she nearly shouted. Cressie scrambled onto her knees, collecting her damp hems as she did, which only served as a reminder of Jem's regard. "I ... Mama brought me to London to find a husband ... I know I must marry," she rambled, "and I do not want to be wed to someone horrid ... I know Mama wants me to be happy and to find happiness ..." Cressie's words began to blend together as her nerves affected her tongue. She did not have any idea how her thoughts were becoming words, and she felt as though she had no control over what she was saying. "She would approve, wouldn't she? If she knew I was happy? I feel like I would be ... I feel everything ... I think this is how one is supposed to feel. Do you? I ... I would ... I think you do ... and I cannot fathom ... me! Who am I? I ..." Cressie huffed, "... I fantasise about oceans and would rather have a laugh than participate in stuffy conversation and I find running a far more efficient method of getting from one place to another and I think I love you, Jem Denham, and I quite enjoy food Mama thinks is 'peasant food' and I –"

Jem clapped a hand over Cressie's mouth, stifling anymore of her nonsense. As she had rambled, she had looked away from him, but his action brought her gaze back to his. Jem's lips were clamped shut as an impossibly gleeful smile filled the bottom half of his face. His cheeks were flushed completely red, but Cressie did not think that Jem had ever looked happier.

Jem exhaled shakily before his lips parted, his smile only growing. "In a moment, I am going to take my hand away, and I want you take a breath, and say that again."

Jem gently removed his hand, and Cressie forced herself to take in a deep breath. Her lungs suddenly felt like shallow pockets as her rapid and thundering heart took up all the room in her chest.

"I ... I like peasant food," she whispered. "Mutton pies are delicious when prepared correctly."

It wasn't cowardly. It was calculated. Cressie wanted to make Jem laugh because she loved the sound. It was startling how easily that word was coming to her now.

But she had been right. A laugh had ripped through Jem's chest and he fell forwards onto his hands. As he did this, the sun caught his dark hair, and it appeared almost chestnut in the light. Cressie thought that she could even see some undertones of red. It was as though her eyes were anxious to notice and memorise everything all at once.

"I think love is what it is," Cressie murmured. "I think that's what it might have been all along. I love you, Jem."

Jem's laughs quietened as his blissful smile returned, his eyes boring into hers. "I can't believe it," he breathed.

Neither could Cressie, and yet she felt it with more conviction with every passing second.

"I think I have been in some form of love with you since the moment I saw you," Jem confessed sincerely. "But since being granted these moments, this time with you, while we have been in London, I have known it." Jem took in a shaky breath. "Lord, I am terrified I might wake up in a moment and this will have all been a trick my mind is playing on me."

In hearing his words, Cressie felt a warmth that wrapped around her in an intoxicating, consuming fashion. And yet, it all seemed so obvious all of a sudden, as though she had sudden put on spectacles for the first time. How blind and oblivious had she been?

"It's not a dream," Cressie replied, returning her own joyous smile. She reached forward and lightly pinched the skin on the back of Jem's hand to prove it.

Jem was quick to capture her hand in his, immediately interlacing their fingers together. He then slowly brought her hand to his lips, and he kissed her palm gently, his eyes never leaving hers.

Cressie's heart quickened even more, if that were even possible, and her breath caught in her throat. She felt his kiss on her skin for several seconds.

"This is what it is, isn't it?" Cressie whispered, her voice crackly with nerves. "This is what it feels like?"

Jem knew exactly what she was meaning to say. "I believe so," he whispered back, nodding his head. "I have never loved anyone else, so I have nothing to compare it to. But I do know I never want to feel this way towards anyone else. Ever."

A stupid smile twisted Cressie's lips as she felt her cheeks flush crimson. But as soon as he had spoken the words, Cressie could only agree with him. The very idea of being so swept up in feeling for another seemed wrong. How could she ever feel this way for someone else? She didn't want to.

"I can't believe that you are looking at me like that," Jem uttered.

"Like what?"

"Like they do," Jem said simply. "I've seen the way my sisters look at their husbands for years now ..." Jem shook his head in disbelief. "I never thought I would ... I never thought someone like you could ..." Jem trailed off, but his eyes never wavered, searching her, memorising her, taking in everything.

"Do they look at their husbands the way you are looking at me?" Cressie wondered.

"I think I can confidently say 'yes'," he chuckled, nodding.

Yes. The word rung in her ears as she was once again reminded of the Winter Assembly back in Ashwood. What might have changed had she said 'yes' on that night? Would they have been married by now?

Cressie had always imagined her marriage to be an affair of manners and properness and suffocation. A life sentence, really. But the idea of marriage to Jem had quickly begun to eclipse that vision. There would be laughing and silliness and love. She had a vision in her mind of Jem twirling her in dance before a hearth. It was happiness, something she had so long been denied. It was as though she could reach out and grab it if she wanted to.

"Tell me what you are thinking. I have to know what thought has brought that smile to your face."

Cressie wouldn't lie. "I am wondering what our life might have been like had I accepted your original proposal," she confessed.

Jem grinned devilishly. "Whoever would have thought panic proposing would be the way to win over the Cressida Martin?"

Panic proposing, was it? "Hush," she commanded. "I am not the anything. Really, I am of no importance." Cressie had not meant her words to sound as though she was searching for assurance. She meant them in all sincerity. She knew that she was not special or important in any way. She could not save a life, nor contribute in any way to academia. She would be forgotten when she was gone from this world. She was just a girl.

"I beg to differ," Jem countered softly. "You are completely important to me."

Cressie was just a girl, she thought again, and it was enough for her to be important to one man. Smiling, she repeated, "Panic proposing? Is that what you call it?"

"I believe so," confirmed Jem. "When one proposes instead of converses like a normal person, I think the label fits." He rolled his eyes at himself. "But I don't regret it. I feel like my own tomfoolery and wayward tongue have brought me here."

Cressie smirked. "Certainly," she agreed. And she could not have been gladder for it.

Jem's eyes quickly flicked to their surroundings for a brief moment. "Will you allow me to take one final liberty today?"

Before Cressie could ask what he meant by that, she realised. Jem had checked their surroundings for onlookers, and once he had seen that nobody was paying attention to them, he edged closer to her.

He began slowly, testing her, testing her tolerance and her conviction. When she did not move away, he drew even nearer.

Cressie was frozen, completely unsure of what to do. She had never done this before. What did she need to do? Did she need to move closer as well? What was she supposed to do with her hands?

"Stop thinking," Jem whispered. He was so close to her now that his words brushed over her face. "Close your eyes."

Cressie obeyed, finding that she was grateful for the instruction, even if she was still unsure of what to do with her hands. She sat them in her lap so that they did not flop at her sides.

A few moments after her eyes closed, Cressie felt a warm pressure upon her mouth. She smiled uncontrollably, and she felt Jem's lips upturn as well. She was kissing. They were kissing. This was kissing!

Her instinct seemed to take over as she mimicked what she felt, pressing her lips to Jem's just as tenderly as he did hers. She felt his hand cup the back of her neck and she was suddenly aware of the goose pimples there, but she was too swept up in the moment to feel embarrassed by them.

All too quickly, it was over, and her eyes fluttered open. Jem was still very close to her, and he looked exactly like she felt.

"I've never done that before," she confessed almost dreamily.

Jem chuckled. "I have never done that before, either."

"You are very good at it."

Jem's cheeks flushed perhaps the same colour of her own as they looked upon the other. "So are you."

"I didn't know what to do with my hands." Cressie turned them over in her lap.

"Put them in mine." Jem turned over his own palms and Cressie grinned as she rested her hands flat against them, enjoying the contrast in their sizes.

"Are you going to panic propose to me again as a birthday gift?"

Jem immediately closed his hands around Cressie's, holding them in his grip. "I'd like to think I've become a little more articulate since November," he chuckled. "But I ought to do it right, shouldn't I? Ask permission? I know your mother expects more, and I certainly wish I was more, but –"

"You are important to me just as you are," Cressie said fervently, interrupting him. "And Mama will see that. I know she will."

CHAPTER 14

"I don't think I could ever articulate what this day has meant to me, Jem," Cressie whispered as the carriage brought them back on to the familiar Mayfair streets.

Even thought she could not properly express her pure elation in everything that had been this day, this perfect birthday, something in Jem's blue eyes told Cressie that he understood. He understood her. His spirit knew her spirit. It was a connection, perhaps, that did not need words to explain it.

"Will your mother be very angry, do you think?"

Cressie hadn't liked to think of her mama much during their expedition, purposefully pushing Mrs Martin and Cressie's obligation to her out of her mind. But she knew there would indeed be consequences, and that she would need to work her hardest to pacify Mrs Martin before Jem could approach her.

"I have spent the day alone with a man," Cressie replied. "Any mother would be furious, I imagine." Especially a mother like Mrs Martin, a mother who had such plans for Cressie's Season. Behaviour like this could ruin her reputation. It could drive away suitors.

In fact, that did not sound at all dreadful …

Cressie shook away those thoughts. It would not do to hurt her mother deliberately. She would need to apologise and help Mrs Martin to see that Jem was her choice, and that he was the only reasonable choice for her.

The carriage stopped at the corner of the street where Cressie and her mother were staying. The sun had set, and the streetlamps had been lit. It would be a quick walk to the house and would require a quick prayer that nobody was lingering by their windows waiting to spread gossip.

Cressie took a deep breath and looked at Jem with sadness, reluctant to leave him, and hesitant to face her mother's ire.

"I wish I could come with you," he murmured softly. He raised his hand, pausing for only a brief moment, before the backs of his knuckles grazed over her cheekbone. Cressie felt a shiver run down her spine as her eyes closed. "Messy Cressie," he uttered.

With her eyes still closed, Cressie smiled uncontrollably, and she felt his thumb dip into one of the dimples underneath her eyes. Cressie opened her eyes and said, "I will get word to you tomorrow. I will tell you what happens, and I will tell you when it is best to approach Mama. Will you wait for my letter?"

"With bated breath," he confirmed.

Cressie wanted to kiss him again, but she didn't know how to do it, or how to say it. The very thought of articulating this wish felt like it went against every lecture of propriety her mother had ever made her sit through. But it was a day for breaking the rules. It was her birthday.

And Jem seemed to be able to read her mind. He leaned in closer to her, tilting his head slightly so that their noses did not collide, and he pressed his lips to hers. Cressie was so excited for a moment that she forgot to respond. But she closed her eyes and followed her instincts, allowing the emotion of it fill her with felicity.

When they parted, Jem laughed, and Cressie immediately froze.

"What did I do wrong?" she snapped fearfully.

"Nothing!" he assured her. "I just can't believe this is happening. I'm allowing myself to be deliriously happy for a moment before I worry, I am about to awaken."

With a spark of mischief, Cressie reached forward and pinched the skin on the back of Jem's hand.

"Ouch!"

"You are wide awake, Mr Jem," she quipped, before she turned to the door of the carriage and unlatched it, allowing it to swing open. She took it upon herself to lower the step, and she climbed out as quickly and as gracefully as she could manage while trying to be quiet.

"I'll await your letter tomorrow," Jem called in a hushed tone as he reached down to collect the step.

Cressie nodded. As she went to hurry away, she was called back.

"And Cressie!"

Cressie stopped and turned around.

Jem smiled a beautiful smile at her. "Happy birthday."

Cressie felt her cheeks flood with everything from happiness to embarrassment over her own inexperience. So, she curtseyed, and completely without realising. A look of horror filled her face when she realised what she had done, and Jem snorted with entertainment, saying something that sounded an awful lot like, "Finally, it isn't me!"

She felt an urge to take off one of her shoes and throw it at him, but she knew that she had been on the street for too long already. Cressie hurried away from the carriage, running towards her house.

The moment Cressie was inside, she leaned against the front door and sucked in several deep breaths. For the briefest of moments, she felt safe and free from embarrassment. But that was the least of her worries.

"Cressida Martin!"

Cressie had never heard her mother speak her name in such an irate tone before. She had never heard her mother sound so angry before. Mrs Martin was quick to appear in the small entryway of the house, her grey-green eyes hard and cold. Her mother was not a remarkably tall woman, but she was holding herself with an imposing posture.

Cressie shrunk down against the door. "Mama, please –"

"What is the matter with you, child?" Mrs Martin asked furiously. "You scare me half to death, abandon me," she clenched her teeth, "risk everything! I couldn't look for you! I couldn't raise the alarm! I couldn't let anyone know you were missing to protect your reputation! And I hated myself for every minute of it! It made me sick! You forced me to make that horrid choice! I had assume that you had gone off on an escapade and that you were not in any danger ... I had to pray that this was the case! And I can see that I was right. But that only makes me more furious with you, Cressie. How dare you behave in such an unforgivable way!"

Cressie felt like a hound with its tail between its legs as shame and remorse filled her. She hadn't meant to punish her mother ... and she certainly had never considered that Mrs Martin would fear something dreadful had happened to her.

"I raised you better!" Mrs Martin continued in her seething tone. "I raised you smarter!"

"Mama!" Cressie appealed weakly.

"I can't bear to look at you!" Mrs Martin hissed. "I am ashamed of you. How could you do this? How could you risk everything that we have worked for? Don't you care?"

Tears filled Cressie's eyes and her lower lip trembled. This was horrible. She felt horrible. Every coherent thought, everything she had planned to say, all vanished from her mind. Her wonderful, beautiful, perfect day was all but a distant memory in an instant. Her mother had never been so angry with her ever, and Cressie felt completely rotten.

"Mama, of course I care!" Cressie blubbered. "Please don't say such things. Don't say you are ashamed of me."

"I had to pretend that you had suddenly taken ill!" Mrs Martin shouted. "Mr Delaney called today, and I had to lie! I had to pretend that you were sick in bed, all the while having not one iota of an idea as to your true whereabouts!"

Cressie's tears spilled over the tops of her eyelids and ran down her cheeks.

"So, where were you?" Mrs Martin demanded to know. "And whom were you with?"

"I don't know exactly, somewhere in London," Cressie replied, her voice trembling. Despite her shame, she could not bring herself to name the Diana Fountain. She wanted to protect it. She wanted to protect Jem. But she knew she could not save the latter. How naïve she had been to think that she would be able to talk her mother around so easily. Cressie had no skill whatsoever in coercion.

She hated to have her mother angry with her. She hated that her mother felt ashamed of her, and all she wanted was for everything to be alright.

"And who accompanied you?" Mrs Martin asked insistently, her voice firm and tense.

"Jem Denham." Cressie whispered his name. In her mind, she wrapped her arms around the words as soon as they had escaped her mouth, drawing him back in and keeping him safe.

Mrs Martin was eerily silent for several moments. Cressie dared not meet her eye.

"I thought as such," Mrs Martin said coolly.

Cressie clamped her eyes shut. "Mama," she said shakily. She willed herself to find any courage, any at all. "Mama, I love him."

She heard Mrs Martin take a breath, one that sounded as though it was filled with pity. "No, Cressie, you don't."

Her response made Cressie look up, her brows furrowing as she met the stern gaze of her mother.

"You don't know what love is. You are too young to know," Mrs Martin said dismissively.

"But I am old enough to marry?"

Cressie hadn't known where that rebuttal had come from, or where her rebuking tone had erupted from, but it had shocked Mrs Martin.

"Love will grow in marriage as you do," Mrs Martin replied tersely, before she shook her head. "Why are you determined to hurt me, Cressida? Have I not done everything humanly possible to give you the opportunities you deserve? Have I not sacrificed all but my own dignity to put you on this stage, in this town, to give you the sort of life a lady should demand?"

Her mother's words slapped her back down from the brief moment of gumption that had filled her, and Cressie's shame was quick to return when she saw the pain and disappointment on her mother's face.

Cressie covered her face with her hands, and she heard her mother's footsteps approach. Mrs Martin collected Cressie's wrists with her own hands and pulled them away, forcing Cressie to meet her eyes.

"This isn't love," Mrs Martin said firmly. "I will not allow that boy to fill your head with nonsense. He doesn't know what love is either. I forbid you from seeing him again. Am I quite understood?"

Her mother couldn't be right. She just didn't understand. She didn't understand yet. She didn't know that it really was love. Surely, she would come around when Jem spoke to her. Jem would be able to make sense of their feelings where Cressie's tongue was tied. Because she could certainly not fathom never seeing him again. Not after today.

"Mama..."

"I forbid it," Mrs Martin repeated icily.

Dear Jem,

It was terrible. Mama was furious. Far angrier than I thought she would be. It was my own fault, my own misjudgement. She was worried that something terrible had happened to me and I never considered this.

But that was only the beginning of her fury.

She told me that she was ashamed of me, and I forgot everything that I wanted to say. I hated seeing my mother like this. I hated feeling that I had let her down so dreadfully.

I will not tell you all that she said. I fear I will ruin the paper with my own tears if I write it down and re-live it.

I wish you had been there to explain. I fear I did an abysmal job of articulating myself. I really couldn't formulate my words at all. But I told her about you.

Mama says that I am forbidden from seeing you again. She is angry. I have to tell myself that. I have to believe that she will come around when she is calmer and when she has listened to everything properly.

It would be wise, I think, to wait a while for Mama's anger to ease. I feel awful in every way for hurting my mother. I never want to hurt her or anger her after what she has endured.

But I have not changed my mind. That is what I am writing to say. I know my mind. I know yours, I feel.

With all my love,

Cressie

The letter, written in the middle of that first night, was stowed in Cressie's pocket and had been for several days. She had almost broken the seal to make amendments and apologies for the delay in getting word to Jem, but Mrs Martin had confiscated her correspondence tools the following morning.

Cressie dared not even try to use Nelly as means to send her letter for fear that it would end up in the hands of her mother.

No scandal broke and Cressie's callers continued, and this seemed to settle Mrs Martin's nerves considerably, though she still have not spoken a word to Cressie when they were not in company. Mr Delaney had purchased honey for Cressie's phantom sore throat and Mrs Martin had fussed over it immensely.

After four days of silence, as well as sickness in the pit of Cressie's stomach, she'd had an idea. When she reached the bottom step of the staircase, Cressie trod on her hem deliberately and stumbled forward, feeling it rip away from the waistline of her dress.

"Oof!" Cressie cried as she hit the floor with a thud.

She heard her mother moving in the neighbouring drawing room. She appeared in the entryway quickly and gasped with surprise at the scene of Cressie on the floor.

"Cressie, what happened? Are you hurt?" she cried.

Cressie's fall was perhaps a little too realistic, and she rubbed her elbow with a wince. "Yes, Mama, I am alright. I think the hem of this gown is a little long. I tripped over it and it ripped." She motioned to the horribly damaged seam that left her stays and chemise on display.

Mrs Martin tsked and frowned at the damage. "It seems the modiste did not hem this gown to your proper measurements. How careless. You could have been seriously hurt! Go and change. Nelly will help you. We shall take this dress back to Belle Desjardins immediately and have her mend it."

Cressie certainly did not want her mother to scold Belle Desjardins, but a trip to the modiste had been her goal. "Yes, Mama," she replied obediently, hiding her smile at her triumph. She would soon be with her dressmaker, a woman who just happened to be Jem's sister-in-law.

CHAPTER 15

Jem had not heard from Cressie the day after her birthday as she had promised. And that had caused him to worry himself sick. What was worse was that he knew it would be foolish and reckless to call if indeed Cressie was in deep trouble with her mother.

He had taken himself on several walks the days after and had found himself on the corner of her street, but he could not bring himself to even walk past her house just in case it caused Cressie more trouble. For the very fact that he had not heard from her, he knew that something was amiss and there was not a thing he could do to help her.

After all, he was the reason.

Jem had promenaded with his sister each day as well to no avail. Cressie was nowhere to be seen.

But despite this, he could not regret sneaking away with Cressie. He could not ever regret that time spent with her. She had been happy, truly happy, and he had seen it in her beautiful brown eyes every minute that they had spent together. To know that he had given her that happiness was a great comfort to him in and amongst the anguish and guilt.

When Jem's mind wanted to frighten him by imagining Cressie with someone older and richer and better than he was, it was a comfort to know that she had known happiness and silliness and freedom, if only briefly, with him.

After four days of hearing nothing, Jem was ready to ask Grace to call on Mrs Martin with some invented reason. Jem imagined that a lady could call upon another to ask advice over lace or hats or something like that.

"You desire me to visit with Mrs Martin and ask about her hat?" Grace stared blankly at her younger brother with a quizzical brow. "Do you really admire it so, Jem?" Grace was seated with her tea tray in the drawing room and had promptly abandoned her sandwiches when Jem had asked the question.

Jem huffed impatiently. Grace did not know of his expedition. Had she known of it beforehand, he would have wagered she would have tried to talk him out of it. Only a fool would risk a lady's reputation. Grace had been amenable to Jem's requests to go walking in the park over the previous days and had accepted an invitation at his insistence for the coming Saturday. She had done everything he'd asked of her despite her own discomfort at being around the gossips who still found her to be an inferior choice for the Duke of Ashwood.

"I'm worried about Cressie," Jem confessed to his sister. "I haven't seen or heard from her in days and I am concerned that her mother is ..." What was he thinking? Did he really imagine that Mrs Martin would chain her daughter to her bed? There had not been any rumours spread about their expedition by some miracle. "... hiding her from me," he concluded.

"Hiding her from you?" repeated Grace, her blue eyes widening slightly. "Oh, my." Her lips pursed. "Your attachment runs deep, doesn't it?" She asked the question as though she hadn't believed it until now. Perhaps she had been humouring him as a young boy with an infatuation.

"You told me that you would do everything in your power to help Cressie and I," he reminded Grace of her promise to him before they had come to London. Jem prayed that Grace did not interpret his reminder as guilt. He hadn't meant it as such, and he would be eternally grateful for all she and his brother-in-law had done for him.

Jem just needed to know that Cressie was alright!

"Have you done something very terrible so as to offend Mrs Martin?" Grace queried softly.

Yes. "Please, Grace?" Jem begged.

Only moments before Jem was about to get down on his knees, did a footman open the door to the drawing room.

"Mrs Peter Denham, Your Grace," he announced.

Both Grace and Jem turned to see Belle cross the threshold into the drawing room, dressed in a fine blue day dress and an ivory spencer coat, the colours of which contrasted to her skin beautifully.

After the footman bowed his head and shut the door behind him, Belle remarked, "I do not think I will ever be used to hearing myself introduced as such."

Grace laughed. "I know exactly what you mean!" She rose from her chair to greet Belle with her hand extended. "Welcome. We were not expecting you."

Jem noticed that Belle still had an expression of surprise and humbled pleasure whenever one of their family would receive her as Grace had just done. Nonetheless, she took Grace's hand and allowed herself to be led into the room.

"I'm sorry for calling unannounced," she apologised, "but I have some rather pressing business with you, Jem."

Belle's golden eyes found Jem, and he immediately saw her sense of urgency. He furrowed his brow as he stepped towards his sister-in-law. Belle produced two sealed letters from her pocket and held them out to him. She seemed to eye Grace momentarily before deciding that she was in trustworthy company.

"Miss Martin and her mother came by the shop earlier today," Belle told him. "When her mother was distracted, she bade me deliver her letter to you. She confided in me," she continued, "and I made her an offer, which I imagine she will tell you about in the second letter. She pretended to write me some requests for a dress she needs mending, but it was really an additional letter."

Relief momentarily flooded Jem as he heard any sighting of Cressie, even more so now that he had two letters from her. He could only imagine what her trouble was if she could not even post a letter normally.

"I feel I am missing some information," Grace murmured, eyeing Jem with a knowing gaze, "but I am reminded of another love story with similar beginnings." Her eyes dropped to the letters that Jem had just taken from Belle. "And with similar opponents," she added. "You have my help, Jem. You have everything you need from me, so long as you look after that young girl."

Jem adored his sister. He promptly kissed her cheek and hugged her tightly, feeling the protrusion of her expectant belly against him. He couldn't know exactly the parallels she was drawing, but he could infer she imagined the opponents to his own courtship similar to that of her own.

"You know I will," he promised.

"I'm glad of it," interjected Belle. "I struggle to bear the sight of an imprisoned woman."

"You must be more careful, Cressie," Mrs Martin urged as they approached Desjardins. "We barely have been able to afford your wardrobe this Season, and therefore reparations to those dresses are out of the question. We are only lucky that the modiste is so grateful for our business."

"Yes, Mama," Cressie agreed blindly as she focussed forwards on their destination. Her heart fluttered in anticipation.

"We have so much to do before this evening," Mrs Martin continued. "It will be your return into society after your illness. I imagine you will have a bevy of gentlemen well-wishers and you shall entertain them all. But, of course, you must pay your dues to Mr Delaney. He has been most attentive with gifts this week."

Cressie was almost excited to be let out of the house for the ball that evening after a week of being kept indoors save for her one trip to the modiste. Her excitement wavered at the knowledge she would once again be returning to the lion's den with Mr Delaney at the helm.

Mr Delaney had been very attentive throughout her sham illness. He had visited every day that week with flowers and treats to wish her well. While grateful, Cressie was really unsure of what she had done to warrant such attention. Could this man not see that her smiles were false, and her conversation forced? Mrs Martin had blamed Cressie's lack of eloquence on her headaches but what could be said for that evening?

Mrs Martin stepped up to the door of Desjardins and pushed it open, the little bell above the door jingling. Cressie followed her mother inside the shop and they were greeted with the familiar room filled with bolts of fabric and the large table covered in catalogues and design books.

Belle Desjardins emerged from her fitting room at the back of the shop and greeted them both with a smile. "Good morning," she said with a smile.

"Thank you for fixing my dress so quickly, Mrs Denham," Cressie said gratefully.

The beautiful modiste's golden eyes warmed in a knowing way. Cressie felt a thrill inside her chest. God bless this woman. God bless the women who helped other women.

"We are thankful for your quick work," agreed Mrs Martin, though she seemed reluctant to call Belle by her married name.

"Not at all," Belle replied. "Please, come back and allow me to fit the dress, Miss Martin. I want to ensure it is just right," she beckoned. "Please do take your time browsing, Mrs Martin."

Mrs Martin hurried Cressie along, and Cressie gave her mother an obliging nod. She then followed Belle across the threshold of her fitting room, where the door was promptly shut behind them.

Out of the corner of her eye, Cressie did spot the mended dress that she was meant to try on, but her attention was immediately drawn to the tall young man waiting for her beside a silk clad mannequin.

Cressie felt her heart swell in her chest as her legs propelled her towards him, completely without any instruction from her racing mind. Jem received her immediately, and he wrapped his long arms around her just as soon as she collided with his chest. Cressie clung onto the lapels of his coat, her knuckles whitening with her grip, as though she was afraid that he would disappear if she let him go.

"You got my letters," she whispered.

"I got your letters," he replied, his voice just as quiet.

Without a word, Belle slipped outside into the small courtyard that was accessed through the back door of the shop, leaving Jem and Cressie alone. Cressie was acutely aware that her mother could walk into the fitting room at any moment and discover them, so she knew that she had to savour this private moment for however long it lasted.

Belle had offered her shop as a rendezvous point for the both of them, and Cressie had jumped at the opportunity. It was a risk, certainly, while her mother was still so angry, but Cressie had wanted to see Jem. Nay, she had needed to see Jem.

"Are you alright?" Cressie felt one of Jem's hands leave her back before it rested on her chin. With his finger, he gently tilted it up to look at him. "I have been worried sick about you this week."

Cressie had always dreamed of the ocean, of swimming in it and feeling the pull of the currents and the rush of the waves. But she had heard the ocean in Jem's conch shell, and she could see it in his lovely blue eyes. If she never made it to the sea, she would recall the peace she felt in this moment.

It was right with Jem. It was the only thing she had ever experienced in her short life that had felt right. Perhaps she hadn't known was right felt like before now.

"I haven't changed my mind," Cressie insisted.

Despite a relieved smile tugging at the corner of his lips, and a slight red flush to his face, Jem replied, "That wasn't what I asked. Are you alright, Cressie? I feel like I have abandoned you and am quite helpless to render you any assistance."

"I'm alright," she confirmed, nodding her head. "Mama is still angry, and very distrustful of me. But I think when she sees how unhappy I will be with another, she will understand. I know Mama wants me to be happy."

"You haven't changed your mind?"

"Didn't I just say that?" A wicked grin spread across Cressie's face, and it was perhaps the first time she had smiled since her birthday. She exhaled rather blissfully as she pressed her cheek against Jem's chest, releasing his lapels so that she could encircle his waist with her arms. Cressie felt Jem rest his chin on top of her head.

Cressie knew her mother would understand eventually. After what she had ensured at the hands of Mr Martin, Cressie knew her mother would want her to find someone with whom she would be truly happy.

"We must avoid each other at the ball this evening, if you will be in attendance, that is," Cressie murmured.

"I will be there," Jem confirmed quietly.

"I don't want Mama to feel ambushed," Cressie explained. "She needs time, but I know her. I know she will see my side. And when she does ..."

"And when she does, I will go to her," Jem concluded Cressie's thought.

Cressie smiled against his chest at the very idea. How strange it was to think the notion of marriage practically sickened her at the beginning of the Season. It was exciting to view it as an adventure to take on with a precious companion.

She felt such surety. She felt it in her bones. She knew that everything would be alright.

CHapTer 16

T he following weeks passed quickly, and the end of May drew nearer. The Season, of course, did not slow, and the endless procession of balls, soirees, garden afternoon teas, luncheons, and whist parties continued.

Unfortunately for Jem, his invitation to such events relied upon his sister's attending, and as Grace's pregnancy progressed, her strength and stamina waned. Though these functions were not the only place that Jem would have occasion to see Cressie.

Belle, the saint that she was, had continued to allow them both to use her shop as a rendezvous point. It was at Belle's shop where they could talk, albeit briefly, and where they could continually affirm their feelings for one another. This, all the sneaking around and longing, would all be worth it in the end when they could be together openly.

Jem had not merely spent the month of May pining, for he did have a responsibility to Adam. Not only was he dedicated to the vocation his brother-in-law provided, but he was determined that this income would facilitate his ability to marry. He was not stupid. He knew that he could not ask for a woman's hand without a home to give her or an income to support her.

Adam and Grace were both privy to Jem's clandestine meetings with Cressie, and whether they disapproved or not they kept to themselves. Both, however, wanted Jem to be successful in his pursuit.

Jem was not the only one in pursuit of Cressie Martin. Everett Delaney had publicly declared himself in pursuit of Miss Martin's hand shortly after Cressie's birthday. They were, essentially, courting. Though there could never have been a more one-sided affair in London's history than Mr Delaney's quest for Cressie's hand. At least, Jem needed to tell himself that constantly whenever he saw them together during the London evenings.

Cressie continually assured Jem that her mother would come around that Mrs Martin would understand eventually, but Jem felt as though there was a clock rapidly ticking on his time with Cressie if he did not act. He felt like he had already let her go with one hand when he had agreed to wait, and he was very quickly losing his grip on the other hand as they delayed.

As May came to a close, the decision was made for Adam and Grace to return to Ashwood to await the birth of their third child before it became too challenging for Grace to travel. Jem could never begrudge them this after everything that Grace had done to assist him in entering Society.

"I don't want you to return with us, Jem," Adam informed Jem from the seat behind his desk in the study. Jem sat across from him as he always did, a bevy of documents in between them.

Jem had not planned on returning with them. In fact, he had been thinking of reasons not to go since they had announced their departure at breakfast that morning. Perhaps his brother could not do without him and absolutely needed him to stay in his newlywed marital home for a month.

But Adam seemed to have other ideas.

"Oh?" replied Jem, completely intrigued.

"You have done excellent work for me since your training began," Adam complimented. "You and your brother share a penchant for numbers, it seems. I am fortunate, I know, to have your keen eye on my books."

"Thank you," Jem said gratefully.

"I am going to leave you in London for the remainder of the summer," Adam decided, "in charge as my House Steward. Officially. This title will grant you responsibilities over my household staff, and the butler will answer to you. This role will also pay you a salary of a hundred pounds per annum.

"When your experience grows, as does your age, I will want to raise you to be my Land Steward. This is the role that you have been working towards and is a serious undertaking in the running of an estate like Ashwood. You would be responsible for managing my farms, collecting rents, and ensuring that my estate remains profitable. When you are ready, it will be yours. You will have a house on my estate, and an annual income of three hundred pounds per annum."

Jem gripped the desk in front of him to hold himself steady. He could barely speak for shock. He had been working tirelessly towards this role for months. That income, while not a landed gentleman's income, was ten times that of what his father or sister had ever earned. And it was only the beginning. He had direction. He had a goal that Adam and laid out before him. In time he would rise to be Ashwood's Land Steward. He would have three hundred pounds and a house.

Jem would have an income and a house to offer.

"I would not give this to you had you not earned it, Jem, nor if I believed you were not capable. You are incredibly so." Adam seemed to chuckle to himself at the sight of Jem's shock. "But

I know this is also what you needed. What are you waiting for, another man to swoop in? Go on then!" he encouraged, waving Jem away with his hands. "Don't do what I did and wait twelve years to wed the woman you love. Don't waste a minute. I would call you a fool."

"Right." Jem nodded his head and got to his feet, rather unsteady like a newborn fawn.

"If you're in need of a minister, I happen to know a good one who could unite you in holy macaroni." Adam laughed then, properly, slapping himself on the stomach at a joke only he understood.

Jem was too excited to think on it for more than a second. He knew exactly what he needed to do.

Jem knocked on the door of the Martin residence with a bouquet of flowers in his hand. He had not made the same mistake of bringing chrysanthemums.

He was dressed in his Sunday best, in a new coat that artfully concealed the disproportionate length of his arms, and in shiny new boots that cleverly disguised his too long legs. He rather hoped that he looked like a smart young man, and not a boy who was still growing into his body.

Jem hope was necessary as inside he felt like a bumbling pile of sawdust.

The Martins' maidservant opened the door and Jem cleared his throat as he offered her a polite smile.

"Good afternoon," he greeted. "I have come to call upon Mrs Martin, please."

Would Cressie be angry with him that he had come to call without consulting her? Jem certainly hoped not. He hoped that she would understand this was what he had needed to do. He did not have any other choice. However unwanted the attentions of

Mr Delaney were, she was still being pushed towards him. Jem needed to try.

"May I ask your name, sir, so I may relay the information to my mistress?"

Jem frowned slightly seeing as he had already called upon this house before. "My name is Jem Denham," he replied. "Please tell your mistress that I must speak with her."

The maid nodded, before saying, "Please wait here, Mr Denham." And then she promptly shut the door.

Jem did not want to feel disheartened that he was not invited inside, but it was hard not to be. He would persist, gripping the stems of his bouquet a little tighter.

The door suddenly swung open a few minutes later, and Jem was greeted by Cressie's frantic brown eyes. She practically leapt onto him, gripping hold of his arms with panicked fists.

"What are you doing here?" she hissed.

"What do you think I am doing here?" Jem countered. "I am here to speak to your mother."

"I cannot believe you are being so contrary at a moment like this!" she stressed. "Mama needs time –"

"Your mother has had time, Cressie," Jem insisted, interrupting her. "We do not have any more time to give. I have to something to offer you now, something to offer her."

Cressie stepped back on her heels. "What?" she prompted.

Jem needed to be optimistic. "When she agrees, I will tell you."

Cressie's brows knitted together in worry as her eyes flicked around, clearly searching for an escape for him. She did not share his optimism, and Jem wondered if, subconsciously, she knew her mother would not come around on her own.

The door to the house opened wider, and Cressie and Jem were joined by Mrs Martin, who looked upon them both with an unreadable expression.

"Mama!" cried Cressie, jumping with surprise at her mother's sudden appearance. "I was just —"

"Go up to your bedroom, please, Cressida," Mrs Martin instructed calmly.

"But Mama —"

"Now," Mrs Martin said, this time more firmly.

Cressie bit down on her bottom lip, her worried brown eyes finding Jem once more. He wished that he could comfort her. He stupidly wished that he had not concealed his news from her only moments ago. It might have brought her some comfort in this moment.

Cressie obeyed her mother and disappeared inside. The moment she was gone, Mrs Martin said, "Please come in, Mr Denham."

"Thank you, Mrs Martin." Jem followed Mrs Martin inside and was led into the parlour, the room where he had fumbled his way through his first call what felt like an age ago.

Mrs Martin ordered tea and then invited Jem to sit down in an armchair. Before he did, he held out the bouquet of flowers to Mrs Denham.

"I have brought these for you, Mrs Martin." Jem was surprised at how evenly his voice was sounding considering his heart was erratically trying to escape his ribcage. He was surprised that Mrs Martin could not hear the beat of it when he opened his mouth. Lord, he hoped he did not begin sweating.

"How kind," remarked Mrs Martin delicately as she accepted the flowers, looking over them with an inquisitive eye.

"Irises and white lilies," he explained.

"I can see that, Mr Denham," replied Mrs Martin. "White lilies for purity of love, and irises for hope. You have been studying the language of flowers, it seems."

Jem nodded once as Mrs Martin delicately laid the bouquet down on the small table in front of her own chair. He took a breath. And then another. "I must thank you for seeing me. I understand that I have made choices in the past that have brought you grief and stress, and for that I am sorry."

Mrs Martin did not reply. But she listened. And she watched.

Jem placed his hands on his knees and cleared his throat. "Mrs Martin," he said, beginning again. "I have come here today to ..." It was too late. He was sweating. "I have come to ask you to ... I have come to ask for your daughter's hand so that we may be united in macaroni."

Jem froze just as Mrs Martin recoiled.

"Matrimony," he corrected. "I mean 'matrimony'. I wish for us to be united in matrimony, please forgive me. I don't know where that came from." Curse Adam. Bless him, then curse him.

Mrs Martin drummed her fingers on the arm of her chair rhythmically as she pondered what Jem had just said. She might had done this for a minute further, or an hour, Jem wouldn't have known. Every tap of her fingers was agonising.

"I thought this would happen. I was right," she seemed to say more to herself than to Jem. Mrs Martin's grey-green eyes settled on Jem, and to his agony, she looked sympathetic. "You are a boy, Mr Denham," she said pitifully. "I forgive you for your ridiculous behaviour with Cressida because it is what a child with no sense of the world would do." She sighed and shook her head. "If forgiveness is what you seek, you have it. For Cressida's hand, I must refuse."

"I am not a child," Jem responded indignantly. But if he was, what did that make Cressie? For he was older than her by a year!

Mrs Martin exclaimed a noise of impatience. "Where would you live?" she proposed. "How would you live? With what income?"

Jem swallowed his indignance and frustration and prayed he would speak clearly. He could answer these questions where Mrs Martin was expecting nothing. "Mrs Martin, I implore you to hear me. I have something to offer. The Duke of Ashwood has made me his House Steward and he has afforded me a good income. In time, he will raise me to be his Land Steward where I will be in possession of a house on the Ashwood estate, and an income of three hundred pounds a year. I can and will support Cressie."

"In time," repeated Mrs Martin in an almost condescending tone. She shook her head. "Mr Denham, do you hear yourself? My dear boy, say what you like, but you are a child! You are barely eighteen! You have not the circumstances nor the resources to marry anybody in good conscience! Let alone my daughter! You cannot yet support yourself, let alone a wife. And what of children? For they inevitably follow. How could you support a child? Would it live with your mother until you find yourself this house?"

No. Had Mrs Martin not heard him? He had an income! He would have a house. Of course, not immediately, but with his income, he would be able to afford to rent a small cottage for them until they could move onto the Ashwood estate. She so determined to dismiss him as a poor child that she would not listen.

"I have the circumstances to marry, Mrs Martin," Jem said insistently. "I just do not possess Mr Delaney's circumstances." Was a hundred pounds, three hundred pounds, not enough? Was it not more than Mrs Martin had now? Had she not been relying upon the generosity of friends, clergymen, Belle, to survive and make it through?

Jem saw the truth of his words in Mrs Martin's eyes. "You never could have Mr Delaney's circumstances, Mr Denham," she said sympathetically.

"Cressie doesn't love him," he snapped angrily. "She has told me repeatedly that all you desire is her happiness. Prove it to her. She loves me, as I love her. I will love her for the rest of my life."

Mrs Martin sighed exasperatedly. "Dear boy, your life has barely begun! Live! Go out into the world and experience it before deciding on a wife! In a year, five, ten! You will be in a better situation, and a young lady will appear who is lovely and amiable, and you will marry. But that young lady cannot be Cressie. I am sorry to disappoint you, but my word is final. I do not consent, and I do not give you my blessing. I beg you would take leave of this house now, and you do not call upon Cressida again."

CHAPTER 17

C ressie watched the street from her small bedroom window and felt a pang of pain in her chest as she saw Jem stalk away from the house, the bouquet of flowers still in his hands.

It was hard to name the emotions that began to flood through her as she watched him disappear around the corner. His shoulders had been slumped. His head had hung low. It was the walk of a dejected man. Tears flowed down her cheeks freely as whatever hope she had deluded herself into holding quickly fizzled out, like the last remnants of a fire.

She could infer quite easily as to what Jem had asked her mother, and she could thus imagine what Mrs Martin had told Jem in reply. It was 'no'. Would it have ever been 'yes'? Could it have ever been 'yes'? Cressie has been certain of it for a time. She had been certain that given enough time, her mother would understand that Jem was her choice. Mrs Martin's greatest desire for Cressie was for her to be married, and she was accepting a man with no resistance.

Only, Cressie sadly accepted, her mother's true wish was for Cressie to be married well.

A painful hiccough ripped itself from Cressie's throat as she let out an unholy sob. She pressed her forehead against the glass of the windowpane and gripped hold of the sill as her shoulders shook violently. She still could not name the feeling that was tearing through her body, but for what she had heard of it, it could only be considered heartbreak.

Cressie felt soothing hands on her back suddenly, before one gently lifted her face off of the glass to turn her. Cressie met the sympathetic grey-green eyes of her mother as she frowned with pity.

"Cressie dear," she said knowingly, before she brought her into a hug.

Cressie wrapped her arms around her mother for a lack of knowing what to do. She needed to hold onto something, some-one, as she wept violently. The front of her mother's bodice became saturated almost instantly. Mrs Martin held Cressie com-fortingly, rubbing her hands over her back as she had done when Cressie was small.

"Mama, please!" Cressie begged, her voice thick with emotion, and muffled as she spoke into the fabric of Mrs Martin's dress. "Please, change your mind, I beg you! I won't be happy with anyone but him. I love him!"

"Shh," hushed Mrs Martin calmly, continuing to rub Cressie's back. "Oh, my girl, my sweet, sweet girl," she cooed. "You are so naïve, darling child. You do not yet understand love, especially the fickleness of first love. What you are feeling is not love, and it will pass, I promise you."

Cressie pulled her head away and rubbed her eyes free of her tears so that she could look upon her mother clearly. She sniffed as she said, "I don't agree, Mama!" Cressie challenged. "I think you're wrong. Naïve, I may be, but this is not fickle. Don't you want me to be happy? I know you do! Please, Mama, please change your mind. You need to help me. You are meant to help me."

Mrs Martin sighed, shaking her head. "And this is your very naivety showing, my love! You do not see how I am helping you! You do not understand that every choice and decision I make is for you. Mr Denham is a lovely boy, a charming boy, I am sure. He is a credit to his lovely village mama, but he is nothing more, he will not ever be more than he is now, and that is not enough for you, Cressie!"

"But it is! He is!" Cressie cried.

Mrs Martin fished a handkerchief from her pocket and sat Cressie back down on the stool she had been occupying by the window. She proceeded to dry Cressie's eyes and wipe her nose for her as though she were an infant.

"One day you will understand," she murmured, "and I pray you will thank me for this." She rested her hand on Cressie's cheek briefly, before uttering, "I would never steer you wrong in marriage, Cressie. I would never subject you to the humiliation I suffered at the hands of your father. I would not be able to live with myself if you were forced to bring up a child in poverty as I have had to raise you. Do you not see how much of a failure I feel I am already?" It was Mrs Martin's turn now. Her own eyes became glassy as tears began to well up. "Can you not see, Cressie?" Mrs Martin implored, her voice breaking. "Can you not understand what it is I am doing for you? After everything I have done to bring you up a lady, as best as I could, this is the final test. You ... you would not spit in my face after everything I have done! Would you? You would not! I know that in your precious heart you know and understand what is right."

Cressie could not do a thing but cry. She hated to cry. She hated that she did not know what to do but cry. She felt like she did not have any choice, any say. Her mother was reminding her of her obligation, her responsibility to care for Mrs Martin after everything she had done to bring Cressie up in their situation.

"Oh, my dear," sighed Mrs Martin again as she returned to cuddling Cressie comfortingly. "I know you are upset, but this is why you are so good. Because you will do the right thing. And I promise that you will be happy."

Cressie whimpered, powerless.

"Do you know what? I think you are ill," decided Mrs Martin. "I think we shall remain at home for a few days to recover. A little time away from the pressures of society will do you good, I think. And when your absence is noticed, it will prove to you just how much you are cared for by some in particular."

Cressie spent the next several days in the same position, sitting in the stool by the window, watching the street. She did not expect Jem to return, but that did not mean that she did not hope to see him once more.

She couldn't imagine what her mother had said to him. Was she cruel? She had never known her mother to be cruel, but what could she have said to Jem Denham to make him leave and not come back?

Cressie still felt a keen pain in her chest, as though there was a chain fixed around her heart connected to another, and the further away he pulled, or was pushed, the more her heart hurt.

Three days after Mrs Martin had sent Jem away, another gentleman arrived at the house on horseback. This was the first time that Cressie had seen Mr Delaney arrive at their home as she was not usually looking over the street as she was.

She had heard him speak of his horse before in passing, when he had mentioned some of the animals he kept on his estate. Cressie believed the horse's name was Dabney, or something along those lines. He was certainly a striking, chestnut coloured animal.

But as the horse slowed, he seemed to spook at something. He must have spotted something frightening as even from where she sat, Cressie could hear the horse cry out as it reared, and Mr Delaney fell from its back onto the street.

She watched as Mr Delaney, with an irate expression on his face, got to his feet and brushed off his breeches, before he seized hold of the horse's reins and yanked them down roughly.

He suddenly had a riding crop in his hand, and that only made the horse more panicked. Mr Delaney did not use the crop, but he kept a very tight hold on his horse's reins as he controlled him.

A gentleman passer-by soon came to assist, and together the men managed to calm the horse and tie his reins to the lamppost outside of the Martins' home. Mr Delaney then approached the front door and Cressie finally looked away as she heard a knock from downstairs.

Cressie touched her cheeks but felt that they were dry. She was not crying. She tried to smile, but she physically could not do it. She was incapable of even pretending to be happy and charmed.

She heard Mrs Martin's delighted welcome travel up the stairs, and she knew it would be only moments before she would need to appear delighted as well.

And then Cressie realised something. She realised something that was plainly obvious now that it had occurred to her. Her life was not her own. It never had been.

Cressie's life would belong to Mrs Martin until it could belong to her husband.

And then the tears fell.

Mrs Martin's footsteps quickly travelled up the stairs, and she said an admonishment under her breath when she saw the state of her daughter. "Cressie!" she huffed. "Control yourself. Mr Delaney has come, and he wishes to speak with you alone." Mrs Martin dried Cressie's eyes with a handkerchief and pulled her to her feet, before she fluffed the hem of Cressie's dress.

"Mama," Cressie whispered, "please do not make me go to him."

"Be a good girl now," Mrs Martin insisted. "Listen to your conscience." She quickly surveyed Cressie's appearance, tucking a stray tendril of hair back into her braided bun, before she turned Cressie's shoulders and nudged her towards the stairs.

Before she could even think, Cressie was shut inside the parlour room, where Mr Delaney was waiting for her, facing the lower window out onto the street. The moment the door was shut, Mr Delaney turned, smiled, and bowed his head.

"Miss Martin," he greeted. "My dear, Cressida, how good it is to see you looking well." His cool, grey eyes appraised her appearance, and the widening smile on his lips told her that she pleased him.

Mr Delaney was always dressed immaculately, but today he wore a fine navy coat with delicate silver embroidery, the handiwork alone showing it to be an expensive garment.

"I have worried after you," Mr Delaney said when Cressie did not respond. "You have had dreadful luck with illnesses."

"Y-yes," Cressie confirmed her mother's lie. "Yes, I have."

"Well, you would be pleased to know that it does not show," replied Mr Delaney. "Your youthful beauty is to be envied wherever you go."

Cressie was meant to be thankful for the compliment. She felt anything but. She wanted to run. She wanted to run to Jem and be saved. But nobody could save her. Nobody was coming to save her. Not even Mama.

"Miss Martin, won't you sit down?" Mr Delaney invited. "There is something that I wish to discuss with you."

Cressie thought that this was a good idea as she was afraid her legs might buckle beneath her. She nodded and elected to sit in the available armchair so that Mr Delaney could not sit beside her. He chose to stand before her rather proudly.

"I understand your shyness, Miss Martin. Cressida," he uttered. "Women, lovely, young girls like you, are always shy when it comes to matters of the heart. Believe me, my dear one, you only endear yourself to me more with your ... reluctance." Cressie's eyes were focussed down on the rug on the floor, but she could hear the smile in Mr Delaney's voice. "In coming to know you this Season, I have found you to be exactly the type of young lady I would want to select for my wife. You are beautiful and endearing, and so amenable. You are a clever girl who does what she is told. I find myself in a fortunate position where I am able to choose a wife without care for her financial circumstances. I am well aware you would come to me with nothing, and I am gentleman enough to be willing to take care of you, as you will take care of everything I desire."

Was the chair shaking? Or was Cressie trembling? She could hardly make sense of anything that Mr Delaney was saying as her mind and heart raced. She was beautiful and he was a gentleman and someone was amenable and ... desires ... what ... what desires?

"Look at me, Cressida," Mr Delaney commanded in a calm tone.

Cressie's eyes found his steel grey irises quickly, and he smiled pleasingly. "Good," he uttered. "Now, I have a rather important question to ask you. Cressida Martin, will you please do me the honour of becoming my wife?"

Cressie was frozen still as she stared up at the waiting gentle-man. As she exhaled her last breath, she did not take another.

She felt as though her autonomy had left her just as the air had escaped her lungs. Though she was not looking at them, she felt him reach down and secure her hands in his, using them to pull her to her feet. She was unsteady as she had not been expecting the movement, and Mr Delaney's hand was suddenly on her hip, steading her. He was close. Too close.

Her mind seemed to take her to Jem to calm her. To imagine that he was the one holding her, he was the one standing so close to her. Cressie basked in the comfort of those memories, in the safety and freedom that she had felt in those blissful moments of possibility. But as quickly as they had come, her memories were overshadowed by the hulking presence that was her duty to her mama. Cressie knew that Mrs Martin was listening at the door, praying for this very moment. This is what she had sacrificed all for. This is what would finally make her happy.

As the last little piece of her heart died, Cressie nodded her head, accepting this man as her betrothed.

CHAPTER 18

At a complete loss of knowing what to do, Jem could not allow his sister to stay any longer in London. Grace had supported his every endeavour, and Adam had done everything in his power to give him a position and a foundation to support a marriage. Unless a long lost relative spontaneously died and bequeathed him ten thousand pounds, there was not anything more his sister of brother-in-law could do for him.

Grace, Adam, and Cecily departed London for Ashwood shortly after Jem had returned from asking Mrs Martin for Cressie's hand. When Grace had learned of Jem's failure in his mission, she had not wanted to leave him. But Jem, after a season of selfishness where his sister was concerned, could not allow it.

And so, Jem was left alone in the big house in London to wallow in his first taste of monumental heartbreak. He had heard about. He had read about. He had certainly seen tastes of it in the flickering memories of his mother's grief after his father's death. But he could never have known the gut-wrenching pain that it was to have one's heart broken.

All optimism was gone. Hope was lost. What, indeed, was hope? It seemed like a distant memory now, and Jem felt delusional that he had ever thought himself good enough for Cressie Martin.

Mrs Martin's words infuriated him, and only added to the pain that he felt. He felt incredibly condescended to. How dare she suppose to understand the depths of his feelings, or the depths of her daughter's affections? Young love was still love. Age meant nothing.

Why, Adam had remarked on several occasions how he had known that Grace was the one to be his wife when they were both in the school room as children. Age meant nothing. It was irrelevant.

Mrs Martin seemed to believe that his feelings would pass, and that Cressie's would also. But the gaping hole in his chest where his heart used to be seemed to suggest otherwise. Unless Cressie came to return it, Jem was certain that his feelings would never change.

And that was what made this whole ordeal so much more painful. There was nothing to be done. Cressie was underage. She could not marry without permission. And Jem was never going to be good enough for her mother.

Jem made feeble attempts over the next few days to distract himself. He needed to do anything that would not tempt him to climb through Cressie's window. He hated to think of her own pain when he thought of his own. He knew that she would be suffering as well, and that was what made it terribly worse. He couldn't bear the thought of her pain.

Jem caught up on his correspondence with his mother. He had been a dreadful son in that respect, and Mrs Denham had written faithfully to remind him that:

You still have a mother, you know.

And:

A note to assure me you are still living would do my nerves the world of good.

Jem wrote a letter to his mother, creating a narrative of a charming stay in London, and how he had been to parties and balls and seen Peter and Belle, and Jack and Claire. Her granddaughters were well, and everything was fine.

The lie of it all made him want to throw the damned letter in the fire.

And Jem began to assume his role of House Steward. Despite this role not being enough to secure Cressie's hand, that did not mean that Jem did not take his new responsibilities seriously.

Though managing the house finances did not distract him well enough for the morning newspaper a week later.

His eyes seemed to find the engagement announcement by themselves. Or perhaps he had sought it out. Perhaps he had been waiting for it, and fearful that it would come. And today it had.

Mr Everett Delaney of Henshaw House, Yorkshire, heir to the Delaneys of Suffolk, to Miss Cressida Martin, daughter of Mr and Mrs Martin, after a brief courtship are to be wed at St Agatha's Church on the thirtieth day of June 1812 at ten o'clock ...

Jem could not read any further.

He was numb. He forced himself into numbness as he could not experience the full weight of what he had just read.

Cressie was engaged. She was engaged to him. The man was two decades older than her, but so long as he had a weighty purse, he would do.

Cressie was to be another man's wife. Jem abandoned the paper and buried his face in his hands. Never did he imagine that there was something below helplessness and despair, but there was, and it was this. Whatever this feeling was, it was ferocious in its toxicity. It threatened to swallow Jem whole.

Cressie existed for the next month. She wasn't living. Living required purpose, determination, and feeling. Cressie certainly had feeling, but it was not of the living variety. She was utterly despondent, and nobody seemed to notice or care.

Especially not her mother.

Mrs Martin, on the other hand, had never been happier. She had access to all of Mr Delaney's accounts, and had been busy planning a grand affair for the wedding at the end of June. Cressie was not involved in any of the decisions, not even the dress, which had been commissioned at Desjardins, just as every other of Cressie's dresses.

Belle was delicate in her interactions with Cressie, but Cressie was unable to speak. For what could she say? What could she do? Nothing. Hope was lost. Her life was gone. It had never even been hers to begin with.

Mrs Martin happily purchased ribbons and lace and bonnets and every other frivolous thing that Cressie supposedly needed for her trousseau. An elaborate wedding breakfast was planned, and the horses would have their manes braided and everything would be perfect, as when this marriage occurred, they would be saved.

Cressie did not feel saved. Cressie felt as though she was clinging to a precipice and was slowly losing her grip one finger at a time.

On the night before her wedding, as she held onto the precipice with her very last finger, Mrs Martin entered Cressie's bedroom quictly. Her mother's cheeks were rosy in the light of her candle, and she wore such an expression of pride. Cressie had seen her own reflection as she had taken her hair pins out before bed. She looked as dead outside as she felt on the inside.

Mrs Martin delicately sat down on the edge of Cressie's bed and she placed the candle down carefully on the table beside the bed. "I cannot wait for you to know how happy you will be," she murmured. "Just you wait, my darling. Just you wait. It will all be alright, and you will be happy. I know it."

Cressie said nothing.

"Now, I have come to have an important discussion with you." Mrs Martin stroked the back of Cressie's limp hand. "There are things that you need to be aware of. Things you must know before your wedding night tomorrow."

Cressie sat and listened as her mother described what she called the marital act. She explained in detail what would be expected of Cressie, and what, indeed, her new husband would do to her the following night. It was an act that created children, her mother explained, and she hoped that Cressie would be blessed with children to love very soon.

"You will find that your husband experiences certain desires for his wife," Mrs Martin said conclusively. "Our role is to be amenable. It is easiest, dear, if you lay quietly."

Cressie was horrified. She was horrified that she would be expected to be so ... so exposed before a man she hardly knew. She was horrified that this man would know her so intimately. She could hardly speak, and weakly shook her head when her mother asked if she had any questions.

The word 'desire' triggered several memories in her of when Mr Delaney had used such a word. Had he been referring to this?

Mrs Martin left Cressie alone as her mind flooded with equal parts panic and horror. This was what it led to. Kissing and desire led to this. But the very idea that this act would take place between her and Mr Delaney felt criminally wrong. She didn't want it. Not with him.

It was too much. It was all too much. Cressie had kissed before. She had experienced desire, now that she knew the name of it, before. And along with that desire, she had experienced the type of love and security that people dreamed of. Only it was not with Mr Delaney.

Cressie was unsure of for how long she sat in her bed panicking. It might have been hours, for the street below from her window was eerily silent. She moved quickly, donning only a hooded cloak overtop of her nightgown, and she stole down the stairs and out of the front door quickly and quietly. She had not even stopped to put shoes on her feet.

Her mother and Nelly had not seen her, and they had certainly not stopped her. They both had to have been asleep as Cressie donned her hood and took off in a sprint.

Cressie could barely concentrate for running, for breathing so heavily that she might have brought up a lung. She did not have the space in her mind to be panicked at the fact that she was running alone down the London streets of Mayfair, with only the dim streetlamps for light. She knew the way to safety, and that was all she could focus on.

When Cressie came to the iron gates before Ashwood Place, she thanked God that the gate was unlocked, and that the servants kept it well oiled. It did not make a sound as she pushed it open. She could not knock on the door and risk waking the house, and she could never guess which one of the many windows belonged to Jem.

Like a thief in the night, Cressie stole around the side of the house, her feet hurting as she stepped on brambles and pebbles. She cried out soundlessly. Pushing through the foliage of the Ashwood gardens, Cressie made it to the servants' courtyard outside of the kitchen, and she could still smell the remnants of tobacco in the air from the footmen smoking. But the kitchen was dark through the windows as the servants had all gone to bed.

Cressie closed her eyes and wished as she approached the wooden door of the kitchen and breathed a sigh of great relief as it opened without struggle. As quick as a mouse, Cressie stepped inside the dark kitchen and closed the door behind her. The kitchen was still warm from the hearth and the gorgeous smells of supper lingered around her. But Cressie did not stay long to imagine what might have been Jem's meal. On the counter, however, was an extinguished candlestick. Cressie seized it and dashed to the embers of the hearth to light it. The flickering flame immediately illuminated her surroundings, and Cressie found the narrow staircase in which she had to climb. She darted to the stairs and sprinted up them as quietly as she could.

Cressie had no idea of where she was going, and she chose to exit out of the first door that she found. When she stepped out, it was terribly dark, but the candle helped her to see that she was in a wide corridor dressed with a luxurious rug as well as tapestries and portraits on the wall. This was no longer the servants' quarters. This was part of the main house. When Cressie turned to the left, she could dimly see the first floor landing from the staircase. To the right was a wing of rooms with ten-foot doorways. Could these be the bedrooms?

Which could be Jem's? Which would house the duke and duchess, or the dowager duchess? She could not dare risk waking them.

But she had little choice but to check. She had come this far, and whatever was coursing through her veins in that moment gave her the bravery to open the first door. Cressie quietly cracked the door and held the candlestick inside. But she was met with an empty bedroom.

The next three doors yielded the same results.

When Cressie opened the fifth door and used the candle to light the room, she nearly fainted when she saw that this room was occupied. In the bed against the far wall, she could see a figure lying there. Only he wasn't asleep. His eyes reflected the light of the candle, and he was looking right at her.

"Who goes there?" His voice was defensive, his hand reached for the drawer beside the bed.

Defensive or not, Cressie knew Jem's voice, and something washed over her in that moment of realising that he was there. It was almost enough to make her delirious. She nearly dropped the candlestick as he legs gave way beneath her and the fatigue suddenly found her after running all this way. Her heart could not slow and she could not breathe in enough air as she slumped against the door, the click of the latch sounding as it shut behind her.

"Jem," she whimpered.

"Good God! Cressie!" Jem cried. He leapt out of the bed and crossed the room in seconds, owing to his large strides.

"Did I wake you?" she asked rather pathetically as he reached her, his hands hesitating for a moment, before they settled on the sides of her face. Cressie leaned into his touch automatically, without even realising, as though her body knew it was safe before her mind could comprehend it.

"How could I sleep when you are getting married tomorrow?" Jem murmured softly. "Cressie, what are you doing here? Are you alright? Are you hurt? What can I do?"

Cressie couldn't help herself as she climbed onto Jem's lap, wrapping her arms around him as she rested her head against his chest. His heart was beating nearly as quickly as hers was. "I had to see you," she whispered against him. She felt his arms tighten around her. She then felt his lips brush her hair. It made her smile with the first feeling of peace she had experienced in weeks.

"Cressie, what do you want?" It was not a demanding question. She could hear the pain in his voice.

Her heart squeezed tightly in her chest at the knowledge that she had caused him pain. They had both experienced the same pain.

What she wanted and what could have were two entirely different things. She was behaving like a fool, but she could not care about anything else in that moment except for Jem. What he had awakened inside of her these last months was entirely intoxicating.

"I wanted to be safe," she replied softly. "My mother told me these things, and I just wanted to be safe with you. I am sorry if that is selfish. I know I am being selfish, but I wanted to be with you."

"You are never selfish," Jem declared rather fiercely, his grip, if it could be imagined, tightened even further. Cressie relished in his security. "You are the least selfish person I have ever met. In fact, I wish you would be selfish."

Cressie moulded her face to Jem's chest as she felt tears begin to trickle down from her eyes. Lord, how he knew what to say. She felt his truth in his conviction, and he wasn't angry that she had come. "I have to get married tomorrow," she whimpered.

"You don't have to do anything. You can be selfish, Cressie," Jem whispered back.

"I have to," Cressie whispered back. "Mama ... I have to. And that is why I know I am selfish for coming to you, because no matter what, I have to get married tomorrow."

Jem was silent for a long moment, but he never released her, and Cressie thanked God for it.

Cressie couldn't say 'no'. Her mother could not afford to support them beyond the Season without Cressie marrying, and she was never going to allow her to marry Jem. She had to be married to Mr Delaney, or else she and her mother would be living on the street come summer's end.

"You are not selfish," Jem said finally. "I hope your mother thanks you every day for what you are willing to do for her. You could never be selfish, Cressie Martin."

Cressie dared to look up at him, and she found his beautiful ocean eyes looking down upon her in the flickering light of the candle. But then she proved him wrong. She could be selfish. She knew it was selfish. But she kissed him. She stretched up her neck and she kissed Jem with everything that she had. She held onto him for dear life.

She felt such overwhelming emotion, such fluttering in her stomach, as her passion overcame her. And she felt it reciprocated from Jem exactly. This was what it was supposed to be like. Cressie felt like she knew nothing, and everything, when she was held by Jem. What her mother had explained to her made little sense when she was with him. Cressie could hardly think of what would be expected of her tomorrow night, but it was there in the back of her mind as she suddenly pulled away.

Cressie remained close to Jem, their noses touching as they each felt the other's rapid pants. "Can I ask you something?"

"Anything," breathed Jem.

"Do you know what happens between a husband and wife on their wedding night?" Cressie genuinely had no idea if Jem would know. She, herself, had only learned of it a few hours earlier.

Though she supposed men were more learned in these matters than women.

Jem nodded cautiously, a slight grimace on his face. "Yes, I do know," he confirmed quietly.

"I don't know if it works if you're not married, but ..." Cressie fumbled with her words. Now was not the time for bashfulness. She knew exactly why she had come here, and that was why she knew that she was selfish. "I want it to be with you."

Jem's brows furrowed as he reached up to cradle one of his cheeks with his large palm. "Are you certain?" he asked her seriously.

"I have never been more certain of anything in my life," she replied, nodding. "I told you I was selfish."

Jem leaned down and stole the words from her lips with a soft kiss. "Stop calling yourself selfish. I won't hear it," he instructed softly. "I will take you home."

Cressie froze as he went to move. She became dead weight on his lap. "No!" she said entirely too loudly.

"You will hate me tomorrow," Jem reasoned.

She shook her head with conviction. "I will love you tomorrow, as I love you now, and I will love you always."

Jem stared into Cressie's eyes for a long moment, searching for any crack in her determination. But he wouldn't find any. Her conviction grew by the second. And then he kissed her, his arms encircling her as he lifted her against his chest, before he carried her over to the bed.

Jem stretched his arms lethargically as his eyes fluttered open. His bedroom was illuminated by a single beam of sunlight breaking into the room from a gap in the thick drapes at the window.

It took a moment for his eyes to focus, and another to realise that last night had not been a dream. Cressie had been there, and she had been his in every way but the one he wanted most. His bride. But she had fallen asleep in his arms, and he had been the happiest that he had ever been.

God, she couldn't marry him. She simply couldn't. As he rolled over to declare this, to tell her that they would travel to Scotland and wear the consequences of her mother's ire, he was shocked to see the other side of his bed had been abandoned.

Cressie was gone.

Jem sat bolt upright in bed, panicking, and searching frantically for Cressie elsewhere in the room. But she wasn't there. As he threw back the bedclothes, his fingers brushed over a stiff piece of parchment, and there on the bed beside him, he found a letter.

It was folded over once, and simple read Jem on the outside.

Jem fearfully unfolded it and read her words. In tear-streaked ink, she had written:

I was right. I told you I would still love you in the morning.

I love you now. I love you always. Thank you for showing me what it is to love and to be loved. You have my heart, and I leave it with you for safe keeping. It will never belong to anyone else.

I am sorry to leave you. You cannot know how I wish it could be different.

I will imagine it as you.

C

"No." Jem couldn't accept it. He couldn't lose her now. It wasn't right. It wasn't fair.

What time was it? Jem's darted to the clock on the mantle, and nearly emptied his stomach when he saw it was twenty minutes to ten. The ceremony was at ten o'clock. He couldn't be too late. IIe just couldn't!

Jem dressed as quickly and as sloppily as he ever had in his life. He pulled on his boots as he ran down the stairs and past the servants asking after him with concern. He had not the time to wait for a horse to be saddled. Now was the time for his extraordinarily long legs to become of some use. Jem ran. He knew exactly where St Agatha's Church was. It was a few miles away, and Jem had travelled there soon after he had read the engagement announcement in the newspaper. Why, he did not know. But perhaps it was for this moment.

What would he do? he wondered as he ran. The fine gentry of Mayfair looked upon him with confusion. The ladies turned their noses up at the chaotic young man running past them. Would he storm into the church? Would he steal her from the altar?

Lord, he would fight that man, her intended, with pistols at dawn if it meant she didn't have to marry him.

He passed the last few familiar corners. The church was close. He had no idea of the time. Finally, Jem rounded the right corner to where the little church was situated. But just as he did, the church bells began to ring, and he stopped in his tracks across the street. The wooden doors of the building opened, and the guests of the wedding began to spill out. Jem stood frozen, paralysed completely, as the wedded couple emerged as well.

She walked, as beautiful as an angel, draped in lace, silk, and flowers, on the arm of another man. On the arm of her husband.

Jem was too late.

CHAPTER 19

I t was not a week later that Jem received a letter from Grace to inform him of the birth of his nephew. He had only known it was a week later as the newspaper was dated, and it seemed to have the story of the Ashwood heir printed in record time. Cecily Beresford worked quickly.

It was announced to the world that Charles Adam Beresford had been born, but Grace's letter had revealed that he had already been given the moniker, 'Charlie'.

And Jem felt little more than fleeting affection for his newest nephew in and amongst the utter despair he was experiencing. Jem did not know what to do with himself. He did not know how to handle it. He could barely breathe for the pain he felt in his chest.

The newspaper, the birth announcement, confirmed that it had been a week. Cressie had been that man's wife for a week. She was God knows where doing God knows what with that man. It made him want to bring up the pitiful breakfast he'd managed to get down that morning.

Jem did not blame her. He could never blame her. Not in the slightest. Cressie was a victim of her own mother's selfish manipulation. Cressie had gone and married a man she could never love to ensure her mother's living conditions did not fall below that which would make her comfortable. Cressie had felt as though there was no way out. No alternative. Her duty to her mother outweighed her own happiness. Cressie had given away her own life for her mother, and Jem furiously wondered if Mrs Martin could even comprehend the gravity of such a sacrifice.

But Jem did not only blame Mrs Martin. He also blamed himself. Jem blamed himself for not fighting harder, for not standing his ground with Mrs Martin. He blamed himself for allowing her to treat him like a child, and not the young man he was. He blamed himself for not simply taking Cressie away, running away with her to Scotland, to Gretna Green, and wearing the consequences. He'd let her slip right through his fingers, and now she was unhappy, and quite potentially unsafe, in the grasp of that man, and all because he was wealthy.

Jem did not think that he would ever be able to forgive himself for that.

And so, he did the only thing that he could do. The only thing that he could control. He threw himself into his work. Every day, he got up out of bed and shut himself away in the study and did everything that that he could to earn the role that Adam had bestowed him with. His work was the only thing that could entice him to get out of bed in the morning.

Several letters had arrived from Peter, and he and Belle both had called at different times, but Jem had always claimed to be too busy to see them. Claire, as well, had come to visit, but Jem had dismissed her as well.

Jem did not know which of the servants had subsequently sent for his brother a time later, but Peter walked into the study entirely unannounced.

Peter stopped dead in his tracks the moment he laid eyes on Jem, and his face fell with genuine sympathy. Jem hated that look instantly. He didn't want pity. He deserved punishment.

"You look terrible," Peter remarked, gasping as he slowly approached the desk.

Jem stared at his brother and could see the concern in his eyes. Truthfully, Jem had not paid much attention to his own appearance of late. Were he able to grow a moustache and beard, he would have wagered that one would have grown in with the attention that he had paid to his hair of late.

"Jem, we're all worried sick about you. Fancy using the servants as guard dogs to keep your family from seeing you." Peter sighed as he reached the desk, before he placed his palms down on the mahogany and leaned forward. "I am sorry this happened to you, Jem. I really am."

"Nothing happened to me," Jem bit back angrily.

"Of course, something happened to you," Peter replied sadly. "You are allowed to mourn."

Jem slumped in his chair and glared at the inkwell for something to concentrate on that was not his brother. This is not what he wanted. This would not help. The only thing that would help would be a miraculous ability to turn back time.

"I do know a little of what you are feeling, Jem," Peter appealed quietly. "I cannot pretend to know exactly, but I know a little. I know what it is to feel as though you have lost the one you love. I know that longing and pain intimately –"

"I do not mean to belittle your own pain, Peter," Jem interjected coolly, "but you will go home to your wife tonight. Your pain, no matter how terrible, is but a page in your story. Mine does not have a happy ending. Mine has ended. The woman I love married somebody else because she is so bloody unselfish!"

Jem seized the inkwell and threw it against the wall in frustration. The crystal shattered on impact, and black ink began to trickle down the wall, soaking into the wallpaper as it travelled down towards the floor. The moment he did it, he knew it was stupid, and he immediately got up and attempted to dab the mess with his handkerchief.

After a minute of feebly attempting the rectify the mess, Jem collapsed, his legs giving way beneath him as he fell to the floor. And he cried.

Jem cried for the first time since seeing Cressie walk out of that church as Mrs Delaney. He cried at the pain he felt inside having lost her so soon after finding her. He cried for the future he had so quickly imagined between them. But most of all, he cried in fear for her. Was she safe? Was she alright? Was she frightened? Was she miserable? The not knowing was agony in itself.

Peter quickly dashed around the desk and knelt down on the ground beside Jem, wrapping a secure arm around his shoulders and Jem rocked in his sobs.

"Jemmy, I'm sorry," he whispered.

Peter did not tell Jem that everything would be alright.

Perhaps they both knew that it would be a lie. Peter could never make such a promise. This pain felt like one that would never leave Jem. It filled every facet of his body, drowning him from the inside out.

"I have to know she's alright," Jem finally stammered. "I wish I could write to her. I wish she could write to me."

"Belle saw her a few weeks ago," Peter murmured.

Jem flinched, his head snapping up. He forced himself to blink away the tears so that he might concentrate on Peter properly. "What?" Jem tried to piece together exactly how much time had passed since the wedding. What was the date? There was a newspaper up on the desk, but he was far more concerned with what Belle had seen in that moment.

"She came with her mother to collect her trousseau and to pay her bill. This was a few days after the wedding," Peter informed him. "She was ..." Peter looked to be searching for the right word, as though he was deciding what sort of word would help Jem. Peter seemed to decide upon honesty. "She was sad."

Jem's head fell once more as he buried it in his hands. He really had no idea what word would have helped him in that moment. But perhaps nothing short of Mr Delaney suddenly dying of a mysterious bout of cholera would help him. Jem did not even have the inclination to chastise himself for such a wicked thought.

"We're going home, Jem," Peter then announced.

"What?" Jem grumbled. "I can't."

"I've come to take you home. There is only a little more than a month left in the Season. Besides, I have Adam's permission. He requests your presence in Ashwood. You might have slackened a little in your correspondence." Peter produced a letter from his breast pocket and unfolded it before he cleared his throat. "Grace insists that Jem return home as well. She would not have our son Christened without his godfather present."

Jem could not really remember the letter he had read from his sister regarding the birth of little Charlie. It was, perhaps, the last letter that he had read from home. But godfather? Him? The young man crying on the floor of her husband's study did not seem like the type who could guide a young one.

"Susanna and Alex had their child also. Did you hear?" Peter asked carefully.

"No," muttered Jem.

"A boy also. Henry," Peter informed him. "You can imagine how the dowager duchess is pleased. She ..." Peter laughed lightly, "...

she seems to think she has discovered a magic concoction to ensure males. Claire, apparently, has been in receipt of a recipe from her." Peter sighed. "Jem, it's time to go. For your health, you need to leave, to get on with your life and responsibilities away from London for a time."

There was nothing so much wrong with London. What Peter meant was that Jem needed to get away from memories of Cressie for a time. And as much as Jem wanted to deny him, Jem knew that he was right. He was going to go mad with pain. The reminders did not help.

He wondered if anything ever would.

Charles Adam Beresford and Henry Alexander Whitfield were christened into the Ashwood parish a few weeks later. Belle arrived at the conclusion of the Season, and just in time to perform her role as godmother to wee Henry as Adam stood up as his godfather.

Kate stood with Jem as godmother to Charlie. Jem noticed the dirt caked under Kate's fingernails as the baby was placed into her arms for the blessing. Tears of joy filled her eyes as the vicar did so. Jem thought that she must have been tending her latest sycamore tree just prior to the christening. Kate had a fondness for them and had been in the midst of planting her sixth when Jem had been dragged by his mother down to the forge to see the Ellis'.

When it was Jem's turn to hold the baby, he was once again dumbstruck at how small and innocent he was. Of course, this was not the first baby he had held. He had several nieces and a nephew already, but he had never gone out of his way to lather them with affection. But he was honoured that his sister had entrusted him with this role in guiding her little son.

The small, pink infant, with a tuft of dark hair and the lungs of a much larger being, was a light in the darkness.

Returning to Ashwood had been the best thing for Jem. While the work of a steward distracted him well enough, the people around filled in the rest of his time. What little time alone he had reduced the amount of time that he wallowed and yearned.

But it did not take up all of his time. And so, there was a time every day where his mind would be exclusively on her, worrying about her, missing her, loving her.

Eventually Jem's family stopped asking him if he was alright. Perhaps they presumed that enough time had passed that he ought to be. Jem had improved his ability to mask his pain, to pretend as though he was back to his old silly self. To still be as in love with Cressie as the day he had lost her over a year ago probably seemed to others rather ridiculous.

But not to Jem.

Jem remained a diligent worker, dedicated to proving himself to Adam. He worked day in and out to know the estate backwards and forwards. Jem made himself indispensable, and on his twenty-first birthday Adam gifted him the keys to his own house as he became Ashwood's Land Steward.

This moment was promptly interrupted by a now eight-year-old Perrie as she burst into her father's study with a new horrid tale about the nemesis boy she went to school with.

Life moved on. People moved on and went about their lives.

In 1814, two years after Jem's first and last Season in London, Adam and Grace added to their family once more. The arrival of Alice Grace Beresford had disproven Cecily's belief that a pâté made from the liver of a goat held magical male properties. Perrie and Lily both attended the village school at the behest of their parents, with Charlie still a little too young to follow in his elder sisters' footsteps. Perrie often talked of little else but her mortal enemy and whatever terrible deed he was up to on his vicious mission to bother her to death.

Jack and Claire remained happily in London with their two girls. Jackie, now seven, and Maria, now six, had their father quite at their mercy. Jack and Peter had worked to make Beresford Press a very successful publishing house. They had since relocated to a larger warehouse in London where they could house more printing presses and employ more printers. Any book with the Beresford Press stamp embossed upon it was sure to sell. Their taste was often touted as second to none.

Peter and Belle, too, lived very happily in London. Belle had developed an extraordinary reputation in the five years she had been designing in London. She was booked completely every Season, often months in advance, by debutantes desperate to wear something divine that could only be made by Belle Desjardins. But at home she was Belle Denham, a wife and mama. A few days after Christmas in 1812, Peter and Belle welcomed Eloise Armande. She was the first grandchild to bear the Denham name, something which had made Mrs Denham ... and Cecily, rather oddly ... very emotional. The little family quickly outgrew the flat above Belle's shop, and Peter, using his keen financial sense, put their finances together to purchase a townhouse for them in Mayfair. It was nowhere near as grand as Ashwood Place, but it was a home that they could grow into. His forethought was necessary, as in 1814, William François Denham was born, followed by Edward Pierre Denham in '16. Once again, Mrs Denham and Cecily were nearly inconsolable as they blubbered through wee Edward's christening service.

Like Jem, Jim and Kate remained in Ashwood where they raised their now eight-year-old son James. They were as happy together now as they had been when they had wed years ago.

Nearby on their farm, Alex cultivated his exotic crops in his greenhouses, while also farming his and Susanna's land with traditional English crops. Master was a title that suited Alex well, but not so much as he revelled in the title of husband and father. The year after Henry had been born, a second son, George, was born. Two years later, in 1815, Amélie, or Amy, came along.

Life moved on. Jem often thought this whenever he looked upon the lives and worlds of his family members. He saw them all the time. Some more than others. He watched as their marriages and children grew. Even his own mother, with all of her children grown and gone, enjoyed the friendship and companionship of Alex's mother, Amélie, and of Cecily.

Life moved on for everyone but him. While he had aged, now three and twenty, and his responsibilities had grown with him, Jem still felt entirely and completely lost. He had lost the person he was, and he hardly recognised the man he was now.

But his family had grown used to the person he was. They seemingly accepted that maturity was to thank for Jem's transformation. Nobody asked anymore. Nobody wondered. Why would they? Jem was fine.

Everything was fine.

Except it wasn't.

CHAPTER 20

Cressie had dreamed of the sea again the night before. It was the same dream she'd had on many occasions. It began with the feeling of water around her ankles, the feeling she had created in her mind from when she stood in bathtubs. She could feel the cool breeze against her skin, her hair whipping around her face uncontrollably. And the sounds. She could hear the sounds the ocean made ever so clearly. The sounds were ones she had collected from pressing her ear to the conch shell that she had kept hidden safely in her trunk.

The dream usually came after she had listened to the waves in the conch shell. And she usually listened to the waves when she really needed them.

And as time went on, Cressie found that she relied upon that beautiful shell more and more. Because when Cressie dreamed of the sea, her mind could always find the pair of beautiful ocean eyes in her memories.

When Cressie awoke, she was shocked to find that she had fallen asleep with the conch shell beside her. The shock alone was enough to get her to launch out of bed and quickly stow it away in her trunk underneath several layers of her unmentionables.

Cressie had learned that it was not safe to seemingly possess anything of value.

Cressie quickly pulled on her robe and climbed back into bed just as the door was opened to her room by her lady's maid, Imelda Wrigley. Imelda carried with her a breakfast tray and Cressie's mail.

"Good morning, Mrs Delaney," Imelda greeted.

"Good morning, Wrigley," she replied carefully. Imelda placed Cressie's tray down in front of her on the bed and took a step backward, surveying the room, before she went to open the drapes.

Cressie surveyed her tray to find a selection of eggs, ham, fruit, and tea. Her mail was opened. It always was.

Her only correspondence came from her mother. Mrs Martin now lived in Suffolk in a small cottage paid for by Mr Delaney's family. By all reports she lived comfortably and wanted for nothing.

Cressie had not seen her in five years.

She chose the letter first, which seemed to prick Imelda's interest. "The eggs first, ma'am," she reminded her.

Cressie put down the letter and picked up the teaspoon before using it to crack the shell of her first egg. She hated eggs. Cressie had not always. But she hated them now.

Before digging into the egg, she reached for the small, silver dish of salt which had been provided.

"Just a pinch, remember, ma'am?"

With her thumb and forefinger, Cressie collected a pinch of salt and sprinkled it onto her egg, leaving the rest behind.

Once Cressie would have facetiously asked her maid if she would have liked to spoon feed her like an infant. In fact, she had asked her first maid that when these rules were first introduced.

That maid hadn't lasted. Imelda had. Imelda liked the rules. And so, Everett liked Imelda.

Cressie didn't fight anymore. She couldn't. Fighting required will, and Cressie had none of it.

So, she ate her eggs, and then the ham, and then her fruit, before drinking her tea without sugar. And once her dishes were cleaned, she then opened her already opened letter.

It was from her mother.

There were several lines crossed out. Blotted with ink so that they were illegible. Cressie had long stopped wondering what they might have said once. She wasn't to know. She would never know.

The news she learned from her mother's letter was that the weather in Suffolk was tolerable as summer approached and that her cook had produced a delectable gooseberry pie.

"Have you finished reading that, ma'am?" Imelda asked.

Cressie nodded, before passing the letter over into her maid's waiting hand. Imelda pocketed it before removing the tray so that Cressie could get up out of bed. She was helped to bathe using only approved scents and dress in only approved colours. Her hair was pinned in the appropriate way and by all accounts, she was a perfectly acceptable mistress of the house.

Once she was ready, Imelda began to run through the list of responsibilities that she had to take care of that day, but Cressie's mind began to wander as she caught sight of the fountain out the window. That had been her favourite part of Henshaw House when she had first been brought here. It was not nearly as grand or as sentimental as the fountain that it reminded her of, but the sounds of the water had brought her a sense of calm that had been a saving grace in the beginning.

The fountain was not on. It hadn't been on for several years. It was not broken or in need of repair. It had simply been taken away from her.

Cressie had searched for anything to bring her peace in the beginning, to take away the utter misery she had felt in being married to another. The morning that she had left a sleeping Jem in his bedroom still haunted her. But she had known true happiness when she was with him, so she knew exactly what it was she was living in now. Purgatory.

Cressie wished that she had been selfish now. She wished that she had listened to Jem and had chosen her own happiness in spite of her mother. For while Mrs Martin lived comfortably in her own home, Cressie's every bite of food was controlled by a man who ...

Everett Delaney had been delighted with his bride for all of a few hours. He had held her like a trophy, guided her every movement as though she were a prize, his prize, at the wedding breakfast. And then had come the wedding night. Cressie could still cry at the thought of it.

She had believed that the thought of Jem would be enough to get her through it, but it wasn't. Everett was not Jem, and he never could be. She felt foul within herself to be before this man, and Cressie's lack of enthusiasm left Everett incapable. She had come to learn quickly that a man's failure in the marital bed was a source of humiliation for him. Everett had cursed her. He had called her names and declared she was as enticing as a 'dead fish'. And then he had thrown a burning candle and saucer at her head.

It had been the one and only time that Everett had ever directly struck her. The cut from the saucer and the small patch of discolouration from the hot wax, both located on her temple, had been enough to convince him that he could not leave visible scars on her body.

Everett managed to get over his performative issues in time, and he made certain to visit Cressie regularly, much to her disgust. But as she lay there, crying uncontrollably every time, it would infuriate him. He would shake her, curse at her, and declare her a devil girl. And when she failed to fall pregnant month after month, she would be labelled a 'barren bitch'.

Cressie never thought that she would be thankful to be barren. Every time her monthly courses came, she felt such relief. How could she ever care for a child? Everett had stripped her of everything that she had ever held dear to herself or about herself.

That was how Everett punished her. After the candle, he had never struck her, and he reminded her of this frequently. He reminded her that he never hit her where other husbands would. She was a disobedient and disappointing wife. She deserved it, after all. So, Everett found other ways to intimidate and control Cressie.

Everett rarely called her by her name unless they were in company. In private she would be called all sorts of things. She was told repeatedly how lucky she was to be with him, and how other men would have turned her out of even had her killed for her failures. When she refused his advances, Everett threated to have her taken to an asylum to get her to comply.

Cressie's failures as a wife led to Everett becoming obsessive. He gradually began to control everything around her. He had final say over what she ate, how she dressed, and to whom she spoke. He read her incoming post and edited it how he wished, the same as he read and edited her outgoing letters, so that Cressie was entirely trapped. Cressie was not allowed any money of her own. Not a penny. Everett strictly controlled her spending. If Cressie wanted to purchase a ribbon, she would have needed express permission.

And when he wanted to punish her, he would destroy or take away the things that she loved. The fountain had been one of them. He had burned the Messy Cressie poems that she had kept from Jem. He had done so in a fit of rage with her without reading them and had immediately regretted this. He had then demanded to know the contents, and Cressie had made up a lie about them being from her father in France.

Everett had taken everything from Cressie. She was not at all certain that there was anything left for him to take from her. Save for the shell. If Everett destroyed the conch shell, then Cressie would have little else to do but throw herself from her bedroom window.

"Did you hear what I said, ma'am?"

Cressie's attention reverted back to her lady's maid. Imelda stood before her with her stern brow furrowed. Imelda reminded Cressie of a strict schoolmistress. She was the right age and had just the right amount of condemnable disappointment in her dark eyes to play the part.

The servants were all loyal to Everett. And if they were not, or they questioned any of his rules or behaviours, they were dismissed and moved on to another household. Everett retained those, like Imelda, who would uphold his rules and control his wife just the way he wanted.

"I'm sorry. My mind was elsewhere," Cressie murmured.

Imelda sighed quietly. "I said that Miss Delaney is arriving from school today. Mr Delaney expects you to receive her and host her until he returns from the mills."

Cressie had not needed the reminder. She had quietly been looking forward to the visit of Everett's niece. Zara Delaney was the seventeen-year-old child of Everett's late younger brother. She was in the care of her grandparents, Everett's mother and father, and had been away at school until recently finishing. Cressie met with her annually during the Yuletide festivities and found that she was the one redeemable figure within the Delaney family.

Every time that Cressie met with Zara, she was reminded so much of herself when she had been youthful and hopeful. Despite only being two and twenty herself, Cressie felt that the days where she had enjoyed running and playing and laughing were the memories of someone else.

"I haven't forgotten," Cressie muttered in reply.

"Excellent," said Imelda.

Cressie dutifully performed the list of pre-approved tasks throughout the morning, and ate her midday meal, before the carriage carrying Zara Delaney arrived shortly after two in the afternoon.

Zara was a beautiful young lady with a gorgeous, pale complexion, soft, red hair, and pale blue eyes. She wore a gown made of the same shade of blue that suited her slender figure heavenly.

Cressie greeted Zara in the foyer, Imelda by her side. Zara immediately bounded up to Cressie with a big smile on her face and collected her in a hug.

Cressie had first met Zara when she was twelve and had disliked being called 'aunt' when she still felt so young herself. So, Zara knew her by her Christian name. It was something that Everett had not challenged. Yet.

"Oh, Cressie!" cried Zara. "How nice it is to see you again! You look well!"

Zara had never known Cressie before. Her current state must have appeared 'well' to her.

"You look delightful," countered Cressie. "A well-educated young lady, I would wager."

Zara smiled happily. "I am so pleased to be finished with school. I am so pleased to be finally of age!"

Cressie did not think that seventeen was enough years to be considered of age. Zara was still a child. Or she should be. What Cressie would have given to be allowed a few more years as a little girl before she had been thrust out into society.

"Being of age is not all roses, Zara. There is still much merit in your youth," Cressie quietly reminded her.

But Zara did not appear convinced. "I simply cannot wait to go to London!"

"London?" repeated Cressie.

Zara nodded. "For the Season. Has Uncle Everett not told you? Oh, he must have forgotten. Grandmamma is too old to escort me. She has written to Uncle Everett requesting that you be my chaperone for the Season. I am going to find a husband, Cressie!"

CHaPTer 21

Cressie's young niece animated chatted about what she was anticipating for the upcoming Season and making oral lists of everything that she would need to procure before their departure.

"Oh, we simply must visit Desjardins as soon as we arrive!" Zara declared insistently. "Everyone at school says that one simply has to be dressed by Belle Desjardins upon their debut. To be seen in anything else is practically a social faux pas!"

Cressie had not been engaged in the conversation with Zara, and not for a lack of interest in what the young lady had to say. Her attention had been listening out for the sounds of gravel under hooves. She could recognise Dabney's footing every time as Everett rode the poor beast as hard as he could.

But her attention had been grabbed upon hearing Belle Desjardins' name. It was a name that had not crossed her mind in several years. Why would it when it was her husband who decided what she wore and when. But the minute she was reminded of the dressmaker, a sudden flurry of memories filled her mind.

"Belle," repeated Cressie, almost dreamily, as she recalled just how instrumental that woman had been to Cressie's happiness for such a short period of time five years earlier.

Zara's blue eyes found Cressie's. "Yes," she confirmed, "Belle Desjardins. Have you heard of her? You must have. All of my school friends, the ones who are coming out this year, are having her make their debutante gowns. I cannot miss out on my chance. What a sight I would be if I were the only one dressed otherwise."

"How would you ever find a husband?" Cressie's question was soft, but facetious. Belle's name had thrown her, but she could see how intent Zara was on being a successful debutante, and an eventual bride. Cressie would have wagered that a daughter like Zara would have been her mother's ideal.

Though, despite her own protestations, Cressie had married at seventeen and had saved their fortunes, just as Mrs Martin had wanted.

This was what Mrs Martin had wanted.

"Exactly!" cried Zara. "I am so pleased you understand. Grand-mamma, bless her, doesn't know these things. I am secretly pleased that she is too fragile now to take me to London. And having been a debutante yourself only ... what ... five years ago now? You will know exactly what to do so that I might find myself a husband like Uncle Everett."

Cressie felt her face physically fall, and she could do nothing to stop it. All blood drained from her face as she saw the optimism in Zara's face as she described a husband like her uncle as her ideal. She saw rich and influential in a husband like Everett Delaney. She could not see the chains around Cressie's wrists, ankles, and neck.

Zara needed protecting. Zara could not be failed.

"What is it?" Zara asked.

But at that moment, Cressie heard that all too familiar sound of the gravel crunching. She rose from the wing back chair that she had been occupying and went to the window of the drawing room which overlooked the front of Everett's estate. Galloping down the hedged row was Everett atop Dabney.

It was odd, perhaps, for a gentleman, and particularly one as wealthy as Everett Delaney, to so often travel on horseback and not by carriage. Cressie had certainly wondered about it for a brief time during the early days of their marriage. But the answer had soon come to her without the need to ask. It was clear.

Control.

There was little more that Everett Delaney enjoyed more than controlling everything around him, including the poor horse he would one day bully to death.

"Is that Uncle Everett coming?" Zara asked, coming to the window to stand by Cressie. When she saw her uncle approaching, she gasped gleefully. "Oh, it is! I am so pleased. I cannot wait to start making plans to travel."

Cressie felt her blood cool, as though a dark hand had reached itself inside of her chest to stop it beating. Ice flowed through her veins quickly as her emotions tried to panic her.

But Cressie numbed herself to nullify the dread. It was how she had survived all these years. Nobody was going to save her. Nobody was going to help her. There was no escape. There would be no leaving. She simply had to survive, she had to find a way to live. And the only way to survive was numb herself. She would have died years ago if she had allowed the dread to eat at her soul.

It did not take long for Everett to join the both of them in the drawing room. The moment he crossed the threshold, he removed his hat and welcomed his enthusiastic niece's greeting with a smile. The butler, Burnley, followed his master, and stood by the door.

"Welcome, Zara," he beckoned as he leaned down to allow Zara to kiss his cheek. "You are looking very well. Very much the proper young lady."

Zara beamed at the affirming compliment. "Thank you, Uncle. I am so pleased to be finished with school and to be ready for my debut."

Everett's cool eyes flicked to Cressie, and then they narrowed. She had remained by the window, feet firm in place. "Cressida, come and greet your husband," he instructed in a firm, but almost playful tone for the benefit of his niece.

Everett rarely, if ever, called her anything by 'Cressida' or 'Wife'. Never Cressie. It was childish, he had claimed, and Cressie was secretly grateful. For a man that was her husband, calling her by the name she preferred seemed far too familiar. It was reserved for those she cared for.

But nevertheless, Cressie obeyed him. Her legs began to move, and she crossed the room to Everett, coming to a stop a few feet in front of him. Everett's grey eyes began their usual appraisal of her appearance, certainly searching for any fault, for anything of which he did not approve. He was not above sending her to change.

But he said nothing. His eyes returned to her face, and he stepped forward, suddenly collecting her chin in a pinch between his thumb and forefinger. "Smile," he uttered. His tone might have suggested otherwise, but Cressie knew that it was an order.

Cressie held her breath and smiled. Somehow. She felt the corners of her lips upturn, and she held them in place for a few seconds until Everett was satisfied. When he released her,

Cressie immediately put another foot of distance between them and released the breath that she had been holding.

"Mother writes and tells me that you are ready to make your debut, Zara," Everett the addressed his niece.

Zara seemed pleased to have the opportunity to once again speak about the prospect of travelling to London. "Yes!" she said enthusiastically. "Oh, Uncle Everett, I am so excited by the idea. Grandmamma wants Aunt Cressie to chaperone me as well. Won't that be divine?"

Cressie said nothing.

Everett's eyes said everything.

He had known about this. He had clearly received word from his mother and had been mulling over this idea for a while. Of course, he had said nothing to Cressie. This would not be her choice. She could only imagine what he would have been thinking. How could he control her from London? Would Everett even be capable of relinquishing control?

Would Cressie even know what to do with herself without Everett's hand on every choice in her day?

"Burnley," Everett barked, without looking back at the butler.

"Yes, sir?"

"Show Miss Delaney to her room. She will need to wash and change before dinner this evening. We are to have a special welcome meal prepared for her."

Zara did not see that she was being dismissed. She was so excited at the prospect of a meal in her honour that she could not see her uncle desired her gone. Zara dutifully followed the butler out of the drawing room, and the door was closed behind her, leaving Everett and Cressie alone.

The moment the door closed, Cressie felt the temperature in the room drop. A chill washed over her as though she had just lowered herself into an icy bath.

Cressie tangled her fingers together to give them something to do, and to give herself something to focus on other than her husband's intense stare. As she did so, she felt the hard, thin band of gold around her left ring finger. While her chains were invisible, this one was clear for everyone to see. And Zara so eagerly wanted one of her own.

"I have been thinking very – look at me when I am speaking to you!" Everett snapped angrily.

Cressie forced her eyes up, and she met Everett's glare, his brows knitted together in disgust.

"Disrespectful, ungrateful," he muttered under his breath before he continued. "I have been thinking very long about this. Mother has requested that you escort Zara for the Season as she is not able to. There are no other women in the family ranked highly enough. I do not have the time to spend months in London, however."

Cressie could not at all predict where Everett's mind was going to go. Would he allow it?

"So," Everett said, stepping forward to close the distance between them, the distance that Cressie had created, "begs the question, can I trust you?" He came to stand right in front of her, with barely a few inches separating their chests as he looked down upon her. He liked looking down. He liked making Cressie feel small. He had never directly said this, but from the smile that spread across his cheeks during these moments of intimidation, it was not challenging to infer. "Can I, Cressida?" he asked.

"Yes," she replied, her voice weak.

Everett sucked in a breath. He was battling with something, and Cressie wagered it was the potential loss of control. "I don't believe you," he suddenly snapped, his voice going from calm to irate in a matter of seconds. "I know what goes on in your little head. Don't you think I don't. I know that you think that you are better than me!" he hissed. He laughed mockingly. "You're nothing. Your entire existence relies upon me and don't you forget that! I have but to snap my fingers and I could have you thrown into an asylum if I wanted to. I keep you here out of kindness. I keep your barren body here because of my own decency."

Cressie said nothing. She gave him nothing. She had fought back before, but fighting often rendered the same result as not. It only made him angrier. This was why she had learned to numb herself. Only she could protect herself.

Her physical existence, perhaps, relied upon Everett. But her sanity and her soul? Those were Cressie's to keep and protect.

She never had to worry about her heart. Everett had never gotten his hands on it, and it had not been in Cressie's possession for a very long time.

Everett clapped his hands on either side of Cressie's face, tangling his fingers in the hair at her temples. His hands entirely captured her head and held it in place as he forced her to stare up at him. "I will know," he uttered. "I will know if you step one toe out of line. Do you understand me?"

With the grip that Everett held, Cressie could not nod. She could not even move her neck. She was forced to say, "Yes." And she did not doubt it. She did not doubt that Everett would find out even if she donned a colour that he did not approve of.

CHAPTER 22

Cressie ate her supper in silence as Everett laughed with musical delight as Zara regaled him with stories from school.

Everett was so charming. He was so, so charming with others. It made Cressie feel like nobody would believe her if she told them what he was really like.

Usually, the lady of the house would take her place at the opposite end of the table. But not Cressie. Everett liked to keep Cressie beside him on his right. When dining with some of Everett's friends or relatives in the past, Cressie has heard comments about her husband's attachment, and how theirs must have been a love match. In reality, it was so that Everett could closely monitor what Cressie was eating.

"I was certain Mary would be spotted leaving that frog in the kitchens, but she wasn't!" Zara giggled as she took in a spoonful of her soup. "It serves that wicked cook right! She promptly quit the school, and the headmistress was forced to hire someone else."

"They certainly did a marvellous job bringing you up to be delicate young ladies, did they not?" Everett replied in an amused tone.

"Oh, please, Uncle Everett. I know French and Latin. I can draw and sing and embroider, and I am told I am excellent on the pianoforte," Zara retorted with a smile. "I would make an excellent bride."

"You certainly are accomplished," murmured Everett. "You could learn a thing or two from her this summer, wife," he added under his breath for Cressie.

Cressie said nothing. She did not rise to the comment. She did not refute it. She did not defend it.

She simply pooled her soup onto her spoon to take another mouthful, before Everett placed his hand atop of hers and said, "That's enough."

Zara did notice this, and she frowned. "But Cressie has not finished."

Everett chuckled. "Cressida doesn't like to spoil the next course," he replied dismissively. But he kept his hand on Cressie's until she released her spoon and submitted to his order to stop eating. "I have already sent word ahead to the house in London to have it prepared for you. You will, of course, take Cressida's maid, Wrigley, with you. There is nobody I would trust more to keep the both of you safe."

Cressie heard the word 'safe', but she knew that Everett meant 'in line'. Imelda Wrigley would act as Everett's bloodhound while he was not there. Right down to the amount of food she took in to ensure that Everett would not be burdened with a fat wife.

"Oh, I have never had a maid before," Zara said excitedly. "Of course, I understand she would not be my maid, but still, it is all so exciting! I cannot believe that I am to come out!"

Zara did not understand that Imelda was not a maid but a watchdog. Would Everett force his niece to undertake his rules? Cressie thought on it for a moment, but then decided that he would not. Everett was not obsessive over any other aspect of his life. Not his family, not his work, not his friends. It was how he appeared to be so charming. It was only Cressie. She was his only victim. Because he could not have her exactly as he wanted, he had become this.

"When do we leave, Cressie?" Zara asked with a wide grin. "Tomorrow? Oh, please say tomorrow!"

Everett chuckled before he took hold of Cressie's hand atop the table. His grip quickly tightened to a point where her knuckles began to crunch together. Cressie wore her pain well, and her face did not contort beyond a brief grimace.

"I am not yet ready to part from my dear wife," Everett replied. "I will make arrangements for your departure next week."

"I thank you, Mr Greenwell," Jem said cordially as he delicately removed the Greenwell family's rent payment from his desk. "Give my best to Mrs Greenwell, would you?"

"I will, Mr Denham," confirmed Mr Greenwell, a greying farmer who rented his land from the Ashwood estate.

As Mr Greenwell departed, Jem made certain to record the payment of rent in the ledger and added the banknotes and coins to his lockbox to be deposited when he was next in London. He would make the trip soon as he'd nearly collected all the quarterly rents from the Ashwood tenants. It was the most important job he had as the Ashwood Land Steward. It was his responsibility to ensure the financial viability of the estate, and to manage its income.

Jem left his small study, which had once been the front reception room of his small cottage and walked towards the kitchen where his cook and housekeeper, Mrs Edwards, had prepared his midday meal. Mrs Edwards was the only servant he kept, purely because if he were to cook for himself, Jem would more than likely burn down the house that had been so generously provided for him. It also gave his mother peace of mind to know that he was being looked after. He was still seen as the baby by most of his family members, no matter how old he got. Nevertheless, Jem had not behaved like the youngest in a long time.

Out of the kitchen window, Jem could see Mrs Edwards beating the rug that usually resided on the floor of his sitting room. She had flung it over a tree branch and was getting an alarming amount of dust out of it. She had left Jem some cut sandwiches beside his post.

Jem picked up one of the sandwiches, enjoying the feeling of the freshly baked bread under his fingertips, and took a large bite, before reaching for the first of his letters.

It was an invitation from Grace to dine at the main house that evening. The second was a letter from Peter updating him on the family. The last was a letter from his mother reminding him that he could come to see her without it being an obligatory church visit.

Jem rolled his eyes, and then secretly hoped that his mother's four other children were in receipt of the same guilt-filled letters. Despite this, Jem knew that Mrs Denham was right. He did tend to stay away until he came to collect her for church on a Sunday morning. He adored his mother. Of course, he did. But she could be oblivious in the same way that Jem could be clever at shielding his feelings.

Jem was a single man with a steady income and a house of his own. He was an amiable young man despite not being a gentle-man. And there were plenty of lovely young women around who would be glad to take him. Only Jem had little desire to be 'took'. He knew that Mrs Denham only desired to see him settled happily like her four other children. Jem would be her failure. Jem knew he would be her failure. No amount of nagging would persuade him to marry anyone. Anyone else.

Any hope of that sort of happiness was lost. And he had accepted that. He'd had to for his own sanity.

A knock on Jem's door startled him, as he had not been expecting any further tenants that afternoon. He abandoned his post and his lunch, and he went to the door. When it swung open, Jem was surprised to see his nine, nearly ten, year old niece, Perrie, standing before him alone.

Perrie was dressed in a rather mismatched riding ensemble, with a flouncy, formal white blouse tucked into the sturdiness of her stiff riding skirt. It appeared she had dressed herself, and quite hurriedly, too. Her dark hair was a mess of untidy ringlets and her cheeks were flushed from the ride in the afternoon sun. Her bright blue eyes met his with a flash of determination.

"Uncle Jem, I've had a thought," she announced in a tone that only Perrie could produce.

"I really don't think you have," Jem replied as he looked around the front garden of his house. He could only see Perrie's horse, its reins tied to his gate, and not a servant or parent in sight. Did Grace know she had gone out by herself? "Not a single thought, indeed. Where is your mother?"

Perrie huffed impatiently as she walked past him into the entry hall of his house. "Not important!" she retorted. She rounded on Jem and placed her hands on her hips, the expression on her face serious. "Mama said that you used to spend a lot of your time swimming when you were a boy. You are a good swimmer, yes?"

Jem had no clue as to where Perrie was going with this line of conversation. All he knew now was that his afternoon would be spent escorting his niece back to her house where she could be berated by her parents for going out alone. And then, knowing Perrie, she would do it all again tomorrow.

"Do you want a swimming lesson, Perrie?" Jem inferred. "I am to come to the house to dine tonight. You might have asked me then instead of going out alone. You really have no qualms for your safety, do you? Your father ought to take you over his knee."

They both knew that Adam never would.

Perrie, again, ignored him. "It is not I who needs the swimming lesson," she replied. "Rather, I wondered how hard it might be to let someone accidentally drown and in doing so, do you think I would be in very much trouble?"

Had Jem been eating in that moment, he would have choked on his food. As it was, he nearly swallowed his tongue as the words came out of this nine-year-old's mouth. And she was perfectly serious.

"Perrie, what on earth is the matter with you?" Jem exclaimed once he finally found his words.

Perrie's blue eyes flared. She looked so extraordinarily like her mother, and yet her temperament was about as far from Grace as she possibly could be. Were they not so alike in appearance, Jem would have put money on Perrie being adopted from a family of wildlings.

She hissed in frustration as she stuffed her hand into the pocket of her riding skirt, and she pulled out a folded piece of fabric. At first glance, it looked like a rather pretty, lacy handkerchief. But as Perrie unfolded it, Jem could see that something was clumsily embroidered across the centre of the material.

In red thread, the words, 'LITTLE IMP', had been stitched across the handkerchief.

"Papa refuses to teach me how to shoot a gun, so I thought drowning would be the next best thing to get rid of my horrid, good for nothing nemesis." Perrie glared down at the handkerchief in her hands, most likely willing it to burst into flames. "That's what he calls me, you know! Little Imp! Little Imp all the time! I will grow!" Perrie growled.

Not likely, Jem mused, in knowing the short statures of his sisters. "Perrie, I am not about to allow you to drown your nemesis, accidentally or not."

Perrie stomped her foot. "But he is so infuriating!" she exclaimed impatiently.

Jem snatched the handkerchief from Perrie's hands and inspecting the handwork of Perrie's nemesis, whatever his name was. The stitchwork was obviously subpar, but a lot of effort had gone into this little prank, and it had clearly had the desired effect. Jem had heard a lot about Perrie's enemy, not only from her, but from Adam and Grace as well. They both seemed to believe that Perrie was a tad dramatic, and that she contributed to the friction equally as much as the boy did. Perrie claimed complete innocence.

In knowing Perrie, Jem was more than inclined to side with her parents. Perrie, after all, was here to plot his demise.

"Grandmamma Cecily seems to think that when boys are cruel it is because the secretly have affection for you," Perrie snapped angrily. "She doesn't understand that this one is absolutely evil."

That comment struck Jem rather oddly, in a way that surprised and startled him. It actually really bothered him that his niece was being told that this boy's actions were being dismissed as affectionate. In his hands was a prank, obviously meant to be funny and to get a rise out of Perrie, which it absolutely had, but to scc namc-calling as affcctionatc was wrong. They both clearly went back and forth with each other, determined to make the other suffer, but that should never be how two people in love treated one another.

Jem knew it. He had felt it. He'd had it in his arms. Cruelty had been the farthest thing from his mind. He could have never been cruel to her. To have her was precious. "Perrie," Jem said seriously, looking down at his niece with an expression of determination. "Cruelty is never a sign of affection. Cruelty should never be seen or accepted as affection."

And while Jem had been suddenly overcome with the need to declare this to his young niece, Perrie simply frowned at him. "I know," she stated plainly. "He hates me. He told me so when I showed this handkerchief to the vicar. He got the cane five times and was then locked in a cupboard for an hour." Perrie sighed, before she smiled slightly. "He deserved it so much. But I really, really want to try the drowning idea. Please, Uncle Jem?"

Perrie was too young to understand. So was this boy, most likely. They probably equally hated one another and would indelibly go their separate ways in a few years when their village education concluded. Perrie wouldn't need to worry about cruelty in her future. She would have the money and freedom to make her own choice. Jem hoped that one day, Perrie appreciated this. It was a luxury not afforded to everyone.

"No," said Jem firmly. "I don't think that your father really wants the next Ashwood scandal to be his nine-year-old daughter being tried for drowning a boy in his pond."

"Well, what do you suggest I do then?" Perrie protested, pouting.

"Put pins on his chair like a normal person," Jem urged. "Come on then, I had better get you back to the house." He tapped Perrie's shoulder to get her moving as an inspired grin spread across her face.

CHAPTER 23

Cressie delicately sat down in the carriage, dutifully shielding any pain from her face as she had learned to do so often throughout her marriage. Everett had visited her bedroom the night before, and he had been particularly possessive.

But no matter how sore she was, she felt a very odd sense of relief as the carriage began to move away from the home that had so quickly become a prison to her. She felt no freedom. How could she when Everett's hound in her maid, Imelda, sat atop the carriage with the driver? But there was relief in knowing that for a time, she would be free from him.

"Why were you so interested in Dabney being one of the carriage horses?" Zara asked curiously.

Cressie sat beside her young niece, who had been positively shaking with excitement until she had posed her question. Cressie had wanted Everett's poor horse to be free from his master for a while also.

"It matters not," replied Cressie. "Your uncle could not do without him." It did not surprise her. How could Everett ever live if he relinquished both of his prizes in one day? She prayed for that poor animal.

"Well, I am glad that Uncle Everett could do without you," Zara emphasised. "I cannot tell you how pleased I am that it is you escorting me this Season, and not Grandmamma. Bless her, but I cannot imagine that she would have the will to attend the number of balls and parties that I intend to. I want to meet all the eligible gentlemen, every one of them! I cannot wait to dance and be complimented and called upon. I hear that when gentlemen call, they bring gifts for the mother, or the guardian, too! That's you!"

Zara's brief curiosity over Dabney disappeared, and she returned to her usual rambunctious and romantic notions of what a London Season entailed. And while she was right in the way that there would be balls and gifts from callers, she was so terribly naïve in the romanticism of it all.

"Zara," Cressie said tenderly. "You must keep your head on as we enter this market, for that is what it is. You are for sale, and there will be bidders, and not everyone will be who they seem. You must be clever, and I will endeavour to help you weed out the would-be rakes and blackguards." And Everetts. Cressie would help to weed out the Everetts.

Zara's pale blue eyes widened as her torso turned towards Cressie curiously. "Rakes and blackguards, really?" she gasped, before her lips upturned in a mischievous way. "I cannot wait to reach London."

Perhaps Zara's grandmamma might have been the wiser choice for a chaperone. Nevertheless, Cressie had no stake in Zara's marriage, not as her mother had done with her own. She did not have to fret about the cost to live. She could fully focus on ensuring her niece found a sweetheart, an emerald, in and amongst all the coloured glass there was to be found in London.

***

Cressie and Zara stopped frequently on their trip from Yorkshire to London, staying at inns in small villages while the horses were changed or rested. Imelda dutifully wrote a missive to Everett at every stop to report their location before they were off again.

After nearly a week and a half of travelling, Cressie began to recognise the familiar outskirts of London. Or, at least, they had been familiar at one point in her life. The moment the buildings came into view Cressie was transported back, back to when she had travelled to the city with her mother and she felt quite the opposite to how Zara was feeling. Cressie had approached her Season with dread and trepidation. Her instincts had been superb.

All of a sudden, such memories that had been long forgotten came flooding back. Cressie could hear the arguments that had taken place between her and Mrs Martin, as though her mother was in this very carriage. Cressie had cursed the fact that she was being shopped, and her mother had reminded her that to marry was her obligation to save them both.

Was this what it was like to be saved? Was this being saved? How could it be? Despite the fact that it would not be her who was shopped to the eligible gentlemen of the ton, Cressie's stomach began to clench.

Though Cressie had never been as enthusiastic to find a mate as Zara was, she still saw a lot of herself in her seventeen-year-old niece. Cressie had once had the energy and zest of ten women. She had desired to run and play and laugh until her sides hurt. She had been the type to she had been the type to run into a fountain just to imagine it was swimming. She had been the type to rebel against every formal convention of what a lady should be. She had been the type to ...

She had been the type to fall in love with a man who didn't seem to want to change a hair on her head. A man who made her feel listened to, treasured, worthy and alive. A man who encouraged her energy and spontaneity. A man who was precious in every way.

Precious, and yet lost.

If Zara could but find someone who made her feel such a way, Cressie would make certain that she did not have to suffer the same fate. Even if she did not, Cressie would never allow Zara to settle. She would not stand for Zara being imprisoned in a house, in a marriage, for the rest of her days. It was too late for Cressie, but it was not for Zara.

When the carriage arrived at Everett's London home in Mayfair, Zara asked, "How long until we go to the modiste?"

How long indeed? Cressie had not been entirely ignorant living in Yorkshire. She was well aware of the success that Belle had made of her business. Women, young ladies like Zara, were desperate to be seen in one of her gowns. Anything else was simply unacceptable. With this success, would Belle be at her shop? Or would she have seamstresses working for her?

Vivid memories, again, came flooding back into her mind of the secret liaisons that had taken place Belle's fitting room.

"Let us get our bearings first," Cressie replied in a pacifying tone. "Maybe unpack a little, have some tea, and then we might venture out."

Zara did not seem to be elated with the idea of tea over a visit to the dressmakers, but she participated well as the servants helped them into the house, carrying their trunks and belongings up the stairs. Once Cressie was shown to the master's rooms, Imelda was taken upstairs to the servants' quarters by the housekeeper, leaving Cressie alone in the bedroom.

Cressie looked around the room, noticing the expensive furnishings and tapestries that seemed to align with Everett's taste.

It was not as large a room as she had at the house in Yorkshire, but neither was the house as large. It was still divinely decorated with a large canopied bed, embellished with golden drapery. A fireplace and hearth dominated much of the south wall, and two plump, wingback chairs were situated before it. Cressie spied a writing desk near the privacy screen and walked towards it tentatively. She opened the compartments with nary a flicker of hope and saw that it was empty. Not a scrap of paper, nor a quill, to be found. If she wanted to write, she would need to ask permission, and whatever she did write would be read. Why would she have ever thought otherwise? Though he was some two hundred miles away, Everett's reach was never ending.

The door opened suddenly, and Cressie found herself shutting the writing desk in a guilty manner, as she spun around to face whomever it was that had barged in. She needn't have fretted as it was only Zara, and she did not seem to notice Cressie's odd behaviour at the desk.

"Settled?" Zara asked, her eyebrows raising. Her blue eyes travelled to Cressie's as yet unopened trunk situated at the end of her bed. "Unpacked?"

Would Cressie ever know the feeling of being settled? She doubted it entirely. "Alright," allowed Cressie with a nod of her head. "To the modiste we go."

Cressie did not think that Imelda would have predicted that they would have departed for the modiste so soon after arriving. Imelda was still with the housekeeper. But to ensure that neither of them would be in any trouble, Cressie informed the butler of their destination, before she and Zara climbed back inside the carriage.

It was not a long journey to Belle's shop, not compared to the distance they had just travelled from Yorkshire, but Zara was positively shaking with excitement and desperation to arrive.

"Oh, I hope she is not too busy," Zara stressed. "I hope I am not too late. I imagine there are far richer debutantes, from much better families, whom she would prefer to dress. It is not as though I am titled."

"Belle Desjardins dressed me during my Season," Cressie recalled soothingly. "She is decency and modesty itself, and I do not think she possesses a high nor a mighty bone in her body." She happily dressed Cressie for a pittance that summer. The woman was a saint.

"I wonder if I might practise my French with her," Zara thought aloud. "Don't gentlemen prefer ladies who speak more than one tongue?"

In Cressie's experience, gentlemen seemed to prefer women who held their tongues. "I do know that Mrs Den – Miss Desjardins' – mother tongue is French. I imagine she would enjoy the conversation." Cressie couldn't say the name. Her mind couldn't let it escape her mouth.

The outside of the shop looked much like Cressie remembered it, though the designs in the window had changed to reflect the change in society's fashion tastes. Through the glass, Cressie could see that there were several parties inside, all as ambitious as Zara was to have their debutante Season blessed with Belle Desjardins gowns.

The footman opened the carriage door and let down the step. Zara barely used it as she practically leapt from the carriage and down onto the street. She impatiently waited for Cressie to climb out before they approached the door of the shop. Cressie felt her breath hitch in her throat as Zara pushed open the door to the little jingle sound of the bell.

The front room was much the same as Cressie remembered as well, save for the furniture having been rearranged here and there. Several young ladies and their mothers were perusing design books and bolts of fabric. The young ladies all looked to be around Zara's age, and Cressie felt her stomach drop as, once again, the vivid memory of her own journey here with her mother appeared at the forefront of her mind.

What was different about the shop, however, was that Belle no longer seemed to be the only seamstress. She now had, if Cressie counted correctly, three other young women working in the shop. They all were engaged with a debutante and her mother, and it did not escape Cressie's notice that these girls were all women of colour. They were dressed finely, though they donned aprons, and their constitutions and complexions were bright and healthy. Had they come from a similar place as Belle had? Had they experienced similar trials? Had Belle rescued them and given them safe harbour?

Zara darted immediately over to a collection bin of fabric bolts and began to sort through them, running her hands over the silks in admiration and awe. "This feels like butter, Cressie," she whispered excitedly.

Cressie did not respond as she felt her eyes drift to the curtained dressing room at the back of the store. She knew it well. She had known it for reasons other than fittings. Her stomach, once again, clenched tightly, as the pain and heartbreak threatened to expose itself right there on the shop floor.

The curtain was suddenly drawn back, and a mother and daughter pair emerged, followed closely by a beautiful, dark-skinned woman. Cressie had always thought Belle and extraordinarily striking women. Her skin was so cool and perfect, and her eyes were like molten gold, and were unlike any others that she had ever seen. But in the five years that had passed, Cressie observed that she appeared healthier, ever so slightly fuller in the face and figure, that she no longer bore any remnants of a gauntness from a horrendous start to life.

Those molten eyes seemed to find Cressie immediately, as though they were magnetised. Belle stared at Cressie for a long moment, perhaps matching her to a memory. Or to the ghost of one.

CHAPTER 24

"Is that her?" Zara whispered to Cressie, her excitement evident in the way her voice rose an octave as she spoke the pronoun. "Oh, this is another reason as to why I am pleased it is you escorting me this Season, and not Grandmamma. I do not think her prejudice would allow me to be dressed by a woman like Belle Desjardins."

Cressie briefly wondered how many mamas and grandmammas prevented their daughters from being dressed by Belle due to their own shameful follies. She then wondered how many of the women in this shop still held those prejudices but would dismiss them long enough to secure a couture gown for their daughter's debut.

Fools be damned. "She is an excellent woman," Cressie quietly informed her niece as Belle began towards them. "You would be lucky to know her grace, and not the other way around."

Zara did not have time to reply as Belle reached them in mere moments. Though, by the expression on Zara's face, Cressie could guess as to what her niece would have replied. Zara appeared utterly and completely starstruck. For the poor debutante, though, Belle's eyes could only find Cressie.

Belle had news of him.

The thought crossed through the forefront of Cressie's mind so suddenly, it caused her to stumble backwards, as though someone had slapped her across the face with the notion.

Zara gasped as she laid a hand on Cressie's arm. "Are you alright?" she inquired with a furrowed brow.

"Yes," murmured Cressie, "I merely momentarily lost my footing. I am quite alright."

But the thought had not left her mind. Never in the five years that had passed had Cressie ever been so close to news of him. She had to but breathe the words, to utter his name, to learn something, anything. How was he? Was he well? Was he happy? Was he married?

"I am Belle Desjardins. Welcome to my couturier," Belle said, finally tearing her golden eyes away from Cressie, before settling them on a very appreciative Zara. "Congratulations on your impending debut, Miss ...?"

"Delaney," replied Zara helpfully. "My name is Miss Zara Delaney. And thank you. I am very excited."

"It is a pleasure to meet you, Miss Delaney," Belle said tentatively, speaking over Zara's surname, and indeed Cressie's, with heightened caution. Her eyes flicked back to Cressie, before she said, "I am glad to meet with you again ... Mrs Delaney." Cressie could still hear the deep French inflection on her words, but it was not as pronounced as it had been five years earlier.

"Oh, Cressie!" exclaimed Zara. "She remembers you! How delightful!"

Both Cressie and Belle had to have been thinking the same thing. Belle did not remember Cressie because she had purchased one or two of her dresses. Cressie could ask her right in that moment. She could say the words, articulate his name, find out anything, anything that had happened to him since they had parted.

Did he still care?

Oh, what a wicked thought!

Cressie hoped he didn't. She knew that she should hope that he did not care. She would not want him to feel what she had done. The good part of her should wish that he had moved on and found the happiness that he deserved. Why should both of them have had to suffer? Cressie would never wish that on him.

As these thoughts flooded her mind, Cressie began to feel the deep, crushing, searing intensity of her old wounds, the wounds that had since been eclipsed by Everett. She felt them like they were healing scabs, and if she were to pick at them, they would bleed and never stop. Cressie couldn't bleed. She didn't have the strength to bleed any more than she had.

Cressie took a subtle, quiet breath, and pushed it away. She pushed the memories, the questions, and the pain to the back of her mind, and put all of her attention and focus on Zara.

Zara took her opportunity then. She said something in French, her tone indicating that it was a question.

Belle tore her eyes from Cressie and replied to Zara in flawless French. Zara's smile broadened and Cressie could only infer that the two ladies had begun to speak about what Zara desired for her debut gown. Belle led them over to her large worktable and brought over a basket of neatly folded scraps of material. They were not really scraps, Cressie supposed, as the edges were all neatly sewn in. They were samples, and Belle laid them out in front of Zara to inspect and feel.

Belle reverted to English as she said, "These are some of the newest fabrics that I have received from the Continent. They are all so very beautiful and will make an elegant debut gown."

"They are!" gushed Zara as she reached for an embroidered sample of white silk.

Belle momentarily ducked down and reached for something that was stored underneath the worktable. She returned promptly with a few sheets of parchment and a charcoal pencil. As Zara continued to look through the fabrics, Belle began to draw. It was hard not to be entranced as Cressie watched Belle scrawl line after line which quickly began to resemble a woman wearing something magnificent.

Belle began to articulate her thoughts on the neckline, bodice design, and the type of sleeve to Zara, all based on her observations of Zara's figure and complexion. Zara agreed with it all, though Cressie suspected that Belle might have suggested she wear a potato sack and Zara would have enthusiastically agreed to it.

After a little more time selecting a few fabric samples that would work with the idea for the design, Belle had one of the other women who worked for her take Zara into the back room to take her measurements, which left Belle with Cressie on the shop floor. Of course, they were not alone. There were several other parties about, but for all Cressie could feel, it was her alone with the inquisitive golden eyes of Belle Desjardins, Belle Denham.

"Cressie," Belle breathed softly, "may I still know you as that? I suppose not."

"No," Cressie said abruptly. "Of course, you may." Very few people in her life now knew her by her preferred name.

"Cressie," Belle said again, as though she was testing the name on the tip of her tongue. Her brows furrowed as her appraising eyes swept over Cressie quickly. "I recognised you immediately but ..."

Belle did not finish her sentence, as though she was deliberately holding her tongue. Cressie felt herself suddenly on edge. "But what?" she prompted.

"It does not matter. It is not for me to say," Belle dismissed.

Cressie could see that Belle did not want to remain quiet. She was asking permission. She had something, clearly, undesirable to say, and was wanting Cressie's approval to do so. "Please," invited Cressie. What was one more comment to add to the armoire of verbal licks that her husband had so lovingly filled.

"From a distance, you look as you did when I knew you," Belle murmured carefully. "But upon seeing you now like this, I can see great change in you."

Cressie knew that Belle was not offering her a compliment to her growth and evolution in marriage. She was conveying her sympathy towards Cressie, no doubt looking upon her eyes and seeing dullness where there was once fire. This thought affected her like a searing burn. And one's instinct when they were burned was to get away.

Cressie did this on instinct, immediately retreating from Belle abruptly. She instead walked towards the curtained room where Zara was being measured. "How are you going in there, Zara?" she called.

"Fine, thank you!" Zara replied back through the curtain.

"Cressie," Belle's sympathetic voice sounded from behind her. "Please, forgive me. I spoke out of turn."

Cressie took a deep, composing breath before she turned around to face Belle. She ensured that her face was blank and free from any evidence that she had been so affected only moments ago. "Do not think anything further of it," she replied coolly. "It was nice to see you again, Mrs D-Denham."

Cressie cursed herself internally for stammering over Belle's married name. It was the first time in five years that she had uttered it aloud, and the charade of her composure threatened to crumble. She needed to turn away. Cressie felt foul for her behaviour towards a woman who had been nothing but good to her, but Cressie feared that she would potentially crack in front of a room full of strangers if Belle persisted. She had done so well to master this façade and it could not unravel already.

Belle did not speak again. After a few moments, Cressie subtly checked over her shoulder to see that she had begun speaking to another young lady who seemed just as excited to receive her attention as Zara had been.

It did nothing to dissipate Cressie's guilt. But at least her charade was safe.

When Zara concluded her measurements, the order for the dress was placed, and was promised swiftly.

Belle locked the door to her shop just as soon as the last customers had left and leaned against the door, feeling more exhausted than she had done in months. Of course, the lead up to the Season was her busiest time, but today had been different, and she knew exactly why. Her mind had been racing ever since she had laid eyes upon that familiar face.

After taking a breath, she dismissed her three seamstresses, Nadine, Marie, and Marguerite, and allowed them to retire to the flat above the shop which had once been the home she had shared with Peter. They had each come to her at different times over the past few years, having heard of her story and possessing one of their own. They each had either escaped enslavement, or had been freed from it, and had made the treacherous journey across the Atlantic from varying islands in the Caribbean.

This shop had been Belle's dream, but for Nadine, Marie, and Marguerite, it was a safe harbour. Belle knew all too well the need for a safe harbour. She wondered if Cressie Martin knew that she still had one with Belle as well.

"Bonne nuit, mes amis," Belle called as the three went to the stairs. They all replied a similar parting greeting.

Belle busied herself tidying while she waited for her carriage. She organised the workbench and straightened the bolts of fabric that had been brought out and shown to the customers. She then came to the material swatches she kept and ran her fingers over the ones that had been shown to the young companion of Cressie's. Who was she? Belle wondered. A stepdaughter?

She was obviously a relation as they shared a surname. Belle ought to have asked, but she had been so caught up in the fact that she was seeing Cressie again that the idea hadn't occurred to her. She had been truthful in what she had said to Cressie. When Belle had first seen her, she had recognised her instantly.

Cressie was as beautiful as the day her mother had all but begged for Belle's assistance during her Season. She had the dress and style of a married woman now, but the fair face was quite the same. But as soon as Belle had drawn closer to her, she had seen that the woman who had walked into Desjardins was perhaps the furthest thing possible from young Cressie Martin.

She was the ghost of Cressie Martin.

Cressie's eyes were dead, soulless. It was almost harrowing to look upon, and it twisted Belle's insides with concern. She was pale and expressionless, and looked as though she had not felt and emotion in decades. She held herself with a strange, unnatural poise, and she spoke with a voice that sounded nothing at all like her own.

Of course, it had been five years, and so Belle's memory could be a little foggy, but it was hard to forget a voice as musical and spirited as Cressie's. She made an impression. She had been an impressive young lady with an energy to match.

Whomever that woman was, she was not Cressie.

And Belle could only begin to imagine what had happened to cause such a change in her. She, herself, had enough experiences of her own to begin to paint a picture of Cressie's potential last five years.

A knock at the door made Belle jump, and her head snapped around to see Peter through the glass as he stood at the door. The moment he registered that he had startled her, his eyes narrowed with concern. Peter was so very aware of her. Belle adored his perceptive nature nearly as much as she adored how he managed to stumble through an affectionate affirmation. Peter seemed to read her mind, read her every expression, and he knew exactly how to care for her, sometimes better than Belle knew herself.

She flitted to the door and unlocked it, and Peter pushed it open immediately.

"Are you alright?" he asked, his voice filled with as much concern as Belle had predicted. His hands cupper her cheeks as he looked upon her with his lovely blue eyes.

"Yes," she assured him. "My mind was elsewhere. I was not at all present." In seeing her husband, her mind went to his brother for the first time all day. The resemblance between the brothers could do that, and Belle suddenly felt quite guilty for not thinking of Jem earlier. But her first concern had been for Cressie. Seeing such lifelessness in her had been quite unnerving.

What would Jem think if he knew that Belle had seen Cressie? Jem never spoke about her. He hadn't in years. Nobody brought her name up in conversation, and the accepted belief amongst the family was that Jem was fine.

In Belle's opinion, fine was not a feeling. Fine was not an emotion. Fine was not a state to be in. To be fine was like living in limbo, teetering one way and then another.

Jem had not married himself. He had not courted. He had never shown an inkling of interest in any other woman. He had simply returned to Ashwood and had thrown himself into his worker as Adam's Land Steward.

"You look like you've seen a ghost," Peter murmured, the alarm not leaving his face.

Had not Belle just thought the same thing only moments ago? Peter really could read her mind. "I think I have," she said quietly. "I think she was a ghost."

"Who?" pressed Peter.

"Cressie Martin," Belle replied as her stomach clenched. "I saw her, the ghost of her, today. Here. Peter ... Peter, I don't think she is alright."

CHAPTER 25

"In my defence, I did not actually think that she would put pins on the boy's chair."

Grace had arrived at the same time that Jem's post had done, but his sister's angry mood had seemed a little more pressing than the small stack of letters that now sat idly on his small dining table.

Grace folded her arms across her chest and looked at him in the way that only mothers could. She possessed that same disappointed, 'you ought to have known better' glare that Mrs Denham had mastered in Jem's youth. Considering Jem stood more than a foot taller than his eldest sister, Grace knew how to hold herself to make him feel every one of the eleven years between them.

Despite this, however, Jem could not help but find amusement in the situation. And it felt oddly nice to find amusement.

"Perrie is an impressionable child!" Grace protested. "The only reason she did not get the cane is because of who her father is!"

Jem could only imagine how filthy that nemesis boy of Perrie's would be after that! Perrie put pins on his chair and then escaped punishment because she was the child of a duke. She was a marked young lady, for certain. Jem wondered what his revenge would be.

"Grace, if it makes you feel any better, Perrie asked me for helpful hints on how to drown the boy. I would wager you would much prefer this than your nine-year-old being carted off to the gallows for murder, don't you?"

It clearly did not make Grace feel any better. Her blue eyes narrowed. "I'm furious, Jem," she snapped. "I've got her sweeping the kitchens for Mrs Hayes, but she enjoys every bit of the attention she gets from the servants who think her boisterousness is darling. Why did you not tell me any of this? Why did she not?"

"I imagine Perrie did not disclose it as she knew you would have stopped her. I did not say anything because I had meant it as a joke. How was I to know she would actually go through with it? Perrie is just a little bit mad." Quietly though, Jem was proud of his niece. He hoped the boy who called Perrie the 'Little Imp' had a sore rear as well as a bruised ego.

Grace sighed with exasperation, before she murmured, "She reminds me of you, you know."

"Of me?"

"Of how you were when you were a child. Of how you were ... up until a few years ago, really."

"Before I grew up."

"Before you grew up." The anger in Grace's voice seemed to shift as she realised that she was treading on terrain that had not been disturbed in a very long while. They both knew that it was not time that had resulted in Jem's change, in his sudden maturity.

"Then that should give you hope for Perrie."

It was not change, but heartbreak. And Jem could see in his sister's eyes that she did not want that for her daughter.

"Are you alright living out here by yourself, Jem?" Grace's question was entirely loaded with nuances, and she was treading as carefully as she could. She was the first of their family members to do so in a long time.

Jem took a breath and almost retorted, "I'm not alone. I have Mrs Edwards," referencing the housekeeper and cook that kept him alive. He had not meant to sound so defensive.

Grace laughed awkwardly. "Of course. But I do wonder ... might you ever feel the inclination to have a female presence who is not your housekeeper?"

Jem shifted his weight onto his back foot, and he looked away briefly as he composed himself. "I have enough sisters and nieces and a mother who make certain that I am never starved for female company." Jem quickly discovered that he could not touch the subject. His family had not asked about her in years, and now that he was so close to speaking of her, Jem found that he couldn't. He felt that wound so keenly, it being still so fresh and raw, that if Grace poked at it, he would bleed uncontrollably.

Grace seemed to sense this as she nodded in an accepting fashion. "Yes, well, please make sure to direct my daughter to me should she require any more guidance in her homicidal pursuits."

"You have my word," Jem confirmed. Unless Perrie's plans would directly or indirectly cause the death of this nemesis, then Jem would certainly inform his sister. Harmless pranks, however, could stay confidential.

"I had better return to the house and find something more mind-numbing for Perrie to participate in as punishment," Grace mused, clearly thinking of what she could do. "I might have to enlist Cecily's assistance."

Jem farewelled his sister, before closing the door and taking a breath. He suddenly needed to take a moment. And in taking that moment, he wondered if he had secretly wanted Grace to ask. Jem soon abandoned the thought, as he tended to do with any hope that surfaced, and he decided to resume his day.

He would first deal with his correspondence, and then he would return to his study. What was the time? He was a little hungry and wondered how far away luncheon was. Jem approached the table and began flicking through the letters.

Quite a lot of his role as the Land Steward for the Ashwood estate was correspondence with the tenants, and so Jem received word from them quite often. When he reached the final letter in the stack, Jem noticed the hand immediately. He did not need to check for the sender.

"Belle," he mumbled to himself as he turned the letter over, choosing to read that one first. Belle's hand was childlike, but neat and legible despite her occasional spelling mistakes, indicative of a person learning to read and write in adulthood. Jem admired her perseverance, however, and considered his own literacy a blessing. He broke the seal with his finger and unfolded the letter.

Dearest Jem,

I can hardle begin to find the wrds. I can hardle write.

I have resseld with myself and the desishon of wether or not to tell you about this. But I must. I feel that in my heart.

I saw Cressie today. She came to my shop with anuther lady and I culd not beleve my eyes. She has chanjed so much I hardle recogniz her, but it was her, and my heart just new.

She is not safe, and I do not no what to do or how to help. I do not no what you can do ether, but I had to tell you. I will keep an eye on her this season, and I will tri to get her to tell me. But my heart compelld me to tell you to.

I hope this duz not hcrt you, Jcm.

You no we love you.

Yours,

Belle

Jem read over the letter again and again, ensuring that he had understood Belle's words completely. Little mistakes aside, he comprehended her words, and there could be no misunderstanding. Jem's heart completely withered, shattered, and fell from his chest all at once, his blood running cold.

He had come to close to being asked about her not ten minutes earlier when Grace had been standing right here in his cottage. And as if Fate was listening, here it was, news of Cressie. For how long had he wanted news? For how long had he avoided news for fear it would hurt even more?

Lord! He had been able to bear it! Somehow, on some unconscious level, Jem had been able to bear it knowing that she was looked after, safe, content even, living in a manor somewhere, even if she was the wife of somebody else.

But this was clearly not the case. Jem could hear Belle's fear in her written words. That same fear settled in his bones the instant Jem had read her name. Cressie wasn't safe. It did not matter from what. She wasn't safe, and that was enough to make him sick. It was enough to take him right back to the morning that he had woken up without her. It was enough to make him wish that he had awoken, that he had managed to hold her and to keep her safe.

But what could he do?

He knew what he wanted to do. Jem wanted to storm the bloody manor of Everett Delaney, torch the place, and steal Cressie away to safety. He wanted to bring her here, where she would be safe and loved and treasured, and ...

Jem threw his hands down on the dining table and he took a breath, willing his mind to stop racing, and to think practically.

Cressie had not written a word in five years. Not a peep since she had left his bed that morning. There was a chance, a great chance indeed, that she had forgotten about him. She might not love him anymore. She might not have ever loved him in the way that he had loved her.

As soon as these thoughts entered his mind, Jem decided that he did not care. They did not matter. Cressie owed him nothing. What she deserved, however, was something else entirely. She had given up her life for her mother, and now, for whatever reason, she was unsafe. Belle had not specified that the reason was her husband, but it was not hard to jump to conclusions.

Jem could never be the sort of man to take from Cressie.

Jem had asked his brother-in-law for permission to take his office to London for a few weeks. What he would find there and what he would do when he got there were something else entirely. Adam had responded by granting him a summer holiday.

Adam clearly was not as perturbed about the nails on the chair incident as Grace was.

When Jem asked what his expected return date was, Adam had responded by saying, "When you feel like it. You have not had an hour off in years, Jem."

And so, Jem packed his things. He packed everything without having a plan, an idea, an iota of a clue of what to do. What he wanted to do, and what was possible, were two separate entities. But he knew one thing was for certain. He had to see her. He had to see her with his own eyes and make sense of Belle's words.

Jem had not forgotten a thing about her. He could still see her face as clear in his mind as though she had left him that very morning. He would know. He would know if she had changed. He would know if something was wrong. He would know if she was unsafe.

The selfish, the very selfish, part of him wanted to find a reason to stage a gallant rescue. But the decent part of him wanted Belle to be wrong. He couldn't live with it if she truly were unsafe. He hoped, he sincerely did, that she had forgotten about him. He hoped that she was happy, that she had found some happiness in the life she had married into.

Whatever the truth was, Jem was about to find out.

CHaPTer 26

It had been two weeks since Cressie and Zara had arrived in London. They had only been back to Belle's shop once to confirm Zara's debutante gown, as well as to order a half dozen other designs for subsequent invitations that would undoubtedly follow. They expected Zara's debutante gown to be delivered in the coming days, ready for the presentation ball this coming Friday.

It had also been two weeks since Cressie had been in the presence of her husband, and yet she felt just as caged as she had done in Yorkshire. Distance had done nothing to loosen the chains that Everett had on both her body and her mind.

"... I saw Anne Kimpton walking today from my window. I went to school with her, you know. I swear she was wearing one of Belle Desjardins' gowns. I feel I would know them anywhere now." Zara spoke, often to herself, as she filled the silence at mealtimes.

It was the morning, and breakfast had been served. Cressie would ordinarily have been served up in bed as a married woman, but she could not well leave Zara alone to eat. So, her maid served Cressie her tray in the dining room each morning and stood there to watch exactly what she ate.

Zara, on the contrary, was served a full portion for every meal.

Cressie had become used to eating so little that she did not suffer from hunger anymore. Or perhaps she had managed to somehow talk herself out of hunger. It had been a realisation she had made some time ago. Everett preferred her thin, of course. But he loved her weak.

"... It really makes me wonder what she will be wearing at the presentation. I know that we will all be wearying varying shades of white, but I hope my lace – Cressie!" The way in which Zara's tone shifted made Cressie jump. As if she had been able to read Cressie's mind, she said, "Cressie, you are about wasting away in front of me, and no wonder!" she exclaimed. "You pick at an egg each morning and consume nothing of substance. I have been noticing, you know!" Zara lifted the dish that was in front of her, only to reach over to Cressie's, before she passed over two thick slices of ham and cheese. "Please, eat them!" she urged.

"That won't be necessary," Cressie's maid, Imelda Wrigley said, stepping forward from the side of the room to reach for Cressie's plate. "Mrs Delaney does not require anything further."

Zara frowned at the sudden and unorthodox interruption from Imelda. "I think Mrs Delaney can decide for herself if she requires anything further. Don't you have anything better to do this morning than to stand there, Wrigley?"

Cressie could hear the frustration in Zara's voice, and it sounded completely foreign as she was so used to her young niece's excited and optimistic tones.

But Imelda ignored Zara's question and took Cressie's breakfast plate from her. She then disappeared through the servant's entrance with the remnants of Zara's breakfast upon it.

Zara was dumbfounded, and Cressie said nothing. She did not fight it. What was the use?

"I ... I have never had a maid of my own before," Zara murmured, "but I do not think that I would allow her to ..."

"You're right," Cressie said, interrupting her. "You have never had a maid before. You don't know." Zara didn't know what it was to have a husband either. Perhaps Everett could not be called a husband, as Cressie had observed husbands in her time who were not at all like her own. Zara had never had an owner before.

And it was her responsibility this Season to ensure that Zara never was subjected to the life that Cressie had fallen victim to. Zara did not need to know. She was innocent, optimistic, with a joy about her spirit that reminded Cressie of the remnants of her own soul that were buried deep within her.

Cressie's soul had been taken, along with everything else that she possessed. Zara could yet live. She could yet be happy. There was hope for her where there was none for Cressie.

So, she took a breath, picked up her teacup, and changed the subject. "Have you thought about what you might say should the Queen address you on Friday? She has been known to verbally acknowledge some of the young ladies each year."

An invitation to Ashwood Place for the opening ball of the Season had become quite the coveted honour for the debutantes and their mothers. After being presented before the Queen, the ladies paraded and pranced around the Ashwood ballroom in their finest ensembles as guests of the Duke and Duchess of Ashwood.

As Grace had not set foot in London in years, it was often Cecily who made the trip to London as host, but to enjoy the social chess matches of the summer. But as Cecily had not made the trip this year either, it had been left to Jack and Claire to host the ball.

Despite the fact that Jem was the only member of the Beresford family in residence at Ashwood Place, he could not host. Who would accept an invitation from a Land Steward?

A voice in Jem's head bitterly retorted probably the same amount of people who would accept a proposal from one. It was fresh. The pain was fresh and raw, festering and inflamed, as he combed over the guest list for the four hundredth time that day.

Mrs Everett Delaney

Miss Zara Delaney

She had accepted. She would be here in a matter of hours. He would see her for the first time in five years. Would she see him? Would she know him?

Would he know her?

Belle had repeated her worries to Jem in person when he had arrived in London, and Jem had all but to retrain himself from calling upon her there and then. But he couldn't. She was a married woman and there were rules. Jem hated them.

He had been counting the hours until this day, going over in his head of what he might say to her when they met again. But in his heart, Jem knew that what he would say depended entirely on what he saw in her. If she was happy, if Belle was wrong, then perhaps it would not be right at all to even approach her.

Jem wished her happy. He could lose her if it meant that she was happy.

"Jack, you know those biscuits are to be served tonight!"

Claire's voice disturbed Jem's thoughts, and he looked up from the guest list to see his sister's family waltz into the ballroom.

"I had to be certain the biscuits weren't poisoned," Jack replied with a shrug.

"So, you decided to test them on our daughters?" Claire challenged, folding her arms over her chest.

Jack grinned sheepishly as he looked down at their two girls who had followed their parents inside. "What do you know, they're right as rain. They're safe to eat." Jack then fished another biscuit from his pocket and popped it into his mouth whole.

"You're impossible," Claire declared, but she could not hide the burgeoning smile that teased her lips.

"Yes, yes, impossibly handsome, I know," Jack agreed. "It's a burden, but one I endure."

Claire shook her head as she rolled her eyes and went to turn away from her husband. But he was quick with a devilish smile as he caught her hand and captured her in a tight embrace.

"I am also impossibly in love with you. It cannot be helped."

The ease and declaration of affection between husband and wife was so intimate that Jem knew he ought to have looked away. But for a moment, it was also such a clear reminder of what he did not have, and yet what all his siblings had found.

Why was he forsaken?

Jem heard his nieces exclaim noises of disgust as their father kissed their mother. Jack laughed lightly as he pulled away from Claire only for a moment, before fishing two more biscuits from his pockets to give to Jackie and Maria. "Don't tell Mama," he whispered, though still right in front of Claire who, again, was rolling her eyes with a smile. Jack's eyes then flicked to Jem across the room. "Why don't you two go and make Uncle Jem smile for me? Mama needs to see to some last-minute details for this evening," Jack encouraged artfully.

Jackie and Maria obeyed their father immediately, allowing Jack to steal Claire from the ballroom in as much time as Jem devoted his attention onto his nieces and not onto his sister's business with her husband.

They would be a welcome distraction, anyway. There was only so many times Jem could stare at the words 'Mrs Everett Delaney' without the inclination to set something on fire.

His sister's girls were so different. Really, the only similarity between the two was their height. At seven and six, Jackie and Maria were about the same height, with Jackie having perhaps a half inch on her younger sister.

Maria was Jack's double in female form. The whole family declared it whenever they saw her. She had the same dark, unruly hair and mischievous hazel brown eyes. She had even inherited her father's wicked smile, though Maria's was still filled with little baby teeth.

Jackie, on the other hand, was very fair, with very light blonde hair inherited from her Aunt Susanna. Her delicate features were very elfin-like, but what was most remarkable about her were her expressive green eyes.

They were nothing at all alike but were as inseparable as sisters and best friends could be.

"Can we come to the party, Uncle Jem?" Maria asked him sweetly.

"No, Maria," whispered Jackie, elbowing her sister softly in the ribs. "Papa said we had to make Uncle Jem smile."

Maria pursed her lips, before suggesting, "Should we tickle him?"

But Jem did smile, he chuckled even, at the two little girls before him. While he could and did feel envy and sadness at what his siblings had found, he would never take his own happiness over theirs. "It's been a long time since I have danced. Would you two help me practise?"

Jackie and Maria eagerly agreed, and Jem entertained them for a little while by humming tunes that he knew while twirling them around the empty ballroom. They girls laughed hysterically and joyfully as they watching their skirts fan out around their legs.

"You're smiling, Uncle Jem!" Jackie declared cheerfully as Jem spun her.

"Do you think Papa will give us another biscuit then, Jackie?" Maria called out to her sister excitedly as she was twirled on Jem's other hand.

"Maybe!" Jackie said enthusiastically.

And at the idea of another treat, both girls sprinted from the ballroom, leaving Jem standing in the middle of the dancefloor.

A few hours later, Ashwood Place was alive with noise and gossip, just as it had been during the first Season Jem had been in London. Speculation was already running rampant about which lady would make the best match, which debutante made the best impression, and which poor girl had the most unfortunate appearance and connections.

Jem possessed neither Cecily's talent for dressing down these women with her tongue, nor the inclination at that moment, as he kept a keen eye on the arrivals.

Jack and Claire were dutifully hosting, greeting their guests with polite attention, though neither of them looked especially pleased to be the centre of such attention. Claire had always been a little awkward about the nobility of the Beresfords, and Jack had certainly never aspired to be his brother. But nevertheless, when called upon, they represented the family well, and looked exactly the part as Lord Jack and Lady Claire.

It was hard for Jem not to sense eyes on him. He was a young, well-dressed man who appeared to be a gentleman, even though he was not one. Though the ladies in attendance did not know that. It was easy for them to assume that he was one of the eligible bachelors in attendance that evening out to sample what this Season had to offer.

Of course, he could not be introduced to any one of them as he had no acquaintances here. Unless Jack and Claire came over to introduce Jem to anyone, he would be left alone to watch the door.

Jem's only interest in marriage was the already married woman he had travelled to London to see, the check on.

A few minutes after the clock had chimed eight, another two of the invited guests arrived. The young, red-haired lady stepped into the ballroom on the arm of her blonde chaperone, a lady far too young to be her mother.

She was a lady far too young to look like ... to look like a ghost.

"Presenting Mrs Everett Delaney and Miss Zara Delaney!" cried the announcer.

Cressie.

CHAPTER 27

Cressie watched as a servant tied the ribbon of Zara's dance card around her wrist. Zara was positively elated as the next step was to be introduced to the hosts of the evening.

Cressie knew them immediately. Of course, she had expected to see one of them, any of them, as this was an Ashwood ball. She had expected the Duke and Duchess, but the duke's brother was as fine a host as any. And he and his wife certainly would not remember meeting Cressie five years earlier.

She felt relieved if anything. The very idea of attending an Ashwood ball had tied her stomach up in knots, and she felt all sort of apprehension and dread at faltering, at breaking behind the perfectly disguised mask of indifference she had applied to her face and body all these years.

Cressie thought that if anyone were to know her, it would have been the duchess. But thankfully, she was not here. She took a breath and refocussed her attention on Zara, and gently guided her towards Lord Jack Beresford and his wife, Lady Claire.

Zara curtseyed deeply, and Cressie followed suit. Jack smiled and nodded his head in acknowledgement, and Cressie could have sworn that Claire appeared a little out of place. Her charade was not as well-practised as Cressie's was.

"You are both very welcome to the Ashwood ball, Mrs Delaney, Miss Delaney," Jack greeted them formally. "Have you travelled far to be here in attendance this Season?"

Zara looked to Cressie for approval, and Cressie nodded encouragingly for her niece to answer.

"My aunt and I have travelled from my uncle's home in Yorkshire, my lord," Zara replied, nerves lacing her voice.

"My, what a journey," remarked Claire, sounding genuinely shocked. "I certainly hope you find your happiness in London, Miss Delaney. I must say, your gown is absolutely lovely. Is it by Belle Desjardins?" she inquired.

"Yes!" gushed Zara. "Oh, thank you, my lady," she added quickly, realising she had not accepted the compliment politely. "I am a great admirer of Miss Desjardins' craft."

"As am I," replied Claire with a wry smile. "I do have a rather precious attachment to her as my sister-in-law. She is married to my brother, Mr Peter Denham."

Denham. Crack.

Cressie flinched. Visibly, uncontrollably, and rather dramatically.

Zara could not continue her conversation with Claire as her attention quickly reverted to Cressie. She latched onto Cressie's arm as she gasped. "Oh, are you alright, Cressie?"

"Cressie?" Claire repeated in a questioning tone, her brows furrowing in confusion as her blue eyes began to inspect Cressie's face.

Cressie averted her eyes, instead offering her niece a look of assurance. "Yes, yes, I just lost my footing for a moment. Perhaps I ought to sit down."

"Alright." Zara nodded.

At that moment, the next invited guests had arrived and were being announced, and Cressie and Zara were being ushered along by a servant. Cressie was thankful to be away before Claire connected her name to the distant memory that seemed to be teasing her mind in that moment.

"Shall we find a chair?" Zara turned her head to look around the ballroom to find a vacant seat.

"No." Cressie shook her head. "It must have been a momentary lapse. I am quite fine. We ought to begin your evening. I am certain the gentlemen here will be eager to gain your favour and a place on your dance card." Cressie, herself, took a breath. It was fine. She was fine. Her mask was intact, and she had a job to do.

Zara nodded, her smile returning to her face. As they began to operate inside the ballroom, she was quick to reconnect with a few of her school friends, who were able to begin the task of the introductions. Zara was introduced to Mr Gilbert Avery and Mr Frederick Dixon, both of whom were handsome, young gentlemen who took an immediate shine to the beautiful debutante.

Cressie, herself, formed acquaintances with the mothers of Zara's school friends, who were quick to inform Cressie of the virtues and values of Zara's upcoming dance partners.

"Mr Avery comes from an excellent family, I am so informed," Mrs Liston, mother of Mary, uttered to Cressie. "Good connections but I have heard their fortune has somewhat dwindled this last decade. The elder Mr Avery is to blame. It is now the responsibility of the younger Mr Avery to marry well."

Cressie nodded in understanding. She would be keeping her eye on that young man, then. She felt suddenly foolish in calling them 'young men' when there was a high likelihood of them being several years older than her. She was most definitely the youngest chaperone in the room by at least two decades.

"Mr Dixon, I hear, has a modest income of about three thousand a year," added Mrs Beswick, mother of Charlotte. "But he is heir to both his father and his maternal uncle. I believe their lands combined are worth some ten thousand a year." Mrs Beswick's eyes were practically dancing as Mr Dixon claimed her daughter for the next dance, as Zara was escorted by Mr Avery.

Mrs Liston grinned with satisfaction as another young gentleman came to claim her daughter for his dance. "And that is Mr David Ferris, of the Shropshire Ferrises," she informed them both. "He has just inherited twenty thousand pounds from his grandmother."

"How fortunate he was that she died right in time for the Season!" exclaimed Mrs Beswick.

"From your lips to God's ears, my dear," agreed Mrs Liston ruthlessly.

As the women talked, despite their scheming and gossiping, Cressie felt herself relax a little into her role. She was able to let go of the shock at hearing the 'Denham' name and she had not seen or spoken to the hosts at all since their entrance.

Even if Claire had pieced together her memories, perhaps she did not care to reacquaint herself with Cressie. It was the best possible outcome.

Zara returned to Cressie after each dance, a little more flushed every time, and gushed over each one of her partners. There was a delighted sparkle in her eyes as she became swept up in the romance and grandeur of the evening, and Cressie listened diligently to the information provided to her by the mothers.

Zara was clearly a very desirable prospective wife, owing of course to her name and fortune. She was not without a partner for several hours.

But as the clock neared midnight and the band took a hiatus for refreshment, the guests mingled and meandered into the palatial dining room. Zara hung on Cressie's arm as she spoke about the dazzling eyes of her previous partner as they followed Mrs Liston and Mary, and Mrs Beswick and Charlotte.

The tables were laden with divinely presented savoury and sweet dishes. Guests stood about with silver plates piled high with the exquisite food, and Cressie did not know quite where to look. She had not seen so much food in a very long time, and it was quite overwhelming.

Mr Avery appeared at Zara's side rather gallantly and offered her his arm so that he might assist her in putting together a plate. And the minute Cressie wasn't by Zara's side, the overwhelming feeling quickly began to consume her.

It was the food. There was so much of it. And it all felt prohibited and illegal and wrong. She felt as if she were to touch any of it, he would know, and she would be vilified and cursed and made to feel as though she was worth nothing at all.

Cressie's lower lip trembled uncontrollably for a brief moment as her composure waned. She wanted to leave, to run, to be anywhere that wasn't here. Except she couldn't. She had a responsibility. Her life was not her own. It had never been. It had once belonged to her mother, and now it belonged to Everett, and he had loaned her to his niece. She was property, and always would be, and she could not lose her composure before dishes of biscuits.

This was not a new discovery for her. She had come to terms with it long ago. It was just the food. The food had been shocking for her, and she was already in a heightened state after meeting with Jack and Claire again. This night would be over soon, and she would be able to sleep, and when she would wake, Cressie was certain her mask would be firmly back in place.

"Do you know who that gentleman is?" Mrs Liston asked Mrs Beswick.

Cressie barely heard them.

"No. Did you know I was wondering about him myself? I noticed him earlier. Fine young man, very handsome and well looking. A little tall, but Charlotte could always have some heeled slippers made if he had a fortune to tempt." Both mothers laughed deviously.

"I noticed him earlier as well," Mrs Liston replied once she had regained control of her laughter. "He hasn't danced at all! But he has been looking this way very often. He is only human, though, and my Mary is looking very lovely."

"Perhaps he is shy," theorised Mrs Beswick. "We ought to find someone to make an introduction. I wonder who knows him. I wonder if they know of his family or his income? Mrs Delaney, do you know him?"

"Pardon?" Cressie's voice sounded like a crackly whisper. She promptly cleared her throat and feigned a slight cold.

"That gentleman there, do you know him?" Mrs Beswick repeated, subtly gesturing in the direction behind Cressie.

"I highly doubt it," Cressie replied, without bothering to turn. "It has been many years since I have been in London."

"I would wager he is very rich indeed," Mrs Liston declared quietly to them both. "Don't you agree? He has not been attaching himself eagerly to the young ladies with dowries. It is highly likely he has no need of a dowry. What's to say that he is not spending this evening observing the young ladies, waiting to find the prettiest one? He does himself a service by mysteriously refusing to dance with anyone. Whomever he calls upon tomorrow will be very fortunate indeed."

"Yes, yes, I quite agree," Mrs Beswick said with wily enthusiasm. "And as you noticed, the gentleman has been looking this way quite often. Charlotte has received quite a bit of attention herself. He must see that she is quite the prospect."

The poor gentleman, whomever he was, ought to run away if he knew what was good for him. These women knew nothing about him, not even his name, and they were quite prepared to sign their daughters over to him. Had her own mother had similar conversations with the other mothers during her Season? Had she spoke of Everett in such a way?

Cressie felt foolish for even wondering. Mrs Martin had spoken about Everett in this way directly to Cressie. His money had been enough to erase any doubt in Mrs Martin's mind as to his character. Cressie would never be so naïve.

Cressie turned her head then, determined to see this man, to know his face so that she could steer Zara clear. "Which one is he?" she asked Mrs Liston and Mrs Beswick quietly. They all appeared the same to her.

"He is by the urn of flowers near the door," Mrs Liston replied quietly. "Carefully now, he is looking this way." She averted her eyes nonchalantly as she went to peruse the offerings on the tables. Mrs Beswick followed her.

Cressie's eyes found the urn featuring an elegant arrangement of greenery and chrysanthemums. There was a figure standing beside it, a tall figure dressed just as sharply as every other gentleman in the ballroom. Except that he was not like every other gentleman in the room. She could tell that immediately by the way that he carried himself. The way he stood, taller than everyone, but not looking down, sparked something deep within her.

She knew it immediately. She did not need to see his face to know. Except she did so unwittingly. Her eyes found his with a mind completely their own. And there they were. Oceans. And for a moment, Cressie felt that if she never saw the sea with her own eyes, the colour of his would be enough. His eyes were the same as they always had been, and they were trained solely on her.

His eyes had not changed, but his face had. His figure had.

Jem.

He looked older, more mature, with a wise brow and a stronger, more defined jaw. He looked like carried a great weight, a great many responsibilities to place the lines there permanently.

It was Jem.

Faint lines crossed his forehead, while his dark hair was cut neatly in the style of a gentleman. There was still curl to it, as though it would fall into his eyes if he ran his hand back through it.

Jem was here.

He had grown into his limbs, his torso was now broad like his shoulders, and his arms and legs appeared proportionate, when once that had made him prone to clumsiness.

Jem!

He was as handsome this evening as he had been the morning that she had left him sleeping soundly. And as that memory consumed Cressie's mind, she realised that she had not been breathing. And it was too late. As her overwhelmed head became starved of air, Cressie stumbled, falling, and her mind fell away before she hit the floor, eclipsing her world in total darkness.

CHAPTER 28

Jem had watched her all night. He had watched her helplessly, forlornly, powerlessly. He kept looking for glimpses of the girl he had once known, of the girl he had once been hopelessly in love with.

But she wasn't there.

Cressie wasn't there.

Belle had been right. She was a ghost of a woman. How could they not see it? How could all of these people around them laugh and dance and converse and flirt and not see that there was a woman in their midst who appeared as lively as a corpse?

This woman, Mrs Delaney, as she had become, appeared to be about two stone lighter than when he had seen her last. She had already been a small, perfectly proportionate young woman when he had known her, and yet now she looked as though a small gust of wind would blow her over. She was pale and frail, with the bones in her cheeks and collar bones far too pronounced.

Her brown eyes were not warm and vibrant, but dull and lifeless, and even the way she carried her figure was demure and reserved, entirely lacking in any sort of confidence. It was as though someone had taken Cressie's entire spirit from her body and had beaten it with a wooden stick like they would a dirty rug.

Cressie's entire being could be found in her spirit. It was something that he had loved entirely about her. She found joy in everything, even when there was much in her life that lacked joy.

For a moment, while standing in that ballroom looking upon the woman she had become, Jem was transported back to the day where she had smiled as big as the world while they stood in the fountain. She dreamed of the sea, and he had taken her to a fountain, and she had found such joy in it.

What had happened to Cressie? Jem could only speculate. He could only worry and imagine. But she had gone to that wedding his Cressie. Jem could only hope that his Cressie was still in there somewhere.

Jem had wanted to be wrong. He had wanted to see her, to lay his own eyes upon her once more and see that she was happy and content in her new life. It would have provided him some peace, he had theorised. He would have been able to close this chapter of his life and potentially not yearn for Cressie any longer.

But now that was entirely impossible. Cressie was here, and she was very real to him once again. He could no longer pretend she was safe and happy. He did not exactly know what to do, but he had to do something.

Jem had not been able to approach her. He had done barely anything all evening but skulk on the edge of the room and observe her. Cressie had not noticed him. She kept her attention focussed solely on the red-headed debutante she was chaperoning, occasionally entertaining whatever the mothers with whom she was standing were saying.

Every part of himself yearend desperately to approach her, to take her hand, and to whisk her away somewhere safe where he could make certain she was alright. But he couldn't. Be damned these rules, these expectations. He hated them. He hated every one of them, for they were what had separated them in the first place. Jem had not spotted Cressie's mother this evening. Was Mrs Martin proud of the waif her daughter had become?

"Jemmy," hissed Claire.

Jem had not at all noticed his older sister approach him, and so he practically jumped out of his skin and into the vase of chrysanthemums which he was standing beside.

"You ought to wear a bell, Claire," he murmured, unwilling tearing his eyes from Cressie to give his attention to Claire.

"I haven't been able to get away to speak to you. I do not know how Grace, or the dowager duchess do these sorts of affairs. They are entirely taxing." Claire shook her head as she dismissed the thought, before she returned to her point. "I did not realise it was her, not until the young Miss Delaney called her 'Cressie'. I did not recognise her!" Her blue eyes filled with sympathy as she placed her hands on Jem's arms. "This must be very difficult for you."

Jem did not know how to answer his sister. The fact that it was difficult, the fact that it was seemingly against some unwritten law that Jem could not simply walk across the ballroom and speak to Cressie infuriated him.

Jem turned back towards Cressie, and she had not moved. She was still standing with the other two mothers as they talked. Cressie seemed to be listening, though she was not contributing to the conversation.

"She is here as a chaperone to Miss Zara Delaney," Claire explained from behind him. "Miss Delaney must, of course, be a relative of her ... her husband's."

Jem said nothing.

"Jemmy," Claire said helplessly, "this will not do. Why don't you go upstairs to bed?"

"Because I am not eight years old anymore, Claire," Jem bit back. He was doing perfectly well torturing himself by looking upon the woman he'd let slip through his fingers.

Claire said nothing further, and Jem would make certain to apologise for snapping at her later when he was not so infuriated. But at that moment, he noticed the two women who were standing with Cressie periodically looking over at him, making rather unsubtle attempts to be nonchalant.

Were they speaking about him? Did they know who he was? How could they? Jem was not acquainted with anyone at this ball, and he had made no attempt to be introduced to anyone despite the questioning looks and glances he had received throughout the evening.

And then Cressie looked at him.

It happened so quickly, it caught Jem entirely off guard. Her brown eyes were looking into his directly for the first time in five years, and everyone around them might have disappeared.

He had observed so much that was missing from her already, but in the moment that she looked at him, Jem could see her. For a split second, Jem could see Cressie again. She knew him and he knew her. They knew each other in a way that would always remain between them.

Could this be the moment? Could he make a case to speak to her now? Could he feign some need to –

Before Jem could even finish his though, Cressie's brown eyes disappeared into the back of her head so frighteningly quickly. Her legs completely buckled beneath her and she crumpled to the floor in a heap of petticoats.

Everyone in the immediate vicinity became immediately alarmed. Ladies swooned as their gentleman admirers caught them and fawned over them. The chaperones Cressie had been standing with produced fans as they attempted to rouse her with the breeze, and Cressie's young charge reappeared with a terrified expression on her fair face.

"Cressie!" she exclaimed with a scream.

Jem launched from his position, practically pushing through the crowd in order to reach Cressie. "Send for a doctor!" he shouted over his shoulder to Claire, though at this point in time, he could not care who sent for the doctor, so long as one arrived.

Jem bumped into the mothers accidentally as he fell to his knees beside the unconscious Cressie. They made noises of discomfort, and a few remarks of, "Well, I never!" but Jem ignored them.

"Who are you?" her charge frantically demanded to know as Jem's hands hovered over Cressie's body.

"I am the brother of your host this evening," Jem uttered, "I will ensure that this woman is properly cared for until a doctor arrives." He needed to play the part. "What is her name?"

"Cressie," Miss Zara Delaney replied, before she immediately corrected herself, "Cressida! Mrs Delaney. She is married to my uncle."

Her name was Cressie and in another life she could have born another surname beginning with 'D'.

Jem gently lifted her torso and supported her back with one of his arms, while he hooked the other underneath her knees as he gathered up the layers of her skirts. It required no effort at all to lift Cressie. Honestly, he worked harder to carry some of his nieces and nephews. Jem was gentle all the same, acutely aware that several hundred pairs of eyes were watching the display before them.

What would they do with the knowledge that Jem had been passionately in love with the woman in his arms five years earlier? What would they do if they learned that his feelings were practically unchanged?

Jem held her closely as he whipped her out of the ballroom. He could hear that Miss Delaney was following, as well as a few others. His sister, he would have wagered.

Jem carried Cressie up the stairs, and without even concentrating on to where he was bringing her, he took her directly to his own bedroom, the bedroom that they had shared together for just one night. Miss Delaney was helpful in opening the door for him, and Jem took a deep breath as he carried Cressie inside. Claire was quick to assist in lighting the dark room as she lit an oil lamp that was sitting idly near the door.

Jem gently laid Cressie down on the bed atop the linens moments later.

Cressie's head flopped to the side against the pillow.

"It's probably because she hasn't eaten anything," Miss Delaney stressed. "That can happen, can't it? She picks at her food like a bird!"

Jem could hear the genuine concern that Miss Delaney had for Cressie, and the anguish upon her face was entirely sincere. Claire had been behind them, and she was flanked by Jack, as well as a housemaid who had arrived with cloths and water.

Claire stepped in to put a gentle arm around Miss Delaney as Jem stepped backward. The housemaid placed the basin of fresh water on the table beside his bed and dipped one of the clean cloths into it, soaking it. She wrung the cloth out and leaned over the bed to dab Cressie's forehead. Jem longed to be the one to do that.

"Mrs Delaney will be just fine," Claire promised. "It was awfully warm downstairs. I will have some food brought up so she might eat if you are so concerned."

"I don't know why she picks like she does ... it's something I noticed ... and her maid ... her maid takes her dishes when she's not finished and ... oh, please be well, Cressie!" Zara stressed as she rushed to Cressie's side, taking hold of one of Cressie's limp hands.

Immediately Jem began to hold onto the details of what Zara was saying, in and amongst her hysterical tone. He had well noticed how thin Cressie appeared to be, and here was an eyewitness to attest to the fact that she didn't eat.

Why?

When the doctor arrived, the bedroom was cleared save for Zara, Claire, and the housemaid so that she could fetch anything that the doctor required.

Jem couldn't bear to the return to the ball as Jack needed to. He found himself pacing in the hallway, waiting for news, and imagining up whatever reason that there could be for Cressie's eating habits.

Jem was halfway down the corridor towards the duke's bedroom when he heard the door open to his own room. Claire's voice carried down the space between them as she said, "We shall just let her rest now. It is excellent news that she is awake. You both will stay tonight and go home in the morning when Mrs Delaney is well enough."

Jem stood frozen in place as he watched the doctor and the housemaid follow the two women out of the room and down the hallways in the opposite direction. They had not seen him standing there.

Cressie was awake. And she was mere feet from him.

Jem's legs began moving before he could even consciously take note of what he was doing. He practically sprinted so that he could get to her faster. He paid no mind to decorum when he pushed open the door without even thinking to knock.

He paused in the doorway as he looked inside, his eyes settling on the bed immediately, and finding the same pair of brown eyes that had been looking at him only an hour or so ago downstairs.

She was sitting up in the bed, though underneath the covers this time, her face ashen. But she didn't appear surprised. "You shouldn't be here." Her words were barely more than a whisper.

Jem stepped into the room carefully, as though he were testing the waters of a dangerous river, but he never dropped her gaze. "Are you alright?" he asked, his voice far hoarser than he had realised. He nervously cleared his throat.

"The servant is going to return with a tray. You shouldn't be here," Cressie reiterated, her tone more forceful.

Jem could not stop himself. He continued to put one foot in front of the other as he approached the bed carefully. As he did, he could see the flimsy façade of Cressie's determination chip, threatening to crumble completely.

"Cressie," Jem whispered, stopping at his thighs touched the edge of his bed. His hands at his sides were mere inches from her left, which was lying flat atop the bed linen.

He could have sworn that he saw a tremor rush through her as she mouthed his name, though no sound escaped. Her fingers twitched ever so slightly in his direction, as though she wanted to reach out to him, and yet she couldn't.

Jem's heart flipped in his chest as he took a chance of his own, reach down to collect her cold, thin hand in his own and squeezing it tightly. As he did so, he felt his heart swell as he saw a glimpse of her, a glimpse of warmth in the depths of her eyes. She was looking at him, looking into him. She was there. His Cressie was there with him. Jem slowly knelt down, taking one knee at a time, keeping hold of Cressie's hand before he held it to his chest.

"Tell me," he murmured gently, not elaborating further on what he wanted to know. He wanted to know everything, but he would listen to anything.

But the moment he did this, he saw Cressie visibly harden. She snatched her hand away from him and her eyes grew cold and dull. Cressie vanished just as quickly as she had appeared. "Get out!" she demanded forcefully.

CHAPTER 29

Cressie's heartbeat rung in her ears as she watched Jem Denham retreat from the bedroom, his bedroom. It had not escaped her attention as to what room she had been placed in. The very memories that they had created in this room were entirely intoxicating and quickly began to contribute to the overwhelming feelings that were consuming her in that moment.

As soon as the door closed, tears began to stream down Cressie's face, her eyes producing more and more than could seem humanly possible. Every part of her wanted to scream for him, to call him back. It was Jem, her Jem. Jem had once, briefly and entirely, been every good thing in her life.

Cressie quickly buried her face into the pillow next to her and screamed, sobbing as a scent she had long forgotten filled her senses. Her screams were muffled by the silk and feathers, but the fabric absorbed her uncontrollable tears.

Please, come back, Cressie willed into the darkness, though no words escaped her mouth. Please, come back and see me. Come back and notice what has become of me. Find me. Help me.

But Cressie remained alone. She was alone as she always was. Never physically. Cressie was rarely alone physically. Her gaoler was always near to keep an eye on her. But the isolation was crippling. She was isolated from anything and anyone. She could not even speak to her own mother. It was crippling to the point where it had robbed Cressie of who she was. She couldn't speak, couldn't eat, couldn't dress how she wanted. She was not permitted her own money or to travel without permission, and she could not even send a letter without it being read –

Cressie's head suddenly turned to the writing desk in the corner of Jem's bedroom. Even in the dim candlelight, she could see the papers atop of it. Cressie felt fear and trepidation before the idea even crossed her mind. The rules were so ingrained into her that she felt sick before she had even formed a plan.

She had been broken in, broken down so many times, as though she were one of Everett's poor horses. Her will and spirit and determination had been erased from her being after every little rebellion. And as much as a younger Cressie would have been shocked to see the ghost of the woman she had become, it had worked. Everett's conditioning worked. Cressie lacked any fight. To fight made her afraid.

Cressie looked upon the writing desk with fear. She saw an opportunity, and yet her legs did not move to get up and out of the bed. She whimpered as her weakness overcame her and Cressie through herself back into the pillows in shame.

A few minutes later, there was a knock at the door and Cressie's heart stopped.

Jem. Could it be? While she had not been able to cry out, had he heard her cries, her pleas anyway?

But her hopes were dashed the next moment as two housemaids entered the room. One carried a food tray and the other went directly to the fireplace to begin building it up.

"There you are, ma'am," the housemaid said as she placed the tray down across Cressie's legs in the bed. "Eat up, and your strength will be returned in no time."

"Is there anyone out in the hallway?" Cressie asked shakily, completely disregarding what the housemaid had said. Her voice was thick with emotion, evidence that she had been crying, and she shivered at the sound.

"No, ma'am." The young maid shook her head. "Did you send for someone? Would you like for us to summon someone for you?"

"No," Cressie replied all too quickly. Her eyes fell to the dishes that had been brought up for her and her heart sank. It looked like a collection of puddings from the ball, as well as a cut gammon sandwich made from one of the main courses of the evening. There was a class of jelly and cream, and a perfectly decorated chocolate torte, and three Queen's biscuits. What was delectably presented food made Cressie's stomach turn, and she could barely stomach the sight of it.

She could hear Everett's voice in her head if even one biscuit touched her lips, belittling her and criticising her, mocking her. Cressie's lower lip trembled, and she tried as hard as she could to get a handle on it so as not to cry in front of the maids.

Retreat.

The word repeated itself inside of Cressie's mind. The overwhelming emotions that were flooding her mind, that were terrifying her and crippling her, made her want to retreat to what was familiar. It wasn't safe, but it was familiar.

"Would you be so kind as to ask the butler for my carriage to be brought around?" Cressie asked, gently pushing the tray away and out of her sight, before she pushed back the bedclothes. She was still lying in her ballgown, which was now terribly crumpled, but she did not care. "I am quite recovered, and I wish to leave. I need to find my niece."

"Are you sure you are alright, Cressie?" Zara asked her again for the seventeenth time that morning while they sat down to breakfast.

"Yes," Cressie assured her impatiently. "It was terribly hot in that ballroom and I was momentarily overcome. I am perfectly alright."

"Should we send for Uncle Everett at least?"

Cressie's back stiffened as she shook her head. "No ... I would not want to worry him. He is terribly busy, and as you can see. I am fine." Cressie continued to eat her egg knowing that Zara's worried eyes were firmly upon her. "You need not trouble yourself!" she exclaimed as she set down her spoon. "I am fine! I am, however, terribly ashamed about ruining your first experience at a ball." Genuinely, this was not how Cressie had wanted to see Zara look and behave the morning after a ball when they were to expect callers. Zara appeared as though she would not have cared if five and thirty gentlemen appeared at the door.

"Your health is more important than a silly ball," Zara insisted.

Cressie felt a genuine smile turn up the corners of her lips as she felt the care and compassion from her young niece. How she could ever be a relation of Everett's, Cressie would never understand. She knew how important the Season was to Zara.

Cressie was determined to refocus herself. The previous evening had been a shock to the senses. It had been overwhelming to say the least. Seeing Jem again had been something that she had never expected. The feelings that had come along with setting eyes upon him again had been incredible and devastating. To yearn for help and to have no power to seek it was entirely demoralising to the soul.

And so Cressie had retreated. She had retreated to her prison. But it was here that she knew the rhythm. She knew what to expect. She knew what to say and how to be and if she did those things, everything would be fine.

She would be fine.

"We must get you ready for your callers. I imagine the first of many will be here soon," Cressie theorised, changing the subject. "Was there a particular gentleman who caught your eye last night?"

Zara appeared a little uneasy as moving away from the topic of Cressie's health, but nevertheless, she humoured her aunt.

"Well, I quite liked Mr Avery," she confessed coyly. "He was terribly attentive and complimentary. "He told me that my eyes were the colour of forget-me-nots, and that he was not likely to forget that he had seen them."

"How charming," mused Cressie, recalling the fact that Mr Avery's family were in some financial distress and that his marriage would need to be a rich one. Cressie wondered if he had also compared the eyes of any other lady to flowers the previous night.

"There was another gentleman, however," Zara continued.

"Mr Dixon?" asked Cressie. "You danced with him, did you not?"

"No," replied Zara, before she quickly shook her head, "Oh, yes, I did dance with Mr Dixon, but he was not the gentleman to whom I was referring."

"Oh?"

Colour began to trickle into Zara's cheeks and Cressie's brows furrowed.

"I don't actually know his name. We were not introduced, but I do know he was the brother of our hostess." Zara smiled wistfully as her eyes widened. "Oh, Cressie, you should have seen the way he swooped in to rescue you. He was quite the gallant hero!"

While Zara was flushed with colour, Cressie felt all the blood drain from her face.

"He was so handsome and mysterious. He did not dance with anyone that I recall." Zara shook her head bashfully. "I am certain that he did not notice me at all."

Cressie, who had been in the midst of masticating on a piece of egg, inhaled a large lump and began to choke. The air completely vanished from her lungs as she leapt up from the table, coughing and spluttering.

And yet, while she was physically suffocating, the only thoughts that could pass through her mind was the panic that her niece had expressed interest in her Jem. That was how she thought of him. Hers.

Choke. Mine. Choke. Mine.

Her mind would not function with any semblance of logic as the tears pooled in her eyes. Meanwhile, a footman had rushed to her aid as Zara screamed in panic. Cressie felt a great blow on her back from the footman's fist, propelling her forward with a great cough. Disgustingly, the egg that had been lodged in her throat flew out of her mouth and bounced down the table in a soggy mess.

Cressie nearly collapsed, leaning forward on the tables as she rested on her arms. She took several deep breaths to collect herself and to settle her racing mind.

"Goodness, Cressie! Are you alright?" Zara exclaimed. "I think you are determined to frighten me to death! I fear London is not doing any wonders for your health." Zara placed a comforting hand on Cressie's back where the footman had no doubt left a bruise.

"Shall I inform the butler to send for a doctor, ma'am?" the footman asked cautiously.

"No, no," said Cressie dismissively. "Just a little breakfast mishap. I am quite well. I thank you for your assistance." She took a final breath and then sat back down in her chair.

Zara returned to her chair as well.

Cressie looked up into the caring blue eyes of her niece. Like her, Jem also possessed blue eyes, but they were quite different in hue. Perhaps she was biased, but eyes that were like oceans were unparalleled. But she would never deny that Zara was extraordinarily pretty. She was a beautiful young lady with exactly the spirit that Cressie had once enjoyed.

Zara was terribly naïve in her youth, but she was a very good soul. She had a great deal of compassion in her heart, and she would, indeed, be a good wife to whomever she chose.

It was selfish, really, for Cressie's immediately reaction to be so possessive. Jem was not hers. On the contrary, she belonged to Everett Delaney. Cressie had made that choice five years earlier to save her mother. Zara would never be put in that position. Cressie would ensure that she chose entirely to suit herself.

And Cressie could attest before God that if Jem was Zara's choice, then she would have found a truly decent man. Lord, even the thought brought an ache to her stomach. But she shook it away.

"His name is Mr Jem Denham," Cressie informed Zara, her voice a little raspy. "The man you are speaking of, the one who rescued me. Mr Denham is his name."

Could Zara hear the pain in Cressie's voice as her tongue spoke Jem's name? Or had Cressie yet mastered the skill of masking her grief?

"Mr Denham," repeated Zara, smiling at the knowledge. "Are you acquainted with him?" Her brows rose with curiosity.

"Yes," Cressie replied as casually as she could muster. "Years ago. My ... my mother and I once lived in the village from whence Mr Denham hails. We knew each other ... very briefly."

"Really?" Zara sounded very eager. "Did you ever dance with him?"

Cressie's mind involuntarily returned to the bedroom where she had laid the night before. The walls of that bedroom held the shreds of Cressie's reputation together. "Oh, we might've once," she murmured. "It was so long ago, I hardly remember."

Before Zara could ask another follow up question, they were interrupted by Imelda, who entered the dining room carrying two bouquets of flowers, as well as a card.

"It begins," said Cressie, watching as Zara's questions disappeared from her mind. Her eyes widened with delight as she took in the lovely arrangement of blooms.

As Imelda set the flowers down, she delivered the note to Zara while simultaneously removing Cressie's breakfast plate from in front of her. "A letter has been sent to Mr Delaney informing him of your condition, Mrs Delaney." Her words did not sound as though they were meant to be reassuring, or even courteous. It was as though Imelda was informing Cressie that her husband would still know all despite the distance between them.

Cressie said nothing as her stomach twisted. She focussed her attention on Zara as she used her butter knife to break the seal on the note she had received.

As she unfolded the letter, Zara smiled as she told Cressie, "These are from Mr Avery. He has sent you flowers also, Cressie. He writes to wish you well! He asks if he may call upon me this morning."

Mr Avery's token was not the only favour showered upon Zara that morning. Before eleven o'clock, every surface in the drawing room of the house was quite covered in floral arrangements, each seemingly grander and more expensive than the last. Cressie assumed her role as chaperone dutifully as the gentlemen arrived alongside the flowers and gifts.

It seemed that every young man who had been introduced to Zara the night before had come to call. Mr Avery and Mr Dixon had both attended, as well as a succession of other very nice-looking gentlemen. Cressie pretended to occupy herself with her needlework by the window as the men showered Zara with compliments and questions, asking after her interests and accomplishments.

She was asked to display her talents at the pianoforte by one gentleman, while another asked to hear Zara sing. His praise after hearing Zara's attempts to reach a soprano note told Cressie immediately that the lady's dowry was more than attractive to him.

Nevertheless, Zara appeared blissfully happy to be in receipt of such attention.

But Cressie's attention was entirely captured when the butler showed Zara's next caller into the drawing room shortly after three o'clock that afternoon. They stared at one another, each having a thousand things to say without parting their lips.

What was Jem doing here?

Cressie froze as her eyes flicked to Zara, who appeared entirely delighted at the appearance of the man who seemed to have been her favourite from the evening before. Had Jem come for Zara?

Zara darted to Cressie's side and collected her from her chair, forcing her to abandon her needlework. "Introduce us!" Zara hissed under her breath.

Cressie was practically pulled to the reception area of the drawing room, her legs dragging almost to the point where she tripped over her feet. Her mouth had gone dry from the shock as her heart flipped and flopped in her chest.

Jem carried no flowers or gifts, and the butler had not presented them with a calling card. He was there by himself, his hands behind his back as he looked between the two women with an anxious expression on his face. His eyes, however, reverted solely to Cressie. He looked over her, inspected her, the concern evident.

"Forgive my intrusion," Jem said formally, however, Cressie could hear the plea in his tone. He was asking her for forgiveness after she had dismissed him the night before. "I had to make certain that you were well." His voice was soft, and yet a little hoarse. He sounded as though he had meant to stay away, to obey her, but he could not. "As the hostess' brother, it is my duty, of course," he added, seemingly for Zara's benefit.

Or perhaps Cressie was in denial.

Zara subtly elbowed Cressie in her ribs as she had been so startled that she had forgotten to respond.

"I ... I am fine," she stammered.

"Fine?" Jem repeated with a furrowed brow. He looked upon her with an even sterner, more anxious gaze, as though he was making no effort to shield –

Cressie stopped the thoughts immediately. It was entirely speculation and she was only torturing herself with the notion of his care. "May I introduce Miss Zara Delaney," she said, her voice firmer as she brought Zara forward. Zara's smile was most pleased. "Zara, this is Mr Denham."

Zara curtseyed, and Jem appeared quite startled at the sudden change in Cressie attention that he fumbled a bow after a long moment.

Zara did not seem to notice. "I am delighted to formally make your acquaintance, Mr Denham. I must thank you properly for your gallantry yesterday evening. I am entirely indebted to you after the service you rendered my aunt."

"Oh ... not at all, Miss Delaney," Jem rebuffed, shaking his head. "Though, of course, I am happy to make your acquaintance as well. I am just happy to know that your aunt is ... fine."

Jem's ocean eyes bore holes into Cressie's that she could not hold his gaze. He was looking at her, trying to see, trying to know. Only yesterday had Cressie wanted to scream into the darkness for him to see what had happened to her. But today she had retreated. Cressie looked away.

"My aunt tells me that you once knew each other in your village, Mr Denham," Zara continued, blissfully ignorant. "You must tell me what Cressie was like when she was my age, or was she always so serious?"

"Y-yes, we did know each other once," Jem confirmed. Cressie could still feel his eyes despite not looking. "I would not ever have used the word 'serious' to describe your aunt."

"Really?" Zara exclaimed. "Please, won't you come and sit down on the sofa, Mr Denham," she invited. "I would love to hear more of your experiences in your village."

Zara turned to go back to the settees, leaving Cressie and Jem momentarily out of her earshot. Cressie dared to look up at him, just as he whispered, "I know you sent me away, but I had to come. I had to check on you, to see if you were alright."

"I am fine as you see," Cressie uttered in reply.

"Cressie," Jem pleaded softly.

"The unmarried young lady desires your attention, Mr Denham." Cressie's voice unwittingly cracked as she spoke, so she quickly turned on her heel and walked back to her chair at the window. Out of the corner of her eye, she spied Jem slowly move to join Zara on the sofa.

"Would you care for some tea, Mr Denham?"

Cressie stared at her embroidery as she swallowed loudly.

"Please," he allowed quietly.

"Tell me about your village. Where was it that you grew up?"

CHAPTER 30

"**I**'m worried out of my mind." Jem discarded his fork, which rather dramatically cascaded to the floor of Peter and Belle's dining room with a clatter of noise. Jem winced, hoping that the children, who were sleeping not far from them in the nursery, would not awaken. "You should have seen her last night. You should have seen her today!"

Jack and Claire had joined Jem in dining with Peter and Belle that evening, and all had become well versed in Belle's theory. Jem had about confirmed it without any concrete evidence of his own save for knowing Cressie better than anyone.

"But what did she say?" Peter pressed.

"Nothing outwardly," Jem huffed. "That is my point. It is in her looks. You all remember her from five years ago, don't you? I know Belle at least does. Forget her thin appearance, one need only see in her eyes that there is no life in her."

"I confess I did not recognise her until I heard her young charge refer to her by name," Claire added. "She was, indeed, very gaunt. But I do recall her spirited nature. Don't you, Jack? She had a rather wicked way with her mother."

Jack sheepishly shook his head. "I have probably met several dozen young ladies since then so I must admit that my memory of the girl is rather foggy. But the lady last night was very reserved and skittish, almost like a doe who'd given up before a hunter."

"How many women you have occasion to meet in your business, dear," Claire said nonchalantly as she took a sip from her wine glass. Jack appeared ready to defend himself before Claire winked at him, setting him at ease. Everyone knew that Jack was a champion of women writers.

"Can we please focus?" Jem begged, reclaiming the attention of his siblings and siblings-in-law. "Won't you trust me? I saw her in there briefly, in her eyes I mean. It was as though her body was a prison and she was trapped inside. When I knew Cressie, there was never a girl more filled with life and ambition. She liked to run to get places faster and she dreamed of seeing the ocean!" Jem cried with exasperation. "Please. Something is happening, or has happened, and I don't know what to do. What am I allowed to do? What is appropriate? How can I ever speak to her?"

Both couples exchanged glances of sympathy, but nobody offered Jem any words of wisdom for several moments. Jem was so panicked that he was panting, his hands balled into fists atop the table near where he had abandoned his supper.

"Jem, I do not know if there is anything you can do," Jack said quietly. "Cressie is not a distressed maiden, but a married lady. A lady, I might add, who now belongs to a very rich and influential man."

"She doesn't belong to anyone," Jem snapped back with frustration. "What sort of idea is that? Do you consider Claire your property? Do you consider it of Belle?" he charged Jack and Peter both.

"Of course not," Jack replied immediately, his voice firm as he took Claire's hand, holding it between their place settings.

"Jem, you know exactly my position on such a notion of human ownership," added Peter tensely. Belle had reached out to him as well.

"I would never profess to own my wife, to be her keeper or her master," Jack continued. "I would never control her, and should she decide to pack up and leave me tomorrow, she would be free to do so." Jem knew that Jack was speaking theoretically for the benefit of his point, but he could see a flash of pain and fear in his eyes as the words escaped his mouth. Jack did not appear to be able to stomach even the idea of Claire leaving him.

Claire rose from her chair and came to stand behind Jack's, placing her hands on his shoulders reassuringly. Jack reached back with both of his hands and collected hers tightly.

"But," he continued, "in the eyes of the law, Claire belongs to me. In the eyes of the law, Cressie belongs to her husband as well. We may not like it, but that is the way marriage works. One simply must pray that they manage to forge a match that is at least based on mutual respect, let alone affection."

"I understand that," replied Jem, "I truly do. But what is clear is that something has happened to Cressie." Sighing, he admitted, "Of course, I cannot confirm that it is the fault of her husband. That is only my assumption. But what else could it be? She would not be the first woman to be ill-treated by her husband!"

His exclamation made Belle flinch, and Jem bit down on his tongue hard. He only released it when he tasted blood. But as his eyes met with the golden irises of Belle, Jem's suspicions were as set as stone. For a brief moment, the compassionate and kind Belle that they had all come to know and love had vanished, and in her place, Jem saw a ghost. In her eyes were her demons, and Cressie appeared exactly the same.

Jem felt a considerable pang of guilt for his outburst being responsible for taking Belle back to a horrid and unthinkable time in her life. While he had never heard the tale from Belle's lips, the papers had covered it quite comprehensibly. He was only glad that she was now under the protection of his brother and was now able to live a fulfilling life.

Cressie, however, was most likely still in the midst of her terror.

"Belle, forgive me," Jem murmured apologetically.

Peter made a move as though he was going to escort Belle from the dining room, but Belle shook her head. "No, I am alright," she assured him quietly. Belle looked back to Jem, and she offered him a sad sort of smile. "I shared my suspicions, my fears with you, Jem, because I thought as you do. I feel a sense of responsibility to help people, women especially, where I can. When I saw Cressie in my shop that day, I saw myself. Women who have suffered at the hands of a man carry that burden with them every day. Even when he is not present, that man can have a way of choking the life out of us, of haunting us and destroying us in ways we never thought imaginable." Belle swallowed loudly as her eyes became glassy. She took a shaky breath. "I believe that Cressie needs help, and I believe that she is too frightened to ask for it."

Belle's reality helped the party to come to the mutual agreement that something had to be done to ascertain Cressie's safety, even if nothing could be done to intervene with the fact that she was married.

Jem, however, was not above snatching her away in the middle of the night and escaping to the Continent if it was discovered she was being mistreated by her husband, but he had not shared that plan with his family.

"How does Jem realistically go about speaking to Cressie again?" Peter asked with a furrowed brow. "He cannot call upon her as though she were a deb."

"Well, he could call upon the niece," Jack jokingly suggested. "If my eyes were not mistaken, I would have thought that the young Miss Delaney was rather taken with our Jem."

Jem could awkwardly attest to Jack's amused insinuation. He had sat through a conversation with Miss Delaney that very afternoon completely unintentionally. Miss Delaney had innocently presumed that Jem had been there to call upon her as though he were a suitor.

He supposed that would have been a very convenient way to meet with Cressie again. Was his determination to help Cressie greater than his conscience?

Claire seemed to answer this question for him. "I rather think Alex and Susanna would have something to say about such deceptive charades," she added in a displeased tone. "I will call upon Cressie tomorrow, and Jem can escort me. I was the hostess of the ball. Really, I should have called upon her today, but I was neglectful. I will distract Miss Delaney and you will have your chance to speak with Cressie again, Jem."

Jem's nieces, Jackie and Maria, held onto one hand each as they approached the front door of Cressie's London home. He was glad for the hands of the girls, as they helped to calm him. Certainly, no butler would have admitted him were he has outwardly frazzled as he was feeling inside.

"Best behaviour, girls. Please keep your dresses this way for at least an hour," Claire instructed her daughters as the door was opened for them by the Delaney butler. Claire smiled at the servant as she entered the foyer, Jem and the girls following her.

Jackie and Maria were both dressed in white summer dresses with matching bonnets. Jem could only imagine what colour his clothing would have ended up were he wearing white shirts and breeches at their age.

"Good morning," Claire greeted the butler. "We have come to call upon your mistress and her charge."

"Yes, ma'am," the butler said, bowing his head respectfully. "Miss Delaney is currently indisposed, but I shall alert the mistress. Whom shall I announce has come to call?"

"Lady Claire Beresford, Miss Beresford, Miss Maria Beresford, and Mr Denham," replied Claire.

The butler showed them to a sitting parlour in a hallway off the foyer to wait and promised a servant would attend them shortly with tea and refreshments.

Jackie and Maria abandoned Jem and ran over to pounce on the fine sofas, to which their mother immediately scolded them for having their feet on the furniture. The girls were occupied shortly thereafter when a housemaid arrived with a tea tray filled with sweet biscuits.

Five minutes after the tea service had been laid, the door to the sitting room opened once more by the butler, and Cressie entered alone.

She was dressed immaculately, wearing a gown the colour of rosemary that fitted her thin frame perfectly. The neckline high-lighted the obvious protrusions of her sternum and collarbones. She was beautiful. She would always be beautiful to Jem, but she was not the beauty he had known. Today, she appeared as though she had not slept. There were dark shadows underneath her brown eyes, amplified by the pale, ashen transparency of her skin.

"G-good morning to you all," Cressie greeted formally as both Jem and Claire stood to come towards her. "We were not expecting you." Her eyes avoided him, and instead focussed directly on Claire.

"I hope we are not intruding," Claire said regretfully. Jem would not have cared if they were. "I imagine Miss Delaney is experiencing a bevy of callers today."

A forced smile tugged at Cressie's lips. "Oh, yes," she confirmed. "She is entertaining Mr Avery as we speak. My maid is acting as chaperone so that I could greet you. Zara will be along ... if it is she whom you desired to meet." Again, she did not meet Jem's eye, but that comment had been directed at him, Jem was certain.

Did Cressie really think him so fickle? Did she really imagine that he would come to call upon her charge when she was right there possessing everything he wanted?

"Of course, we would be glad to meet with Miss Delaney again, but our purpose for coming here this morning was to ask after you, Mrs Delaney," Claire replied, appearing to struggle with addressing Cressie as such.

Jem, likewise, wanted to choke every time he heard them.

"Oh, how kind." Cressie sounded formal, dutiful, and forced.

Go away, Claire, Jem willed.

His nieces seemed to read his mind, as behind them a clatter sounded.

One of them, Jem did not know which, but one of the girls had tipped the biscuit dish, sending the biscuits in every direction. They had likely been tussling over who got to have more.

Claire apologised as she flitted to scold her children once more, ordering them to pick up every crumb off of the rug. She did not re-join Cressie and Jem, and Jem presumed that was by design.

They were not alone, but they were out of ear shot.

Cressie's formal pretence appeared to be teetering as she finally brought her brown eyes to meet Jem's. Jem could have sworn that he saw a shiver pass through her.

There she was. She was there. She was frightened, but she was there. Lord, he wanted to protect her. God grant him the power to protect her.

"Cressie, do you feel safe?" he asked her quietly.

She was trembling. Jem yearned to reach out, to pull her into his arms and hold her. But finally, Cressie nodded. "Yes," she whispered. "I feel safe right now."

Jem felt no reassurance by the way that she had worded her answer. She was telling him everything and nothing at the same time. His stomach was in knots as he asked, "Have you felt unsafe at any moment since I saw you last five years ago?"

Cressie's eyes flicked around, her lips parted and wobbled. Jem could see her shoulders rising and falling rapidly. She was panicked and he couldn't hold her. But she tried to calm herself. Jem could see that she was conditioning herself, punishing herself, pushing this emotion away as she tried to regain control, to become the emotionless waif that he had seen at the ball.

"No," Jem said firmly.

Cressie's eyes widened, and he saw her resolve vanish. She was there again in those brown depths. Frightened, terrified, but she was there. She couldn't speak, but Cressie nodded.

And that was all the confirmation Jem needed.

But a moment later, Cressie stepped backwards, bumping into the door in her rush to get away. She was panicking, the emotion that she was determined to hide appeared crippling. Jem felt completely powerless, and that sense of helplessness was not one he wanted to keep.

"Cressie, be calm," Jem said gently. "Please, you can tell me what's happened. You can talk to me." Jem willed himself to remain calm, to remain gentle. He could not outwardly express his desire to hang the man who called himself Cressie's husband.

"I can't talk to you," she hissed. "I can't talk to anyone." She shook. "No one."

Could she not verbalise it? Was it too difficult to say? Jem swallowed the bile that rose in his throat as his thoughts briefly travelled to Belle and what she had endured. The very notion of Cressie experiencing anything remotely similar was unthinkable. It was unconscionable, and yet it was very likely.

"Could you write it down?" Jem quietly suggested. "You could write to me, and I will find a way to help you."

"I can't write," Cressie snapped. She was not curt or rude but panicked. She was still entirely frightened. Her eyes were wide and searching for escape. "They ... they read my letters. Everything I say, I can't ..."

Jem was taken aback by Cressie's abrupt confession. Her letters were read. By whom? Her husband? Someone else? Regardless, such close monitoring of her correspondence was evidence of a wicked controller. It was also evidence of Cressie's isolation. Her tongue was being held, and not by her own hand.

Jem held up his hands before slowly and gently lowering them in a calming motion.

"You need to leave," Cressie urged, her tone terse as she reached for the door handle. "Go away." Her hand rested on the gold hilt, but she did not turn it. Her shoulders were riding and falling rapidly, and her eyes closed as she tried to calm herself. "Go away!" she snarled, forcing her voice through clenched teeth. She was trying to soothe herself back to the blank woman she had become, but she was struggling immensely.

"I will not," Jem said firmly. He longed to hold her, but he knew that he could not.

"Stop it!" Cressie begged, her voice cracking.

"You can't speak of it now, and you cannot write it, I understand," Jem assured her. "I will not force you to tell me anything, though you must know I would hear anything you had to say. But you must also understand that I now know you feel unsafe, and I cannot live with that. I will help you." Just how, Jem did not yet know, but he would.

"You cannot." Cressie's voice was barely audible, but it was just loud enough for Jem to catch it. She did not look at him.

"Take Miss Delaney to Belle's tomorrow afternoon at two o'clock," Jem instructed. "Please."

Cressie stared at the floor, her hand still on the hilt of the doorknob. She was concentrating, the rise and fall of her shoulders slowing as her breathing settled.

"Will you come, Messy Cressie?" Jem probed.

The reminder of their courtship, if it could be called one at all, was enough to collect Cressie's gaze once more. She nodded, only once, but it was enough. She then finally turned the door handle and opened it.

"It seems Miss Delaney is still occupied. Perhaps you can call again another day," she said, louder this time, and for the benefit of the servants.

It made Jem wonder how many of them knew.

CHAPTER 31

B elle's shop was always a place to be seen in London as it was the most fashionable place to procure the latest couture. Cressie, thus, was not at all surprised that it was quite busy as she and Zara passed through the doors the following day at two o'clock in the afternoon.

That fact only made Cressie more frightened. She was already in pieces. Internally, of course. She had become an expect as masking her anguish outwardly. Inside these walls were so many eyes and so many opinions belonging to hideous gossips.

They had been inside for all of nine seconds and they had already been seen and spoken off by a half a dozen mothers and daughters.

'Look who it is. Zara Delaney.'

'I wonder what she is coming to collect. Is she to order a new gown already?'

'A wedding gown perhaps? Her trousseau?'

'Has she had a proposal already?'

Cressie heard the whispered questions, and she supposed she was thankful that all attention was focussed on Zara. She was also thankful that Zara seemingly enjoyed the attention.

"How silly they will all feel when they see we are only here to purchase ribbons," Zara mused to Cressie quietly.

Zara believed that she and Cressie were at Belle's to procure ribbons. By the way Cressie's heart was attacking the inside of her ribcage with how rapidly it was beating, one would have easily formed the opinion that ribbons were highly offensive and terrifying to Cressie. She could hardly concentrate on anything beyond her next few steps.

Cressie felt the need to look over her shoulder. She felt the need to look around the room and search the faces there. She felt the need to check her appearance and her dress for faults. She felt like she was being watched, as though someone knew what she was really there to do.

What was she there to do?

Jem had asked her to meet him. Cressie felt such conflicted anguish in her chest at what Jem wanted to know. He knew. Somehow, he knew. He could see it in her, see what others didn't, and he knew that something was wrong.

And Jem wanted to help her. He believed that he could help her. Cressie had looked into his divine, pure ocean eyes, and had seen the faith there. The faith that he held in his own ability to save her.

Jem did not understand that Cressie was beyond saving.

And yet she was here. Despite the fact Cressie had long abandoned all hope in ever escaping the prison in which she was held, and the husband she was shackled to, she was here.

What a foolish girl she was.

Belle descended upon Cressie and Zara almost immediately with a smile that anyone else would have interpreted as friendly as hospitable, but Cressie could see it was knowing. Of course, she knew.

"So lovely to see you both again so soon, Mrs Delaney, Miss Delaney," she greeted warmly in her accented English.

"And you as well, Miss Desjardins," replied Zara with enthusiasm. "I do have to tell you, I never received as many compliments in my life as I did when I wore your gown to the presentation ball. Thank you ever so much for your tireless work and your meticulous attention."

Belle's smile widened in its sincerity. "I am so pleased to hear it, though I must say that it is the lady who makes the gown, and not the other way around."

Zara was utterly delighted with such a compliment, and Belle expertly steered her into the arms of her seamstress employee, Marguerite. Cressie momentarily pretended to occupy herself with some of the open catalogues on the large tables, showcasing the possible ensembles that could be ordered. Just as she was about to make an interested, 'oh, how pretty' comment, Belle returned to her side.

"Mrs Delaney, I have some more ribbons upstairs which you might be interested in perusing." Belle's golden eyes were once again knowing. Too knowing. All knowing.

Was Cressie entirely mad with paranoia and panic or did Belle Desjardins – Denham! – know everything? It was like this woman was a seer or a mystic or a witch, someone who could read minds, invade minds, and know all their deepest secrets.

But then Belle delicately placed her hand on the small of Cressie's back in a guiding manner, just as she had done a moment ago with Zara, before she whispered, "You are safe here, Cressie." Her voice was so soft, so quiet, that not even Cressie thought that she had heard Belle correctly. But the look on Belle's face confirmed the words were hers.

"You can't know that," Cressie whispered back, the words leaving her mouth involuntarily.

Belle guided Cressie gently through the shop, weaving through the parties of ladies in an inconspicuous way, before they came to a door that blended into a back wall. Belle opened it and closed it, bringing them into a very small room that served only as a stairwell to the rooms above.

"But I do," Belle replied, her voice a little stronger now, and yet still filled with compassion. "These walls are a safe harbour as I have meant them to be for every person who comes to me for care." Taking a breath, she said, "I know your pain. It took a hurricane for me to escape, but I escaped. So will you."

Cressie didn't know what to say. She did not know at all if she would be able to speak without crying. And Belle seemed to know this to.

"Go upstairs and fight."

"I'm not strong enough." The words sounded as though they came from someone completely foreign to Cressie as the thickness of her voice sounded entirely unlike her.

"You have survived!" Belle declared. "Dying is simple. Do you know how much strength it takes to live? Every day that you awaken and choose to live you are showing your strength. You are choosing to not let your demons defeat you. You have survived this long, and your hurricane is coming."

Cressie felt the wetness of her tears spill over her eyelids as she whimpered, "He has taken everything from me."

"Take it back," Belle said emphatically.

Cressie trembled as she closed her eyes, blinking more tears, before she took a deep breath. And then she walked up the stairs. And in mere moments, Cressie found herself standing in a small room with tidy, yet tired, furnishings that were situated towards a dormant hearth.

The kitchen consisted of a stove and a small wooden table with four chairs. Where there might have been baking utensils of food meant for supper on an ordinary dining table, this one was laden with sewing baskets, darning, knitting, and embroidery. Not even the chairs were free from the evidence that the mistresses of this home were seamstresses.

Two little sofas, repaired with mismatching patches, were crammed into the tight room before the hearth, with one of them being occupied by a very tall, nicely dressed young man. He was quick to his feet, however, and showcased his full height.

"You came," Jem breathed, relief flooding his face as he approached her, though his steps were cautious as he clearly saw the state that was Cressie in that moment.

Cressie was still trembling, frozen to the spot, while staring at Jem. Belle's words rang in her mind. Take it back. Take it back.

How she wished she could! But Cressie didn't know how. She felt helpless as she stood there shaking, and the words, "I'm scared, Jem," tumbled out of her mouth.

Jem threw caution to the wind as closed the distance between them, enveloping Cressie in his arms and crushing her to his chest in mere seconds. Cressie melted into him entirely, her legs losing all integrity as they collapsed beneath her. Jem easily bore her weight.

It took a moment for the shock of the action to pass before Cressie realised what position they were in, and it took another moment for her to reciprocate. Her arms regained some of their authority, and they slowly encircled him as well, and for the first time in five years, Cressie felt as though she was holding something real, and something precious.

His strong hold on her was so steady and constant, that Cressie knew shew would not fall. Jem would never let her fall, and that faith should have alarmed her, but it didn't.

And with that faith, Cressie began speaking. Her speeches and stories were a ramble, incoherent and undoubtedly confusion as she told Jem events that had happened as they popped into her head.

And once she had stared, Cressie found it difficult to stop. She told Jem everything. She told him how Everett's desire for her had turned into an obsession, and how he controlled every part of her life.

She relayed Everett's incessant need to belittle her and humiliate her with his venomous words. Everett controlled what she wore, what she said, and what she ate. If he could not personally watch her, one of his servants, namely her maid, would, and her every move was reported back.

If he did not read every one of her letters himself, he ensured that they were read before they were posted, and if she dared write something untoward, she would have suffered for it. Every letter she received had the same treatment, and she had not heard a proper word from her mother in years.

Cressie was never allowed any money of her own. She was solely dependent on Everett, and that was another way that he lauded control over her.

Cressie had also failed to produce a son and heir, or any child for that matter. She had never been pregnant, and Everett had declared her barren, which was another monumental failure on her as a woman. Cressie found admitting this last story to Jem particularly confronting and shameful.

She shivered and whimpered when she finally realised that she had nothing left to say. She had said everything. She had confessed everything. Jem had heard it all, every sordid detail of the last five years of Cressie's life.

Jem's grip never loosened, though he did gently move her back towards the sofa that he had been sitting on. He had been holding her for that long. He delicately helped Cressie down onto one of the sofa cushions and then took his place beside her, their thighs touching, as he then returned his arm to its rightful place around her.

"I feel watched," Cressie whispered. "I feel so frightened that he will know I told someone. I feel like I am standing on a precipice."

"You are not being watched," Jem promised her. "We are alone, and you needed to tell someone, and I feel a considerable amount of privilege to be the one whom you trusted with the truth." Cressie felt Jem's fingers gently travel up and down her arm in a soothing motion. "I won't let him hurt you again. I won't let him control you or keep you. You never have to feel unsafe again, I promise you."

"Please don't make promises you can't keep," Cressie implored weakly. "When the Season is over, I have to go back." The very idea of travelling back to Yorkshire, to that house, turned her stomach over.

"No, you don't." Jem shook his head emphatically. "Cressie, I ... I have never stopped loving you. Not for a minute in these five years. And if you think I am going to let him take you back to a place where you are unsafe, then you, my dear one, are not very bright."

Cressie froze upon hearing Jem's declaration. She had heard it. He had said it. And it made the tears come all the more violently. Cressie buried her face in her hands as Jem cuddled her closely. He hushed her soothingly.

Cressie had not allowed herself to experience the depths of her feelings for the pain that it brought. If anything, what she felt most keenly was the pain and regret from the morning she had left Jem sleeping in bed. But she had not allowed herself to feel the love that she had once had for Jem. Cressie had buried that safely away and had stowed the key in another hiding place for additional security measures.

Love did not fill her. That love was still safely stowed.

And yet, Cressie still managed to stammer, "You won't love me anymore when you realise how broken I am."

"I will love you all the more," Jem replied simply and as quickly as a heartbeat.

For the first time since Cressie had begun talking, she looked at Jem. Her brown eyes found his oceans watching her with constancy.

"You do a good job of hiding for anyone but me," he continued gently. "I can see you in there." He lifted his other hand to softly brush his knuckles across her cheekbone.

But before another word could be spoken, Jem and Cressie heard the sounds of footsteps marching up the stairs with considerable purpose. They both were too shocked to alter their compromising position at all as the door to the flat burst open and Zara entered the room, closely followed by Belle, who appeared incredibly flustered.

Zara's blue eyes settled on Cressie immediately, and they widened with shock and disbelief as she looked between her aunt and the young man whom she'd briefly expressed interest in.

"I ..." Zara stammered, "...I wanted to know where you were. What ... what on earth is going on?"

CHAPTER 32

C ressie was frozen still, her mouth agape as she stared at Zara with wide-eyed shock. Her expression, Cressie was certain, was mirrored in Zara's own astonishment at her discovery upon entering the flat above Belle's shop.

The ever-present fear that existed within her paralysed her, perhaps even stopping her heart from beating. Whatever little minute ounce of hope that Cressie had accidentally manufactured had vanished, and she felt like the hands of Hades were reaching up to seize her, and to take her back where she belonged.

Jem, perhaps, felt the panic and fear from Cressie, and his arm tightened protectively around her. But this did nothing to settle Cressie's dread. She could not look away from Zara.

"I'm sorry," apologised Belle emphatically, her voice wracked with guilt, "I tried to stop her."

"Miss Delaney," Jem said, his voice alarmingly cool and calm, "would you please sit down?"

Zara was just as paralysed to the spot as Cressie was, and it took Belle leading her to the second sofa to get her to move. Zara nearly tripped over her own feet on the way, and she rather ungracefully plopped down into seat, her blue eyes never leaving the scene in front of her. Belle took a seat next to Zara, though she was merely resting on the edge of the cushion. She looked about ready to run to the door and block it if Zara meant to escape out into the street and shout this secret affair at the tops of her lungs.

But it wasn't an affair! It wasn't. It was innocent. Cressie and Jem were both innocent. They were both victims of this wicked place, and their wicked customs and rules.

"Your aunt has done nothing wrong," Jem began firmly. "Cressie and I have known one another for a long time, and –"

"You can't tell him!"

It took Cressie a moment to realise that the horridly panicked shriek of a sentence had come from her lips. Her tone so shocked Zara that she jumped.

"You can't!" she willed again, seeming to find her voice, no matter how terrifyingly shaky it was. "Please, you don't understand. You can't tell him."

"Cressie," Zara stammered, her voice equally as shaky, "he is not your husband." She lifted a trembling finger to point at Jem. "My uncle is. What are you doing?"

Cressie didn't have the words to explain. She didn't know how to explain this situation without revealing Everett's true nature to Zara, and how would that be to ruin whatever bond her niece had with her uncle?

Jem, however, had no such qualms.

"Your uncle is a blackguard and a wretch," he spat angrily. "He does not warrant the title of man, let alone the honour of husband."

Zara had probably never heard a man speak with such a vicious tone before, and she was visibly affronted. She recoiled into the stuffing of the sofa and all colour drained from her face. Her blue eyes searched Cressie, trying to find the truth in Jem's accusations.

"I cannot believe this," Zara whispered.

"You can," Jem urged forcefully. "Think back to our conversation," he prompted. "What did I say about her? What did I tell you about Cressie?"

Cressie was momentarily confused but recalled the brief conversation that Zara had shared with Jem when he had come to call. She had chosen to amuse herself on the opposite side of the large room, purposefully humming to herself so as not to hear one iota of flirtation from either party.

"I asked you what Cressie was like when you knew her in your village," Zara recalled quietly.

"And what did I say?"

Zara was trembling, her lips chattering, and she couldn't speak.

Jem answered his own question. "I said that she was the sun in human form. A bright, warm light, filled with life and wonder." His tone was not reflective of the beautiful compliment that he had just paid Cressie. He was furious. "Do you see that person here?"

Cressie's eyes shut as Jem's words felt like a blow. She understood that he was proving a point, but perhaps she did not realise how altered she was until now. Her seventeen-year-old self would not recognise the quivering, weak, little waif that she had become.

"No," Zara said weakly. "No, I don't."

The four in the room were silent for a moment as the reality of what had just been discovered settled upon them all. Jem, after all, had not long learned the truth before Zara.

"Cressie, tell me, is this true?" Zara's eyes had begun to fill with tears as she asked the question. "Has my uncle hurt you?"

Cressie felt herself fill with hesitation, the fear that was second nature, once again began to cripple her.

"Take it back," Belle implored, repeating the words that she had said to Cressie downstairs. "Do not let him take one thing more from you."

And so, Cressie nodded, confirming the truth to her niece. "Yes, it's true," she whispered. "All of it. Everett has hurt me ... he has hurt me in every way that a man can hurt a woman. He has stripped me of everything that once made me me. He is cruel, Zara. He is a cruel man. He enjoys, thrives off of control. He has controlled every moment of my life for five years, from what I wear, to limiting my correspondence, to –"

"To what you eat as well?" Zara guessed fearfully.

Cressie regretfully nodded. "Yes, he has tightly controlled what I eat."

Jem's hold on Cressie did not relent once as she relayed her tale for the second time that day, though she did protect Zara's innocent ears with some of the horrible details. Despite her fears and panic and anxiety, Cressie could not deny that there was a small feeling of catharsis in unburdening herself to the people for whom she cared.

Zara cried silent sobs as she heard every word. Tear continued to fall freely down her face, though she never looked away as she listened intently.

"What must you think of me?" Zara asked, ashamed, once Cressie had concluded. "How ridiculous you all must see me, fretting about over suitors and dresses and hair ribbons, when all the while you have been suffering!"

"Zara, please," implored Cressie, "those are the things someone your age ought to be focussing on! And I do take my responsibility as your chaperone very seriously in ensuring that you find a man who loves you incomparably."

"Someone like Mr Denham, you mean."

Cressie stiffened, and Jem seemed to do the same beside her. Did ... did Zara still think of Jem for herself?

Zara seemed to read Cressie's horrified and affronted expression immediately, and her eyes widened. "Oh, dear, no!" she exclaimed. "I meant, simply, that I ought to find a gentleman who might love me the way that Mr Denham loves you." Zara took a breath, before saying, "I did suspect it, you know, on your part, Mr Denham. Cressie hides her true feelings well, but –"

"Not as well as you might think," Jem interjected. "Cressie's in there." His statement brought her eyes to his, and he smiled at her reassuringly. After everything that had been said and discovered, Jem smiled at her with care and compassion. "I can see you."

"Did you love each other back then?" Zara then asked curiously, her voice vulnerable.

"I loved her." And then Jem waited, not answering for the both of them. Cressie wondered if he was unsure of how she had felt about him five years ago.

"I loved him," she confirmed softly.

A smile tugged at the corner of Jem's lips.

"Well, then why would you marry Uncle Everett?" asked Zara. "Why would you not marry each other?" Zara posed the question as though it was the simplest decision in the world.

And really, it was. Love and happiness ought to be the route motivation behind every decision made in one's life. Duty was a wicked thing, indeed.

"Because I was a poor steward, and Cressie was expected to marry a rich gentleman," explained Jem simply.

Jem had never courted a woman in his life. Not properly, anyway. His clandestine excursions with Cressie all those years ago could not be considered a proper courtship, even if he wanted it to be.

Which was why it was so odd that his first proper courtship was with a young lady he had absolutely no intention of marrying.

And yet, here he was, walking through Hyde Park with Miss Zara Delaney on his arm, in full view of every other important debutante and gentleman in London, letting them all know that Miss Delaney had selected her suitor for the foreseeable future.

And she had. This had been Zara's idea. She had volunteered to pretend to be rather infatuated with Jem so that he would have a reason to visit the house, and a reason to be near Cressie. It had also been Zara who had emphatically stated to Cressie that she was not returning to her husband.

Jem, of course, had wanted this. He would have moved heaven and earth to prevent Cressie returning to that beast of a man. But ultimately, Cressie was responsible for her own life. Or at least, Jem wanted her to have the free will to decide.

Zara, however, did not possess that desire.

But Cressie had made that choice. Fearfully, but she had made it. Belle had implored her to take back her life. Jem had refused to let her go. Zara had been the one to provide the opportunity.

The young seventeen-year-old debutante warranted a lot more credit than she was given. When Cressie had worried over Zara's own chances for a match, Zara had replied, "I want to meet the Cressie Mr Denham described to me. If this is what I must do to meet her, then I am happy to pay any price."

Jem knew that it would not be long before half of London viewed him as a deceitful fortune hunter. He was not a gentleman, after all, and he was courting a lady with a very handsome dowry. But he would wear the gossip if it meant being able to call on Zara, and Cressie, each and every day.

Cressie walked a few steps behind them, shielding herself from the sun, and the public gaze, with a white parasol. Zara played her part dutifully, laughing musically at any observation Jem made as though she had been trained to do it. He wondered if that was what girls were taught in those fancy finishing schools.

But Jem's mind was on escape, as it had been from the moment that he had suspected that Cressie was in danger. He needed to get her out. He needed to find an avenue to smuggle her to safety. He needed an ally who would equally move heaven and earth for Cressie.

And while she had once been Jem's foe, and the reason for his first taste of heartbreak, Jem couldn't imagine that Mrs Martin's ambition for Cressie's marriage had ever been this.

Jem stopped on the path and pretended to be admiring the view of The Serpentine, motioning to several of the ducks that were swimming along the surface of the water. He pointed at them with a smile as he stole a glance back at Cressie, who had lifted her parasol ever so slightly.

Her brown eyes were warm, and there was a glimmer, a persistent glimmer, of life in them. Never would he allow that life to be extinguished again.

CHAPTER 33

I t arrived. Jem had been waiting weeks for this letter. He had written in hope shortly after he had begun courting, or rather the façade of courting, Miss Zara Delaney.

The charade had allowed Jem intimate and frequent access to Cressie's drawing and parlour rooms, where they had been able to converse freely. Of course, the conversation could only flow as freely as Cressie could manage, and over the weeks she had begun to share more and more of the prison marriage that she had been kept in by her scoundrel of a husband.

It had become clear to Jem that Everett Delaney viewed Cressie as some sort of caged bird, a pet, whose wings he'd clipped out of sheer delight to keep her solely dependent on him.

Despite being separate from him in London, Cressie still very much felt the bars of the cage around her, and her wings had no strength. Her maid, Jem had learned, was an extension of her husband, employed essentially as a spy. Letter travelled back and forth detailing Cressie's movements and habits, and Everett would write to say if he approved or not.

And all Jem could do was sit and listen to her and wonder at how this wicked man could possess such a woman as Cressie was, and could be again, and treat her thus. How could anyone know Cressie's spirit and not love her? To snuff her spirit, to snuff her soul, was a crime.

Everett Delaney would never again lay his hands on Cressie. Jem had already decided that. But he had not forgotten his conversation with his brother prior to learning the truth of Cressie's situation. Cressie was still the legal possession of her husband, no matter how abhorrent the notion was. Things would not be as easy as Jem simply snatching Cressie away and refusing to give her back.

Jem had returned from his daily visit to the Delaney house to find that a letter had arrived after that morning's usual post. And it had been the one he had been waiting for. Jem broke the seal in the entry foyer and began unfolding the letter as he bounded up the stairs, taking them two at a time. He could hardly read for the speed in which he was moving, and yet, he managed to focus on the neat and elegant script of Mrs Martin.

Dear Mr Denham,

I can hardly believe that I have just addressed this letter thus. It has been such a long time, and yet I find myself filled with equal parts hope and anguish at the prospect of our correspondence.

I am truly grateful to you for sending me word of Cressie. You cannot know my grief at being separated from her all these years, with barely a scrap of news as to her wellbeing in letters than can hardly be described as such. I have wanted to travel to see her, but I have been unable to leave.

When Mr Delaney established me in Suffolk, he told me that if ever I were to leave this house, that it was forfeit. He promised me that Cressie would be well taken care of and I truly have prayed every day for this to have been the case.

I have written Mr Delaney dozens of times over the year begging for him to send Cressie to me for a visit, or to allow me to travel to Yorkshire to no avail. Cressie's letters to me are re-written, and I receive no answers to my questions. I can only presume that she does not receive the letters I write.

At first, I was able to convince myself that Cressie was swept up in marital bliss and had no time to write to her dear mama. That notion allowed me to sleep at night.

But it has been a long time since I have slept well, and your letter has confirmed my deepest fears.

You must know that I only ever wanted the best for my daughter. I only ever wanted to secure her future so that she never had to worry about where she was going to find her next meal, or her next bed.

But in doing so, I traded her happiness, and I traded her safety, for security. My own security. I will have to live with my own wicked mistakes, but I will try to atone for them.

I cannot help but wonder at what my Cressie's life would have been like now had I granted you permission five years ago. The mother in me still knows that I thought I was doing what was best for my child. You could not have provided for Cressie, or anyone, five years ago.

But if I had allowed you the time to earn your living

The sentence was unfinished. Almost as though the thought had been too painful, too regretful, for Mrs Martin to commit to paper.

I will forfeit this house, and I will travel to London to collect my daughter. I failed her once, and I will not do so again. I will make her safe.

I will journey as soon as I am able. I will need to sell a few of my possessions in order to procure a carriage and horses for the journey. I am afforded very little.

Please watch over my Cressie for me. Thank you from the bottom of my heart for getting word to me.

Yours gratefully,

Anne Martin

Jem folded the letter and stuffed it in his breast pocket. He had stopped on the landing to read, and he then proceeded to march towards his bedroom so that he could reply, and send funds, so that Mrs Martin could arrange her travel as soon as possible.

Her mother was a way out. Mrs Martin could take Cressie back. It happened all the time. Well, possibly. He had heard of wives leaving their husband's homes and returning to their parents when marriages of convenience turned sour. Cecily had gossiped about such matters before.

Jem knew that he could arrange housing for them in Ashwood and everything would be as it was.

Aside from the fact that Cressie would have a husband elsewhere ...

But so long as the man could not get within a hundred miles of Cressie, Jem did not care. He was only glad that Cressie did not have any children with the wretch.

As Jem sat down to write the woman who had once refused him permission to marry her daughter, Jem knew that the likely outcome of the entire situation would not be won for him. He knew that he would not get to wed Cressie. That was not the object, no matter how it disappointed him.

Jem loved her enough to be entirely satisfied that she was safe and happy. He knew that if Cressie was safe, then he wouldn't need anything else.

A servant collected Jem's reply a little while later, and Jem subsequently sat in his bedroom drumming his fingers atop the desk in agitation. Jem couldn't tell Cressie the news. He had already been to call upon them that morning. He could not call twice in one day without arousing some odd suspicions amongst the servants.

If Cressie's maid was a spy, then others probably were, too.

By the time Jem had eaten his supper, the agitation and urge to speak to Cressie had been festering inside of him all day, and he had made a rather foolish decision.

A ridiculous, reckless decision, really, and if any one of siblings had been aware of his plan, then Jem was certain that they would have tied him to a chair in order to slap some sense into him.

But they weren't. Grace and Kate were happily at home in Ashwood with their families. Likewise, Peter and Claire were in London with their own lovely broods.

Jem was alone. And senseless.

He waited until the sun had disappeared beyond the horizon and set off from Ashwood Place while the sky was still lit faintly with purple and pink auroras. The streetlamps had already been lit as Jem walked with purpose along the familiar route.

Darkness had enveloped the city by the time he turned onto the Delaneys' street, and Jem began to slow his strides as he recalled his conversations with Cressie surrounding her placement in the house.

The slept in the master's bedroom. Cressie had described walking down the hall toward it like walking to the gallows every time. A double door entrance guarded her cell at the end of the hall.

"Upstairs," muttered Jem as he looked at the house through the entry gate. "End of the hall. Which end?" he wondered aloud quietly.

The gate squeaked. Jem was aware of this after entering through it each day. He would not risk alerting any of the household as to his presence. Jem stepped up, placing his booted foot upon one of the crossbars or the gate, and hoisted himself up and over. His long legs made for an easy jump down onto the stone path.

Jem prayed that there were no servants looking out of any windows at that moment. Not all the drapes were drawn, and Jem could see the glow of candlelight and fireplaces from within.

"What am I doing?" he asked himself as he began to jog around the side of the house. What was he looking for, something to scale? "You're an idiot, Jem," he told himself as he spotted a set of garden stairs leading up to a patio on the first floor. He prayed there was a door leading inside, or an open window, or something. He then prayed for some wisdom after this ridiculous and foolish gamble.

His anguish over Cressie clouded his judgement.

Jem climbed the stone steps quickly. The dim light meant that he walked directly into a stone bench on the first-floor patio, banging his shin, and it took every bit of self-control not to shout out a vile expletive, alerting the entire household as to his presence. After a few deep breaths, Jem composed himself and continued. There was a door and two windows level with the patio, and Jem went directly to the door. He could not see anyone through the windows, though how they could not hear the ferocity of his heart rate and come running, he would never know.

Saying another prayer, Jem turned the handle of the door, but it didn't move. It was locked. He clenched his teeth in frustration before he moved over to one of the windows. Through the glass, he could see that the window was latched with a small hook. He ran his fingers down the wooden middle of the two separate panes of glass, and gently manoeuvred the window out a little to give himself a better grip. And then he wrenched it, and the hook snapped with a little crack. It then opened, and it thankfully did not squeak.

And within seconds, Jem had stepped inside the house, uninvited, like a common criminal. He was without sense in that moment, and neither his mother nor his siblings were there to stop him. Jem closed the window again and then looked both ways down the dim hallway. Which way? He had not been on this floor of the house.

Jem had never prayed so much in his life as he quietly opened the first door he saw. But as he poked his head inside, in the shadows he could see that he was looking into an upstairs drawing room. Cressie's room was at the end of a hallway. He hoped it would be this hallway. Jem began to walk quietly, keeping to the side of the windows so that he might dart behind a thick pair of drapes if someone were to appear.

There were several closed doors at this end of the hall, and at any moment Jem expected them to open, for someone to see him, and their scream would mean his downfall, and Cressie's, too.

At some point, he would need to revisit his thought process, or lack thereof, that had led to this event of him skulking down a hallway having broken into a house. Perhaps the law would treat him better if they knew that Cressie had done this first.

Jem managed to make it to the end of the hallway uninterrupted, and sure enough, he was greeted by double doors.

"Let this be hers," he whispered as he turned the door handle.

The bedroom was empty, though it was illuminated by the fire which had been lit. The bed had been turned down, so Jem must have barely missed the maids who had attended to this room. But what it Cressie's?

Jem quickly shut himself inside the stately room and looked around for any sign of Cressie. It was quite a startlingly bare room for one so large. It had everything, of course, that a great bedroom needed, though it lacked any warmth of personal touch.

He spotted the trunk at the end of the bed, and Jem knew he would find confirmation there, despite how intrusive such an action would have been. Cressie would want this news, he told himself. Jem knelt before the trunk and opened the lid. He was greeted by layers of folded linen and ... unmentionables. He would about to slam the lid shut out of decency, despite his great intrusion, when his hand felt something hard underneath the clothing. His own curiosity gave way as he uncovered the object. It was cool and smooth to the touch, and Jem knew it instantly.

It was the conch shell that he had given to Cressie years ago. He had given her the shell to give her the ocean. And here it was, with her, even after all this time. She'd kept it. She'd brought it to London with her. Jem was in a daze for a moment too long that he had not heard footsteps approaching the bedroom. The sound of the door handle turning alerted him, and he slammed the trunk shut and dove behind Cressie's privacy screen to conceal himself just in case she was not alone.

His hunch had been correct. From behind the screen, Jem could hear that Cressie was accompanied by her spying maid, Imelda Wrigley.

"You ate quite a lot at dinner this evening, Mrs Delaney," Imelda stated in a disapproving tone.

Jem had never had a servant of his own, not including his housekeeper and cook, Mrs Edwards. But a personal servant, like a valet or a maid. But he'd seen the way Grace and Adam interacted with their servants, and the way their servants treated and spoke to them. There was nothing but respect between servant and master.

Imelda Wrigley spoke to Cressie as though she were a naughty schoolgirl, and she were the headmistress and disciplinarian about to beat her with a cane.

"I was hungry," Cressie retorted sharply. "One tends to eat when they are hungry."

Through the small gap in the privacy screen, Jem could see that Cressie was seated at her dressing table, and Imelda stood behind her, taking out the pins from her hair.

"You need to listen to my authority when I say to stop," Imelda demanded as she rather roughly pulled at one of Cressie's hair-pins, making her wince. "You know the rules."

"Please inform Everett that I ate three slices of pork instead of two. He will want to know." There was a facetious bite to Cressie's voice, a spark of something that had previously been missing.

As a smile spread across Jem's face, he knew that this was something that Imelda was entirely unused to from Cressie. It was fight.

"Do not you worry," Imelda said tersely as she wrenched the last of Cressie's pins from her hair, causing her to yelp. "I shall. Come on. Up. It is time to change."

Jem froze as he watched Cressie stand from her dressing table and head towards the screen, her hair now down and curly. Imelda was following her with a nightgown in her hands. He had to be clever. Jem crept to the side of the screen and popped around just as the two women disappeared behind it. He could hear Imelda given Cressie instructions of where to stand and how to hold her arms as she unfastened and unlaced Cressie's dress. As soon as it was off, it was thrown over the top of the screen, and unbeknownst to the women behind it, Jem was about near suffocated with layers of silk as it enveloped his head.

"Change into that, and then straight to bed with you," ordered Imclda.

Jem realised the maid was about to leave, and so he quickly moved back around the privacy screen to shield himself from her. But in doing so, he surprised Cressie, who was standing in nought but her drawers, her nightgown pressed up against her naked torso.

Before Cressie could even recognise him, she went to scream, dropping her nightgown in shock. Jem leapt to her, slapping his hand over her mouth to silence her fright, averting his eyes to maintain any minute chance he might ever have at being considered a gentleman. Cressie's brown eyes were flared with shock, and he could feel her hot breath against his hand. He silently placed his index finger of his free hand to his lips, hushing her, as he waited for the sound of her door opening and closing, telling him that Imelda had gone, and that they were alone.

Jem then slowly took his hand away and Cressie stared at him, her mouth agape. Jem forced his eyes away, as Cressie seemed to have no idea of her present state before him. "Your nightgown," he whispered.

"Oh!" Cressie gasped as she promptly turned around. She bent over to collect the garment from the floor, and Jem couldn't help but notice the bumps of her spine, and the lines of her ribs protruding from beneath her pale skin. Cressie fumbled with the nightgown, before finally pulling it on over her head. By the time she had turned back around, her cheeks were scarlet. "Are you mad?" she accused in disbelief.

"Probably," Jem confirmed, nodding.

CHAPTER 34

Cressie was quite certain her heart had ceased to beat the moment that Jem had rounded her privacy screen, and it had not restarted in the several moments that she had been standing before him in a scandalous state of undress.

Jem had to have lost every bit of his sanity to have found his way to her there. What on earth was he thinking? How had he managed to get in? Did he not realise the danger that he was in? The danger that they were both now in. Had Imelda caught him in her bedroom, Cressie could not even fathom the consequences.

And yet ...

And yet, Jem was still standing before her, with her, even after all this time. His coastal gaze washed over her as she stared into the hue of her favourite colour. His dark hair was curlier at the ends near his forehead, where the sweat from his exertion still glistened. He was not so formally attired as he had been, and as he usually was, during his calls. His cravat had been abandoned and the top buttons of his shirt were undone. He had also forgone his waistcoat. The linen of his shirt clung similarly to the planes of his chest in a way that Cressie found to be blush-inducing.

Jem was terribly handsome. He was also terribly foolish. In that moment, Cressie wished she were not so preoccupied with the former thought.

If Jem was any bit as distracted by her form, he did not display it. Cressie had not realised that she had been standing before him in nought but her drawers for the shock. Her scarlet cheeks had to have betrayed every reckless thought that was racing through her mind.

"I am sorry for frightening you," Jem uttered quietly. "I realise ..." he paused sheepishly, "I realise how incredibly peculiar this intrusion is, and that ..." His eyes shifted, and his composure waned for a second, and Cressie felt a stir in her stomach.

Cressie bit down on her bottom lip to focus on something that was not her erratic thoughts or the nervous fluttering in her stomach, but the moment she did, she heard Jem suck in a breath.

"Don't do that."

"What?" Cressie whispered.

She watched as Jem's jaw clenched and unclenched, his eyes boring into hers. Her heart still felt as though it was suspended in time, though she had long theorised that it no longer resided in her own chest. Perhaps the reason it felt this way was because the person to whom it had always belonged was standing right there in her bedroom.

Cressie knew she ought to have been afraid. She had spent the last five years of her life learning to be afraid of things that no usual person would ever find frightening.

She had learned to fear food. She had learned to fear certain styles of dress. She had learned to fear the dressmaker's tape measure. She had learned to fear her own voice and her own thoughts. Cressie had learned to fear her own shadow, and in doing so, she had completely lost herself.

She had been schooled by a man who had vowed before God to honour her. Everett had broken every vow he had made, though, could a man of honour ever make such a vow?

But in Jem's presence, Cressie was not afraid. She felt no semblance of fear. For the first time in a very long time, Cressie felt more herself then she did the weak lamb that Everett had moulded her into. The fog that had been clouding her mind for the longest time was clearing. The shackles were loosening. She was swimming up towards the surface, ready to finally take a breath.

Cressie did not know what reason had brought Jem to her bedroom, but it could wait. She took one step towards him, and then another, those two being all she needed to find his hands. The moment she reached for them, Jem bypassed her fingers, and his hands found their way to her waist.

The feeling of his hands on her waist, separated from her skin by only a thin piece of cotton, sent a shiver down her spine. Cressie could see Jem's kiss in his eyes before his lips found hers, but the moment they did, Cressie completely lost any inhibitions that may have been lingering in the back of her mind.

She felt the floor disappear beneath her feet as Jem lifted her up into his arms, and Cressie felt completely bathed in a sense of safety that should not have felt so foreign to her.

Her fingers found their way into his hair as she kissed him with a passion that had been long forgotten. She smiled against him as her hands travelled to his cheeks, where she could feel the subtle prickle of his jaw. Cressie was barely aware of her surroundings, or the fact that Jem had carried her out from behind the privacy screen.

But all too quickly, she was suddenly returned to her feet, completely breathless, and Jem was ten feet away from her.

He was near her dressing table, equally as breathless, his cheeks flushed and his eyes ablaze as he stared at her.

"Why did you stop?" Cressie asked, her voice embarrassingly thick.

"Cressie," Jem said, in a tone that he had probably meant to sound firm, yet it came out just as husky as her own. "You deserve more respect than this. You deserve everything."

Cressie felt a spark of defiance, of fire, deep in the pit of her stomach. She felt the flicker of the fight that had long left her, and it filled her lungs as she spoke. "I deserve to choose my own fate. I deserve a say in my own life. I deserve to decide, Jem!" Cressie said emphatically. A tingling sensation travelled down all of her limbs, right to her fingertips and the tips of her toes. It felt like power, like she had regained control over every morsel of her body.

Jem's expression softened as he looked upon her, in a way that only he could. It was as though he was seeing Messy Cressie, the person she truly was, and the person only he could appreciate.

"You kept the conch shell," he whispered.

It took Cressie a moment to comprehend his words. Her eyes briefly flicked to the trunk at the end of her bed, where, indeed, the conch shell that he had gifted her five years earlier was hidden. Perhaps at any other time, she would have chastised him for opening her trunk, but she could only assume that he had a good reason.

"You gave me the ocean," Cressie whispered back.

"I would give you anything." Cressie could hear the love in Jem's voice as he uttered the most devoted of sentences. But in his eyes, she could see that something was keeping him from crossing the room once more to her. And then he said it. "You are another man's wife."

Cressie shook her head. She wouldn't hear that word; she would not hear herself be described as a wife. What she had become was not a wife. "I am another man's caged bird," she bit back as she lifted her left hand to look upon the wedding band that resided there on her ring finger, "and I have had enough." Cressie pulled the ring from her finger, and as it passed over her knuckles and then settled into the palm of her hand, it felt as though she had untied her own noose.

A smile tugged at the corners of Jem's mouth, before it spread across the lower half of his face as he looked upon her with such pride. "Messy Cressie," he breathed, shaking his head. "There you are."

"I'm here," Cressie said with determination, "and I am not going anywhere."

"Oh, yes, you are." Jem marched towards her then and collected her once more in his arms.

Cressie decided then and there, that there was nowhere she would have rather been.

Cressie awoke with a start. What time was it? For how long had she been sleeping?

She was immediately aware that she was not alone in her bed, as she could feel the warmth of the hard body beside her.

"Are you alright?" Jem whispered into the darkness. His voice was not tainted by sleep. He had clearly been awake.

Cressie felt a comforting hand trail down the length of her back, and then back up again. Lord, how easy it would have been to imagine that it all had been a dream. But it wasn't. Jem was here, beside her.

Cressie turned to the table beside her bed and reached for the oil lamp that she knew was there. She immediately illuminated it, and her bedroom flooded with golden light. She blinked several times as her eyes adjusted to the light, before she rolled back over to find Jem watching her.

He was sitting up a little, leaning against the quilted headboard of the bed. His lower half was covered by the bed linens, but his upper torso was bare. Jem appeared pensive, his eyes more serious than the passionate blue they had been some hours ago.

Cressie's throat filled with dread. "Do you regret staying with me?"

Shock crossed Jem's face as he reached out for her immediately. He found Cressie's waist underneath the covers and pulled her to his side, cradling her into his chest in seconds. "Never," he promised her. "I only wish that this was going to be easy for you. I do need to tell you about why I came in the first place ... but I cannot help but worry about something else."

"What?" Cressie whispered against his warm skin.

"If ... if there's a child ..."

Jem could not even complete his sentence before Cressie interrupted him. "There won't be." Cressie's mind immediately brought her to the memory of the relief that she felt every month when her courses came. Her barrenness had been a source of joy for her, one of the only sources. She had never carried Everett's child.

And she would never bear Jem's. And that realisation did not bring her joy. Not even close. In fact, Cressie felt a pang of a sort of pain that she had never felt before.

"I cannot have children," Cressie confessed, almost soundlessly.

Jem was quiet for a moment. Cressie was certain that it had been over an hour before he spoke again. And all that he said was exactly what she had needed to hear.

"I love you." And then he leaned down and kissed the top of her head.

Cressie blinked away a wayward tear which dropped down onto Jem's skin. When he felt it, his grip tightened on her ever so slightly.

"I'm going to get you out," Jem uttered quietly. "That was what I came here to tell you. I was always going to need help, and so I wrote to your mother."

Cressie stiffened, before sitting bolt upright in the bed. "Mama?" she gasped. "You have heard from her?"

"I have." Jem nodded. "And she is coming to help."

CHAPTER 35

Jem continued to call upon Zara every morning, and Cressie every night. It was a dangerous sort of game, entering into what would be considered an affair, but neither of them could see any other way around it.

In some ways, many ways, in fact, it seemed that Jem and Cressie finding their way back to one another was inevitable. They did not, could not, consider their actions wrong.

Foolish, most definitely, but not wrong.

"I was never ... I'm not allowed any money of my own," Cressie confessed into the darkness some nine or ten days later. "If I want to purchase a mere ribbon, I must ask for permission. I was afforded no opportunity to put anything away for myself. I understand that it is his money, but –"

"But nothing," Jem interjected. "You were his wife." Jem used the word 'were' very purposefully. In his heart, and everything else besides his good sense, Cressie was no longer the wife of another. "Even servants receive a wage."

Cressie shared moments, rules, incidents, or stories sporadically, when they popped into her mind, or when she was ready to share them. She paused sometimes, often trailing off in thought, and were it not dark, Jem would have wagered that her brown eyes would have been illuminated by their ghosts.

But with each memory she shared, Jem heard a little more of his Cressie in her voice. It was as though she was conquering each and every moment once it was spoken and was no longer allowing that particular point in time to have power over her.

And Lord, he was proud of her. He was furious, and grief-stricken, and entirely torn apart with guilt that any of this had ever happened in the first place, but Lord he was proud of her. Cressie had survived. No matter what had happened, she had survived, and despite everything, she still had fight in her. It had been hidden, trodden down upon, and belittled, but the fight was still there.

And she was going to need it.

"What if he locks me up in a madhouse?" Cressie suddenly worried. "Men do that, you know. I've heard of it. Women who deprive their husbands, or desert their husbands, they're captured and locked away in asylums simply because their husband declares she is mad. What if Everett does that to me when I leave?"

The fear in her voice, despite her fight, was deafening. Jem had had enough of the darkness, and he leaned across Cressie and felt across the bedside table for the oil lamp. He turned up the flame and illuminated the room. Cressie's eyes were as fearful as he had predicted. Jem pulled her close, hugging her to his chest and feeling her tremble against him.

Truthfully, Jem had not considered that. Now that Cressie had spoken of it, he, too, had to admit that he had heard of men committing their estranged wives to insane asylums as means to unburden themselves from them.

And in hearing Cressie's accounts of Everett Delaney, locking her away in a madhouse did not seem like such a farfetched abuse.

Cressie was going to need to be well hidden on their way out of London. Jem's plan was to escape the hour of Mrs Martin's arrival. Jem could not travel with Cressie. He knew that would attract too much suspicion. Mrs Martin and Cressie would travel to Ashwood House under an assumed identity as distant cousins of Cecily. Both Mrs Martin and Cressie had not been Ashwood residents for very long when indeed they had resided there and most likely would not be recognised after so many years.

And maybe ... maybe Jem could marry her then. It would not be a legal union, but who was to know?

"Cressie, there is a plan," Jem reiterated to her. "I have a plan. Just as soon as your mother arrives, we will leave. You will never have to see that man again, and you will never see the inside of a madhouse. That I can promise you."

Once Jem had received word from Mrs Martin, Jem had properly formulated his plan, and he had advised his family of it. He spared them the more intimate details of their tale, as he was not certain his mother would take it well, but he knew that Grace would put into motion whatever Jem needed in order to keep Cressie safe. She had promised him once to do all that she could to help. She had never broken a promise to him. Not in his three and twenty years had his eldest sister ever let him down.

Cressie took a shaky breath and she nodded.

Imelda Wrigley watched in displeasure as Cressida Delaney, Mrs Everett, served herself a second helping of bacon, a dish that had been prepared for her charge, Miss Zara.

Imelda, of course, had tried to intervene, but she had been dismissed, rather rudely, and rather forcefully, by Mrs Delaney. She was obstinate of late, and Imelda was entirely uncomfortable at the sight. Truthfully, she was utterly disgusted.

She was a Christian woman, and it seemed Imelda respected the vows Mrs Delaney had promised on her wedding day more than her mistress did. Mrs Delaney had vowed to obey her husband. There was a sacredness in making such vows before God, and it was a dreadful, disgusting sin to steer away from them.

Imelda saw it as her Christian duty to obey Mr Delaney herself, and to ensure that Mrs Delaney abided by the expectations of a woman in her position. She was the wife of a great gentleman, and such wives had to mind their husbands.

The man was the head of the house. It had always been the way. It was what was right. Her own father had commanded the Wrigley household, and had been blessed with the eternal devotion of his wife and children. Mr Delaney was no different, and Imelda saw great similarities in him to her father, despite their difference in station.

Cressida Delaney, however, was about as far removed a woman from Imelda's mother as one could be. She was a failure as a wife in her constant displays of disrespect towards her husband, and she was a failure in her sacred duty to bear her husband's children.

Imelda felt important in her role. She felt needed. She felt as though she was an irreplaceable cog in the Delaney household machine. It was she, after all, who had moulded and maintained the wife that Mr Delaney expected this girl to be. Without Imelda, Cressida Delaney would have been no more than a pretty sort of urchin without any prospects.

Imelda was the one to keep house. Imelda was the brains if Cressida was the puppet.

Only, her puppet was no longer doing as she was told. Imelda could remember back to when Mr Delaney had first married Miss Martin. She had understood why. He was a man, and he preferred beauty above everything.

As had her father.

But it was what the woman could become after marriage that would make the household. And anyone with eyes and an ounce of intellect could tell that Cressida Martin was not going to become Mrs Delaney without a little breaking in.

Mr Delaney's expectations were communicated throughout the household, and Imelda immediately assumed her responsibilities as the lady's maid. Every one of Mrs Delaney's foolish little rebellions were quashed. Mr Delaney could never be blamed for his anger or his frustration towards his wife.

Were Mrs Delaney obedient in her Christian duty as a wife, she would not have had anything to fear. Imelda taught and taught as much as she could, obeying Mr Delaney herself in every aspect.

And for a time, Imelda had felt completely successful. But lately ...

Her insides felt sick and twisted at the look in Mrs Delaney's eyes. She had seen it before, that horrid, stubborn, blasphemous rebellion. Imelda felt Mrs Delaney's disobedience as a personal betrayal, and she longed to reach out and slap the tempestuous child across the face.

What sort of role model was she for Miss Zara? She was in London for the sole purpose of finding the young lady a husband, and all she was managing to do was to teach her to defy her husband.

Well, all would be put to rights soon enough.

Imelda subtly brushed her hand over her dress pocket and felt the stiff, folded paper there. She had been in receipt of a response to her letter first thing that morning. Imelda had taken it upon herself to warn her master of what was happening to his wife.

Mr Delaney was not going to stand for it, and he was coming to put a stop to it.

"If I am supposedly courting Jem, then why must we continue to attend these soirées?" Zara asked the following evening. She was sitting atop Cressie's bed as Cressie pulled on her gloves.

Imelda had stepped out, in a rather haughty fashion, to ensure the carriage was ready,

"Have you tired of them?" Cressie asked curiously, observing that Zara had certainly changed her tune from the beginning of the season.

"No," she replied with a sigh. "Of course, I enjoy them. I love to dance and wear fine dresses ... and I certainly like to be admired," she admitted with a flush of her cheeks. "Only, I have been watching you, watching you and Jem both. The way you look at one another is unlike anything I have ever seen before. No one has ever looked at me like that before. Not one of the gentlemen I have become acquainted with this Season has even remotely appeared enamoured with just me, and not my dowry."

Cressie could see that a little of the naïve excitement had faded from inside Zara, and she was quietly glad of it. Cressie never would have allowed Zara to accept just anyone, but it seemed that Zara was beginning to find such standards for herself.

"There is no rush, Zara," promised Cressie. "You are still so young. You have time. There is always next year." Her only concern with any delays was that next year, Cressie would not be Zara's chaperone. Zara did not know that. Cressie did not want to frighten Zara with any of the escape plot yet. It would undoubtedly be more complicated than they had initially planned.

Zara nodded. "I suppose you are right."

The carriage awaited them outside the house. There was a chill in the air, which could only mean it was an English summer, and Cressie motioned for Zara to enter into the carriage first. As Zara did, another carriage, a public one, rounded the corner and turned onto their street.

Cressie would not have taken note of it had it not slowed to a stop mere feet from where she was standing.

It was a tired looking carriage, as most public ones were, and it was laden with luggage atop the roof. The driver and footman jumped down onto the street with a youthful energy that did not match their weathered skin, and they began to pull down a large trunk.

It was lugged onto the path with a loud thud just as the door to the carriage opened. A cloaked woman emerged from within, and she took ownership of the trunk, though she would have no way to move it without assistance.

Cressie knew her immediately. She could see past the streaks of grey in her hair, of the lines that had deepened in her cheeks or on her forehead. She could see past the stress that had aged her a few years more than the five that had passed between their meetings. She did not need to meet her grey green eyes to know it was her mother.

Mrs Martin froze to the spot when she finally saw Cressie standing there, staring, awestruck herself.

A confusing twist of emotions turned in her stomach as she took in the sight of her mother. She felt love, overwhelmingly, as she always would for her mama, and yet that love was peppered with another feeling, a vile one. Resentment.

The seventeen-year-old she once was longed to run to her mother, to be once again in her arms and safe. But she didn't move. She couldn't.

Even though she had been expecting her mother, Cressie had not expected this.

"Cressie!" Mrs Martin exclaimed first, cupping her hands over her mouth. "Oh, my darling, my dear, dear Cressie. It's you!"

"Mama," whispered Cressie in response, her voice sounding entirely foreign to her.

Zara stuck her head out of the door to see what had caused Cressie's delay, and she saw the strange woman standing near Cressie. "Mama. Did I hear that correctly?" she asked.

"Yes," breathed Cressie. "Yes, it is Mama."

Tears filled Mrs Martin's eyes as they looked over Cressie completely, searching her, memorising her, taking in all that she had become. What was she thinking? What did Cressie look like to her? She knew that she was entirely altered. Surely her mother, of all people, would notice it all.

"Cressie, there is so much to say," Mrs Martin's tone was filled with heartbreak, and her arms reached out for her daughter.

Cressie's stomach was still twisted, and the resentment was rich and poisonous, but in that moment, she wanted to be held by her mother. She closed the distance between the both of them, and she wrapped her arms tightly around Mrs Martin. Her mother immediately reciprocated and held onto Cressie as though she might have floated away when released.

The sound of horse's hooves barely entered Cressie's consciousness as she hugged her mother. She was not aware that another carriage had turned down the street, led by a solitary rider atop a beautiful, misused stallion called Dabney.

CHaPTer 36

"Ah, it seems it is the evening for reunions!"

Cressie's blood ran cold as she heard that voice. She froze immediately in her mother's arms as all manner of dread consumed her immediately. No. It couldn't be.

She dared to look, only so she could be wrong. She prayed to God in that very instant that her imagination, her wildest nightmares, had simply come to spook her, and that Everett was still half a country away from her.

But it wasn't to be. The moment she looked up, she was meet with the cold, calculated eyes of her husband as he dismounted Dabney, keeping a tight, wrenching hold of his bridle.

Cressie, who was still holding her mother, felt Mrs Martin begin to tremble. Despite her own fear, she stepped in front of her mother.

Everett arched one of his eyebrows for the briefest of moments before he released Dabney's bridle to a servant and made his way towards them. With every step that he drew nearer, Cressie's pulse heightened, racing at an impossible pace as it rung in her ears.

Before Everett could reach for her, however, Cressie felt herself being pulled backwards. Mrs Martin had grabbed Cressie by the waist and had switched their positions, putting herself between Cressie and her husband.

"Come now, Mrs Martin," Everett said in a condescending tone. "I, like you, am anxious to be reunited with Cressida."

"Cressie does not want to be reunited with you," Mrs Martin said fiercely, before she added, "right now," to protect themselves. "She is very clearly expected somewhere."

Everett chuckled coldly. "How fortunate is it then that I am the one who decides what Cressida wants."

Cressie wanted to run, but her legs were like lead.

Everett clicked his fingers to catch the attention of the footman on the back of the carriage. "You there. Fetch a servant to collect Mrs Martin's things and see that she is brought inside. I will attend to her later." It was an order for the servant as much as it was for Mrs Martin.

Mrs Martin looked upon Cressie with a fearful, helpless expression on her face. She didn't know what to do or say, the same as Cressie did not. Neither of them had anticipated Everett's arrival in London, and their plans were very quickly becoming impossible to achieve.

"I ... I have accommodation elsewhere," Mrs Martin announced.

"Nonsense," Everett refuted. "I will not have my mother-in-law stay anywhere but here." His tone suggested that he had wanted to add 'where I can keep an eye on you'.

Something was different. Something was off. Everett knew something, and Cressie did not know what it was. He was always controlling and patronising, but Cressie could feel it in her bones. Everett had come to London for a reason, and it was not because he had missed his wife.

Several servants emerged from the house, and Mrs Martin was ushered inside, along with her trunk. It was as though Everett now had a very convenient hostage. Cressie could not run now at all, not while her mother was inside this house.

Everett and Cressie were not standing on the footpath alone together for more than four seconds before the door to the carriage practically came off of its hinges as Zara launched herself out. She all but threw herself into her uncle's arms in a warm greeting.

"Uncle, how good it is to see you!" she cried. "We have just missed you so! How was your journey? Are you tired? I imagine you must want to rest. The trip to London can be so arduous! I must say, you are looking very well. You must share your secrets with me in the morning. For now, Aunt Cressie and I must be off as we have an engagement to keep." Zara sang her questions and comments all in one long breath as she artfully occupied Everett for Cressie's sake.

But Everett was not in a pacifying mood, not even for the sake of his niece who had always historically been fond of him. "I shall join you," he decided, staring down at Cressie with an almost menacing taunt in his grey eyes.

"But you are not dressed, Uncle!" cried Zara.

Everett promptly removed his travelling coat to reveal a fine suit that was only slightly creased from travel. Of course, Everett would have ordinarily chosen a finer ensemble for a formal social occasion, but Cressie could see that he was determined.

He threw his coat at an unsuspecting servant as he stepped around Zara to finally stand before Cressie. He looked down upon her as he reached for her, his hands settling on her waist, squeezing her there, his eyes narrowing. Was he measuring?

"B-but you are not on the invitation!" Cressie managed to find her voice, and much to her shame, it was weak and rattled.

"There is not a ballroom in this city that I would be barred from. I cannot bear another evening away from my wife," he murmured. "I have no desire for you to leave my sight."

Throughout the Season, Jem had managed to make many acquaintances. He had needed to as without the status of a gentleman, he relied upon his conversation and his personable demeanour to forge connections that ensured he received an invitation to the next occasion. Having a familial link to the Beresfords would only get him so far.

Jem knew that he was a curiosity. For certain, his connections were brilliant, but he was set to inherit nothing from his own family estate. What exactly did Miss Zara Delaney see in him?

Jem was more than happy to let them gossip so long as he received that next invitation. He circulated around the ballroom as he awaited Cressie and Zara's arrival. Jem speculated that that would be one of the last, if not the last engagement that they all attended before they fled London.

Certainly, Mrs Martin would arrive any day now.

But as soon as that thought crossed Jem's mind, he heard Cressie's name called by the door. Only she was not referred to as simply 'Mrs Everett Delaney'. No. Jem heard, "Mr and Mrs Everett Delaney".

His head whipped around so quickly that he was certain that his neck had cracked. Jem's eyes found Cressie immediately, and his stomach seized when he saw that she was not entering with Zara on her arm. Instead, Jem was brought right back to the day that he had watched Cressie exit the church on that man's arm the day she had married him.

The way Everett Delancy was gripping Cressie sent a murderous flicker through Jem's veins. It was written all over his face. It was written all over Cressie's as well. Control.

But as soon as they were received by their hosts, Everett's face flooded with charm and grace, and Jem could immediately recall how the man operated within a ballroom during Cressie's Season five years earlier. Nobody here knew what he was like.

But Jem did. Hang him. Hang the plan. Hang propriety. Jem was not about to let Cressie remain under his thumb for a moment longer. She didn't belong to that man anymore. Cressie belonged to no one.

Just as Jem was about to sprint across the ballroom towards her, Cressie managed to catch his eyes.

Her expressive brown eyes spoke volumes as she looked at him. She was so afraid. But subtly she shook her head, it moving nary a half inch from side to side. Cressie could read Jem's mind just as much as he could read hers.

Cressie was mad if she thought that Jem would be leaving this ball without her.

Zara promptly left her aunt and uncle's side and began to weave her way through the crowd of guests towards Jem, and Lord, was he thankful. Perhaps they appeared to be quite a legitimate courting pair, and Jem appeared so relieved to receive her as she reached him.

"My uncle has come to London," Zara stressed under her breath.

"Yes, I can see that, Zara," Jem said shortly. "The question is why?" He stopped himself. "I do not care. I'm taking you both this minute," Jem decided. "We'll make for Hertfordshire tonight and I will find a way to divert Mrs Martin."

"But Mrs Martin is here!" Zara replied worriedly. "She arrived just before my uncle did. She was sent inside the house."

Jem was taken aback with shock. Mrs Martin had arrived already? And Everett was clearly aware of her presence. Jem felt the hairs on the back of his neck stand up as a panic set in.

"I don't know what to do," Zara continued in a frightened whisper. "Jem, what do we do?"

Jem did not have an answer. He very suddenly felt overwhelmed with his own fears, and he felt completely powerless. He couldn't steal Cressie away, and that was why she had shaken her head. She would not go if her mother was still inside Everett's house. Which meant that no matter what, Cressie would be returning to that house to be at her husband's mercy when this evening was over.

And the very idea of that made his stomach turn over.

"Oh, Lord, they're coming," hissed Zara. She immediately looped her arm through Jem's and took in a deep breath.

Everett had spotted Zara in the crowd speaking to Jem, and he had begun to lead Cressie in their direction. Every other lady in that ballroom who was currently on the arm of a gentleman did so with a delicate hand. Everett had a vice grip on Cressie's arm as though she was a dog on a rope.

Zara plastered on a pleasant expression. Jem hated to imagine what his face looked like. He imagined he appeared much like Cressie, who looked like a doe facing down the barrel of a hunter's rifle.

"Uncle!" Zara cheered in a musical voice. "I thought you were talking to our hosts."

"I am much more interested in the conversation that you were having," Everett replied in a cool voice as he appraised Jem with a steel gaze. Jem doubted that a man like Everett Delaney would remember a low-born man like him.

They had met before, but Jem had not known what this man had been capable of then. But he knew everything now, and it was taking every ounce of self-control that he possessed not to strike him down with whatever he could get his hands on.

"Uncle, may I introduce Mr Jem Denham. Mr Denham, may I present my uncle, Mr Everett Delaney," Zara dutifully, yet awkwardly, said. "Mr Denham and I are courting," she added.

"So, I have heard," Everett murmured.

He knew? How? Cressie certainly would not have said anything, and clearly Zara had not. Who had informed on them? Jem had little time to speculate, his mind briefly taking him to the prison warden that called herself a lady's maid, before his thoughts were interrupted.

"We have met before, have we not, Mr Denham?" Everett recalled.

Jem's theory was incorrect. "I do not recall an acquaintance," he replied stiffly.

"Oh, young man, that was because there was not one. I do not tend to acquaint myself with serfs." Everett laughed as though he had told a great joke.

He, Cressie, and Zara stood silent, motionless, all at a loss of what to do.

"But I do remember you," Everett continued once he had gotten control of his humour. "I believe you were a favourite of my wife once." A wicked smile teased at the corners of his lips. "It seems that you will stop at nothing to ingratiate yourself within my family."

How wrong this man was. Jem wanted to be as far away from his family as possible, and he wanted to take Cressie with him. Everett was trying to be intimidating and condescending; that was clear. But Jem could not be intimidated by such a little man. Anyone who needed to prey upon women to feel important could not even be given the title of man.

"What is it you do?" Everett asked curiously.

"I am not a serf," Jem bit back through clenched teeth. "I am ..." Jem was about to reveal his title and role within the Ashwood estate, but he stopped himself just in time. Of course, there would be ways for Everett to find this out, but once Jem had formulated a new plan, he wanted to have as much of a head start as possible. "I work for a publisher," he lied, his brother's occupation popping into his head.

"In trade?" Everett shook his head with a mocking grin. "No title. Clearly no fortune. You are like so many others who swan about London during the summer months, desperate to attach yourself to a rich lady in order to live off of her fortune." Everett's voice began to rise, capturing the attention of onlookers around them.

"I can assure you that you are mistaken," Jem snapped.

"And I can assure you that whatever understanding you have with my niece is over. You are no longer welcome to call upon her. If you so much as look in the direction of my house, I shall have you shipped off to the colonies. Your association with my family is over."

Cressie watched in frozen horror as Everett belittled Jem, just as he belittled her, in front of a ballroom of people. There were whispers, laughs, and cries alike, immediately after Everett's dressing down as means to humiliate Jem.

Cressie knew that Jem would not have cared. He didn't care about any of this, the same as she did not. But they both knew that they were in trouble, and that their escape was going to be much harder than originally planned.

Everett did not release Cressie at all for the entire evening. If he did not have her arm, his hand was on the small of her back, guiding her as though she were a child in use of leading strings.

The only brief freedom she had throughout the entire evening was when she was seated at the dinner. While Everett was distracted by Zara on the other side of him, Cressie pocketed her knife.

She might still have been petrified, but Cressie was never going to submit to him again. Cressie had found her fight again. Being afraid did not mean that one could not fight.

Cressie saw the look of agony on Jem's face when they took their leave. She knew exactly what was going through his head, but they couldn't run while her mother was inside of Everett's house.

Cressie would fight, and she would live to run another day.

"Wrigley, get out!" Everett demanded of Cressie's maid as he burst into the bedroom once they had returned to the house.

Cressie hadn't seen her mother. Mrs Martin had to be in one of the other bedrooms. She had been seated at her dressing table while Imelda had come to take out the pins from Cressie's hair. She had no doubt in her mind that her maid had something to do with what Everett knew.

"Yes, sir," Imelda agreed immediately as she scurried from the bedroom, closing the door behind her.

Cressie subtly placed her hand over her pocket and held in a breath when she felt the hard line of the knife there. She willed herself to stand her ground.

"You are a hopeless woman, aren't you?" Everett seethed, shaking his head as he began to pace across the room. "I send you to London with one task, and you cannot even do that. I thought I could trust you to have perhaps an ounce of common sense, an iota of intelligence, but alas, I thought too highly of you. You are too stupid to do the simplest of tasks of chaperoning a girl at a party!

"But furthermore!" he shouted furiously. "Don't think I didn't see it in you the moment I laid eyes upon you! You thought that you could disrespect me, and I wouldn't find out? There are rules and you have broken them by showing me your contempt. You are a disrespectful, brainless, fat wench, and I ought to drown you in your bathwater."

This was not the first tirade of verbal slaps that Everett had delivered Cressie. It was not the second or third, either. This was the way he had always dressed her down and demeaned as a means to control her. Everett had spent the last five years making Cressie feel insignificant.

Fighting while afraid was brave, Cressie reminded herself as she sucked a breath of air into her lungs. Everett Delaney would never have power over her again. "Don't talk to me like that," Cressie said through clenched teeth.

Everett's head snapped back in shock.

Cressie stood up from her dressing table and squared her shoulders, her hand still on the knife in her pocket. "Do not talk to me like that," she said again firmly.

Everett stepped towards her, and Cressie gripped the knife.

"Do not touch me!" she hissed.

Everett let out a maniacal laugh. "I will touch you anytime I want to." His hand rose quicker than Cressie's could reach into her pocket. He brought his open palm down hard on the side of her temple, sending Cressie backward.

The blow itself stung, but mere seconds later, her temple collided with her dressing table, and a focussed throbbing suddenly consumed her skull. Her eyes immediately began to blacken and fade as her surroundings rapidly disappeared.

Before they vanished completely, she heard a voice in the distance say, "Wrigley was right. You do need to be broken again."

CHAPTER 37

C ressie's eyes fluttered open, but her vision did not focus as quickly as it usually did in the morning.

It was morning. She could see the light leaks through the gap in her drapes. It was blurry, but she could see the light. Cressie strained her eyes, squinting, as she tried to prop herself up in her bed. The moment she lifted her head, however, she felt the true weight of it. It felt as though someone had tied three sacks of flour into her hair.

A pain, a wicked and vicious searing headache, reverberated between her temples, and Cressie audibly gasped as her hand snapped up to support her forehead.

"Oh!" she cried.

What had happened? It suddenly occurred to Cressie, in and amongst the shock and discomfort of the pain that she felt, that her memory was rather hazy. She could not remember going to bed. She could not remember dressing for bed.

After blinking a few times, her vision slowly beginning to steady, she saw that she was wearing her silk chemise, and not her night-gown. Even then, she did not remember undressing.

But she could feel the tender bruise on her temple, and a hazy memory flashed through her mind. Everett had struck her, and Cressie had fallen into her dressing table. After that, her memories were blank.

An ominous feeling momentarily consumed her at the thought of being powerless and alone with Everett, but Cressie quickly could confirm that despite his assault, he had not touched her again. After five years of marriage, she was used to the horrid feeling the morning afterward.

And then Cressie began to cry. A sob ripped through her chest uncontrollably as she suddenly realised that the hope she had had for escape had completely vanished in the blink of an eye, or the slap of a hand.

No.

Cressie fought with the bed linen and pushed it off of her, no matter how her head protested at the sudden rough movements. She couldn't seem to get her legs to work immediately, and so Cressie fell out of the bed into a crumpled heap on the floor, bringing down some of the linen with her.

She clawed at the rug, pulling herself towards the door sluggishly, the effort feeling gargantuan and yet entirely necessary. Cressie felt as though with every pull, with every movement in which she wrenched her body forward, she was fighting for her life.

When Cressie finally reached the door, she pushed up off of the floor and reached up with whatever strength she could find to secure the door handle in her hand. But as she went to turn it, it would not move. It was locked.

Cressie trembled hysterically as she collapsed onto the floor. She could not help crying, in rage and in sorrow, with her face and hands pressed into the pile of the rug. But this left her able to feel the movement in the floor as someone approached from the other side.

Her sobs quickly silenced as she recognised the proud march of Everett Delaney instantly. Cressie scrambled backwards, reaching the edge of her trunk by the time she heard a key being inserted into the lock. She heard the lock give way and the door swiftly opened as Everett pocketed the key.

His grey eyes found her instantly, and he looked upon her pitifully. "You are pathetic," he declared with a shake of his head.

Cressie sucked in a sharp breath as she glared at him, feeling all manner of hatred coursing through her veins. It felt wicked to hate a person so, but she did. She hated everything about this man. She hated what he had done to her. She hated what he had taken from her. And she hated him for what he would do in future.

But, by God, she would fight him every step of the way. He might have power over her body for the difference in their sizes and strength, but he would never have her mind or her soul. They belonged to her.

Cressie's heart was still safely stored away outside of her body and in the hands of the only man who could ever deserve it.

"You are despicable," Cressie seethed through her clenched teeth.

Everett smirked as he stepped forwards, coming towards her and stopping once he was standing over her. He meant to be intimidating and he succeeded, and Cressie loathed that she felt intimidated. She willed herself not to hide. She did not want to appear weak.

"Where has this come from, I wonder?" Everett mused. "Where has my Cressida gone?" He spoke as though he was wonderful where his favourite handkerchief had disappeared to, and not the woman he had wed and kept as a trophy. He wanted Cressie as his toy, his object, his plaything.

"I was never your anything," Cressie spat back. "The very sight of you makes me sick." Cressie knew that her words were taunting him into a retaliation, and though she dreaded any kind of pain, she refused to cower.

But Everett did not retaliate. He did nothing but throw back his head and laugh mockingly. When he composed himself, he said again, "I don't know where this has come from. London was perhaps a little too exciting for you. But no matter. I broke you once. I will do it again." Everett then knelt down before Cressie, and he smiled. "How I will enjoy doing it."

"Sir, a woman is being abused!"

Jem has exclaimed this statement thrice before a private meeting with a magistrate that he had only secured on short notice through the connections of Jack Beresford. How he was intimately acquainted with a magistrate, Jem was unsure of, but at that moment, he had not cared.

The magistrate, John Peer, appeared sympathetic but powerless as he sat behind his large desk in his office that seemed overrun by papers, books, and files.

"Mr Denham, I appreciate your struggle. But in the eyes of the law, a wife is being managed by her husband, as is his right."

"What right does any man have to lay a violent hand upon a woman?" Jem challenged. He had no proof of this, but he could only imagine what Cressie was going through in his wildest nightmares and he was powerless to stop it. In his desperation, he had turned to the law.

"None," replied the magistrate, "in the everyday sense. But in the sanctity of marriage, it is different."

"That is hogwash, and you know it," Jem snapped. "A husband is bound by God to protect his wife, and I know of one who is in peril. She is an innocent woman! She needs protection!"

"There is nothing that I can legally do, Mr Denham, and I would thank you to watch your tone. A wife is the property of her husband in the eyes of the law."

Jem had entered into this office wanting to accept nothing less than a hangman's noose for Everett Delaney. But he would be leaving with nothing more than a tepid apology. How was that a law? How could women be so powerless?

Jem could remember having this conversation over dinner with Jack and Claire and Peter and Belle, but it had not truly settled in his mind until now. He saw no threat of it when discussing this horrid law with his family because he knew that it didn't matter. Claire and Belle were both entirely safe within their marriages and they were never going to be taken advantage of.

Such was not the case for perhaps thousands of women in this country. Cressie was one of them.

Jem wanted to tear his hair out. He was so afraid and distraught as he left the magistrate's office that he was quite close to scream-ing his lungs out on the street. How had this happened? Why had he waited so long?

Jem had known that something wasn't right with Cressie the second he had seen her at that first ball. Why hadn't he grabbed her then, regardless of what she had initially claimed?

But then, why hadn't he eloped with her five years earlier.

It was easy to blame himself for these events, but he did not, deep down, that there was only one villain. And this villain had won. Jem had no idea how to beat him, none whatsoever.

The carriage promptly returned him to Ashwood Place, and as he walked through the door, he was greeted by a frenzy of two women shouting at him hysterically. The Ashwood butler was there also attempting to calm the situation, but Jem quickly saw that Zara and Mrs Martin had found their way to him, and by the expressions on their faces, the situation was very dire.

Jem had already known that. It had been several days since the last ball and he had not had any news. His imagination was a world of nightmares but in seeing Zara and Mrs Martin before him as they were, his nightmares were all but confirmed.

"Sir, I beg your pardon, but they wouldn't wait in the drawing room!" the butler stressed.

"No matter!" Jem said dismissively, waving him off in a rude manner that he otherwise would have never entertained. "How have you come?" Jem demanded to know. "Where is Cressie?" It was very obvious that they had come without her.

"Miss Zara, here, got me out," Mrs Martin explained, her voice shaky.

"I managed to convince a servant that we were going for a walk and that I had my uncle's permission. He gave me permission to go out with a companion but did not specify whom. My uncle was determined to keep Mrs Martin captive just as he is doing with Cressie!" Zara's blue eyes were brimmed with tears, and Jem could see the guilt in her features as clear as day.

Captive. The word sent a sickening shudder down Jem's spine. Could that word have convinced the magistrate to intervene? Was a husband allowed to imprison his wife? Jem's mind immediately went to the fears that Cressie expressed over her husband locking her away in an insane asylum. It seemed husbands were allowed to whatever they wished to their wives without fear of any repercussions.

"I tried to free her. I promise I did," Zara insisted fearfully, as though she expected Jem to berate her. She most likely was frightened of his horrified and infuriated expression that he had absolutely no control over. "Uncle Everett had the door locked and only he possesses a key! He won't let anybody in. Not even the maids are allowed in."

Jem managed to find a way to place his hands onto Zara's shoulders in an effort to calm her, when he, himself, felt anything but calm. Jem had spent the best part of three days, weeks, the last several months, really, feeling powerless. His hopes had been dashed time and time again, and he really had no plan, nothing that he could do to save Cressie.

Save storming into the house and assassinating Everett himself, Cressie was going to have to save herself. That realisation suddenly dawned on him. Cressie was going to have to save herself. She was strong. She was going to have to be strong. She was going to have to win back her husband's trust so that he would allow her a similar sort of excursion, like this one in London, again. And the moment she was alone, Jem would be there. He would never abandon her.

"Will you go back there?" Jem asked Zara, cutting her off as she continued to cry her worries. "Is it safe for you to return to your uncle's house?"

Zara froze. "But we left," she retorted. "Aren't you going to go and get Cressie and bring her here? You are far bigger than I. You could break down the door!"

"Please, Jem," begged Mrs Martin. "I was wrong about you. You know I was. Please, save my daughter."

Jem tried to push aside his feelings of overt failure at such a statement and request from Mrs Martin. "I can't do anything yet, and it kills me to come to that realisation. Cressie is going to be strong, and I know she is in that room surviving. She won't break." His breath hitched in his throat. "Is it safe for you to return to that house?" Jem asked Zara again. "I need you there to keep an eye on things, to tell Cressie that we haven't abandoned her. But if it is not safe then you can remain here."

"No, I can return." Zara nodded. "My uncle still believes me to be very oblivious."

Jem exhaled. "If you can get word to Cressie, please tell her that I love her, and tell her to fight like the devil."

CHAPTER 38

The quiet little tap of a knock sounded on Cressie's door at exactly ten o'clock in the morning. Everett had already been and gone with her breakfast and his daily deluge of verbal whips to her back. He was still the only person permitted inside of Cressie's bedroom until she was suitably broken.

Cressie did not care if she would need to bathe with a pitcher and basin for the next month. She flatly refused to cower before that man for a second, and he seemed to enjoy every minute of her fight.

Because he was right. Everett had successfully broken her once before. He had not struck her again since the night of the ball. Physical violence was not usually Everett's control tactic of choice. He was a gentleman. He dressed people down with his airs and words. And once upon a time, it had worked on Cressie.

He could call her whatever he wanted to. It would not change the fact that she would one day escape from him while resisting the urge to kill him in his sleep.

But it had been three weeks of this, and neither one of them had relented. With every day that passed, Cressie only became more determined in her resolve. She had tasted life again. In being in

London, in reuniting with Jem, Cressie had come to know what it was to feel alive again, and she was never going to return to the ghost of an existence that she had been living in for the past five years.

Cressie's only connection to the outside, besides her husband's visits, was from the daily little knock on the door that came after Everett had left to shut himself away to work for the day.

Cressie was ready and waiting at the door, crouching down at the lock. "Zara!" she whispered.

"Cressie," came Zara's voice through the lock. "Are you alright today?"

"Yes," she confirmed. Zara has not seen Cressie, as the door remained closed, but the bruise on her head was nearly entirely gone, and the swelling had reduced considerable. Were her hair styled in a particular way, one would never have known. "I haven't given up."

"Good," breathed Zara. "Here. I brought you something."

Zara pushed a sheet of paper underneath the door, which was followed by a pen. It was an expensive looking pen, and Cressie could have wagered safely as to where Zara had procured it from.

"An inkwell would not have fit underneath the door," Zara explained, seeming to pick Cressie's thoughts. I visited Uncle Everett in his study this morning and I pocketed this. It has some ink, though I am not certain how much. I would choose your words carefully just in case it runs out and needs filling."

Cressie snatched up the paper and held the weighty pen in her hands. It was a heavy black and gold pen, and Cressie wondered if the weightiness of the pen could be attributed to perhaps the real gold accents.

"This is for you as well," she added, pushing another object underneath the door.

It was a letter, folded, and it was addressed to, "Messy Cressie".

Cressie immediately smiled, before noting that it felt so nice to smile. She collected the letter immediately and held it tightly. "Zara, you don't know what it means to me that you have been putting yourself in such positions. I am the one who was meant to protect you this Season. How can I ever thank you?"

"Perhaps I am not meant to be a deb," Zara mused humorously. "Perhaps I am meant for the stage." They both knew that Zara would never be allowed to enter into such a career as acting, despite her obvious talent for deception. "I'm a romantic, Cressie. You know this. All I wanted was to find my sweetheart, and it just so happened that you were meant to secure your sweetheart first. I will collect your response tomorrow. I had better make myself scarce just in case one of the servants happens upon us."

"Make haste, dear Zara," prayed Cressie. She heard Zara scurry away from the door and Cressie climbed to her feet. She moved as far away from the door as she could, walking right over to the window, before she broke the seal of the letter and unfolded it.

My dearest Cressie,

I hope that our messenger can find some way to get this letter safely to you. I suggest you burn this after you have read it for your own security.

How are you? I write that question knowing I must wait in agony to find out the answer. Part of me already knows it. You will not be well until you are free, and that day will come.

You cannot fathom how much I believe in you. Just like you cannot fathom how much I love you.

I am waiting for you, as I always will be, until we can be reunited.

Keep fighting, my dear one. He could never know the strength and tenacity you possess. Not in his wildest dreams.

Your mother is well and is praying for you constantly.

I love you.

The letter was not signed, not that it needed to be.

Cressie hugged it tightly to her chest, before she promptly ripped it into tiny pieces and threw the remnants out the window. She watched as the little pieces of paper were immediately collected by the summer breeze and carried off down the street, as though they had wings like a bird.

Cressie looked down from her window into the garden below. It was not the first time she had judged the distance, nor would it be the last, she imagined. Jumping would not lead to her escape. She would most likely shatter her legs from this height. Oh, to have wings.

Cressie decided that she needed to hide the paper and Everett's pen until after his next visit. She did not want to risk him coming upon her while she was writing. She ran to her armoire as her mind began to plan what she would write in her letter to Jem. She needed to be very particular, as Zara had advised. As she pulled open the bottom drawer to hide the contraband, Cressie's eyes immediately settled on the neatly folded rags that were there awaiting her next lot of courses.

She froze immediately when she saw them, suddenly overcome with a horrified sense of shock. The rags were there, as they always were, ready for her courses that came, as they always did. Every month since she was a young girl, she had bled, and never once had she missed it.

And until Cressie had seen the rags, she had completely forgotten about it. She had not noticed at all that her courses had not come. In fact, now that she was forced to think about it, Cressie struggled to remember the last time that she had had need of the rags in her drawer.

The pen and paper fell from her hands. The pen clattered and bounced across the floor, rolling away, as the paper floated to the ground and settled at her feet.

Cressie knew what this meant. Every woman who was expected to produce an heir knew that this meant. And the very fact that her courses had never failed her had always brought Cressie a sense of relief-filled joy. She had never been able to bear Everett's child because she was barren.

Except perhaps she was not. She had never been able to bear Everett's child.

But ... but she was able to bear Jem's. If it was true, then it could only be Jem's. Cressie's hands, which were now shaking quite uncontrollable, travelled down to her stomach, where they settled on her flat surface. Was it truly possible?

There could be no mistaking the identity of the father if Cressie were really with child. The very idea seemed so absurd, and only because she had spent the last five years being cursed by her husband for possessing a useless womb. She had resigned herself, quite happily at the time, to never having to witness a man as cruel and calculated as Everett rearing an innocent bairn. Her useless womb was performing a good deed, a blessing, for their non-existent children.

Except now there was a very real child. Perhaps Cressie was overcome, simply mad, with a flurry of emotions, but she could feel it. She could not feel it kick, obviously, as expectant mothers reported feeling, but she felt like she knew that this was real.

Cressie was not barren. She did not know if it were possible for men to be barren, but perhaps Everett was. Or if he was not, it was simply God protecting a child who did not deserve to be born a Delaney.

Her child would be born a Denham.

The very notion of her child bearing Jem's name brought happy tears to her eyes, and Cressie clapped a hand over her mouth to stifle a sudden overwhelming sob that ripped itself from her throat.

And as quickly as the happiness had come, the reality of Cressie's situation suddenly returned to her. She had lived a fantasy for mere moments, and the fact that she was still locked inside this bedroom brought forth the considerable danger that was now apparent.

Her child could not be born a Denham while she was married to someone else. Cressie quickly realised that there were only a few possible outcomes given her current predicament.

The first was that Everett would acknowledge her child as his own, and give him or her the Delaney name, and it would be brought up as Everett's heir. Everett would know the child was not his, and Cressie could see him doing this to punish her for her infidelity. In doing this, Cressie would have no control, no ability to protect her son or daughter from their would-be father.

The second possible outcome was that Everett would force her to give the baby away as soon as it was born. The very idea of having to hand her child to someone else was heartbreaking. Cressie has known the child existed for all of ten minutes, and that was enough to know that she would love it for eternity. There would be no way to give the baby to Jem. Everyone knew about these quiet pregnancies, especially amongst the aristocracy. Ladies and girls went away all the time for their 'health' and returned nine months later as shells of their former selves. If this option was forced upon Cressie, then her child would be brought up by strangers, and she would never know its fate.

The third and final possibility that came to mind when Everett learned about Cressie's state was that he would actually kill her.

He was that proud a gentleman that Cressie could imagine the knowledge that she was carrying the child of another would be enough for him to hit her a little harder.

All three were entirely unimaginable, and for Cressie, they were entirely unacceptable. Her escape no longer meant her own freedom. Her own freedom be damned. It was now twelve minutes that she had known this child existed. Or perhaps it was fifteen. Regardless, the wee one she carried was innocent and precious, and they were meant for far greater things in this world then what they would get from Cressie's current predicament.

Cressie's letter was ready. She had chosen her words carefully, writing only:

I am carrying your child. I am going to hide it for as long as I can, but I will be running the moment I am let out of this room. I love you.

Everett had already been and gone. Cressie had taken his snide remarks and somehow she had managed to not draw attention to the fact that her instinct was now to protectively cradle her stomach whenever he was near.

But at ten o'clock, Zara's knock sounded, and Cressie practically launched herself at the door.

"Zara!" she cried, not at all taking care to whisper.

"Cressie! Do you have the letter?"

"Yes." Cressie kissed the letter in hope, before she passed it through under the crack in the door. "Please get that to him safely. It contains something very important that he must know."

"I will," promised Zara. Cressie could hear the sound of Zara collecting the letter from the floor.

But no sooner had she done that, Cressie's heart stopped as a third voice joined their clandestine rendezvous.

"Miss Delaney, what are you doing there?" Imelda's voice demanded to know.

"Wrigley!" Zara exclaimed in shock, her voice filling with panic.

"What are you doing at Mrs Delaney's door? What is that you have there?"

Cressie's soul left her body as she slammed herself into the wood of the door in desperation. "Give it back!" she hissed. "Pass it back to me!"

She heard Zara scramble, all subtlety leaving her in that moment as she struggled to pass Cressie back the letter. Cressie couldn't see what was happening on the other side of the door, but she could hear the struggle and the grunts of the two women as Zara strived to protect Cressie and Imelda strived to be Everett's pet.

Cressie banged on the door with her fists, at a total loss of knowing what to do in that moment. There was a thud from the other side of the door that sounded like a body, before Imelda cried, "Thank you!"

Cressie's heart stopped.

"You know that conversing with Mrs Delaney is forbidden, and whatever notes you have been passing are certainly not allowed as well. I will be delivering this promptly to your uncle, and he will certainly see you disciplined accordingly."

Cressie heard Imelda's proud footsteps march away, and she could have only imagined how quietly she must had skulked in the shadows to come across Zara at the door for neither of them to have heard her approach.

"Cressie, I'm sorry!" Zara cried, her voice thick with her tears.

"Zara, you have to go now," Cressie ordered. "Leave the house immediately, before Everett locks you up as well. You need to go to Jem, and you must tell him that I am with child."

CHAPTER 39

Jem was in a sort of limbo. He was no longer participating in the Season. He was no longer pretending to court Zara. He had no reason to promenade in the park to happen across Cressie. But he could not leave London. Not without her.

He distracted himself from his worry over Cressie by completing his work as the Land Steward for Ashwood by correspondence. But the paperwork did little to take his mind off of what might have been happening to Cressie inside of that house.

Lord, in another lifetime he would have been rich enough to study the law. Surely something could be done to prevent this unnatural imbalance of power. How was it that a man could have such power of a woman? How was it that a wife could be at the mercy of her husband without any right to leave him?

A man could desert his wife whenever he wanted. Mrs Martin was evidence of that. As far as he knew, Mr Martin, Cressie's father, was still gallivanting about the Continent with a mistress some thirty years his junior. If a wife wanted to do the same thing, she ought to have the right.

The right to anything. But first and foremost, a woman had the right to her own autonomy, and her own safety.

Jem was pulled away from his worries by the sound of a commotion downstairs. He could hear shouting voices, voices that were filled with stress and anguish, and it prompted Jem to launch out of his chair immediately. Was it Cressie? Had she escaped? Was she here? Such thoughts and hopes flashed through his mind as he all but pulled the study door off of its hinges and ran towards the first-floor landing, towards the source of the noise.

But as soon as he reached the landing, his heart fell when he realised that it was not Cressie who had come, but Zara. His disappointment could not last long, however, as the expression on Zara's face was cause for alarm. She appeared positively terrified, filled with desperation, as she shouted at the footmen in a way that she would never usually address servants.

"Fetch me your master immediately!" she shrieked. "Please, please, hurry! Please, something terrible is going to happen!"

"Zara!" Jem called from above, capturing the young girl's attention instantly.

There wear tears in Zara's blue eyes, and her cheeks were flushed a bright scarlet from exertion. Had she run all the way here? "Jem!" she cried, bypassing the footman and running to the stairs. "Jem, you have to help me."

They both met each other midway on the steps, and Zara grabbed onto Jem in a way that unmarried ladies would never do. But there was not romance or desire in the way that Zara clung to Jem. It was desperation.

"Jem, I fear something terrible is going to happen!" Zara stressed hysterically.

"Tell me!" Jem demanded to know.

"Cressie wrote you a letter, a response to the letter you wrote her," Zara blubbered. "I went to collect it this morning. But her maid discovered us and took the letter from me. The fought it off of me, more like. Cressie was beating on the door, she wanted me to give the letter back to her. She told me to tell you that she is with child."

Jem felt his whole body seize upon hearing Zara's news. A multitude of feelings, shock, confusion, fear, all coursed through his body and mind at once. And one kept repeating. But Cressie was not able to bear children.

Was she wrong? Had Cressie been mistaken all this time? Was she sitting in that house, right at this moment, carrying their child?

"When Uncle Everett learns that Cressie is carrying his heir, she will be trapped forever," Zara continued in her frenzied panic.

It was Everett's child.

Jem gripped Zara's shoulders, partly to settle her, and partly to centre himself from his own shock. It was Everett's child. Of course, it was. Everett had been in residence in London for several weeks now. The blackguard had Cressie at his mercy, and he'd had plenty of time to ...

Jem could not even finish the thought; it was too infuriating. All Jem knew was that Zara was right. The minute Everett found out that Cressie was carrying his heir, she would be trapped forever. Even when the child was born, Cressie would never be able to leave. She would never be able to abandon her child the way her father had abandoned her. This child was a life sentence as much as it should have been a blessing.

But if she could get away ...

Jem knew the answer to the question before he had even asked it of himself. He would love any child of Cressie's body, and he could only pray that they made it in time to liberate her.

The hallway was silent for what felt like an age. Cressie listened at the lock until her back ached from crouching. How her heart managed to keep beating she would never understand. She had put the poor thing through a lifetime's worth of anguish in a matter of hours.

The inevitable would happen. Everett would come. No matter what, he would come. That door would open, and Cressie was going to have to fight with every ounce of her strength to make it through. She had fight in her. It had never left her, only lying dormant for much too long.

No matter what, she would not allow the little child within her to grow up as a prisoner.

The pounding sound of boots marching down the hallway finally came and gone was Everett's usual proud walk. The velocity in which he walked, and the weight behind his steps, was evidence enough of his fury.

Cressie instinctively backed up from the door, but as she heard the violence in which the key was shoved into the lock, she filled her lungs with air. Be ready, she told herself.

The moment the door was unlocked, it was not opened, but kicked right off of its hinged, the door frame splintering, as it fell to the ground. Cressie jumped backwards at the sheer sound of the wood splitting.

Everett seemed to double in size, taking up the entire doorway with his person, as he huffed with pure rage. His cold, usually unfeeling grey eyes, were centred on her, and were filled with crazed indignation.

"Whore!" he seethed through his clenched teeth.

The options that Cressie had considered flashed through her mind with rapid speed, and the first two seemed like ridiculous fantasies. The third option was clearly the only one for a man such as Everett Delaney. He was going to kill her. Her infidelity had wounded his manhood. Her falling pregnant to another, proving that he was the one with useless seed, was probably a fatal blow.

Everett stormed into the bedroom and wished her dead with his eyes, and Cressie knew that now was her only chance. She wouldn't wait another moment. The door was open, or rather in pieces, and she needed to run. Cressie did not hesitate. She charged at the door, hoping to be so quick that Everett would not have been expecting her to run.

And she was quick.

Just not quick enough. As she passed Everett, his arm swung around in an effort to catch her. He missed her arms or her torso, and for the briefest moment, Cressie thought that she was clear. But her head suddenly snapped back, and she fell to the floor like a ragdoll as Everett caught a fistful of her hair and seized it tightly.

Pain radiated from her scalp as Everett's grip only tightened. She reached up in a desperate attempt to loosen his fingers, but it was useless.

"Whose is it?" Everett yanked on her hair, forcing her head back as he leaned over her intimidatingly. He spat in Cressie's face as he forced her head back even further, her neck feeling like it was mere inches from snapping. "I want his name so that I can kill him in front of you before I send your filthy, wretched existence to Hell."

Cressie cried out in pain as Everett pulled on her hair again. She didn't know what to do. She didn't know how to survive this. All she knew was that she would never give him Jem's name.

But she did not have to.

"Is it him? Jem Denham. Is it?"

Cressie's eyes must have betrayed her as Everett swore disgustingly, at her, and at Jem. And then Everett pulled her out of the room, but by her hand, or on her feet, but he dragged her by her hair down the hallway, pulling her too quickly for her to gain any sort of footing. She could not concentrate on much but the pain, but she could not understand how her hair was not pulled from her scalp.

As Everett dragged her, Cressie screamed and cried in pain, and he cursed her with every derogatory word that came into his brain, brandishing her a whore as the end of every disgusting tirade.

All she could do was pray that Zara got to Jem in time. She didn't want Jem to be in any danger, but he had to come. He had to. He had to take her and their child both away from here.

That was the last thought she had before Everett used his booted foot to kick her down the stairs. Cressie tumbled down the wooden staircase quickly, flipping over and over, hitting every square inch of her body. The pain that was concentrated in her scalp quickly radiated all over her body as possible broken bones and bruises began to appear. Cressie landed in a heap at the foot of the stairs, disorientated and weak as she faintly heard Everett screaming orders for Dabney to be brought around.

Cressie felt no control whatsoever over her body. She couldn't feel her hands or her feet with any sort of coherency in order to climb to her feet. Had she hit her head? She felt a targeted, sharp pain suddenly in her back as Everett kicked her again, before he grabbed a hold of her hair once more.

Cressie cried and whimpered as Everett dragged her out onto the street and dumped her in a pile of limbs and dress.

"She's a whore!" Everett screamed fanatically. "This woman is a whore! Don't you tend to her! Spit on her! She's a whore!"

Cressie could vaguely hear the voices of others, perhaps they were neighbours or passers-by. She blinked her eyes repeatedly, but she felt blinded by the sunlight and deafened by the pain ringing in her ears.

After blinking several more times, Cressie's vision began to focus a little and she could see that quite a crowd had gathered at the sensational scene that Everett was in the midst of creating.

Everett ranted about her infidelity and her pregnancy, cursing her to anyone who would meet his eye. He'd gone entirely mad, and Cressie believed that he would actually kill Jem if he saw him.

Her hazy vision focussed on Everett's poor horse, as the steed was forced to near his master. A servant pulled on Dabney's reins to bring him towards Everett, and Dabney screamed in a way that Cressie could intimately understand.

"Stupid beast!" Everett cursed as he seized hold of Dabney's riding crop and beat him on the rear with it a dozen times, forcing the servant to hold onto Dabney's reins with his entire body weight as she horse tried to flee.

Everett suddenly turned around, riding crop still in hand, and a wicked idea etched across his face.

As he approached to beat her in the same way, Dabney broke free of the servant's hold, rearing to his great, formidable height, before bringing down his heavy hooves upon Everett's head. In a matter of seconds, Everett was silenced, and he crumpled to the ground.

CHAPTER 40

J em saw the events unfold in complete and utter disbelief. As he rounded the corner and came onto Cressie's street at great speed, he immediately saw a crowd of people gathered. The subsequent ranting her heard seconds later told him all he needed to. Their fears were realised, and Jem pushed his legs to move even faster. He would bowl over these people if he needed to.

But before he reached the crowd, before he could use his elbows to push them all out of the way, Jem saw Everett Delaney's horse rear to his almighty height, and he brought his hooves down upon his master's skull. Such a sight stopped Jem dead in his tracks, albeit briefly.

The crowd gasped and swooned as the servant struggled to control the panicked horse. The stallion's uncontrolled thrashing dispersed the crowd just enough for Jem to see that Everett was not alone on the pavement. Cressie was also there, and by the looks of her, she was nearing unconsciousness herself.

Jem nearly brought up his stomach as he sprinted towards her, bypassing Everett without a care. He fell to the ground beside Cressie and immediately lifted her head to support it on his lap. Cressie's golden curls cascaded over his thighs as her groggy brown eyes found his. She had a cut over her right eyebrow and swelling forming on that side of her face. He noticed several other welts across her exposed skin. What had that bastard done to her?

"Cressie, can you hear me?"

Jem barely registered the sounds of the people around him, the ones tending to Everett. How could they render service to such a man?

Cressie's eyes slowly blinked. "He ... knows," she croaked weakly. "You ... need ... to ... hide."

Jem shook his head vehemently. "No. I've had enough. I'm never leaving you again. Hang the law. Hang it all." He tore his eyes away from Cressie when he heard a sudden scream from a woman in the crowd.

Everett had roused, and had pushed himself up using his arms, glaring at Jem with red eyes, as though they were filled with blood. Blood poured from his mouth and his nose, and he began to drag himself along the ground with a clumsy yet mad strength.

"Get ... AWAY!" he gurgled, blood splattering on the pavement.

Jem instinctively seized Cressie. He supported her head as he got to his feet, and he lifted her up into his arms effortlessly. From this height, Jem could see a gushing, gaping wound on the back of Everett's head, and it was as though only his sheer hatred was keeping him alive.

Cressie lifted her head groggily, and she stiffened when she saw Everett pulling desperately at the distance between them. "Help me ... to stand," she asked Jem, and he gently set her feet on the ground so that Cressie was standing a few feet from where Everett lay crawling.

"You whore!" Everett screeched. "You'll get nothing from me. Nothing!" His words were slurred with blood, his teeth now stained crimson.

"I want nothing from you," Cressie said, looking down upon him with pitiful disdain, her voice steadying. "In fact, from the moment you die, I will never think of you again. I will forget you, and you will forever be insignificant." Cressie's knees bent, and she became unsteady.

Jem supported her as she went to kneel down beside Everett. Whatever she was summoning from within her, it was powerful enough to help her remain strong even when she had suffered so plainly.

"You failed, Everett. You didn't break me. I am stronger than you ever could be," Cressie murmured. "But dear Dabney broke you."

Everett attempted to spit at Cressie, but quickly began to choke on the amount of blood that had collected in his mouth. Jem put a protective arm around Cressie as Everett's arms collapsed beneath him and his face hit the stone pavement. His limbs twitched briefly, before they ceased completely, and he was most certainly dead.

Cressie stared at him for a long moment before her legs, too, collapsed beneath her. She did not land on the ground, however, as Jem caught her in time, and turned his body away from the scene so that Cressie was separated from the body of her deceased husband. In doing so, Jem got a good look at the gathered crowed, and the many shocked faces of the men, as well as the swooning women.

The servant who had been holding Dabney's reins had finally regained control of him, and the poor lad looked very frightened indeed at the scene before him. "Send for an undertaker," he instructed, "and then inform whomever it need be that the Ashwood Estate would like to purchase this horse."

Jem had a sudden fear that this horse, abused and broken, much like his master had tried to do to Cressie, would be auctioned for meat after such a display. He knew that Adam would approve of gifting the horse to Alex to live on his farm with him and Susanna, the horse lover that he was. If ever there was a man who knew how to care for one who'd been under the thumb of a cruel master, it was Alex.

Everything hurt. Cressie could barely move her chest to breathe. Her eyes fluttered open and she groaned. She had floated in and out of consciousness for several hours, or maybe days. She wasn't certain.

There had been a doctor present. Cressie could vaguely remember hearing a conversation about a baby, but she couldn't force herself to stay alert. Was the baby gone? Had the baby survived the fall?

A sob ripped from Cressie's half-conscious lips, and she felt her hand being squeezed.

"Cressie, all is well," Jem assured her.

"The baby!" she stressed.

"Is well!" Jem assured her. "A doctor came to examine you and found no evidence of any loss. Your baby is safe."

Cressie's sobs became violent as all manner of emotions rushed through her. She suddenly felt like she was experiencing everything all at once, and it was entirely overwhelming. She felt the pains and aches in her body physically, but the emotional toll was something else entirely.

She felt a dip in the bed as Jem came to sit beside her, and he gently cuddled Cressie to his side. Cressie felt tenderness in her body, as though she was covered in bruises.

It wasn't until a little while later, after Cressie had cried out her sobs and whimpered with relief, that she realised that Jem had referred to the baby as hers.

"Our," she corrected softly.

"What?"

"Our," Cressie repeated. She lifted one of her stiff arms to find Jem's hand, and she gently placed it atop her stomach. "Ours. Yours and mine." When she looked into his ocean eyes, before Jem had understood her meaning, Cressie could see that it didn't matter. Jem loved her, and he would love this child regardless of its parentage. But Jem clearly wasn't certain of the child's father.

But when he realised, a smile spread across his face as his hand began to carefully rub Cressie's stomach. "Ours." He leaned down and pressed a soft kiss to her forehead. "You're healing, my precious Messy Cressie, and you're free."

An uncontrolled giggle escaped from between Cressie's lips, in stark contrast to her sobs from earlier. Simply hearing that name felt freeing. Her bruises would heal, and she would be free to do what she liked. She would be free to make her own choices. She would have her own autonomy.

"I'm free," she whispered.

The following hours were spent with Zara, who could not have felt more terrible for the events that had unfolded. She blamed herself for her uncle learning the truth and for Cressie's being hurt the way that she was.

Cressie did all she could to alleviate young Zara's guilt as someone her age should not have to carry such burdens. After all she had done for Cressie, Zara deserved everything and more. Zara had taken on much more than she anticipated this Season. She had arrived as a naïve, young debutante, and instead of enjoying her time receiving calls and paying visits, she had assisted Cressie in every way imaginable, forsaking herself.

Cressie did worry what would happen to Zara in the coming weeks once news had reached her grandparents of Everett's death. She would return to their care as they were her legal guardians.

Later that evening, Cressie's mother tentatively knocked on her door. As Mrs Martin entered, Jem went to leave, but Mrs Martin asked him to stay.

"Oh, Cressie," Mrs Martin murmured softly as she approached the bed, sitting down on the opposite side to Jem.

"Mama," she whispered in reply.

"I am so relieved that you are safe, my dear child."

The moment those words were spoken, Mrs Martin's grey-green eyes became glassy and she turned away, fishing a clean handkerchief from her sleeve as she wiped her eyes. Once she had composed herself, Mrs Martin turned back to face Cressie and Jem.

"I owe you both a monumental apology," she insisted. "Cressie ... I cannot even begin ... my darling, I failed you. There is no other way to put it. I failed you. I failed you in every way a mother can fail her daughter. I will never forgive myself for putting you in any situation where you were unsafe –"

"But Mama –"

"No," Mrs Martin interrupted. "No, I won't have you trying to ease my guilt. It is mine, and deservedly so. My only consolation is that, at the time, I sincerely did believe that I was making the right choice for you. But I see now that it was not my choice to make. You were perfectly capable of making your choice then as you are now, and you deserve a life that fulfils you entirely.

"I see now that nothing I could have done could ever really have separated you both." Mrs Martin briefly smiled in an accepting fashion as her eyes flicked between her daughter and Jem. "You have a better eye then I ever did, Cressie. I am sorry, my darling girl, and I hope that you can find it in your heart to forgive me one day."

Cressie took a moment to take in her mother's words. They were very overwhelming, as had much of the last several months been. Her instinct was to forgive and appease, but her mother was right. Cressie needed time to sit with what had happened, and then, and only then, could she find her way back to loving her mother as she once had.

And Cressie had faith that she would get there one day.

"For what it's worth, you both have my blessing. I should have given it years ago."

CHAPTER 41

C ressie was able to move about more normally in the days
that followed, albeit stiffly as the purple bruises appeared on
her skin from her fall. She was in a bit of a haze of thick emotions
and she was quite certain it would be some time before she would
ever truly be able to comprehend just what had happened to her.

But if ever she felt herself being caught up in the gravity of it all,
she need only remind herself that she was safe and free, and that
she was in this house by her own choice. Never would she choose
to leave Jem's side again. And how Jem was patient with her.

One needed to only witness Jem's tenderness to know that he
was raised with utter compassion. His nature was to care and
protect, and he was why she felt as safe as she did. She loved him
completely for it.

Cressie loved Jem for a multitude of reasons. She was still
counting the ways. But to be made to feel so safe so soon after
such an ordeal was incredible.

Gone was any pretence of propriety. She rarely left Jem's side,
and never did at night. Cressie could not have cared less about
any sort of scandal. She had taken no notice of that sort of thing,
though she had no doubt that her name was being flown around

London by the gossips after the scene that had been made on the day Dabney had rendered justice.

Widows traditionally wore mourning attire for an age and certainly did not plan on remarrying within the first year after their spouse's death. Cressie would have remarried within hours if it were possible.

In protest, or rather celebration of her own free will, Cressie was dressed in white, the complete opposite to black.

"My brother and sister wish to dine before we return to Ashwood," Jem told Cressie tentatively. He read from a letter as they ate their breakfast together in the dining room, though his expression was uncertain. "Claire and her husband, Jack, and Peter and his wife, Belle. I can refuse them if you are not ready to receive visitors."

"They're your family," Cressie replied softly, "only ..."

"Only what?" Jem prompted once Cressie had trailed off.

She bit down on her bottom lip nervously. "Have you told them? Have you told them about the baby?" It was highly likely they already knew. It was highly likely half of England knew. Again, Cressie did not care at all what strangers thought of her. But she did care what Jem's family thought. And she knew that he would, too. His family were so proper. His eldest sister was a duchess. Cressie couldn't imagine any of Jem's sisters doing something so shameful as to falling pregnant out of wedlock.

"No, I haven't told them," Jem replied tenderly. He seemed to read Cressie's hesitancy and uneasiness on her face and he took her hand. "But we will," he said encouragingly. "They will be happy for us," he promised. "And they will all love our son or daughter." Jem artfully collected Cressie with a gentle pull to her hand, inviting her into his lap so that he could wrap his arms around her, holding his hands on her stomach protectively.

Cressie nestled into his chest and sighed. "Our son or daughter," she repeated in a whisper. "What would you rather?"

"A girl who looks exactly like you," Jem answered almost immediately, like he'd been thinking about it for a while.

His comment brought a smile to her lips immediately. Cressie wanted a girl as well, but for different reasons. The first was because she knew that there would be less likelihood of interference from the Delaney estate if her child was a girl. Her late prison warden (for she was loathed to call him 'husband'), had proclaimed to the world that she was unfaithful, and so there was little chance of any claim on the child, but she did not want to risk it.

The second reason was because she longed to have a girl who could enjoy her own freedom from her very first breath. No daughter of Cressie and Jem would ever be forced to do anything. From eating a Brussels sprout, to entertaining suitors. Free will would always be the order of the day.

"So long as she has your ocean eyes," Cressie decided, looking up at Jem and finding his eyes on her. Aside from her conch shell, they were the closest things to the sea that she had ever seen. "If she has your eyes then I shall be content if I never set foot on a beach."

"You will see the ocean one day," Jem promised, leaning down and kissing her softly on the forehead.

A knock on the dining room door disturbed them, and both Jem and Cressie looked up. Cressie righted herself immediately and shifted herself back into her own chair. The door opened and the Ashwood Place butler stood before them, appearing very awkward indeed.

Before Cressie could wonder if the butler's unease had anything to do with her, he said, "A servant has arrived with a letter for you,

Miss Martin." Jem had insisted that Cressie be referred to by her maiden name. Cressie quite agreed. "She is waiting in the kitchen. She is insisting that she deliver it to you herself."

Cressie frowned, but she did not have to wonder for long. For whom else could it be? Who else would have such a nerve as to make demands of a butler for such a family? Who else would carry such an air of self-importance but the lackey of a prison warden?

"Is it Imelda Wrigley?" Cressie asked, already knowing the answer.

"Yes, ma'am," confirmed the butler.

"Tell her to kindly walk in front of a carriage," Jem snarled.

"No, I want to speak with her," Cressie decided.

"Are you sure?" Jem frowned. "Cressie, you needn't. She can be made to go."

"I want to," Cressie assured him insistently. She stood up from the dining room table and Jem followed suit, taking her hand before they followed the butler out of the dining room.

The servants were all busy below stairs as they went about their daily duties. The moment that they entered the kitchen, Cressie could see the scullery maids attending to the pots that had been used to prepare the breakfast dishes that she and Jem had been enjoying only moments ago. She could see another servant sitting at the long table adjacent to the kitchen with her dress in hand and a sewing kit as she mended the rips that had been made when she had tumbled down the stairs.

Standing in the middle of it all wearing a dark cloak and bonnet was her lady's maid. In her gloved hand, Cressie could see that Imelda was holding a sealed letter. Whether or not it was a legitimate letter, or merely a ruse to speak to Cressie, she was unsure. Cressie, however, wanted to see this woman one last time regardless.

"Wrigley," Cressie murmured.

Imelda did not curtsey. She did, however, nod in acknowledgment as she said, "Mrs Delaney."

Cressie did not correct her, though she could feel Jem tense at her side. This movement in Jem's long limbs captured Imelda's attention briefly, and she did not hide her sneer.

"Don't you dare look at Mr Denham in such a way," Cressie commanded with an authority once lost to her. Her tone startled Imelda, as the maid was taken aback.

Nevertheless, she averted her eyes and focussed on Cressie. Her gaze flicked over the bruises that were very apparent on Cressie's face. "I have been charged with delivering this to you." She held out the letter. "It is from Mr Delaney's solicitor."

Cressie did not accept the letter. She did not reach for it. She simply stared at her maid. "Why do you still do his bidding? He is dead."

Imelda flinched.

"How could you ever comply with such a man? You knew what he was," Cressie accused. "You knew it. Look at me. Look at what he did. You knew it all."

"You vowed to love, honour, and obey your husband, and you broke your word. You deserved what you got," Imelda replied dryly. "It is the way. A husband has the right to demand obedience and respect from his wife."

"If obedience and respect must be commanded from a subordinate, then it is not true obedience and respect," retorted Cressie. "Wedding vows work both ways. He made promises also, Wrigley. Look at me. Look at what he did to me." Cressie gestured to her face.

Cressie could see the conflict on Imelda's face, as though her belief in a wife's submission was ingrained within her. She could not understand how one could ever justify a man's abuse of his position.

"You became another man's whore," Imelda said distastefully. "You deserved it," she reiterated.

"Get out!" commanded Jem, pointing to the door.

"God save you," Cressie uttered in disbelief.

"God save you," Imelda retorted. "I came here not only to deliver this letter, but to offer you the chance to see sense. I have always tried my best to make you the best mistress you could be. I have failed as you have fought me every day, but you have one last opportunity. Mr Delaney's parents are travelling to London. There will be a funeral service conducted where you will be expected to attend as his widow. There will undoubtedly be a widow's pension from the estate, which is what I imagine the solicitor writes to you about. It is time for you to grow up, Mrs Delaney."

Cressie had to put her hand on Jem's chest to stop him from intervening. Had she not, Cressie was quite certain that he would have physically expelled Imelda from the kitchen window.

"You're right," Cressie admitted calmly, nodding her head.

Even Imelda seemed surprised at Cressie's sudden acquiescence. Jem certainly stiffened.

"It is time for me to grow up. For only children, nay, indentured servants so blindly obey." She shook her head. "I will never mourn anyone who wields their power over those weaker than them. I will never grieve a man whose nature was always to be cruel and never kind. I will not pretend to miss a man who never loved me, but collected me, like a trophy on a shelf. I want nothing from him. I want nothing at all. I choose not to read that letter, and I choose to forget that I was ever tied to someone as inhuman as him. God save you, Imelda. I saved me."

Zara knew that she would be eventually summoned back to live with her grandparents, but until she was discovered, she travelled along with Jem, Cressie, and Mrs Martin to Hertfordshire.

After the warm reception she had received by Jem's family in London, she was feeling excited and optimistic, especially as the London environment disappeared, and the countryside surrounded them.

Again, she knew that time would be the true healer, but exercising these freedoms for herself felt like air in her lungs. And she knew that if she demanded the carriage be stopped and diverted all the way to Cornwall, then it would be so.

When they began to travel through the outskirts of the Ashwood village, Cressie began to recognise it, even though she had only lived there briefly five years earlier. Perhaps in meeting someone terribly special, she had committed it unknowingly to memory.

"Oh, my goodness," Zara gasped as they finally came in view of the great house. Cressie's eyes, similarly, widened. She had never seen it either. "What an extraordinary house. You live here, Jem?"

Jem chuckled. "No." He shook his head. "My brother-in-law and sister do. I have a house on their land as part of my duties as Land Steward."

"And I thought that Grandpapa and Grandmamma were well to do," Zara muttered under her breath.

"Do not be intimidated," Jem urged. "Any of you," he emphasised. "Grace is my eldest sister, and were it possible, she would give you the blood in her veins if you needed it. And her husband, Adam, is the most decent man. He gave me a chance and taught me how to be his steward. They are the definition of good people."

Cressie had met them before obviously, but she had never known them in such an intimate setting. Even though her meeting with Claire, Peter, and their spouses, had gone swimmingly, the thought of knowing the Duke and Duchess of Ashwood so informally was daunting.

When the carriage stopped and the footmen climbed down to open the door, Mrs Martin and Zara exited first, and Jem subtly held Cressie back from following. For the briefest moment, Jem placed a chaste kiss on her lips, before smiling and nodding. "We're here," he whispered.

"Do I look alright?" she asked in the same hushed tone. The bruises on her face had yellowed by then, and the swelling from the cut on her forehead had gone down. She simply looked a little discoloured upon first glance.

"You're beautiful," Jem uttered. "I have been mercilessly distracted by your beauty for the best part of my adult life. It is hardly fair."

Jem's grin elicited a laugh from Cressie, and how it felt good to laugh. She was reminded of the days when they had once been able to laugh and be silly and enjoy the other's company under the veil of late childhood. With time as her healer, Cressie knew there would be a lot more laughing in her future.

"I am terribly sorry, Mr Denham. I shall endeavour to make myself uglier so as not to distract you." Cressie subsequently contorted her face into the most ridiculous expression that she could conjury, and Jem snorted, before he pulled her close to kiss her again, more deeply this time.

Before the party had barely even reached the front door, let alone crossed the threshold into the foyer, a young girl moving faster than a flash of lightning burst through the parade of footmen carrying the travellers' luggage.

"Uncle Jem!" Perrie cheered, throwing herself into Jem's arms.

Jem chuckled as he swung his niece around. When he placed Perrie back onto her feet, he was glad to see that she had not grown or changed much in his absence. She was destined to be short like her mother. Perrie's large blue eyes briefly took in the rest of the guests, but she did not acknowledge them. There was determination in her eyes, and Jem recognised that expression of justice.

Oh, dear. What had she done?

"Mama and Papa are being ridiculous!" Perrie exclaimed. "I am being punished until the end of the decade, so I am so glad that you are here, because I need you to go to Papa's study and tell him it was all your idea! Papa likes you. He won't punish you." Perrie scampered around Jem and placed her hands flat on his back, before she pushed him with all her might. Jem staggered forwards a few steps, before he regained his footing. They did, however, move inside the foyer.

"Cressie, Mrs Martin, Zara," Jem called over his shoulder, watching that they had followed him inside. "This is my niece, Perrie. Perrie, won't you greet –"

"Uncle Jem!" Perrie huffed, interrupting him. She ceased pushing and came back around to face him. She put her hands on her hips and stared up at him with gumption beyond her years. "Are you listening to me? I am being punished until the end of the decade! And none of it was my fault!"

Jem sighed with a wicked grin on his face. "What happened?"

"Do you remember when I showed you that embroidery?" Perrie prompted. "The one with 'Little Imp' stitched upon it? That's what he always calls me. Always! Never anything but that. Mrs Hayes measured me, and I have grown one quarter inch this year!" she insisted.

Had she? Jem dared not offend Perrie with his remark seeing as whatever she had done warranted such a great punishment. He managed to mask his smirk.

"So, I put pins on his chair as you suggested."

Jem heard a giggle from behind him.

"And then he removed the nails from my chair so that I fell in front of everyone. So, I snuck dung onto his chair so that he would sit in it and then I accused him of soiling himself in front of everyone. He then cut off a chunk of my hair!" Perrie fished through her long, dark locks to find a large piece that was shorter than the rest. "It was only right what I did, don't you think?"

Whomever this boy was, he certainly brought the competition out of Perrie. But they were clearly as bad as one another. He was nasty, and Perrie gave it right back to him.

"Seeing as I don't know what you did next, I am not so sure."

Perrie huffed. "Mama and Papa said I could invite the school children to Ashwood to swim in the pond because it was hot."

Jem's face fell as he recalled Perrie's original plan that she had relayed to him in his house months ago. She hadn't gone through with it, had she?

"We were playing, honest! He was splashing me and calling me an imp, and so ..." Perrie pursed her lips guiltily.

"So, what?" prompted Jem.

"Promise me you will go and tell Papa it was your idea so I can stop being punished," Perrie begged.

"The pin was my idea. I'm not taking the blame for anything else," Jem retorted. "You didn't try to drown him, did you?"

"Not really!" Perrie exclaimed. "I climbed on his shoulders and sat on him for not even a full minute! He was probably under water for ten seconds and then decided to be a baby." She rolled her eyes and folded her arms across her chest indignantly. "I was never going to actually drown him. And he got right back at me by stealing my clothes! He wasn't even upset. He laughed at me! He's just evil and stupid and wicked and Mama and Papa are overreacting."

"Overreacting?" came a commanding voice from above. "Have you finished your letter of apology, or do you desire to be punished until the end of the next decade as well?" Adam asked with his brows raised.

"Papa, you do realise that giving him an apology letter will only cause him to torture me even more!" Perrie scowled at her father as he descended the stairs.

"Perhaps you should have thought of that before you tried to drown the poor boy," dismissed Adam as he shooed Perrie away towards the stairs.

Perrie gasped. "Poor boy?" she repeated. "Papa, he's wicked and evil! And if I hadn't had the idea to drown him, I mean, if Uncle Jem hadn't had the idea to drown him first, then he would have tried to drown me!"

"My God, we named you girls around the wrong way," Adam sighed. "If ever there was a Cecily-incarnate, it is you, Perrie."

Perrie growled under her breath as she stomped up the stairs dramatically.

"I never suggested drowning!" Jem joked as he held his hands up.

Adam laughed. "Just quietly, I rather enjoy Perrie's colourful creativity. I should prefer that she channels it into more ladylike pursuits, but then I think I prefer her being merciless towards the opposite sex. It is settling me before I have to inevitably think about taking her to London one day for a Season." Adam then looked up at the accompanying guests and smiled warmly. "Do forgive my daughter. That is hardly a proper welcome."

Jem smiled. He rather enjoyed Perrie's spirit as well. "Allow me to make introductions."

"Are you happy, Jemmy?"

"I thought I told you never to call me that." But Jem couldn't be angry at his sister. Never.

Grace had looped her arm through Jem's as she sat next to him closely on the settee in the drawing room after dinner. It had been too long since Jem had been in a room this full. Grace had invited everyone for dinner only after ensuring that Cressie would be alright with a parade of Denhams and Beresfords descending upon her. Jem knew that Cressie would never refuse a duchess, but he had privately asked her as well.

She was sat on the opposing settee in deep conversation with Mrs Denham and Kate, their other family members having dotted themselves around the room in similar conversations with glasses of champagne in hand. It was a celebration, after all.

"But yes, to answer your question. I am happy."

Grace rubbed Jem's arm affectionately. "I might cry." True enough, her voice was thick with emotion.

Jem chuckled. "You haven't been this worried about me, have you?"

Grace rested her head on Jem's shoulder. "I think it's a special something that grows within you when you become a parent. You will learn it soon enough. The capacity to worry amplifies dramatically. And when my sisters and brother have been so fortunate, as have I, myself, to find true love matches, I could only worry that you had missed your chance, or that you would never open yourself up to trying again."

Jem's eyes flicked around the room, finding the spouses of his siblings. Adam and Jim were engaged in conversation with Alex and Susanna, but both men seemed to naturally look back at their wives sporadically, as though they couldn't help it. Jem might have once found such devotion amusing, but he understood it now.

He found himself doing the same thing. He had to look back at Cressie, to make certain that she was really here, and with him. And he felt like the luckiest sod to ever walk the planet.

"Thank you for accepting her," Jem replied. "You cannot know what that means to me, and to Cressie as well. She was anxious about her condition and how you would all feel —"

"Always!" Grace interjected. "Jem, I do not care how the right people find their way to our family, so long as they get here. We get to welcome a sister-in-law and a new niece or nephew. It is a good day."

Jem was still watching Cressie, and at that moment, her brown eyes came up to find his. Jem could see the relief on her face, and the happiness that she was allowing to radiate within her. For someone whose life had been so lived for others, autonomy looked beautiful on her.

EPILOGUE

November 1817

"Can I open my eyes yet?" Cressie asked impatiently.

"No," Jem said emphatically, and for the sixteenth time that minute.

"What if I ask you really nicely, and conclude my request by calling you my sweet husband?" Cressie begged, her hands still obliging him by covering her eyes.

Jem chuckled. Though, he did not think he would ever tire of being called Cressie's husband. "Not even then."

Cressie huffed. "Annoying husband."

"Husband all the same." Jem grinned, and despite Cressie's eyes being covered, he could see a tug at the corner of her rosy lips.

It wouldn't be much longer that he would be torturing Cressie with the suspense of their honeymoon location. They had been travelling for several days to the West Country, only Cressie didn't know that. Their honeymoon journey was a wedding gift from Adam and Grace, brought upon by Jem's idea for a perfect surprise for Cressie.

The wedding, itself, was a small affair. It would have happened sooner had Cecily not arranged for Belle to design and make

Cressie's wedding gown ... for the second time. Belle had worked as quickly as her nimble fingers would allow, and once the banns were read and the dress was finished, Jem and Cressie were married by the Ashwood Parish vicar. By that time, Cressie's figure appeared a little fuller to those who were not the wiser.

Once they were returned to Ashwood, Cressie and Jem were separated, which neither one of them particularly enjoyed. But all was worth it by the time the wedding finally arrived and Jem got to see his bride finally floating down the aisle towards him.

It was hard in that moment of pure joy not to briefly recall the last time he had seen Cressie in a wedding gown. The ache of his shattered heart could still be recalled keenly when he pictured Cressie walking out of the London church five years earlier on the arm of another. Every trial had brought them here, finally. And while Jem would have wished that their road to their marriage had been easier, he knew that both he and Cressie were stronger, more compassionate people for it.

"I've lost count of the number of days we have been travelling." Cressie slumped beside him, the fabric of her dress settling atop her rounded stomach. He was glad that her eyes were closed. He couldn't help but stare at it with a giddy look on his face. "I wonder if Zara has reached Suffolk yet."

Zara had left for her grandparents' home in Suffolk shortly after the wedding, the same as she had been summoned back there shortly after arriving in Ashwood. The Delaneys' solicitor had been running about the country in the aftermath of Everett Delaney's death. The shock of their son's demise had brought on a heart episode, and the elder Mr Delaney had died a short time later. The elder Mrs Delaney had become quite indisposed, and rather neglected Zara despite wanting her home. The heir to the Delaney estate had been located in the last several weeks as a very distant cousin by the name of George Delaney. The young man was educated and free thinking, by all reports, and gave Zara permission to attend Jem and Cressie's wedding despite the observed mourning period. Upon speaking with Zara, Cressie determined that Zara was quite sweet on him.

"I'm certain you'll have a letter waiting for you when we return home telling you all about her new sweetheart."

"I could have given her the address here, or wherever we are going, if only you weren't so secretive, annoying husband," Cressie snapped comically. "Do you know what, I think that carriages ought to be pulled by stallions so that we may get places faster."

Jem laughed. He could not wait to see Cressie's face when he finally allowed her to open her eyes. "I don't know how horses like Dabney would do pulling carriages. There are such things as carriage horses for a reason. Dabney is not a carriage horse."

"Dabney would certainly get us there more quickly."

"Dabney's content in getting Alex around his farm quickly. Be patient. Maybe Dabney will take a shine to Alex's mare, Argent. There could be foals in his future." Jem pressed a kiss onto the top of Cressie's head, just as he felt her shiver.

"I can't thank you enough for that, you know," she said then in a more serious tone. "You weren't going to leave anyone behind, were you?"

"No," murmured Jem. And that's all there was to say.

Jem looked out the window at the beautiful landscape. He was marvelled himself at the beauty of the West Country, as he had never seen this before. They weren't quite at their destination yet, but Jem couldn't deny Cressie this view. Oh, he hoped this wouldn't spoil the surprise. Jem banged on the roof of the carriage to get the driver to stop, and Cressie jumped with fright.

"What's happening?" she cried. "Can I look?"

"No! Not yet. In a moment."

Jem could hear the driver settling the horses as the carriage came to a stop, and a footman jumped down to open the carriage for him.

"Is everything alright, Mr Denham?" he asked.

"Yes, yes," Jem assured him. "Mrs Denham," he would never tire of hearing that either, "would like to stretch her legs."

"Very good, sir." The door was opened for them properly, and Jem immediately climbed out.

He could not wipe the smile off of his face as he took in the breathtaking view. Cressie had to see this. He turned back to the carriage and guided Cressie with his voice, taking one of her hands while she used the other to cover her eyes. Jem didn't risk having her descend down the steps blindly. The minute she was at the door of the carriage, he took her by the waist and lifted her down onto the ground.

"That smell ... what is it?" Cressie gasped. "And I can hear ..."

Jem beamed as he went behind Cressie and wrapped his arms around her waist, settling his hands on her stomach as he guided her forwards towards the grassy path. "What can you hear?" he whispered in her ear. "Have you heard it before?" Perhaps in a dream ... or in a conch shell.

"It isn't, is it?" Cressie's excitement was bubbling within her.

"Open your eyes."

Cressie's eyes fluttered open, and they immediately widened with amazement as she took in the vast blue landscape before them. Nestled in a cove, thickly dotted with mature trees, was an ocean so perfect it might have been painted. The cove protected the beach from the world, and it was completely clean and un-touched, save for the small waves breaking on the pebbled shore.

"Oh!" Cressie cried, covering her mouth with her hands in shock. "It's ... it's ... the sea!"

Jem had never been happier than in that exact moment, and it was hard to believe that his previous happiest moment had happened only days earlier at their wedding. But this, this look on Cressie's face was everything. Jem was watching her dream come true, and he'd had the power to grant it.

"You're giving me the ocean!" Cressie's voice became suddenly very thick. She looked up at him with large, glassy brown eyes.

"You've given me everything. It was the least I could do." He leaned down to softly kiss her trembling lips.

Cressie pulled on Jem's collar so that she might kiss him again, and she did swiftly, before she seized his hand. "We are swimming right this minute!" she exclaimed.

Jem chuckled. "It's November!" he retorted. "It's freezing."

"I don't care!" Cressie declared. "I have waited me entire life to do this." She looked past Jem to their driver and footman, and called out, "Turn around, please!"

As they did, Cressie began to pull at her buttons, rather than unfastening them, with wicked determination. Within the space of a minute, Cressie was dressed only in her silk chemise, and did not seem to feel the chill of the wind off the ocean at all.

"Are you coming?" she challenged, her brows raising. She turned her back on him as she took off towards the water, but Jem wasn't going to let her get far without him.

Jem ran after her, leaving pieces of his clothing in a trail behind him as he followed Cressie to the edge of the sea. He joined her at her side just as a small wave broke and cascaded over the pebbles. The freezing foam then washed over their toes and Cressie shrieked with delight. She then seized Jem's hand, and before he knew it, he was dragged into the icy water.

They both simultaneously lost their footing on the slippery stones of the seabed and cried with shock and excitement as they were suddenly soaked up to their necks with the cold sea water. But Jem did not care at all. The water was liberating, and the look on Cressie's face was worth every bit of discomfort. They found their footing moments later and stood up, their undergarments having been rendered completely transparent.

Cressie's chemise was plastered to her swollen belly, and Jem couldn't help but marvel at her. Would he ever again see a sight so beautiful? He would endeavour to. Happy Cressie was stunning, and he was determined to make her happy for the rest of his life.

www.ingramcontent.com/pod-product-compliance
Lightning Source LLC
Chambersburg PA
CBHW070736190726
48292CB00002B/289